IN THE *Arms* OF A *Woman*

A short story collection

HARPER BLISS

Other Harper Bliss Books

A Swing at Love (with Caroline Bliss)
No Greater Love than Mine
Once Upon a Princess (with Clare Lydon)
Crazy for You
Love Without Limits
No Other Love
Water Under Bridges
This Foreign Affair
Everything Between Us
Beneath the Surface
No Strings Attached
The French Kissing Series
In the Distance There Is Light
The Road to You
Far from the World We Know
Seasons of Love
Release the Stars
Once in a Lifetime
At the Water's Edge

"Reunion Tour" has been previously published in the anthologies *Cougars* (2014) by Ladylit Publishing and *Best Lesbian Erotica of the Year* (2016) by Cleis Press.
"Alphas" first appeared in the anthology *Anything She Wants* (2013) from Ladylit Publishing
"Overtime" first appeared in the anthology *Lipstick Lovers* (2012) from Xcite Books
"Neighbours" first appeared in the anthology *Smut in the City* (2012) from House of Erotica
"Champagne" was first published as a standalone short story by Ladylit Publishing in 2013
"Off the Record" first appeared in the anthology *Bossy* (2014) from Ladylit Publishing
"All of Me" was first published as a standalone short story by Ladylit Publishing in 2013
"Stair Walking" first appeared in the anthology *Gay & Lesbian Coffee Break Quickies* (2013) from Storm Moon Press
"Fit for Forty" first appeared in the anthology *Don't Be Shy* (2015) from Ylva Publishing
"Rather" was first published on harperbliss.com in 2014

"Lovely Rita" first appeared in the anthology *Can't Get Enough* (2014) from Cleis Press
"Wetter" was first published as a standalone short story by Ladylit Publishing in 2012
"Dress Code" first appeared in the anthology *A Christmas to Remember* (2013) from Ladylit Publishing
"Stormy Weather" was first published as a standalone short story by Ladylit Publishing in 2014
"New Girl" was first published as a standalone short story by Ladylit Publishing in 2012
"Bar Service" was first published as a standalone short story by Ladylit Publishing in 2013
"Personal Training" was first published as a standalone short story by Ladylit Publishing in 2013
"The Power of Words" first appeared in the anthology *Opposites Attract* (2015) from Ladylit Publishing
"Fair & Square" was first published as a standalone short story by Ladylit Publishing in 2013
"The Client" was first published as a standalone short story by A Hotter State in 2013
"Match Point" first appeared in the anthology *Sweat* (2013) from Ladylit Publishing
"Freedom" first appeared in the anthology *Forbidden Fruit* (2014) from Ladylit Publishing
"One-on-One" first appeared in the anthology *Bossier* (2015) from Ladylit Publishing
"A Matter of Inclination" first appeared in the anthology *Summer Love* (2015) from Ladylit Publishing
"The Opposite of Darkness" first appeared in the anthology *First* (2015) from Ladylit Publishing
"Stepping Stone" first appeared in the anthology *Al Fresco* (2015) from Ladylit Publishing
"Commanding Officer" first appeared in the anthology *Christmas Kisses* (2015) from Ladylit Publishing
"Not Yet" first appeared in the anthology *From Top to Bottom* (2016) from Ladylit Publishing

Cover design by Caroline Manchoulas
Published by Ladylit Publishing – a division of Q.P.S. Projects Limited - Hong Kong
ISBN-13 978-988-79123-3-0

CONTENTS

INTRODUCTION

Back in 2012, I hesitantly came out of the writer closet with a few short stories, only to discover that I really enjoyed writing them. I went on to pen quite a few before 'graduating' to novellas and novels. I was fortunate enough to have a few of my short stories published in various anthologies and, over the years, published a bunch of them myself. Now, 6 years after my very first short story was published (*Neighbours* in the erotica anthology *Smut in the City*, fyi), I thought I'd put them all together in one big bundle for you to enjoy.

These days, I hardly ever write short stories anymore, so going over these was quite the nostalgia trip for me and… a rather hot re-discovery of what I used to specialise in.

I started out in erotica so, do be warned, all of these stories are much more than just romantic. Some aren't even romantic at all but, overall, even in these short tales, my undeniable romantic streak was already coming through.

I wouldn't be where I am today if it weren't for starting my big lesbian fiction writing adventure with these short stories.

There are twenty-eight of them and I vividly remember

writing every single one. I hope, after all these years, they bring you as much joy and satisfaction as they have done me.

Blissful reading!

Harper Bliss

REUNION TOUR

You're a cocky little thing up there. The way you wriggle your ass—I can't wait to stripe it with my belt. I watch you from the side of the stage. If this were a festival in Europe, my band would be headlining, but here in our home country, yours gets the number one spot. I'd be lying if I said it didn't smart a little. I may have to take that out on you as well. It's a win-win, really, the way you bat your lashes—your head twisted up to me—when my hand comes down on your flesh, always defying me to give more. And, when it comes to you, I never fail to have more to give.

You shimmy to the edge of the stage, lifting your arms high above your head, giving your fans—and me—a glimpse of your pale, taut belly and the little silver ring driven into the delicate skin above your belly-button.

"No one will know what it means," I said when I arranged for Lisa to administer the piercing. "Only the two of us." Now, every time you flash it, every single time you bare this glittering symbol of whatever we have between us for the world to see, something pierces me, too. A wave of something I don't wish to define washes over me. I'm old enough to recognize it instantly, but still foolish enough to deny it.

Because you drive me crazy, make me feel things I haven't felt in years. Not even taking the stage again, after a nine-year hiatus, flanked by Tommy and Matthew and Sam, my brothers in arms since 1981, affected me in the same way as the first time I saw that glint in your eyes. All it took was one glance, and I knew.

You flick your head to the right, momentarily pinning your eyes on me, and the whole motion thunders through me, leaving my panties drenched. Speaking of, you're wearing a pair of mine underneath those leather pants—the ones that hug your ass so sublimely I need to catch my breath every time you present your back to me on the stage.

"Please allow me to present to you the next big thing," my manager said. "The Harriettes." You were obviously their leader, the way you hung back a bit—the way I learned to do all those years ago—to allow the others to shine during moments of lesser importance, like being introduced to a band long past its prime.

"Oh my god," your bass player giggled. "We are such huge fans. You are our biggest inspiration." It sounded a bit rehearsed, what with her not even been born yet the year we broke through. You appeared smarter, more composed, shrouded in that cool sort of silence that no one can take issue with.

When we shook hands, though, I detected the slightest hint of sweat on your palm, and when you met my gaze, I knew. I'm old enough to know.

You take your first of many faux-modest bows. After five months on the road, I know your routine by heart. I can only imagine the adrenaline coursing through your blood right now. Not that it doesn't still happen to me, but the years have taken away the highest highs. I've learned to put it all into perspective more, to see the long-run—the end game. But I hope you're enjoying this moment because it truly is glorious. Unencumbered by self-consciousness, lifted up by the incessant roar of the thousands of people in front of you, that one moment you sang and strutted your ass off for the past forty-five minutes. The higher your high, the more you'll want me after.

You and your band members exit the stage, walking right past me, as usual. The first time it happened after we'd been together, it hurt a little bit, but I never held that against you. It would be like holding being young against youth. You're pumped, ready to go back out there, to soak up whatever precious minutes of adoration you have left after your gig. Yet, for all your bravado, your magnetizing stage presence, and your—admittedly—raw, powerful vocals, you never let it go to your head.

"I need you to do this to me," you said, the first time. But I didn't need you to tell me that.

I wait patiently, glaring into the bright lights of the stage, the corners of my mouth lifting spontaneously as the people out there scream your name, scream for you to come back. Our own fans, like ourselves, are older now, and rarely call for encores in this unbridled, shameless, self-effacing way.

When you shuffle past me again, it's as though I can smell you. Your sweat. The state of arousal you've worked yourself into during your set.

"I'll be there," I whisper to no one but myself. "I'll be there when you come down."

And I am. After you perform two more songs—The Harriettes' first hit 'Boyfriends' and that cover you and the girls always insist on playing of our 1986 song 'It's not me'—I rush to my changing room. At least, due to my status as new wave goddess of the eighties, most venues, even festivals, easily grant me my wish for my own changing room.

If I wanted to, I could count down the minutes it takes from the applause on the other side of the stage to die down, until you knock on my door. It never takes more than five—just enough time to exchange some high fives with your bandmates—and you always knock.

"Come in," I say, in my most earnest voice. No time for smiles just yet.

You close the door behind you and lean against it, sinking your front teeth into your bottom lip. Already, the first pang of hunger, of blind, delirious lust, shoots through me. To this day, it's still unclear if you chose me or if I chose you. Perhaps we just chose each other. Perhaps, in that long first glance we shared, we saw what we could mean to each other.

As per our ritual, your back stays glued to my changing room door. I forbade you months ago to lock it. I get up from where I was sitting—a rather dingy couch, unworthy of the backstage of a festival of this standing—and, slowly, take a few steps in your direction. The first thing I always do, is unhook my belt and slide it, loop by loop, from around the waistband of my jeans.

Your eyes catch on it and your teeth sink deeper. There's a twitchiness to your demeanor, a desire so great it shines through in every tiny movement you make. You don't know this, but I feel it too. It burns through me now, and destroys me a little every time you close the door behind you again, every time you leave. But I don't think of the pain that is to come, because this moment is not about my pain. It's about yours.

I fold the belt in my hands, enjoying the soft caress of the well-used leather. Your eyes are glued to it. They always are. The way you can never look me in the eyes beforehand, and how you make up for that afterwards by sending defying glance after defying glance at me, as though you've just survived the greatest ordeal, the biggest challenge of your young life, always floors me a little, makes the crotch of my jeans go damp in a flash.

"Take them off." As much as I admire how you look in that pair of leather pants, how they cling to you the way I sometimes want to, time is of the essence.

You kick off your shoes first. You know I want you totally naked, not a scrap of clothing lingering on your body to protect you from what I'm about to give you. I don't go for anything less than complete surrender. Your top is next. I'm glad you're not wearing that old faded T-shirt with my face on it. I hate to see myself crumpled on the floor like that. As usual, you're not wearing a bra. And I didn't even ask you this time. The sight of you, naked from the waist up, only clad in those leather pants—and those large, snaking tattoos that crowd the skin of your arms and shoulders, makes my pussy clench around nothing.

I don't need to take a picture of you this way. I carry this image with me throughout the days. I see it in the morning just before I open my eyes and before I drift off into sleep at night. When did it become all you, I wonder? When did the balance I sought so hard to find in my life tip into your direction?

You don't need me to tell you that I love you. I'm about to show you, again.

I arch up my eyebrows, indicating my impatience. Pants. Now. There's no need for me to say these words, either. Your hands are pushing the leather down already, and it reminds me of the leather slipping through my hands, sliding through the gaps between my fingers. Leather and fingers. All you need. Maybe you should write a song about that?

I nod my head in the direction of the couch and, once you've kicked both your pants and panties off your ankles, you patter over there. And, in moments like these, I do wonder where I get the strength to not push you down and ravage you immediately. This display of youth, so present in the smoothness of your skin, the agility of your muscles, the ease with which you take the pain... it shouldn't be for me to touch anymore, but the fact that I can, that you let me, arouses me even more. Because, for as much as you sometimes claim this is a one-way street, that you complain that you barely get to touch me, this—you naked, at my mercy—is about all I can take. Any more of you, and my old, abused heart may give up.

You know the position and you take it without direction. Your ass arched up high, your torso folded over the armrest, your legs spread wide.

I swallow hard as I approach, and take a moment to behold your beauty. The skin of your behind lost its smooth, silken, youthful un-blemished hue after our first night together. When —not if—you ever decide to take another lover, I will always be there with you, and her. I push the thought from my mind, but don't move just yet. I let you stew, anticipate, melt.

Then, at last, I run the side of my belt along the curve of your ass. Up and down, and I need to activate all my willpower to not let my fingers follow the track of the belt. The need to touch you is so much stronger than on any other given night. Perhaps because this tour of ours only has a few more stops left. Because I can feel something is about to end, again. I guess I'll have to write a song about this, too, in veiled terms, and with a contradictory upbeat melody.

I love you, all of you, but when it comes to your body, I love your ass most of all. It's so firm and bouncy—and those tan lines. I told you once, in an unguarded moment, that I found tan lines inexplicably sexy. You've been working on yours ever since, resulting in a white V tapering downward along your crack. It makes me feel things I haven't felt in years.

When I let the belt drop off your side, I can hear you inhale. Your body tenses with anticipation, but I wait. Just a fraction of a second, just to throw you off guard a little. I know that you know why I do this, and you adjust yourself accordingly. You make it look as though you relax, while, between your legs, that clit of yours must be thumping—screaming, like mine. Like your fans earlier. Like my heart when you knocked on the door.

The leather cracks down on your pert flesh, but you take the first blow with a solemn sort of dignity that baffles me. All throughout this secret affair of ours, so many things you've done have amazed me. But this, this stoicism, as though it's the most important part of what we do, has thrown me for a loop the most.

I don't hold back, and a pinkish stripe has formed on your skin already. Time to paint your other cheek. The room is silent, apart from the threatening, exhilarating whoosh of the belt, your intake of breath, and the stifled moan you expel as the leather touches down again.

As much as I admire how brave you are in the beginning, it's the unraveling of you I crave the most. You make me work for it, though—although 'work' is hardly the correct word.

"Is this what you want?" I ask, as I pause and, with the slightest of touches, run a finger over your crack, all the way down to your soaking wet pussy lips. "Is it?" I insist.

"Yes," you groan, your voice a flimsy echo of the one you use on stage.

I let my finger skate all the way down to your clit, and I revel in how ready you already are, but we both know we haven't even started yet.

My finger retreats and I look you over. I can't tear my eyes away from your behind—my biggest prize. I think of the platinum records I amassed over the years, all of them now stashed away in my basement at home, and I consider how none of them ever gave me as much satisfaction as leering at your blushing ass on display right now. My trophy. All mine.

You don't know all of this yet—and, sure, you remind me of me when I was your age, and I didn't have a clue either back then—but fame is always fleeting. And, most of the time, the highs barely erase the lows. This is not how I think about our romance—because, no matter the practicalities and our silently agreed upon arrangements, this is romance. I can ride this high for as long as it takes.

Still, today I need to ask. I need you to tell me what is going on in that pretty little head of yours, underneath the mask of your face, which I can't see right now because you've pushed it into one of the couch cushions. At the previous stop of this tour, I had my assistant buy a T-shirt with your face on it. I was amazed to learn that they even still made those at first, but you and your band members always claim to be so old school, so I guess it makes sense.

I run the belt over the curve where your ass meets your thigh, again and again, marking the spot where it will land next.

"What are you thinking?" I ask, giving voice to my own weakness. It's the first time I ask you this question. I slap the leather lightly against the exact spot I will paint red in a few seconds, so you know I mean business. When I discovered that spot, when I found out how it made your knees buckle when flogged from the right angle and with the right amount of pressure, my clit throbbed so hard beneath my jeans, I wanted to plunge my free hand into my pants and come for you. Only, it wouldn't have been for you. So I didn't do it.

You push yourself up from the cushion you have your head buried in and crane your neck, finding my eyes, but you don't speak.

Whack. The leather finds the spot and, instantly, tears well in your big brown eyes.

"Tell me," I say, but don't wait for a reply. Instead, I let the belt come down again, striking you hard in the same spot again. Every time my wrist flicks, a bolt of lightning runs through my blood.

"Tell me how much you want this." I lock my gaze on you, but your eyes close and open, blinking in that mute despair I can't get enough of. You try to open your mouth, but I don't give you the opportunity to form words. I rain down my belt on your tender flesh, that perfectly shaped mound that I will caress later, after you've gotten as much as you can take.

"Look at me." I put as much threat in my voice as I can muster because your head is starting to drop down again, your forehead almost touching that cushion again, and I need to see your face. You can't speak, so I need to get my answers there.

Time for my fingers to take over again. I let them travel along the fresh stripes on your flesh, before directing them to your puffed up pussy lips.

Immediately, you moan while your pupils dilate. "Fuck me," you whisper. "Please."

I draw my lips into a smirk—the one I used for the picture on that T-shirt of me you love to wear. "I think you need a little more."

"I—" Your breath stalls as my finger slides a little deeper inside. Just the tip. Just to tease. "I want you so fucking much," you manage to say after my finger has retreated and is riding upwards again, smearing some of your juices onto the most sensitive patches of your skin.

"I can tell," I say. This is always the moment where I could go further. Where I could tell you all the reasons why you don't deserve it yet, but I don't believe enough in them myself to try and fake that speech for you—although I'm quite sure you'd like the tone of voice in which I would deliver the words. "Not yet, baby," I say instead, my own bravado quickly starting to crumble. Because the courage in your eyes undoes me, more so than at any other time. Do you feel it, too? Do you feel that this is ending? Or do you have a master plan? The tabloids would have a field day, and believe me, my front page days are over.

I surprise myself with the force of the next slap on your tortured cheeks, but there it is, that glint in your eyes I've been waiting for. You set your jaw, as if to say that, as of now, you can take all I've got. Perhaps you know that I don't have that much left, but I don't think you do. I think you're all in. I think you want more and, this time, I'm happy to oblige.

I let a few well-aimed slaps come down near the highest curve of your ass where, I suspect, it hurts the least. But you don't need time to breathe, I can see it in your eyes. "Is that all you've got?" they seem to say. And this game we play, this charged silence between us, the quiet we fill with our own thoughts and needs and fantasies, they leave me gasping for air more than you are at this point. And I hope that you can read it on my face as well. How much I need this. How much I want you.

It's this unrelenting want that undoes me in the end. I witness my own unraveling instead of yours. I drop the belt to the floor and position myself behind you. Even glancing backward at me, your neck twisted in an awkward, possibly painful position, you have the nerve to sink your teeth into your bottom lip. "Yes. I give in." I don't say this out loud, but I know you get the message loud and clear.

Roughly, I spread your legs as wide as they can go, and I lock my gaze on the wetness in front of me. How long will you last this time? I know you fight hard to make it last; I can feel it in the way you twitch, and in how you push your body away from me when I fuck you, but I always find the spot.

Your beauty floors me again, the smoothness of your youth, the swollen pinkness of your sex. You're no longer looking at me, and your back curves gently into the exquisite nape of your neck—the exact spot I'd like to sink my teeth into right now. But I'm not about to fuck you because you're young, or because it makes me feel younger. I will fuck you because you're you, and uniquely so. Mandy Harrison—you once said your mom was a big fan and named you after me. Frontwoman of The Harriettes. The girl who can't get enough of my belt on her ass. Sometimes, on stage, when you're watching me, I touch the belt and the heat that rises from my core is so great, my voice drowns in it for an instant. But no one ever notices, except you.

I plunge three fingers inside of you at once. I know how wide you can stretch, and I slide in easily, lubricated by all the juices you started producing the moment you took to the stage. I fuck you. I feel you. I watch your back arch inward, your head tilt sideways, your ass slam against the palm of my hand.

Today, you don't resist. Your body meets me as I thrust, so I give you a fourth finger, filling you up—as close as I'll ever come to disappearing inside of you. I watch the reddening crisscrosses on your ass, admiring my work, as you grind your way to orgasm. My fingers are but a tool for you now, or perhaps that's what you want me to believe. Our romance is certainly an unspoken one, as much to the outside world as in this cocoon we're in now.

When you come, the groan you utter is close to your singing voice, that raw, deep howl that has all the critics raving, but this particular guttural inflection of it, is reserved just for me.

"Amanda," you whisper, out of breath. "Fuck, Amanda." And the way you say my name is like I've never heard you say anything else. It's your code for "I love you".

"I love you too," I murmur, but only to myself, as I let my fingers slide from your wetness, and drape my fully-clothed body over your bare back, embracing you as though I never want to let you go.

ALPHAS

Robin's hair looks meticulous again. I wonder if she stops at the hairdresser every morning before work. It must be statistically impossible to have a good hair day every day of the week. Does it fall as gloriously on Sundays?

"Kate?" Bruce cocks up his eyebrows.

"Yes," I say quickly, not having a clue what they're discussing.

"You and Robin will work this case together." He aligns the stack of papers in front of him without taking his eyes off me. He gives me a swift nod to indicate his word is final.

"Of course." I hide behind my best poker face. The last time Robin and I tried a case together, I had to hit a punching bag for at least an hour every night to decompress. The woman is a delight to look at but a pain to work with. It's obvious that she thinks having the cheekbones of an angel makes her the best lawyer in the firm.

I can't stand her, but I can't keep my eyes off her either. Every day she wears another pristinely starched designer blouse, open at the throat, and while I'm sure the direct view at the hollow of her neck influences some jury members, I wouldn't exactly call it expertise.

"I look forward to it." Robin shoots me a mechanical smile —she saves the heart-warming ones for court. Today's blouse is baby blue, bringing out the clear colour of her eyes.

I vow to not let her boss me around this time. To not let her take control the way she always does.

"That's settled then." Bruce ends the staff meeting. Chairs scrape against the floor. I take a deep breath before standing up.

"My office in ten?" Robin asks. She towers over the table. I follow the line of her cleavage because it's impossible not to. It doesn't give anything away though. Robin is all about suggestion.

"Sure." At least I'll have a few minutes to compose myself and check which case we're meant to crack together.

I shuffle out of the conference room behind Robin and can't help but inhale a whiff of her perfume. I've been trying to figure out which one it is—sniffing endless scented paper sticks at Sephora—but I'm a much better lawyer than I am a detective.

Nine minutes later I knock on her open door.

"Come," she says, her voice measured and authoritative. She sits behind her desk like a queen on a throne, illuminated by light streaming from giant windows. Robin started at the firm barely a month before I did, but she's always had a knack for securing things well above her status. My office is spacious and light, but not nearly as big and bright as Robin's. No matter how hard I try—and sample different dry cleaners—my suits are never as crisp as hers. And my nerve always seems to crumble when I'm within three feet of her.

I sit down in a chair opposite her desk without being invited.

"Would you mind closing the door, please?" Robin's eyes

rest on me, a tight smile tugging at her lips. I know she waited for me to sit so she could ask me to get up again. It's how alpha females like Robin assert their power—it's the small things that get under people's skin the most.

"Sure." I stand and turn. Before I head for the door, I tug my skirt down to draw her attention to my legs. In situations like this, they're the only thing I have going for me. My legs are the reason why I so easily agreed to meet in Robin's office. I'll get to cross and uncross them while on full display, as opposed to hidden under a desk.

I sway my hips a bit when I walk back to my chair. Her eyes follow me, but she doesn't flinch. I cross one leg over the other and lean back, legal pad with notes on the case ready in my lap.

We both start speaking at the same time and one of those awkward moments ensues. A small crack appears in her veneer, allowing the beginning of a silly grin to peek through. She dips her head slightly and I take it as a sign that I should continue.

"I think..." I need to glance at my notes. I'm thrown by the unexpected curve of her lips and the twinkle of amusement in her eyes. Just like that, the image flashes through my mind again. The image I fall asleep to most nights. Robin's blouse a crumpled heap on my bedroom floor. Robin face down on my bed, her wrists and ankles bound so she can't move.

"Take your time." The smile she sends me is so condescending it makes my blood boil. It also makes the picture in my head spark to life again in vivid colour.

"Let's start with the witness list." I quickly regroup. "This doctor..." I glimpse at my notes again. "Barnes. He seems—" The beep of her mobile interrupts me. Robin holds up one finger as she scans the screen. Frustration builds in my gut. Not just because of the way she treats me, but also because of how her hair slides off her forehead as she tips her head, and how her eyes narrow while she reads the text message. I envision her looking at me like that. Her eyes narrowing for different reasons and her hair clinging to her forehead in sweaty strands. It's not easy wanting someone you dislike so much.

"I have to go." She pushes herself out of her chair. "Jury's out."

"I'll be in court all afternoon." My body relaxes. "Let's reschedule tomorrow."

"No. We need an airtight strategy before the next staff meeting." She slides her suit jacket off the back of her chair. "Are you free tonight?"

She slips her arms into the sleeves of her blazer, her chest jutting out in the process, and I have an idea. "Why don't you come to mine?"

Her eyes widen in surprise, but I know she won't say no. Her alpha code won't let her. "I'd love to. Around eight?"

"Perfect." I uncross my legs and stand up. Robin is tall, but I have at least an inch on her.

"Great." I watch her strut out of her office, chin up and back straight, as if the world would end if she were to relax a muscle.

I'm still in my heels when Robin rings my bell. Usually, I can't wait to get out of them as soon as I set foot in the house, but I'm planning for a hard-fought battle in which details like shoes can make all the difference.

"Nice place," Robin says as I open the door wide for her. I wish I could see beyond the mask of her face, beyond the standard compliments, to learn what she really thinks. After all, I'm always courteous with Robin, always professional, never letting on that I want her body writhing beneath me in my bed. I may think I hate her as much as I want to, as much as I need to make myself feel comfortable, but the truth is that we're so alike, both so driven, competitive and ruthless, and I've never wanted anyone more. It's not just her regal posture and cool, impenetrable glare that draw me to her—the distance she puts between herself and everyone she deems beneath her. It's what I suspect lies underneath.

One day, when she finally does, I want to be there when she cracks.

I gesture for her to take a seat in the sofa, but she heads straight for the dining room table, indicating this is not a social visit.

"Red or white?" I hold up two empty wine glasses.

"Do you have anything stronger?" She digs inside her briefcase and slips out a folder.

"Whiskey?" My heels click loudly on the tiles as I make my way to the liquor cabinet.

"Oh god, yes please." A chill chases up my spine as she says the words. I realise that the second she sees through me—the instant she figures out what I really want—I will have lost.

I pour us both a double and sit down at the table at a ninety-degree angle from her. She tilts her head back as she sips and the muscles in her neck stretch so gracefully, I nearly finish my glass in one gulp.

"Rough time in court?" She eyes my half-empty glass.

"Just in general." The smell of the whiskey blends with her perfume and I try to recall my plan of action. Then I remember it wasn't so much a plan as a vague idea. Get her to come to my house. Divert the conversation. Have a drink or two.

As if.

"Do you mind if I take off my shoes?" She doesn't press me for more information on the roughness of my day.

"Go right ahead." I hear two quick thuds on the floor beneath the table.

She takes another sip from her glass and our eyes connect

over the rim. I don't look away. I hold her gaze until my blood starts hammering in my veins. Do I have her where I want her already? The image flashes through my mind again. Robin's back arched, her bottom curved towards me, begging for more.

"Everything all right?" The glass lands on the table with a quiet bang, bursting me out of my reverie. Her voice is curt as usual. Her tone doesn't imply that she expects an answer. She's all business again.

"Can I ask you a personal question?" I trace a fingertip over the rim of my glass.

She leans back in her chair. I hear the fabric of her skirt rustle as she shifts her legs. "Why?"

A tiny giggle makes its way out of my throat. "God, you're tough." I heel my shoes off and inch my feet closer to hers underneath the table. "Don't you ever get tired of it?" As I speak the last word, my toe brushes against her naked ankle.

She doesn't even blink. "Why am I really here?" She doesn't retract her foot. Her blue eyes scan mine as she crosses her arms over her chest.

"The same reason you go anywhere, I presume." My toe travels up her shin. "Work." I tip my upper body over the table towards her.

"This doesn't feel like work to me." Her eyes are still on mine. They burn with something new, something exciting, while the rest of her expression doesn't alter.

"What does it feel like?" I trace my foot down again and catch her ankle between my soles. I realise I'm nowhere near drunk enough for this degree of audacity.

At last, she manages a smile. "I suppose I should say 'incredibly inappropriate.'" Suddenly, one of my own ankles is trapped between her feet. She presses hard, making a point I don't really want to get. "But." She uncrosses her arms and slants her body in my direction. Her face is so close I can feel her breath. "Maybe I should teach you a lesson instead."

My pulse quickens; my breath stops in my throat.

"What do you think, Kate?" She pauses, relaxing her muscles, freeing my ankle.

I nod because I can't speak. My mouth goes bone-dry. This is not exactly what I wanted to happen, but I'll take it.

"Good." She pushes her chair back. I do the same. We both stand up at the same time. With one quick step she's by my side, curling her fingers around my wrist. She seems taller than me now, more commanding. My brain stops thinking of ways to get the upper hand. "Where's the bedroom?"

I walk us through the hallway to my room where the blinds are half-drawn. I head towards the window to close them.

"No." She stops me with one word. "Turn around." Her tone is not one to mess with. "Strip."

I should have known this would be the only outcome if I made a move on her. With trembling fingers I unbutton my blouse. My skin pricks up into gooseflesh under Robin's gaze. My nipples poke against the lace of my bra as I unzip my skirt and let it fall to the floor. I stand in front of her in just my underwear—my clit a throbbing mess—and suddenly feel self-conscious about removing it.

"I want you naked." Robin's voice has changed, but her demeanour has not. "Now."

I want to make it sexy, strip slowly, but I can't. I'm fully under her command and get rid of my underwear swiftly. The air hits my nipples and they crinkle into even harder peaks.

Robin tilts her chin with a tiny nod of approval. Already, I want more. She shifts her gaze towards the bed. "Lie down on your belly and don't move until I say so."

I crawl onto the bed and do as I'm told. My breath comes out in shallow puffs. Behind me I hear the rustling of clothes being taken off. I wonder if she's naked and if she'll allow me a glimpse.

"Spread your legs and arms wide."

I feel her climb onto the bed with me. I stretch my arms over my head and part my legs. I watch how she ties my right hand to the bed frame with my bra and my left one with what I assume is hers. My ankles are submitted to the same treatment. From the feel of starched cotton and tiny buttons against my skin, I guess she's using our blouses to fasten them.

I want to snicker at the irony of the situation, at the foolish boldness of my dreams, but I choose to stay as quiet as possible.

"Now, tell me, Kate." The mattress dips again and her voice comes from behind. My backside is on full display for her and I imagine her eyes roaming across my skin. "What have you been dreaming of?" Suddenly, her body covers mine. Her hard nipples prod against my shoulder blades and her lips brush against my neck. "And remember." She trails her tongue along the outline of my ear. "This is no time for dishonesty."

I'm overwhelmed by the abundance of skin she piles on me, by her closeness. All I can manage is a ragged moan as I feel her bush tickle my back.

"What's it going to be?" She asks again. "If you don't tell me, I won't do it."

"Spank me," I whisper, but my voice is too hushed for her to hear.

"Can you say that again, please?" Her knee grazes my pussy lips. "Loud and clear."

"Spank me." The words come out strangled, my voice already shot to pieces.

"Oh, I will." She's all over me and I want to grind my clit against the mattress to release the tension from my muscles, but I know better. "And you know why?"

I nod into the duvet.

"If you're so clever, you'd better tell me." Robin's voice is not all menace—it's tinged with a quiet thrill, with tiny bursts of exhilaration

"Because I deserve it." I know this game so well. I've played it in my head a thousand times. The only difference being that I was doing the questioning then.

"Good." She lifts herself away from me, leaving my skin hot and abandoned. I sense how she positions herself between my legs, near my ankles, far enough to gain momentum for a forceful blow.

"Count." Her hand lands on my behind much harder than I had anticipated. She means business. I should have known.

It stings too much for me to utter the number immediately. Despite not being able to see her, I notice her impatience.

"I'm waiting." The edge in her voice makes my blood beat faster towards my clit.

"One."

Before I have the chance to gather my thoughts, her palm connects with my butt cheek again—the same one. My body tenses, my wrists pulling at their restraints.

"Two," I barely manage, my voice stifled by the duvet I'm biting into. Pain tumbles through my body and my pussy drizzles juices.

She gives me two quick, softer slaps on the other cheek.

"Three. Four," I count.

The fifth one elicits such a loud groan from me, that she lets me get away with not counting out loud. She knows she has me. She's had me from the start.

The skin of my rear burns, but I want more. Of course, she doesn't give it to me.

With the back of her hand, she caresses my cheeks, causing more wetness to trail down my legs. I feel her shuffle closer and arch my back to lift myself towards her—just as I had imagined her doing for me.

Fingers graze my opening, lingering briefly, before plunging inside. The pain, the frustration, the agonising competition between us, all of it is released from me as she twists her fingers deep inside of me.

She withdraws her fingers and lands another blow. All the muscles in my body contract, only to relax in blissful agony as she pushes her fingers back inside.

Slap. Thrust. Slap. Thrust.

I've long forgotten about counting as my mind frazzles to Robin's ruthless rhythm. Each stroke of her hand brings me closer, and every pang of pain is immediately rewarded with the glorious sensation of her fingers in my cunt.

Bound and totally at her mercy, the orgasm takes me. I spasm around her fingers, wanting to keep her inside of me. My skin tingles and aches for more of her. A different image floats through my brain as the final crash of climax leaves me spent. The image of what's taking place in my bedroom right now.

Robin quickly unties me and lies down next to me. She kisses my forehead with surprising tenderness. "There's only room for one alpha female in our firm. I hope you know that." She smiles before she takes me in her arms and pulls me close.

OVERTIME

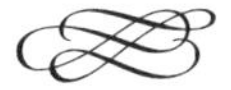

Laura blinked twice. The letters in front of her started to swim. She'd been huddled over the document for hours, trying to find a loophole, a missed technicality, something that would give her an edge in tomorrow's meeting. An unusual office silence hummed around her, closing in. She guessed she was the only one left at this hour. Maybe her colleagues weren't so dead-set on pleasing Cathy, but it was all Laura lived for.

The triple beep of her office phone startled her. She checked the wall clock and wondered who would be calling her after ten PM.

"Burning the midnight oil?" The voice on the other end of the line was deep and throaty and, more than anything else, brimming with effortless authority.

"I'm struggling with the Wallace case." Laura pinched her eyes shut in frustration. She could never keep her cool when Cathy called. Admitting to the boss, especially a boss like Cathy who loathed weakness, that she was getting nowhere with a case was career suicide. "But I'll get there." She tried to correct herself.

"Maybe I can help?" Laura wondered what the slight, almost unnoticeable shift in Cathy's tone could mean. She couldn't be serious, though. It must be sarcasm.

"I'm sure you have better things to do, Miss Turner." Another slip. Laura could hit herself for this one. She was supposed to address her boss as Cathy. Despite being a firm believer in scare tactics and strict hierarchy, Cathy had insisted. She liked to play with people's minds like that. "I mean, Cathy," she mumbled.

"My office in two minutes." Cathy hung up with a dry click. Laura hated that sentence because, so far, it had always meant she was in trouble. She started mentally preparing for the tongue-lashing she was about to receive. If only she had left the office earlier. Her overtime hadn't produced anything useful and now she had Cathy to deal with as well.

She secured some stray strands of hair behind her ear and straightened the collar of her blouse in the reflection of her computer screen. A deep breath and Laura was on her feet. It was still a private audience with Cathy, she told herself. A late night rendezvous. However the psychological encouragement failed and by the time Laura knocked on Cathy's door she was a nervous wreck, palms sweating and knees trembling. She was a grown woman, for god's sake. Graduated at the top of her class. Recruited by Cathy herself.

"Come." Cathy's voice was always stern, but one-word commands made her sound like a vicious army lieutenant with too much power.

Laura opened the door and took a timid step inside. For a woman of her stature, Cathy had ridiculously bad posture. She sat hunched over her desk, her shoulders drawn up and her neck curved in an unnatural position. With icy-blue eyes she peered at Laura over dark-rimmed glasses that had slipped to the tip of her nose.

"I'm sorry, huh, Cathy." It didn't feel right to address a superior like that, especially one as formidable as Cathy. "I didn't mean to alarm you. I'm—"

"Shut the door." Cathy put her pen down and leaned back in her chair.

Her heart thumping in her throat, Laura turned around and gingerly closed the door. To her knowledge, they were the only ones left in the office, so shutting the door could only mean one thing. It was time for one of Cathy's infamous sugar-coated, smooth-voiced scoldings that worked best behind closed doors. Cathy Turner wasn't one to yell. She didn't need to raise her voice to get things done.

Laura shuffled towards one of the visitor chairs and pulled it back.

"I didn't say you could sit." Cathy's eyes scanned Laura's face, her long lips drawn into her trademark sphinx-like smirk.

Laura withdrew her hand from the chair and didn't know what to do with it. What would appear least weak? Crossing her arms over her chest or clasping her hands together in a ladylike fashion in front of her belly?

"Do you have a girlfriend?" Laura certainly wasn't expecting that question.

"What?" she stammered as her cheeks flamed pink.

"A boyfriend maybe?" Cathy didn't show any emotion on her face. She asked the question as if she were inquiring about the weather forecast, as if the answer didn't really matter.

"No. I'm single." Laura had to force herself not to add a reverent "ma'am" at the end of her statement.

"I thought as much." Cathy pushed her chair back and the scraping of its wheels over the floor made Laura jump.

Laura had steeled herself for a chastising speech and these personal questions were throwing her off guard. No doubt it was Cathy's plan to break down her defences completely before she went in for the kill. Nothing was ever straightforward with her and if she couldn't make a game out of it, it wasn't worth investing any time in. At least Laura knew that much.

With a swift movement, Cathy pushed herself out of her chair. She briefly placed her hands on her desk, forcing the shoulder pads of her navy pinstriped blazer to puff up. She reminded Laura of a lion about to pounce, the only thing missing was the audacious licking of lips.

"I see your ambition."

Laura had a hard time keeping her eyes off Cathy's legs. Her boss strutted to the front of the desk, towards her, and leaned her behind against it. Cathy planted the palms of her hands on the table-top and crossed her ankles. From day one, Laura had been enamoured with Cathy's glossy legs. Maybe because they stood in such stark contrast to her manipulative and overbearing personality. Or maybe because, while always on display under Cathy's pencil skirts, they were so untouchable.

"It reminds me of me. When I was your age, I was always the last one to leave the office." Cathy pushed a strand of perfectly coiffed blond hair away from her forehead. "I was single for a long time as well."

Was this advice on romance? Laura's confusion grew.

"Of course, now I'm divorced." At last, a sparse smile tugged at the corners of her mouth. Maybe she thought her divorce was funny—Laura believed Cathy didn't find anything funny. "Don't make the same mistakes I did." After removing her glasses, Cathy pinned her eyes back on Laura. "In the end, it's not worth it."

Laura couldn't believe she was in the middle of a heart-to-heart with the mighty Cathy Turner. Truth be told, it was more of a monologue, really, but still, Cathy was confiding in her. Clearly, she was suffering from some sort of melancholy that was driving her to impart these words of wisdom on Laura. Or maybe her divorce papers had just come through.

"I won't." Laura felt it was a good time to speak, although she couldn't entirely relax. She never could around Cathy. Not just because she was her boss, but also because, even long after office hours, Laura had trouble getting her off her mind. "It's just, I'm still so young and working here—"

"You don't have to explain." Cathy pushed herself up from the desk and put her glasses, which she still held in one hand, behind her.

Laura was glad Cathy hadn't mentioned the Wallace case, but she had no idea what to do now that Cathy was marching towards her. Everything was quiet around them, the soft thuds of Cathy's heels on the wooden floor the only sound. Until Cathy was so close that Laura could feel her breath against her cheek. Her own breathing was suffering and she had to swallow hard. In a year of working for Cathy, they'd probably never stood this close together.

Instinctively, Laura took a step back. She didn't want to and it wasn't a conscious decision, but she had to. Perhaps her body thought it the logical next step in this late night match of office Stratego, or whatever game they were playing.

"Lock the door." Cathy's voice was low, a little menacing and extremely sexy.

"What?"

"Turn the key to the right and lock the door."

Laura stifled her natural reflexes to protest and did as Cathy ordered. When she spun around, her back against the door, Cathy stood mere inches away. Her eyes peered into Laura's as a small smile crept along her lips.

Before Laura had a chance to even consider what was happening, Cathy's hand was on her chest. Her fingers pressed against Laura's clavicle before finding their way down the front of her blouse. Without warning or words, Cathy snuck her hand under Laura's bra and squeezed her nipple brutally between thumb and index finger.

Laura gasped for air. A sharp pain sped through her body as Cathy pinched harder.

Not allowing her eyes to leave Laura's, Cathy leaned in a little closer.

"I'm only going to ask you once." Cathy's lips found Laura's ear. "Do you want me to fuck you?"

Laura nodded. Moving her head was all she could muster. The power of speech seemed to have escaped her the moment Cathy's hand had landed on her skin. It was also hard to decline an offer like that when her boss' strong fingers were squashing her nipple. And besides, she wanted nothing more than to get fucked by Cathy Turner. The deemed impossible prospect of it had fed her fantasies for months.

"Good," Cathy growled in her ear. She'd always had something animal-like about her, something feline. Sly as a cat. Reflexes honed to always come up with a sharp reply. Her eyes looked like they could burn through darkness. And then there was that cold, distant air, designed to keep people at bay and simultaneously lure them in, people like Laura at least.

Laura felt herself go damp between the legs as Cathy kissed her neck. She trailed a path of light pecks along her jaw until she reached Laura's trembling lips. The first thing Laura felt were teeth sinking into her bottom lip. Unsurprisingly, Cathy was not a gentle lover.

Laura responded greedily when Cathy slipped her tongue into her mouth. She latched on as if she'd never get an opportunity to taste it again. Pangs of lust shivered up her spine. Cathy roughly undid Laura's blouse, not caring about the delicacy of the fabric and the way the buttons were sewn into it. Laura was past wondering if she could ruffle her hands through Cathy's sculpted hair. It felt remarkably soft when she let it flow through her fingers, not at all like the hair-sprayed mass she had expected. Yet, she was afraid to touch Cathy in any other place. Frightened to go near her breasts and explore their shape. Way too daunted to even think about opening a button of her starched blouse. It was clear who was in charge, who was always in charge.

Cathy yanked down the cups of Laura's bra, exposing one battered and one perky nipple to the air-conditioned office air. Electricity coursed through Laura's body. It wasn't so much Cathy's touches, which were sparse and rough at best—not that she minded—but the fact that she stood cornered against Cathy's locked office door, her boss all over her. Like most things that went on in this office, it was more a mind-game than anything else. Maybe Cathy thought she had the winning hand again, but at least Laura knew that, for her, a massive orgasm was on its way. She felt it in the shortness of her breath, the goosebumps on her skin and the heat between her legs.

Cathy's hand travelled down, to the button of her trousers. This suit had cost a fortune but Laura didn't care if Cathy ripped it to shreds, as long as her fingers arrived where it mattered soon.

While amping up the pressure on Laura's tortured nipple, Cathy lowered her zipper in a slow and controlled manner—as if there was any other way. As unusual as this situation was, it was still a classic Cathy moment. A demonstration of power from the boss and an extreme act of obedience by the employee. Laura wondered what Cathy would taste like, feel like under her tongue, at her mercy. Despite what was going on, and the possible opening it may bring forth, Laura knew it would never happen.

"You're all wet for me." Cathy's mouth went back and forth between Laura's lips and ear, nibbling and kissing both. "Good girl."

Cathy's fingers rubbed the soaking wet seam of her briefs and they were inches away from Laura's throbbing clit. At last she released Laura's nipple and used both her hands to tug

Laura's trousers down, underwear included. The sudden rush of air blowing between her legs, made Laura's skin break out in goosebumps. Her clit swelled in the breeze of the AC and she could feel juices leaking from her pussy, moistening her upper thighs. She was more than ready for Cathy to fuck her.

Shaking her shoes and trousers off, Laura searched for Cathy's eyes. Their icy stare seemed laced with a tiny sparkle, a glimmer of what usually stayed hidden. Apart from a tousled hairdo and a few creases in her blazer, Cathy's demeanour appeared unaffected. This was in stark contrast to Laura's dishevelled state, with her blouse torn open, her trousers crumpled on the floor, and the cups of her bra pushing her breasts up from underneath.

Cathy repositioned herself. She pinned her gaze on Laura, unblinking and unwavering, like in a deposition with a hostile witness. One hand shot straight to Laura's neck, its thumb tracing the line of her collarbone. Laura couldn't see Cathy's other hand, but she sure felt it. Its fingers skated along her moist pussy lips with overwhelming tenderness. Up and down, they travelled, only inviting more wetness to ooze from between Laura's legs.

During dull moments in meetings, Laura had often inadvertently stared at Cathy's fingers and wondered what they would feel like pressed inside of her. Her breath hitched in her throat as Cathy parted her lips and slipped a finger between her folds, not too deep, merely probing.

"I'm going to fuck you." Cathy peered into her eyes, as if she wanted to stare her down. "Just like you want me to." Her voice sounded lower than Laura had ever heard it. And just like that, Cathy pushed two fingers inside.

Laura gasped and she felt her pussy clench around Cathy's knuckles. She let her head fall back against the door, pulling her eyes away from Cathy's triumphant grin, looking upwards. Cathy retreated slowly, letting her fingers hover at the rim of

Laura's pussy for a split second before slamming them inside again.

"Look at me," she commanded and, as if she had no other choice in the world, Laura lowered her gaze and met Cathy's eyes. They shone with shameless bravado, but Laura swore she could make out something else in them as well. Something she'd never seen in Cathy's glance before, something fragile and akin to desire. Or maybe she was too caught up in her own lust, in her own world of pleasure at the mercy of Cathy's fingers, to see things clearly.

Cathy kept thrusting her fingers inside, pulling out gently and going in with hard determination. Each stroke delivered Laura to new heights. She focused on Cathy's eyes, letting herself drown in the cold blue of them. Her pussy sucked Cathy's fingers in, accepting them eagerly, while her clit roared for attention. She wanted to touch herself. Her hands were idle anyway, hesitating between finding a grip on the door and tugging Cathy's clothes off. But she knew better than to take that kind of initiative.

A mild grimace took hold of Cathy's face every time she delved deeper inside Laura's pussy. Cathy's other hand dipped lower, to Laura's other breast, kneading it roughly before going to work on the nipple. The pinch of her fingers around Laura's nipple sent an electric jolt through her system, connecting with her pussy. Her blood seemed to sparkle, her entire body expanding and contracting around Cathy's fingers.

Just at the right time, just when Laura felt she couldn't take anymore, Cathy flipped her thumb over Laura's engorged clit, setting off a round of fireworks in her brain. Fingers kept stroking her inside, touching her deep down, while the thumb of Cathy's hand expertly nudged her clit. Laura wanted to stay in the moment forever, the moment before all fuses blew, the moment before Cathy would retreat forever.

As her climax approached, crashing into her from all angles,

Laura had trouble looking into Cathy's eyes. Her eyelids fluttered and in between the instances of darkness she noticed how Cathy's cheeks flushed. This crack in her boss' stoic air moved her more than anything. Laura let go and came all over Cathy's hand, no doubt staining the cuff of her tailored blouse.

"God," Laura murmured and when she opened her eyes, Cathy stared right back at her, a relaxed expression on her face. Knowing this illicit office dalliance at least meant a little something to Cathy made it doubly satisfying for Laura. Carefully, Cathy let her fingers slip from Laura's pussy and lifted them between their faces. They glistened with juice and smelled of Laura's musky wetness.

"Open your mouth." Cathy was back to giving commands again and Laura easily complied. She tasted herself on her lips as Cathy ran her fingers over them, before inserting them into her mouth. Laura licked and sucked, savouring the feeling of Cathy's fingers on her tongue. It was her turn to drill her eyes into Cathy's, who, try as she might, couldn't stop an almost inaudible gasp from escaping her.

With her fingers still in Laura's mouth, Cathy inched closer and pressed her lips against Laura's. Despite coming on her boss' fingers earlier, this was by far the most intimate moment they had shared. Laura felt her legs go weak again and this time she couldn't stop herself. Unhinged from her thoughts and inhibitions, her hands drifted to the waistband of Cathy's skirt. She'd barely touched Cathy and was consumed by the desire to do so, to give back. Cathy paid her after all. Cathy stiffened at her touch and retracted her fingers as well as her lips.

"It's all right." She placed her hands on top of Laura's. "Unlike you, I can take care of myself."

Just like that, Cathy slipped back into professional mode, as if this had been a business transaction, or a mere favour bestowed by a boss on a desperate employee. Laura knew fucking her had satisfied Cathy, though. Otherwise, she simply wouldn't have done it. With a last glimmer of goodwill, Cathy bent down and picked up Laura's trousers.

"You'll need to get these dry-cleaned."

Laura discarded her underwear and slipped into her trousers, pulled up her bra cups and quickly buttoned up her blouse. Cathy stood waiting at her desk, leaning against it, mirroring her position to the one she'd taken before coming for her.

"Good night, Cathy." Laura unlocked the door and cradled the handle in her hand.

"If you tell anyone about this, there will be consequences." Cathy's voice had crept back into its most menacing register. "Understood?"

Laura spun around and faced Cathy one last time. It seemed unreal—and certainly implausible—that she'd just given her such pleasure. The aura in the office had gone straight back to its usual frostiness, not leaving any room for sentiments.

"Of course." She shot Cathy a smile, that she expected would be most unwelcome. "I'll be working overtime again tomorrow." Laura licked her lips. "I hope you approve." With that, she turned the knob, and was out of the door.

NEIGHBOURS

Karen had scored the friendliest amongst Hong Kong cabbies again. He sighed and muttered in the front seat as if he were doing her a huge favour by driving her home. Blocking out the driver's dramatic antics, she peered out of the window, still getting used to her new commuter route. After another spike in rent, Karen had chosen to switch neighbourhoods instead of moving down another few stories in her old building—she had almost been at the lowest floor and nearly out of options. Her new place was a few miles further from the office, but it had one unexpected perk.

One night, on her tiny balcony, when searching for the harbour in between the skyscrapers obstructing an open view, her gaze had drifted to the apartment building on the left. It was the usual grey affair with a yellow glow beaming through the windows, creating a scattered pattern of city light. From the showerheads towering over plastic curtains she'd learned she was watching a column of bathrooms. Except, on the twelfth floor—at least she guessed it was the same floor as hers —the person in the process of showering obviously didn't believe in curtains. At first, it didn't fully register, but as her eyes grew wider and her mouth curled into a smile, Karen had realised she was witnessing quite the revealing shower scene.

The woman on the other side of the window, which wasn't even opaque, lathered soap over her arms, producing white frothy bubbles that stood out against her olive skin. Karen deemed it impossible for the woman not to know that she was on display. The easy conclusion was that she must really enjoy it. At least four other buildings had windows or balconies facing her bathroom. Hundreds of eyes could feast on the way the foam was slipping off the woman's skin right now. Karen had checked her watch. It was just past eight, around the time half of professional Hong Kong arrived home from work. Apart from an exhibitionist streak, the woman also had excellent timing.

Karen had soon learned that the showering woman was a recurring phenomenon and she found herself drawn to her balcony every time she stepped inside her flat. Some nights, after a rough day in the office dealing with incompetent suppliers, she'd rush home instead of going for the usual after work drinks with her colleague Andy, finally relaxing with a glass of wine on her balcony, eyes glued to the illuminated window across from her. Once, when stuck in traffic after a gruelling meeting, she'd gotten out of the cab and had half-jogged home, anxious to make it in time for the show. She wasn't exactly proud of it, but Karen felt that her own vices were easily eradicated by the woman's.

Impatiently waiting for the taxi driver to hand her the receipt, she glanced at her watch. It was ten past eight and the spectacle would soon be over. Karen dashed into her building, ignoring Kermit, the jovial doorman with the unfortunate name, and frantically pushed the elevator button. Once inside the lift she wondered if this sort of behaviour could be placed on the same level as a trivial caffeine addiction or if she should consider professional help.

She stepped onto her balcony just in time to see the lights go out in the woman's bathroom. With a sigh of disappointment she sank down onto the little wooden bench she had solely acquired to rest her weary feet when indulging in the peep show across the road. Karen didn't always make it in time and neither did the star player in what had become some of her liveliest fantasies of late. The woman showed up in her window often enough to keep the momentum going and build hope for the next day, but she didn't stick to a rigid schedule. This fact filled Karen with hope because it meant the woman was just a human being like her, with a job and a calendar bursting at the seams. Even though she did seem to prioritise personal hygiene over other activities, like watching the eight o'clock news.

There's always tomorrow, Karen thought and retreated back into the living room. Her stomach grumbled and as she reached for her phone to order food, it started ringing, Andy's name blinking for attention.

"Are you coming or what?"

"Excuse me?" Karen had rushed out of the office, barely saying goodbye to anyone, eager to get home. She'd had a rough week and had been looking forward to the Friday night showing more than ever.

"Deborah's party. Almost everyone is here." Andy sighed. "You forgot, didn't you?"

"Of course not," Karen lied. Her mind had been a bit preoccupied lately. "I was just about to call you to get the address. I seem to have lost it."

"You've lost it all right," Andy scolded her. "Her building's right next to yours. Twelfth floor, apartment A."

When Karen entered the lobby it hit her. This was the building to her left when she stood on her balcony. Her finger trembled when she pushed the button for the twelfth floor. She couldn't help but feel closer to the woman, even though, realistically, ogling her from across the street was probably as close as she would ever get. Before ringing Deborah's bell she looked around for the apartment that faced hers. Her eyes landed on flat C across the hall. Adrenalin surged through her veins as Karen stood there, her feet unable to move and her mouth going dry.

"Are you coming in?" Andy, always the gentle soul, yanked the door open.

Karen took a deep breath and entered the apartment.

"What's wrong with you, anyway?" Andy asked.

"Nothing a few glasses of wine can't fix."

Karen found Deborah and handed her the bottle of Sauvignon Blanc she'd brought. Most people present were work colleagues accompanied by their usual plus-ones. Karen did notice a few unfamiliar faces but, at first glance, no one seemed suitable to attend to the growing ache inside of her. Since she had started shamelessly indulging in her voyeuristic activities pertaining to the shower scenes of a certain resident in this very building, her needs had gone unmet and she was always on the lookout for someone to quench her thirst.

"Is everyone here?" Andy asked Deborah. "I've prepared a little something."

Deborah scanned the living room. "We're just missing my neighbour from across the hall, but she's always late." A moment later the bell rang. "Speak of the devil."

Karen stood closest to the door. "I'll get it." She opened the door and, with clothes on, the woman looked almost unrecognisable. Karen had to swallow before she could speak. "Come in."

The woman pinned her eyes on Karen, narrowing them. "Have we met? You look familiar."

"I'm not sure." Karen extended her hand. "Karen, Deborah's co-worker."

"Joan." The woman slipped her fingers against Karen's. Her skin felt soft and tender. Must be from all that soaping up, Karen thought. "Neighbour." She squeezed Karen's hand firmly. "Pleasure."

Andy's speech and the cutting of the cake happened in a haze. Karen only had eyes for Joan. She wore tight jeans with a blue halter-top and now that Karen had the privilege of standing so close to Joan's exposed shoulders she found herself unable to engage in fluent conversation. Everyone else in the room had paled now that Joan was there. They were all blending into the walls and the words coming out of their mouths held no interest for Karen. Joan's pitch-black hair was tied together in a low ponytail and the sight of it transported Karen's thoughts to the black mound of pubic hair she'd so often seen drenched in foam.

It's quite unusual to see someone naked before you get to know them, she pondered, as she let Deborah pour her another glass of wine.

"In case you're wondering, the answer is yes." Deborah shot her a half-drunk smile. "And don't tell me you haven't been wondering. You can't keep your eyes off of her."

"I have no idea what you're talking about," Karen grinned, her gaze still fixed on Joan. "And even if I did… what are you doing hiding hot lesbians from me?"

"I just haven't had a chance to introduce you, that's all." Deborah winked. "As far as I know, she's single." She turned around and refilled everyone else's glass.

"You obviously don't know much about her," Karen mumbled more to herself than to Deborah, who had reached the other end of the room by then.

Joan stood talking to Andy and Karen realised they weren't making much effort at covertly glancing at her. Andy waved her over and, with her heart pounding in her throat, Karen shuffled towards them.

"I've just been told that for once I'm not the only one in the room." Joan accompanied her statement with a wide smile, revealing a row of immaculate white teeth. Karen thought it a bit daunting to hit on a woman whose near-perfect body she saw on a regular basis. She should be glad it was a hot lesbian and not a chunky Chinese man who lived opposite her, but the sight of Joan had quite the tongue-tying effect on her.

"Have you lived here long?" Karen asked clumsily. "I recently moved into the building next door."

Joan studied Karen's face and pouted her lips before she spoke. "Maybe I've seen you around the neighbourhood then. That wasn't a pick-up line earlier, you really do look familiar."

"Pity," Karen's confidence grew. After all, she'd always been fully clothed on her balcony. "About the pick-up line, I mean." The wine was also ascending to her head rapidly. She'd only had a few crisps for dinner and a thin sliver of birthday cake, her stomach too upset by Joan's arrival to have much of an appetite left. She shot Joan a coy smile and looked around for a bottle of wine.

"I do apologise." Joan moved a little closer and the taut skin stretching around her bicep as she held up her glass brushed against Karen's arm, sending a shiver up her spine. Joan cast her eyes down to the spot where their skin had just touched and bit her bottom lip. "Is this better?"

"Yes." Karen was reduced to stammering again. All the time she'd spent watching Joan in the shower felt like foreplay and, for Karen, there was only one satisfying outcome. She bent her head and sniffed Joan's skin. "You smell divine. Which brand of soap do you use?" Karen remembered the foam trickling down Joan's breasts when she leaned back to rinse her hair.

When their glances met, Karen saw the sparkle in Joan's eyes intensify, as if the penny was about to drop.

"Clinique Happy Body Wash." Joan whispered it seductively in Karen's ear as if she was talking dirty and not just promoting her deluxe beauty products. "Quite pricey, but I just love it."

"I've noticed." Heat rushed through Karen's blood.

"Would you like to try it?" Joan's lips were still hovering around Karen's ear. "I live right across the hall."

Karen swallowed hard, then nodded. "I know." She glanced around for a sign of Andy. When she caught his eye, she winked and slanted her head towards the door, indicating she wanted to leave. Andy gave her an obnoxious thumbs-up, but Karen refrained from rolling her eyes. Instead, she gave in to the lust pooling in her blood and grabbed Joan's hand.

"So you like to watch." Joan closed the door of her apartment behind them and leaned against the small dining table. Her lips curved into an audacious smile. "How would you like it if you were the one being watched?"

Karen stepped closer and peered into Joan's eyes. "But you've only just showered."

"And you weren't there to see."

"I had a party to attend." Karen placed her hands on Joan's hips. "The people you meet at these things." She snuck her hands up Joan's sides, lifting up her top in the process.

"Tell me about it." Joan's breath caught in her throat as Karen jerked her tank top over her breasts.

Karen pressed her body against Joan and kissed her. She could feel Joan's nipples stiffen through the fabric of her bra. Joining Joan in the shower hadn't made it into Karen's fantasies yet—they'd been more traditionally located in the bedroom—but it looked like she wouldn't need to waste any time on imagining that one.

Joan's lips nibbled their way to her ear. "Let me show you to the bathroom."

It was like stepping onto the set of a TV show she'd been following for years. The bathroom was tiny, like most in this city, the tub doubling as a shower. A bright bulb illuminated them from above, preventing them from seeing anything but dots of yellow light beaming from the buildings outside.

"That's your flat." Joan brought Karen's arm up and pointed it to the window. Karen could barely make out her balcony, it was one of so many—then again, most balconies probably didn't have someone appearing on them at eight o'clock every night. "I do love a captive audience."

Joan's nipples probed into Karen's back. All the memories of a dripping wet Joan flooded back into her brain. Karen felt Joan's breath on her neck as her lips drew closer before planting a moist kiss on her shoulder. Her own nipples perked up as Joan rubbed her hands over her belly, snaking them up to her breasts. All eyes on me now, Karen thought as her gaze was lost in the twinkling lights outside. The possibility of other people watching her—them—heightened her senses. Joan's fingers had reached her nipples now, caressing them over the lace of her bra.

"Time to soap up," Joan whispered, and moved her hands to Karen's back where they unclasped her bra. With one swift move, Joan hoisted Karen's top and bra over her head and arms. There she stood, half-naked on display for the neighbourhood. Karen saw their reflection in the window. Joan's hands were on her shoulders, creeping down to her trousers, ready to undo them as well.

Karen spun around to face Joan. Now her trousers had dropped down, her nudity against Joan's half-dressed state felt quite unbalanced. She folded her arms around Joan's waist and dropped her hands to cup her buttocks. Joan's lips tasted of wine and peanuts when she kissed her again. Karen's clit pulsed between her legs and she briefly wondered what her panty-clad behind looked like to casual balcony-standers.

Joan grew impatient and flipped open the button of her jeans. "Nothing you haven't seen before." She grinned and let them sink to the floor, underwear included. Karen had to stop herself from kneeling and burying her tongue in Joan's pussy. Instead, she tugged off her own panties and watched as Joan got rid of her bra.

Joan stepped into the tub first and extended her hand gallantly to facilitate Karen's entrance. The side of the tub was covered by a foldable frosted glass shower screen that, Karen suspected, extended far enough to protect users of the shower from prying outside eyes. Joan obviously had no interest in using it. Joan turned on the tap and the first hit of water was freezing cold, causing Karen's skin to break out into goose-bumps. The pressure was perfect though, massaging her scalp and relaxing her shoulder muscles.

With closed eyes, their mouths met and water dripped down their lips as they kissed. Joan broke the lip-lock and reached for the soap, in the form of an orange, expensive-looking tube. She squirted some in her hands and rubbed them together to make it foam.

"Turn around." Karen was beyond hesitation now. She just wanted Joan's hands to spread the divine smelling lotion over her skin. Facing the window, she leaned back against Joan's breasts to give her neighbour's hands free reign. Joan let her fingers sneak down over Karen's shoulders, exploring her skin along the way, until they reached her nipples. Simultaneously, Joan tweaked both of Karen's nipples, her fingers slippery from the foam. Joan's breasts rubbed against Karen's back and her pubes pressed against her buttocks.

Karen saw herself in the reflection of the window, as if she was watching from the outside but experiencing it all as an insider as well. She pictured herself on her balcony, watching as Joan fondled a woman. Only, she was the woman who Joan was stroking and washing and getting moister in every spot.

Joan's hands travelled down now, transporting the slithery foam between Karen's legs. Her fingers slipped through her pubic hair and Karen followed the mirrored motions in the window. She witnessed her mouth opening wider when one of Joan's fingers skated along her clit. Joan's other hand was on her left nipple, rolling it between thumb and index finger while her mouth remained at ear-height.

"As far as bathrooms go," Joan hissed. "This one has a prime location." Her finger encircled Karen's clit. "And you know how hard that is to come by in this city."

Karen closed her eyes, blocking out the sight of herself getting more and more aroused by Joan's actions and words. She forgot about the people that might or might not be watching. She slanted her body against Joan, who held her with a firm grip around her chest, her fingers at perfect nipple-height.

"Of all the times I've had sex in this apartment," Joan continued and her use of the word "sex", the way she let the "s" sit on her lips before releasing it, made Karen's knees buckle, "I would say seventy-five percent of them started here."

Joan gradually increased the pressure on Karen's clit. It was so swollen and lubricated by both her own juices and the soapy water that Karen knew she wouldn't be able to take much more direct stimulation.

"It's no surprise you're getting so excited." The pace of Joan's fingers increased, half-hovering over and half-caressing her clit. "I've noticed how often you watch me."

Karen's nipple was just as wet as her pussy. Joan's fingers kept manipulating it, squeezing it tightly and then releasing it to the same rhythm as her other hand manoeuvred around Karen's clit.

"Come for me now." Karen never had anyone say that to her and the sheer power of the words made her shiver with delight. Her clit throbbed against Joan's fingers as she climaxed, her legs weak and her head thrown back on Joan's shoulder.

"And that was just foreplay." Joan kissed Karen's neck and chuckled in her ear.

Karen caught her breath and checked herself in the window. Heat flushed her cheeks as drops of water streamed from her hair. She could give as good as she could get and she had every intention of doing so.

"You really love the sound of your own voice, don't you?" Karen turned around and cupped Joan's cheeks. "I know a thing or two that should shut you up." A mischievous grin spread across Joan's face.

"Can't wait." Joan started to get out of the bath.

"Oh no, I don't think so." Karen grabbed her by the arm and pulled her back. "Right here is where I want you." She brought her lips to Joan's ear. "Where everyone can see you."

"Fair enough." Joan leaned in to kiss her, a wet slippery meeting of lips involving teeth and the sucking of tongues. When they broke apart Karen spun Joan around and gently pushed her forward until her hands rested on the narrow ledge above the tub. Her back was arched inward and her behind stuck out, giving Karen ample access.

Karen slicked her wet hands over Joan's back while peering into the darkness of the city. Whoever was watching tonight was getting one hell of a show. She traced her fingers between Joan's raised cheeks and wished she had a strap-on at her disposal. Joan probably had one on offer, but Karen couldn't wait that long. This moment in the shower was theirs. Weeks of peeking had come down to this. She was about to plunge her fingers inside Joan and she had no time for interruptions.

Sitting down on the edge of the tub for stability and a better view—much better than the glowing buildings outside—Karen let her fingers dance across the length of Joan's moist pussy. Drops of water trickled down her legs and clouds of foam clung to her skin.

"Fuck me," Joan moaned and Karen had to obey. There was

something in Joan's voice, an implied authority impossible to ignore, that urged Karen to follow its commands. She couldn't wait for Joan to ask her to come for her again. But she had some unfinished business to attend to first.

Karen positioned one hand close to Joan's clit and the other at the entrance of her glistening pussy. She circled a finger around the rim a few times and then gently pushed inwards. Joan's heat wrapped itself around her, clamping her fingers tight. Desire pooled between Karen's legs again as she saw Joan's back arch, like a trembling wire on a bow, to the rhythm of her thrusts.

"More." Joan's voice grew hoarse as her moans increased. "Faster."

Karen didn't waste any time executing the command. She fucked Joan with three fingers while the thumb of her other hand inched closer to her clit. Joan was captured between her arms, at her mercy, like in the countless fantasies she had given in to lately.

The walls of Joan's pussy contracted around Karen's thrusting fingers. Karen could feel Joan's climax approach as her pussy tightened around her knuckles, driving them together. Touching another woman inside like that, exerting such power over her pleasure, always drove Karen a little crazy.

Joan breathed heavily now. A syncopated moan crescendoed out of her throat, announcing the arrival of her orgasm. She bucked down on Karen's fingers one last time before trembling through the remnants of her climax.

Karen slipped out of Joan, a bit reluctant to leave the intense warmth of her pussy, and helped her up.

"Excellent handiwork," Joan said as she shook her wrists to release the tension from them. "And excellent idea." A sparkle twinkled in her eyes. Karen wondered what else her new favourite neighbour had in store tonight.

"Let me show you my bedroom."

"Can't wait to see the view."

They scrambled out of the tub and exited the bathroom still wet from the deluxe shower.

The curtains were drawn in Joan's room, only allowing for slivers of light to pierce through the cracks.

"Very modest." Karen grinned and started to reach for the curtain, curious to see what lay on the other side. Joan yanked her arm away mid-stretch and pulled Karen towards the bed, where she waited with her legs spread and her skin hot and wet.

"It's your turn now." Joan let her back crash onto the mattress and dragged Karen on top of her.

"For what?" Before Joan could answer, Karen kissed her until her entire body throbbed with desire again.

"You've been ogling me for weeks." Joan pushed Karen up by her shoulders, a dirty smirk plastered across her face. "Don't tell me you haven't been dreaming of this."

"If I have." Karen lowered herself and bit Joan's earlobe before continuing. "The person in my dreams was never this cocky."

With a swift movement, Joan eased herself out from under Karen and straddled her before she could protest. "Speaking of which." Joan cast her glance to the bedside table next to the bed. "I have a new toy I've been dying to try out."

Karen's pussy tingled at the thought of Joan fucking her, again and again. "I'll be your guinea pig on one condition."

"What's that?" The last drops of water splashed down from Joan's hair onto Karen's neck.

"Open the curtains." Just saying the words made Karen's blood sizzle.

Joan snickered and found Karen's ear. "Somehow I always end up with the shy ones."

CHAMPAGNE

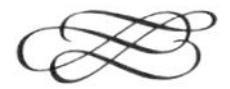

It was the middle of the day when I saw her draining the last of her Champagne. She sat alone at the bar, staring blankly at a row of empty crystal flutes suspended from a metal railing. I don't know why she caught my eye. Maybe it was the way she fiddled with her pale fingers, as if itching for a cigarette, or how her bright red hair seemed to catch fire under the ceiling spots.

I'd just spent half a paycheck on a designer lamp at Lane Crawford and I was feeling quite audacious, in that devil-may-care reckless way, when you've paid a ludicrous amount of money for something you don't really need.

She drank Champagne as if it was the least celebratory drink on the planet, exuding a sort of world-weariness that could only result from having too much of everything. Or not having anything left to dream of.

The bar was an open circle in the centre of the shopping mall, cordoned off by deep-red velvet strings bleeding from the ceiling—like a shredded curtain put up more for effect than privacy. She held court in the middle of it, ennui on obvious display on her face. And I wanted to help her, make her feel better.

Undoubtedly, in this city, there are lots of other people much more deserving of my help. People in actual need, with no money or a roof over their head. Nevertheless, I walked into the bar and I ordered a glass of Champagne. I picked a stool two seats from her, just at the curve of the bar, so it looked as if I had no choice but to glance at her. She kept gazing ahead, as if all the answers to her prayers were to be found in those empty glasses. By the time I had finished half my drink, I still might as well not have been there. She hadn't acknowledged my presence once, despite the two of us being the only patrons.

I had plenty of time to study her. The fingers of her right hand, the one closest to me, sported three obnoxiously big rings, all of them gold. One by one, she kept twirling them around. Age-wise, I estimated her between thirty-five and forty-five. Her skin stretched a bit too tautly around her temples so I guessed she'd had some work done, but not to the point where it looked unnatural.

What drew me in most was that big shock of ginger hair. It stretched out beyond her frail frame, reaching out to the world around her, contrasting sharply against her self-sufficient body language.

I resorted to the oldest trick in the book and had the bartender pour her another glass of Champagne. The lamp I had just bought had financially ruined me already, so I was at a point where I could fool myself into not caring anymore. I pretended that I had gotten a discount and was spending the money I saved on a few victory drinks. It's true that my mind can fool me into believing almost anything, as long as I want to. Or libido is in play.

Her bar stool creaked when she turned towards me, not something you would expect in the lavish establishment we found ourselves in. She fixed a pair of moss green eyes on me, devoid of any hope or sparkle. It's then that I knew I had made the right decision. I also realised it wasn't so much about helping her as it was about doing this for myself. Despite her desperate demeanour, and the lack of life in her eyes, I was strangely attracted to her. Just like that, it had hit me. I'd seen her and I had felt it ripple through me. A shot of desire up my spine. A sudden tingle between my legs. I wanted her. Sometimes it's as simple as that.

"Such gentlemanly behaviour for a woman," she said and lifted her glass.

"You looked like you needed it." I held her gaze, even though I could feel it drifting away already.

"I always do." Unlike her eyes, her voice sparkled. Her accent harboured that New York confidence I always believed to only exist in movies. But she was real and I wanted her even more. "What's your excuse?"

"Do I need one?"

"Not as far as I'm concerned." She let her glance drop down into her glass. "Thanks," she murmured. "For trying to cheer me up."

"Do you want to talk about it?" Part of me was dying to hear her story, while the other part just wanted to kiss her despair away.

"God no." She ended her statement with a puffy chuckle, a sort of resignation to the fact that everything was lost. "I'm not a big believer in verbalising issues. I'd rather ignore them." With that, she chucked back the rest of her Champagne. "Another one?" She nodded at my glass.

"Do you want to go somewhere a bit more upbeat?" I took a chance, hoping she was the spontaneous type.

"Like where?" She shot me a defiant smirk that almost silenced me. I didn't even know her name. It didn't seem like relevant information.

"A taxi to my place." I said it as if it were the only option. I could have suggested the zoo, or the beach, but that would just have been a waste of time.

At last, she smiled. She bared a row of too white teeth, but the unexpected dimples in her cheeks made up for it. "The foolishness of youth." She shook her head, but kept her smile. "What's so great about your place?"

Absolutely nothing, I thought. "It has the most interesting view you'll ever see." It wasn't really a lie. My living room window looked straight into my neighbour's kitchen and he loved to cook shirtless. Not that I found that compelling in the least.

"Well then." She gestured at the barman for the check. "I simply can't decline."

I grabbed the fancy bag that held my lamp and followed her to the exit. Her pace indicated determination, a trait I hadn't yet noticed in her. Then again, I'd only seen the sadness in her eyes and not much else.

As we approached the taxi stand, my heart started hammering in my throat. The first sign of doubt. I didn't question my desire as much as I did my tactics and the state of my flat. She didn't strike me as a woman accustomed to bruises caused by ancient furniture and beds smaller than king-sized.

She hailed a cab with authority and waited for me to give the driver directions. Her eyes rested on me, cool and expectant.

I mumbled my street name in Chinese, a flash of new confidence zipping through me, and shot her a wide smile.

She locked her sad green eyes on me, chewing her bottom lip. "This better be good," she said.

My mental state yo-yoed between panic and brashness. I wasn't exactly in the habit of picking up women at the mall, let alone what looked like an extremely neglected housewife.

"It should be better than a mid-afternoon alcohol daze." I

winked at her, despite beginning to feel rather foolish. "Minus the nasty hangover."

"I visit that bar several times a week, always claiming the same stool." She stared out of the window, her eyes facing away from me and her hair slightly bobbing to the movement of her mouth. "And I wait for something interesting to happen." She shuffled around in her seat, her tailored trousers rustling against the taxi's leather interior. "It seems like my patience has paid off." She spun her head around and, this time, the gloominess in her glance was replaced by hope.

Sparks of electricity buzzed through my blood. I signalled the driver to stop and paid him. Seconds later we stood on the pavement of my street. I could only guess what was going through her mind while mine was racing to come up with a plan of action.

"Interesting." She looked my building up and down. "I hardly ever come here. It's sort of downtown, isn't it?"

That was the first time I'd heard my neighbourhood described like that. I didn't live in a posh high rise with sea views, and the facade was painted a sickly pink, but it was far from the dingiest area of the city.

I punched in the key-code, slightly embarrassed to live in a building without a doorman, and gestured for her to follow me. The flickering of the light bulb in the stairwell, to which I usually attributed a sort of romantic quality, now annoyed me.

"No lift?" She inquired.

I was grateful for the half-darkness covering the sudden blush on my cheeks.

"It's good exercise." I countered, a nervous giggle underscoring my insecurity.

She turned around and gave me a quick once-over with her bright green eyes. "I can see that."

I couldn't afford to pay a fortune in rent, but at least I didn't need a plastic surgeon to make me feel good about myself.

Countless daily trips up and down the stairs took care of the rest.

We climbed the two flights to my floor in silence, just the hiss of our breath and the clacking of her shoes on the concrete steps accompanying our trek.

I unlocked the door to my apartment and held it wide. I wondered if now was a good time to ask for her name, but figured she'd tell me if she wanted me to know. I scanned my living room for any signs of blatant laziness and immaturity. Apart from a Winnie the Pooh handkerchief box, and two empty bottles of wine flanking the coffee table, I didn't detect anything too damaging. If anything, I thought my boudoir looked quite suitable for entertaining unexpected guests.

"How about that view." She strutted towards the window.

An idea flashed through my head. "Sometimes the best view is not outside of the window." I hoisted my T-shirt over my head and presented myself to her wearing only a bra and jeans.

"You don't say." She leaned her backside against the windowsill and eyed me with a piercing glance.

I placed my hands at my sides and shot her back what I hoped was a seductive glare. Underneath my frumpy jeans and T-shirt I always wore quality lingerie.

"What makes you think I partake from the lady buffet?" She painted a crooked smile on her lips.

"Call it female intuition." I was going out on a limb, but I'd already had the audacity to take my top off and could hardly back down now.

"I am a married woman, you know. Unhappily, but still married."

"I learned to ignore a woman's marital status a long time ago." This time I surprised myself. It was as if someone else had taken control of my body and mouth. As far as I knew I'd never shared so much as a kiss with a married woman, let alone what I was hinting at here.

She merely chuckled in reply. I took a step closer to the window. Whatever she said, I didn't pick up the slightest vibe of hesitation.

"Stop," she said and held out her palm, fingers pointed upwards. "You might as well take it all off now so that I can have a good look at you." The light falling through the window caught in her red curls and created a halo effect behind her head. For a minute, I felt as if I was about to strip for a disillusioned angel.

I brought my hands to my back to unclasp my bra and let it slide off me. It fell to the ground with a soft, dry thud. I hoped my neighbour wouldn't suddenly decide to cook a three-course meal in his kitchen.

The woman cocked her eyebrows up. "And?" Her voice dipped a little lower, to that sultry register from which no one can hide.

I flipped open the button of my jeans and ignored how my brain was trying to catch up with how my body was behaving. It wasn't every day that I slowly undressed for a stranger in my living room. Goosebumps spread over the plains of my skin and my nipples creased into hard peaks as I lowered the zipper of my trousers. I always wore matching underwear—as if always prepared for this sort of behaviour.

Out of nowhere, her hand pulled me closer by the waistband of my panties and one of her red-nailed fingers slipped inside, not deep, just browsing the edge of my pubic hair, but enough to jolt my clit into a quick, pulsing action.

I didn't know her name, we hadn't even kissed, but she felt so incredibly close. I held her gaze while she explored beneath the flimsy fabric of my panties. My jeans gaped wide open around the movement of her finger. Her nail scraped my skin as her finger travelled lower.

I inched closer, wanting to lean in for a kiss, but she tilted her head back, indicating kissing was not part of the deal.

"I need to see your eyes," she said and, just like that, her finger grazed my clit.

My breath stopped for an instant as desire crashed its way through my flesh. Was I supposed to just stand there and take it? I let my hands fall down next to her, holding on to the windowsill for support. Her finger slid lower and connected with my wetness. My nipples grazed the silk of her blouse. Her moist Champagne breath landed on my skin. Her lips stretched into the widest smile as she entered me, as deep as she could with the first stroke.

"Ah." I clenched my fingers around the wood of the windowsill. Her eyes were still locked on mine. They seemed much darker than the bright green I'd seen earlier. She couldn't be much closer, yet she was so far away, so distant. It only made me wetter.

Her palm skated along my clit as she delved in and out of me. It was hardly a gentle motion and it surely lacked any kind of finesse, but finesse was the last thing on my mind. The build-up wasn't happening in my panties, it was taking place in her eyes. They narrowed every time she slipped back in, the tiny crow's feet around them deepening with effort.

My ragged breaths mixed with the slapping sound her hand made against my wetness. Apart from that, my flat was silent. I met her thrusts with my body as much as I could, as much as the restraint of still wearing my panties and my jeans let me. I wanted her naked and on top of me. I wanted her red curls splayed across my shivering skin. I knew it would never happen and it made me all the hotter for her in that moment.

She replaced one finger with two and positioned her thumb over my clit. Instantly, I pushed myself forward, my clit eager to be touched more. She let me set the pace and I bucked down hard on her fingers while grinding my throbbing clit against her thumb.

While biting her bottom lip, she brought her other hand

between her blouse and my breast, her palm connecting with my stiff nipple. She cupped my breast and squeezed hard and, as if that was the signal my body was waiting for, my knees buckled and crashed against her. Her heady, flowery perfume hit my nostrils as I came over her fingers, a quick heat thundering through my muscles.

Slowly, she eased her fingers out of me. I stood hunched over her, my body trembling, my breath coming out in clipped gusts.

"You were right." She kissed me gently on the cheek. "Your place does have the most interesting view."

"I'm glad you think so." I straightened my posture and shot her a seductive grin. "It comes with excellent service as well." With the back of my hand, I stroked her neck, but she caught me before my fingers dipped too close to her cleavage.

"Gosh," she said, "look at the time." She brought my hand to her mouth and planted a reverent kiss on my palm. "I must go."

"But—" I started.

"You can't tell by looking at me," she cut me off, "but I'm much better at giving than at receiving."

I stepped aside and let her pass. In two quick strides, she was by the door. Out of it in a second, as if she'd never been there. I looked at the shopping bag holding the lamp I'd bought earlier and considered it excellent value for money.

OFF THE RECORD

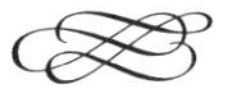

I opened the door myself, not something I usually do, but I wanted to start off on the right foot with Penny Fox, star reporter for The Hollywood Herald. I could see why she would dazzle men and women alike, with her porcelain skin, piercing blue eyes and impeccable Ralph Lauren suit. It satisfied me that she had dressed to impress. I wouldn't be spilling my PR-approved, innermost secrets to someone clad in jeans and a T-shirt.

"Such a pleasure, Miss Arragon." Penny extended her hand as I opened the door wide. I had not expected the British accent. Her hand felt cool in mine, not a hint of sweat.

"Please, call me Jill." I shot her a quick smile. Inviting someone into my home to write a profile on me was not an everyday activity, but at least it beat morosely answering the same old questions from the same old film reporters.

"The photographer will join us later." Her crisp voice cut through the sound of our heels on the tiled hallway floor. "I thought it better to get acquainted in private first."

"Excellent idea." As much as I loved the camera—and vice versa—posing for pictures always made me feel awkward. I led

Penny through the hall to the patio at the back of the house. Somehow, it felt better to conduct the interview outside of the walls that shielded my private life.

"Tea? Coffee?" I asked while inviting her to sit, giving the impression that I always fetched refreshments for guests myself. I knew I wasn't kidding anyone.

"Iced tea would be lovely." Penny's blue eyes caught mine. They were so pale, almost translucent. The way she pronounced the word 'tea' made how I said it appear completely inadequate.

"Coming right up." I all but shot her a wink before I turned and walked inside the house. I poured two glasses from a jug of iced tea my housekeeper had prepared earlier and carried them outside.

Penny had placed a small tape recorder on the wooden table top. "Do you mind if I record our conversation?" She said it the way people say things they're used to exclaiming every day.

"I didn't know they still made these." I sat down and reached for the recorder. It was grey and heavy in my hand, the shine of its glossy exterior having faded years ago.

"They don't." Penny's blue-eyed glare landed on me again. "But I take excellent care of my belongings."

Linda, my PR-person, had sent me a bullet-pointed fact sheet on Penny Fox, along with copies of a few high profile interviews she had done for The Hollywood Herald before, but I felt sorry for not doing my own research. Her eyes gave nothing away either.

"You have a lovely home, Jill." Penny let her gaze drift across the grounds behind me while slinging one long leg over the other.

"Thank you." I sipped from my drink, torn between finding her eyes again or avoiding them altogether.

"Do you live here alone?"

She hadn't switched on her recorder yet, but if this was the icebreaker she had planned, I was in for one hell of an interview I didn't want to have. "I do." I shuffled in my seat, my hand instinctively reaching for the recorder and covering it with my palm. "I take it Linda has informed you about off-limit topics?"

"Extensively." Penny's facial muscles didn't flinch, but her hand found mine across the table. "There's nothing to worry about. I respect your privacy."

Instinctively, I loosened my grip on the recorder and let my hand slip from underneath hers, letting her reclaim ownership of the device. After I let my hand fall back into my lap, my skin seemed to sizzle and a sudden flush shot up to my cheeks. I quickly took another sip from my tea.

"Shall we get on with it?" I asked, after swallowing a few greedy gulps to cool me down.

Penny nodded, her lips still drawn into the same neutral grimace, and pressed a button on the recorder. Without the help of any notes—just that cool stare of her bottomless eyes—she asked me about my last movie, my slow but steady rise to fame over the past six years, my obvious reluctance to comply to Hollywood's body standards and my smart choice of film roles that had contributed to my current position of Tinseltown's leading lady.

I replied calmly and eloquently to Penny's questions, the way Linda had taught me, hearing myself say the same things I say in every interview. Usually, these situations tend to bore me, but the complete absence of emotion on Penny's face intrigued me. I didn't perceive it as lack of interest, which would have been rude, nor as a strategy to lure more out of me than I was willing to say. The more I let my eyes linger on Penny's lanky figure, back straight, one arm casually resting on the table, the other poised on the armrest of her chair, the more I was convinced this was simply how she was. There was no pretense, only straightforwardness and respectful but, frankly, rather disappointing questions.

I had read her other pieces and, unless she was extremely good at selling lies as truth—a skill most Hollywood reporters excelled in—this lame line of questioning was not how she got her interviewees to give her quotes that made the front page every time.

"Thank you," she said after I had responded with the obligatory 'I've been so lucky' phrase to her last question. She clicked off the recorder and put it away in her purse. "Do you mind if I ask you some questions off the record before Steve arrives?"

I arched up my eyebrows.

"The photographer," she offered, while checking her wristwatch—a slim, delicate and understated piece of jewelry I could appreciate.

"Sure." Linda would not approve, but this whole interview with The Herald's often lauded Penny Fox had been so anticlimactic, I wanted more. Maybe this was how she did it. Maybe she had me right where she wanted me as per her secret strategy. And was that a twinkle breaking through the ice in her eyes?

Penny leaned over the table, breaking posture for the first time, and looked me straight in the eyes. "Don't you ever get bored of this act?"

I glared at her in silence for a few seconds, as if in the middle of a staring contest. I looked away first, no match for Penny's blue ice.

"Let me rephrase," Penny said, after I had averted my gaze and failed to answer. "Am I correct in assuming you lead a somewhat lonely life?" She spread her arms, her fingers pointing to the luscious grounds behind us. "All of this and no one to share it with."

"How off the record are we?" She was goading me—in a

very un-British, direct manner, as well.

"Couldn't be more off." She pinned her eyes on me again. "And you and your people will get ample time to approve the article before it goes to press." She leaned back in her chair and crossed her legs again. Even when seated, they seemed to go on forever. "You can be frank with me."

From a distance, we could just be two women sitting in a garden drinking iced tea together. Or, it could even be the most exciting part of a date progressing according to plan. A date. I hadn't been on one since Ari, my agent, hooked me up with Oliver Fitz for the Golden Globes.

He made for an excellent beard—attentive, chatty, even throwing in a few jokes that were actually funny—but we both knew very well why we were paired together that night. I didn't even have the chance to invite him in for a drink because, after the party that Ari made us stick around at for forty-five minutes, we were carted off in separate cars.

"Yes, it can be lonely," I said. "But it's my life."

"A gilded cage." Penny's voice had dropped a bit. I assumed out of sympathy.

"Put yourself in my shoes." I wasn't giving anything away by speaking in platitudes.

"I'd love to." Penny let her gaze slide down towards my feet. "What size are you?"

For the first time, she made me chuckle. Her skin crinkled around the eyes when she smiled—not a luxury a lot of women in Hollywood afford themselves.

"If you don't mind the loss of decorum, I may actually take them off." I started heeling off my shoes without waiting for a reply. I'd never worn them before and they pinched my toes even when seated.

"It's your house."

"Yes," I nodded. "Another gilded cage."

I'd been living in this 'dream mansion' in the hills for over a year and nothing even remotely exciting had happened in any of its eight bedrooms. Even when reading a sexy story online, I was afraid some journalist-turned-hacker would somehow find out, and caution always won out over pleasure. In fact, Penny Fox turning up on my doorstep, albeit completely orchestrated and with the necessary documents signed, was quite possibly the most thrilling event to happen since I'd moved in. Just me, another woman and some innuendo. A girl like me had to get her kicks somewhere.

"Why don't I call off the photographer and you pour us something stronger?"

I lost myself in Penny's stare for an instant before replying. "Indeed, why not?" I was glad to not have to pose and, additionally, this interview was getting more interesting by the second.

While she reached for her phone in her purse, I sauntered inside and stood in front of my well-stocked drinks cabinet. Most of the bottles had remained untouched. Did she want wine or champagne or something stronger? It was up to me and my decision would set the tone, perhaps even dictate the outcome. Wine was too non-committal but, perhaps, if I opened a bottle of Champagne, she would feel compelled to stay until it was empty. But maybe that would come across as a tad too celebratory. I couldn't stomach brandy or Scotch and, in the end, grabbed a bottle of port from the shelf. Elegant, aged port seemed perfect for this afternoon.

Penny gave me a nod of approval when I deposited two small glasses on the table along with the bottle I had picked. I poured and we drank in silence for a few minutes. It started to feel like a date then. But, whereas my life was highly publicized —apart from the bits I carefully and professionally hid from the press—I didn't know anything about Penny Fox.

"Why Hollywood reporting?" I asked, because, truth be told, she looked more like a fashion journalist, or someone who would take an interest in topics more worthy of her time than people like me—the idolized and overpaid who happened to be good at pretending to be someone we were not.

"I've always been interested in people, in what hides behind the public facade. Their secret tragedies." She took another sip. "When I profile someone famous and adored, it's never my intention to bust the myth, although I do tend to subtly hint at that—too subtly for most people in this town to see—but, by then, I've had the chance to see it with my own eyes and that's what makes it worthwhile for me."

"So you're a well-paid voyeur who gets off on being admitted behind otherwise closed doors?"

"That's a bit harsh." She blinked for what seemed like the first time. "And I'm not that well-paid either."

"I'm sorry," I said. "Do you live alone?"

She bit her bottom lip, possibly trying to hide the grin spreading across her face. "Touché." She scanned my face for a split second, then refilled our glasses. "Look, I won't sit here, drink your port and pretend to be your friend to get something out of you that may give me an original angle. I pride myself on treating the people I write about with respect. I don't know if you're familiar with my work, and obviously you don't have to take my word for it, but you can trust me not to spill the beans on you." She took a few big gulps of the port, which isn't really a liquor to knock back like that. "And yes, I live alone. Have done for as long as I've been in L.A., despite a three-year relationship with someone whose name I can't mention."

I wasn't expecting that last bit. Instantly, and rather ironically, curiosity took hold of me. It burned like a broadening flame inside of me, despite my own constant need for privacy. Human nature in the twenty-first century. "A man or a woman?"

She gave me a wry smile. "Bottoms up and quid pro quo?" Her eyes glimmered like blue pearls, her face still pale white.

She curled her fingers around the tiny stem of her glass and brought it to her mouth, already tilting her head back. "A woman," she said, licking her lips. She eyed my full glass.

The liquor burned my throat as I tried to swallow it all down in one go. I couldn't speak for a while, not because I was so afraid to say it—it had been so long since I'd last admitted it to someone, the words were practically clawing their way out —but because my stomach was on fire.

Penny gave me time to recover. She was clearly a more experienced drinker than I was. Maybe being an A-lister's secret girlfriend had something to do with that. She wasn't leaving here before I found out who it was. Maybe Janet Rhyne. I'd always had my suspicions about her. Or Hollie Harper. Then again, it seemed as if my gaydar had stopped performing altogether the instant I scored my first major role and signed with Ari.

"I'm bisexual," I said.

"Sure." Penny nodded. "Almost obligatory these days. It looks good on the resume. Not to mention Twitter."

"What's wrong with being bisexual?" I could tell she wasn't having any of it.

"Absolutely nothing. Just as there's nothing wrong with being a lesbian either."

"Fine." I scanned my surroundings. I saw my gorgeous empty house in front of me, my manicured backyard reflected in the windows. A few birds chattered. In front of me sat Penny Fox, blue-eyed, on her way to being tipsy, and highly attractive. I had nothing to lose. "You got what you came for. I am a lesbian."

"You know," Penny slanted her body forward again, folding her legs under the chair, "I truly believed that was what I had come for, until now."

"Too anti-climactic?" The air around us seemed to change,

the oxygen suddenly sucked out of it, leaving us both a little breathless.

"No." Penny shook her head, while dragging her chair closer to mine. "But now I want to kiss you as well."

As if pondering her confession, I inspected her lips. "What? You're a lesbian and I'm a lesbian and that automatically means we should kiss?" I slipped to the front of my chair. She was so close, I could feel puffs of her ragged breath roam across my chin.

"I understand your cynicism, but I choose to reject it." Up close, her eyes were less mysterious. Or maybe Penny had warmed up to me.

"If I let you kiss me, you'll have to give me a name." Heat tumbled through my veins, pooling between my legs.

"How about you kiss me then?" She leaned closer, her lips almost touching mine.

I pressed my mouth to hers, tasting port, and someone else for the first time in months. I kissed her as if we were the last two lesbians on earth, in the garden of my Hollywood Hills house and I couldn't care less who could see, or who would find out.

Breathless, we came up for air. "Satisfied now?" I asked.

"Not by a long shot." Penny rose from her chair, grabbing my wrists in the process. "How about an intimate tour of your house?"

"Let's start with the bedroom." I laced my fingers in between hers and pulled her inside, straight up the stairway that led to my bedroom. Her heels made hollow noises on the steps, thuds of anticipation behind my bare feet.

From my bedroom window the view over the city was stunning, but Penny only glanced out of it for a split second, all her attention focused on me. Despite not wearing shoes, I still stood as tall as she did.

"Gorgeous," she said, bending the 'r' in a way I'd never be able to. "And I'm not talking about the view."

I gave a chuckle at her corniness. "Was it Eliza Hews?" I asked, suddenly being able to envision them together clearly—in a situation like this.

She shook her head. "I signed legal documents." A new sort of grin appeared on her face as she came for me. It lit up her eyes, leaving them as blue as the sky on the other side of the window. "I really can't say."

I wondered if there was such a thing as a fetish for closeted movie stars.

By the time she let her linen blazer slip from her arms, her eyes still pinned on mine—like some sort of intense tantric foreplay—I couldn't care less about her motivations for being in my bedroom, nor who her secret lover had been. My nipples stabbed into the fabric of my bra. Every nerve ending in my body seemed to throb, leaving my skin ultra-sensitive.

Then, her hands were in my hair. Those long, pale fingers pulling me in. The kiss that followed shot right through me, my lips pulsing as much as my clit was between my legs. Her fingers roamed from my hair, along my neck, to the front of my blouse.

I noticed I was shivering as she undid the buttons, one by one, slowly. Penny's lips were parted, as if ridding me of my clothes was an extremely strenuous activity. I lunged for the hem of her silk top and started tugging it upwards. When I pulled it over her head, I couldn't believe how white her skin was. The most unlikely color for someone living in Los Angeles. I couldn't stop staring at it, but I knew what that felt like, so I quickly refocused my attention on taking off her bra.

Her frame was boyish, her breasts small—barely filling my hands when I cupped them. If I'd been in a magical circus with contorting mirrors showing the complete opposite of me, this would have been the image reflecting back.

Once she unhooked my bra, she started pushing me towards the bed. I unzipped my skirt and let it drop to the floor before sitting down on the edge and watching her step out of her suit pants. When she straddled me, I half-expected her skin to be cold against mine, like porcelain. But nothing but heat sizzled between us. Right before she kissed me again, it occurred to me that her clandestine girlfriend could quite possibly have been Joanne Moz. I'd co-starred with her in... Two of Penny's fingers closed around my nipple, leaving me panting against the skin of her neck.

"Lie down," she said, her tone of voice nothing like the one she'd used for the interview. She pushed herself up so I could scoot back on the bed until my entire body was supported. She lay down next to me, a finger already trailing along the delicate skin of my belly. "I can't share my secrets, but I can fuck you," she said, a delicious smirk pulling at her lips.

I could only nod. If I had known interviews could be such excellent foreplay, I would have taken greater pleasure in them in the past. Then again, I'd never come across a reporter like Penny Fox before.

She briefly kissed my lips, letting her tongue flit inside for an instant, before moving on to my neck.

I ruffled my hands through her gelled, ginger hair. Despite appearing wiry at first, it fell softly between my fingers. Her own fingers were already browsing the waistband of my panties, cruising along the line they'd created on my lower belly.

Before her lips touched my nipple, after having left a moist trail along my breast, she looked up, the tip of her finger dipping under the waistband of my panties. She looked at me as if asking for permission, but didn't wait for a response. It was probably plastered all across my face. How I wanted her. Lips on my nipple, fingers inside.

Her eyes widened as her hand made its way into my panties.

"Fuck, you're wet," she said, her voice all hoarse and raw. As if needing to directly see the evidence, instead of just feeling, she retracted her hand and yanked my panties down. "Spread wide for me," she urged, as if she instinctively knew how it excited me when someone made demands like that.

I let my knees fall left and right for her, just like she asked me to. My one hand was back in her hair, the other behind the pillow—leverage for pushing myself up towards her. I could already feel her fingers skate along my soaking pussy lips, sucking her fingers in.

Her eyes, locked on mine again, narrowed when her fingertips circled my clit briefly. Shots of electricity fired through my flesh. She'd have me begging soon. I didn't see any patience in her eyes though, only hunger and need. She went deep with the first thrust, touching me the way only a woman's fingers ever could.

"Oooh," I moaned, too loud for the bright room we found ourselves in. Too guttural for a supposedly straight film star with a woman in her bed. But it was a cry of release, a moan of freedom. Because in that bed, on that afternoon, with Penny Fox's long fingers inside of me, I was more me than I'd ever been in my life.

Penny's eyes on me were as effective as her fingers inside. I held her crystal blue gaze as long as I could, but she kept thrusting and I kept moaning and years of frustration seemed to seep out of every pore of my skin. When I started to thrash my head this way and that, I felt her shift. Her hair slipped from my fingers and it tumbled across my stomach as her mouth found my clit.

"Oh fuck," I groaned, now holding on to the pillow with both hands. "Oh, Penny."

She fucked me with quick deep strokes of her fingers, while

my clit disappeared between her lips. Every muscle in my body tensed, preparing for release—for freedom. Then she added another finger, spreading me wide, opening me up even more, and I caved.

Everything rolled over me at once. The joy of being with another woman. The desire to experience this on a regular basis. The frustration of hiding. It rolled over me with shocking bursts of pleasure spasming through my muscles and tingling in my belly. The sensitive spots her fingers and tongue connected with spread all over my body, until my climax was complete.

"It was Sandra Wong," she said, after the retreat of her fingers, her face close to mine again, eyes on me.

"I knew it," I said, but, by then, I really couldn't have cared less.

ALL OF ME

Sex with Laila was always dirty, but when she whispered in my ear mid-fuck that she'd be wanting my ass next, my pussy clutched itself around her hand so hard I expected her knuckles to come out bruised. I rode out my climax, my fingers lost in her raven-black hair as colours collided in my brain, my muscles flexing to the rhythm of her last strokes inside of me. Then she surprised me again by turning me over on my stomach, my backside bare and, seemingly, all hers. I'd gathered she meant next time she fucked me. I just hadn't presumed that my enthusiastic reaction to her words would lead to it happening so quickly.

Laila was in charge in the bedroom and in the kitchen, the two rooms of our flat where I was merely required to serve, to not take any initiative. I was a sous-chef at best in both places, but my pleasure always came first. I was well-fed and satisfied, living on a diet of expertly spiced dishes and my girlfriend's delicious golden-brown fingers buried in my cunt at regular intervals. So far, she'd only teasingly ventured in the direction of my ass.

She covered my naked body with hers, her soft flesh moulding over me.

"Your ass is mine tonight," she hissed into my ear, while spreading my legs with her knee. I wondered what she meant with 'mine'. Would she just lick it, finger it maybe, or rely on other objects? Or all of that combined? I knew better than to ask. In the bedroom, Laila did all the talking.

When she pushed herself away from my ear, her taut nipples grazed the skin of my back. They swirled patterns along my spine until they reached my ass cheeks. As Laila guided one nipple along my crack, and despite the slamming orgasm she'd just delivered, I felt myself go moist again. This was more than sex. This was breaking boundaries.

I gasped as she parted my cheeks and allowed her nipple to explore a little further. I imagined how the caramel of her skin —and the dark chocolate of her nipple—was now contrasting with the creamy whiteness of my behind. The gentle probing of her stiff bud was enough to make my asshole pucker with anticipation and, first time or not, to grant her unlimited access to the unchartered territory that my ass represented. Not that she would ever ask. Laila appropriated things. She took them because, within the dynamic of our sex life, they simply belonged to her. Our affair was not complicated. She fucked me and I came.

Her long hair tickled my back and, regardless of not being able to see her, I could easily imagine the smirk edged around her mouth. I'd witnessed it enough, usually with a few of Laila's fingers sunk into me, to know its details by heart. Two fine lines bracketing her lips on the right as they curled up. Intensity burning in her eyes as she got off on my pleasure—and how I always, so easily, acquiesced.

She slipped one hand between my legs, under my pelvis, and found my clit, still a little sensitive from the previous round. Her nipple gently probed my crack while she circled a finger around my clit. Once, twice, just enough to make it perk up and want more, before retreating and focusing on my back door again. Laila was an expert at driving me crazy and, thus, at making me want things I never even knew existed before I met her—like a fist in my cunt and metal clamps on my nipples.

The room smelled of orgasms had and climaxes still to be bestowed. A heady perfume of anticipation blending with dirty delight.

On the way back up from teasing my clit, she coated her finger with juices dripping from my cunt. She traced a line from my pussy to my asshole and replaced her nipple with a wet fingertip. After dark, I always felt as if all of me belonged to Laila, with no exceptions. That she could do whatever she wanted. Possess me, cuff me, whip me. This sensation multiplied by a hundred when she circled the meaty part of her finger along my most delicate passage. If Laila ever asked me to marry her, this would be how she'd do it. By claiming me as hers, completely.

She entered slowly, letting my body adjust to the newness of what she was doing. My clit throbbed and my muscles tensed as the tip of her finger slipped in, invasive but welcome at the same time. I had no reference point for this, no prior experience to measure these sensations against. My asshole sucked at her finger as she pried deeper. I could hear her pant as she worked me with controlled excitement, which was pretty much the essence of Laila.

Before going deeper, she pulled out and started the circular motion again, drawing perfect circles around my rim. Laila knew me so well, as if she could read my body. She knew I'd be wanting more soon. I always wanted more of her.

This time, she pushed her finger in and out, just far enough to have me gasp for air every time she penetrated, stretching my asshole. No doubt preparing it for what was to come.

"I knew you'd like this," she said, her voice dropping into that low register reserved for kinky activities. "You're all mine now, babe." As if I wasn't already. "Mine," she repeated, and widened me further by adding another finger.

I yelped, unprepared for the filling sensation, the thickness of two fingers I could easily take in my cunt—four or a fist were most common—surprising me from the back. But I took it like the good girl she knew I was.

Juices leaked from my pussy, bathing my clit in wetness. I wanted to reach out and rub it, to add to the pleasure I was experiencing from behind, but I was afraid to move. With two fingers, Laila had me pinned down, at her mercy beneath her. The only way she wanted me.

She explored me further, twisting her fingers every time she stroked me inside. Bright white stars popped up on the back of my eyelids as I buried my head into the pillow. Surely, I couldn't climax just by having her fingers in my ass. Either way, I was certain Laila wouldn't let me. She was nowhere near done with me.

Stroking turned into thrusting while I felt her hair dance on my ass cheeks. I pictured the white globes of my butt being parted by her fingers, her brooding brown eyes staring down at me there. No one had ever seen me the way Laila had and I was fairly certain no one ever would.

Her hair slipped down my hips as she lowered herself and planted a tender kiss at the top of my crack. It stood in stark contrast to the way she was handling my asshole, ravaging it with her fingers at an increasingly merciless pace. If my hands had been anywhere near my clit, it would have been more than enough to propel me into another star-shattering orgasm.

She trailed a path of moist kisses along my butt cheek and, when reaching the top of its curve, bit into my flesh. Another shock ripped through my body, tightening my muscles and leaving me breathless. My pussy pulsed like crazy, roaring for attention, screaming for release.

I panted into the pillow as she withdrew her fingers, leaving my ass wanting more.

"On all fours," she commanded and sparks coursed through my blood as I exposed my pussy to the musky air of our bedroom. I settled on my hands and knees and, looking back through my arms, searched for her eyes. I found darkness, pure sexual desire mixed with the will to possess. To have and to give.

She reached for the bedside table where we kept all our toys —her toys—and watched how, from beneath handcuffs and blindfolds, she unearthed a dildo. Not the biggest one she owned, but not the smallest one either.

My throat went dry at the sight of it. Two fingers seemed nothing compared to the hot pink silicone cock she was about to negotiate into my virgin ass. Luckily, she grabbed a bottle of lube on her way back to my rear, on her way back to deflowering me once and for all.

She squirted a generous amount of lube onto the toy, not caring that half of it spilled onto the sheets and her knees. I watched her bring the dildo to my ass and closed my eyes. I had no other option than to submit to this darkness. She rubbed the cock along my crack, spreading the lube around. My muscles cramped when I felt the tip at my rim, not probing just yet, just familiarising itself, as if saying a polite hello before entering me.

I braced myself for impact, but, instead of easing it gently into my ass, Laila rammed it into my soaking wet pussy first, coaxing a loud cry from my throat. My cunt reacted instantly, clamping itself around the slick shaft of the toy, sucking it in. My clit stood to attention, but Laila was much too clever to attend to it. I wasn't clinging to the edge yet, wasn't ready to beg for release. And she hadn't fucked my ass yet.

She kept slamming the cock into me and I bucked down hard, my thigh muscles straining to catch as much of it as possible. When my groans betrayed my level of excitement, she retracted and dragged the tip up to my crack.

I exhaled and tried to relax, my body trapped in a frenzy of lust and sweltering desire. I wanted it now. Wanted her to invade my ass. Wanted her to take all of me. She put a hot hand on my butt cheek while she positioned the dildo. It was warm and slick with my juices, ready to slip in. My asshole automatically widened at its touch, bidding it a warm welcome.

The head disappeared inside me easily, my body parting for Laila, and I heard her gasp with wonder. She must have been soaking wet, her juices leaking onto the fancy silk sheets she'd brought back after her last visit to Morocco. The dildo filled me to the brim as she pushed it deeper. Never in my life had I felt so owned, so enslaved to one person, so at her will.

As she started sliding the toy in and out of me with slow steady movements, my asshole relaxed, contracting and expanding around the girth of the dildo. A simmering fire stirred in my belly, setting off explosions in my blood. The stars under my eyelids returned and this time they blazed brightly, absorbing me. My head spun through nothingness and everything as my body gave itself up to this new intrusion—as I surrendered.

"Touch yourself," Laila groaned, her voice nothing more than tones of pure lust, syllables strung together by passion. Her command surprised me, but I guessed that in subjecting me to her will in the way she was doing—a way she had never explored before but must have fantasised about a lot—she had amazed herself as well.

I let myself slip onto my shoulders, pushing my ass up higher, and shifted my weight to one side. My fingers couldn't reach my engorged clit fast enough. My cunt flexed around nothing while I tended to the aching bud between my legs.

Laila manoeuvred the dildo with more determination inside of me, out and in again, relentlessly driving me to new heights, taking more of me. I felt her free hand shake on my butt cheek as I trembled towards orgasm.

Galaxies collapsed in the darkness in front of my eyes, giving way to torrents of colour. I saw the brightest pink, the same colour as the dildo Laila was fucking me with. I saw myself, willing, loving it, shattering into rainbows as heat catapulted through me.

Feverishly, I worked my clit, rubbing it back and forth with my finger. The sensation of being filled to the brim, paired with the direct stimulation of my clit, was like bursting into heaven.

"Come on, baby," Laila's hoarse voice moaned. "Come for me now." She knew I was waiting for her to let me. I always did. The muscles around my asshole started contracting of their own volition, pulsing electric sparks of pleasure through my bones. I found that perfect spot on my clit, the one that is always the most sensitive, and stroked myself to an obliterating climax. I came then, for Laila, filled with her love for me, and a hot pink dildo.

Carefully, she withdrew the toy and, drained of everything, I collapsed onto the bed. My entire body throbbed and I knew, in that moment, there was nothing I wouldn't do for her—at least not in the two designated rooms of our house where she was the boss of me.

She poured her hot body over me, covering my sweat-soaked back with her chest, her limbs caressing every bit of my skin they could touch. As much as I loved the other-worldly climaxes, the purely physical bit, this part, the magical aftermath, was always the best.

"I love you," she said, her voice back to normal. Her mouth was buried in my hair, her breath barely reaching my ear. I knew I didn't have to say it back. I'd just shown my love for her.

Her nipples, rigid as marbles, poked into my shoulder muscles. "Next time," she continued. "I think I'll strap on." She slithered her body up my back until her lips found my ear. "I think you're ready for double penetration." She bit my earlobe before relaxing her muscles, her body going soft on top of me. I could hardly wait.

That was the first time my girlfriend claimed my ass and took all of me. I've yielded ever since.

STAIR WALKING

Delphine was the shy one. I never heard her come in or go out, yet she was always there, behind a closed door, when I needed to ask her something complicated about numbers. That's how I first started talking to her. Our only introduction before had been a limp wave from behind her desk, me leaning in the doorway with our boss: a loud, brash guy who thought he knew everything. In truth, it's always the quiet ones who know best.

I knocked gently on her door so as to not disturb too much of her inner peace.

"Yes?" The soft response came through the cheap wood veneer.

I nudged the door open only far enough to stick my head in —it felt wrong to expose her to too much of the world outside the safety of her office. She dressed in a butch fashion but in a posh way. Sneakers: dark, expensive ones. V-neck sweaters that didn't hide her breasts. The collar of her shirt always starched to perfection.

"Can you give me the markup on those metal rings?" I

checked the hot pink Post-It note clasped in my hand. "Product AJ457. I keep getting a different number."

There was something aristocratic about her cheekbones and her skin was always tanned, as if she spent her weekends at a remote beach house. She fixed her brown eyes on me and without blinking—or thinking—she said, "Twenty-eight percent."

I wanted to ask if the numbers were in her head, at her disposal at any given time, but Delphine was not one for using more words than necessary. I even believed her to have a daily quota. "Thanks," I said instead, and then padded back to my office, a little mesmerized by the intensity of her gaze.

That was the first time we spoke, and I will always remember it. Not because the conversation was significant in any way—I've asked her for countless percentages since then—but because it was the first time I felt it. My heart compressing a few beats into one and my skin flushing over nothing. She had that way about her, a brooding darkness in her eyes that got to me. A firmness in the way she stacked papers on her desk betraying her reasons to be so withdrawn. This wasn't personality; this was a well-practiced act.

Despite working on the sixth floor, Delphine always took the stairs. I suspected the close proximity to other people in the elevator was a nightmare for her. One evening, after we'd both worked late, I followed her down the staircase. I'd been meaning to do so for a while, but I didn't have a system with which I could track her comings and goings. She was elusive, wearing soft-soled shoes that barely made a whisper as she stalked through corridors. That night was simply a coincidence, highly anticipated on my part.

I couldn't hear a thing as I made my way down the stairs. She had maybe one flight on me, but I could only base that assumption on a silly time calculation—and numbers weren't really my thing. I quickened my pace in the hope of catching up with her and engaging her in some casual small-talk. Or even just walking down side-by-side in silence. That would have been enough for me, a mute camaraderie developing between us whilst at the edge of office hours.

"I don't like to be followed." A clipped voice growled at me through the semi-darkness. She'd chosen a flight with only a flickering bulb shedding scattered light on us to scare the living daylight out of me. She leaned against the wall, her eyes on fire —and terribly mismatched with the bourgeois butch flair of her outfit. Black trousers, white shirt, beige V-neck.

"I'm sorry. I didn't mean to—"

"Don't make the mistake of doing it again."

I'd barely caught my breath before she disappeared around the next corner. I stood there gasping for a while, until the sweat on my back dried up. All I wanted was to see her again.

I hurried down the steps, but by the time I made it into the lobby, she was long gone. I couldn't help but wonder what her punishment would be if she found me chasing her footsteps again.

The next few weeks, I took the stairs at irregular intervals hoping for the same dose of luck as last time. It didn't happen. Noise was not something I could go on, so I had to make it down every time with my heart throbbing in my chest, both hoping and fearing she'd be lurking around the next bend. She never was. But then the team-building event happened.

It was mandatory and stupid, like most of these things. As if putting people in a brightly lit room and pushing their invisible fun-button would ever work. We all gathered in the conference room where five tables of two had been set up in a circle. My boss stood in the middle, a yellow bow-tie straining around his wide neck.

"Welcome to our first annual quiz night. I'll be your host this evening." It was common knowledge that Greg's favorite hobby was playing a ruthless game of Trivial Pursuit—not even letting his children win on their birthdays. "Please divide yourselves into teams of two."

Delphine stood sulking in a corner, her hands in her pockets, one foot crossed over the other. Her eyes looked glassy, as if she were trying very hard to imagine she was anywhere else but there with us, her colleagues, in that conference room on a Friday evening after four. In two strides, I was by her side, avoiding Polly, with whom I shared an office.

"What do you think? I'm good at music, gossip, and geography. You're good at math and scaring people. The perfect pairing, no?" Perhaps my approach was too direct for Delphine, but I was amped up by the prospect of sitting next to her for ten full rounds of racking our brain for useless facts, a bottle of wine shared between us.

"Whatever." She shot me a weary glance, eyes dull and lips drawn into a thin slit. Where did she usually go on Friday nights? Did she have any special hobbies?

"I'll take your lack of enthusiasm as consent." I sat down at the nearest table. "What should we call our team?"

"How about the Stair Walkers?" She didn't smile. She said it as if it was a number she'd just crunched, dry and matter-of-factly.

"Good one."

We didn't win. Delphine appeared to not possess one competitive bone in her body, and we both lacked considerably in our knowledge of spiders, desert plants, and serial killers—three of Greg's favorite topics. We both knew the answers to the easy questions but blanked on the specialized ones, and Greg had prepared a lot of those. In the end, we turned it into a drinking game and downed a good gulp of cheap wine every time we came up short.

After the winners—Polly and Michael—had been crowned, and exaggerated compliments and condolences exchanged, Delphine grabbed her jacket and bag.

"I'm taking my usual route out of here," she said, one hand pushing a stray strand of hair out of her eyes and the other filling her trouser pocket. "Do you want to come?"

"Erm." It wasn't hesitation on my part, just shock. "Sure." I waved goodbye to the others, a boozy mist clouding my brain, and ducked into the stairwell with Delphine. The conference room was on the eighth floor, so we had two extra flights to tackle.

We descended in silence, the only sound the ticking of my heels on the concrete stairs. Click-clack, they went, ominous sounds in the darkness. Click-clack—the same rhythm as the throbbing between my legs.

When we reached the half-lit area of the stairwell, the one where she'd cornered me a few weeks earlier, she stopped dead in her tracks. She dropped her bag to the floor and crossed her arms in front of her chest. Her V-neck was orange today, the shirt underneath pitch black.

"I know why you followed me down here that day." Her voice was lower than usual and a little alcohol-soaked.

"Oh, yeah?" I leaned against the wall, acutely aware of the moist goings-on underneath the carefully ironed fabric of my skirt.

"I could practically smell it on you." She took a step closer. "Like a bitch in heat." I inhaled the wine on her breath.

"Why am I here, then?" The lamp blinked above us, erasing our presence for a split second.

"As if you don't know." Slowly, she let her jacket slip off her arms. It fell to the ground with a rustling whisper.

Of course, I knew. I just hadn't expected it. The sudden authority in her voice set my blood on fire, driving it, beat by beat, to my pulsing pussy lips. In response, I locked my eyes with her blazing brown ones and bit my bottom lip. As a yes, it would suffice.

"Unbutton your blouse," she commanded. I had known it would be this way. I had seen it in her glance that day I craned my head around the door frame of her office. I'd deducted it from the aura of controlled silence in which she wrapped herself. The quiet ones always know best.

I complied immediately, curling my fingers around the buttons of my bright white shirt. Once they were all open, allowing a glimpse at my white lace bra, I yanked the blouse out of my skirt and ripped it open, my chest on full display for Delphine. She didn't move a muscle. My nipples were hard against the fabric of my bra—their own silent scream for release.

"Off," Delphine ordered and, just like she'd done with her jacket earlier, I let it slide to the floor. I didn't follow its path with my eyes, unable to tear my gaze away from her, but I imagined the puddle of whiteness it created on the dirty concrete floor, not belonging there. As out of place as this whole scene.

"Bra." She nodded at my chest. My skin was covered in goosebumps, partly from excitement and partly from leaning against the cold gray wall.

I brought my arms to my back and unhooked my bra. My nipples perked up more as I let it glide off, adding to the heap of discarded white clothes on the floor.

"Hike up your skirt." Despite keeping her body in check, I could see everything happening in Delphine's eyes: a storm of emotions raging in the black of her pupils, darkness on darkness.

I did as I was told; after all, that's what I was there for. My panties were black and unremarkable. I hadn't exactly planned for this. She inched toward me and brushed her fingers against my belly. A high voltage current struck me, hard. It ripped through my flesh and collided in my clit. She slid a finger underneath the waistband of my panties. I understood. I couldn't get them off fast enough. I was naked except for a hitched-up skirt around my hips. She was fully dressed—and fully in command.

"You'd better be wet." Her voice was a mere, but loaded, whisper, a reflection of the turmoil in her eyes—like muted lightning.

Her finger grazed my clit, just an inkling of a touch, and then circled around it. Again and again. Close enough to make me gasp for air, but distant enough to not tip me over the edge. Her eyes were still on me, her ragged breath warming my nose. She must have seen I was hers then, must have seen it in my eyes between the uncontrolled fluttering of my lashes.

The circles became bigger, longer, until her fingers reached the rim of my cunt, a wet throbbing mess at her disposal. One soft sigh and she was in me, her finger going deep with the first thrust. I lost it then, lost my composure, and slammed my head against the wall, grating the skin of my shoulders raw against the uneven concrete.

"Kiss me," I hissed. It was only common courtesy. I knew she wouldn't do it.

"Shh," she said as she added another finger, another level of pleasure. She fucked me hard—there was nothing gentle about it. Just her fingers claiming my cunt. For balance, she leaned her other hand against the wall, and I let my cheek slide against the cotton of her sleeve. At least it was something.

Being an expert at sniffing them out, I'd been with women like Delphine before and I knew better than to come without explicit permission.

She buried her fingers deep inside of me, three now, spreading me wide.

"Oh, god," I moaned as the orgasm started to crash through me, that warm tingle that can quickly spread into wildfire. It roared in my neglected clit and in my puffed-up pussy lips. It shattered my self-control as it roamed across my flesh and trembled through my muscles. And then, she retreated, leaving me with a big, gaping wound of a cunt and a million unfulfilled desires.

"Come for me now." It was more a grunt than a command, the edge of a dying wish clinging to her words, maybe desperation. I knew how women like Delphine got their kicks. I was made for them, my brain especially wired for the likes of her.

She circled my clit again, full contact this time. Fast and confident. Flick-flick-flick.

"Now," she whispered in my ear, her lips grazing my skin, her other hand almost in my hair. My clit reacted to her command. It pulsed violently against her finger as the fire inside tore me apart. Lightning struck my nerves as I came for her. As I obeyed. Then, at last, she kissed me gently on the cheek.

We've been stair walking ever since.

FIT FOR FORTY

"For crying out loud." I can't hold my frustration any longer. "Are you trying to kill me?" But Kate has already hopped halfway up the steep path, as though it's easy for her, which is probably what's pissing me off the most. It is easy for her. For me, it's pure hell. And what's the point of going on a hike 'together' if she walks a few yards in front of me most of the time? I have half a mind to turn back, and let her reach the top—and the glorious view she's promised—on her own. For the life of me, however, I can't remember how to get back. We've already hiked up one mountain and retracing my steps would only lead to the same agony as following Kate. But no vista, no matter how spectacular, is worth the cramps in my calves, and the blisters forming on my big toe that will take days to heal.

She turns around, hands at her sides, smirking down at me. How can she be so sweaty, yet still look so hot? As if she's part of a commercial for hiking gear with the cameras hiding in the bushes beside her.

"Come on, babe." She beckons with one arm. "You can catch a glimpse of the ocean from here."

I don't give a toss about glimpsing the ocean. I've seen plenty of stunning views in my lifetime, and have absolutely no desire to break my back climbing two mountains to see another. The ups don't really outweigh the downs, which is exactly what I wanted to tell Kate this morning before we set off, but it's not really something to say to your wife on her birthday.

"I want to be fit for forty," she told me eight months ago, and suddenly started using her overpriced gym membership again.

"You look fine, babe," I said to her.

"No." She shook her head. "It's not about how I look. It's about how I feel inside."

"Oh, it's like that," I had wanted to say, remembering my own approach to my fortieth birthday five years earlier, but instead murmured some vague words of support.

"Birgit, come on," she insists. "It's really not that bad."

But I hadn't returned with her to the gym. I was glad to point out the new study that had proven a glass of red wine in the evening is just as good for your cardiac health as an hour on the treadmill. And a whole lot more fun. Not that I restrict myself to one serving per night. Hence my current state on this wretched mountainside. I gasp for air while glancing at my wife, who seems so far away. But I have no choice. I took the day off from work for her birthday, and she wants to climb a few mountains and take in a magnificent view together. It's what she wanted. What was I going to say? No thanks, dear, the view from our window is plenty for me? I would have if it wasn't her fortieth. In my defense, when I turned forty, I asked for an evening cruise across the harbor, not a torturously long trek through the wild. And I'm supposed to be the high maintenance one in this relationship.

"We're almost there," she shouts.

So, I straighten my posture and start by putting one foot in front of the other. I'd developed this coping mechanism when we reached the hiking trail more than two hours ago. It feels more like days than hours.

One step at a time, that's how all great accomplishments are achieved. Up I go. I try to ignore the sting in my thigh every time my weight shifts to my left foot and focus solely on the triumphant smile Kate's sure to give me when we reach the top.

"That was worth it, wasn't it?" she'll say. "Don't you think, babe?" And at first I'll be annoyed, but then she'll lean into me with those strong hips of hers and I'll melt a little because she hasn't looked better in years.

I focus on that as my breath transitions to short stutters. On the sight of her dark-skinned arms against the white of her tank top, and the delicious curve of her ass in these shorts she's wearing. I'm here for her. I repeat it in my head like a mantra. I'm here for my wife because I love her and it's her birthday.

Mid-slope, I look down at my feet instead of the top of the mountain. On days off, I prefer not to face reality, especially if that reality promises another hour of unfortunate muscle spasms and further proof of my very pathetic lung capacity.

Kate moves to the side of the path and drinks water from a bottle, exposing the line of her throat as she tilts her head back. Oh, that neck of hers. If I wasn't suffering so much, I'd surely have some raunchy thoughts running through my mind, but alas. I'm too preoccupied with feeling sorry for myself because my wife went on a health-kick to stave off feelings of midlife worthlessness, instead of binging on Champagne and a trip to a tropical island.

I pause again, bending at the waist. I'm almost to her, but not quite. A few short, but very steep, yards stretch between us like hot coals I'm intended to walk over barefoot. I can't say these things to Kate, because she takes too much pleasure in making fun of my theatrics.

I take the twenty—I count them to stop my mind from going elsewhere—steps needed to reach her side, and can't help but say something dramatic anyway. "Jesus fucking Christ, babe," is all that comes out between my ragged breaths.

Kate slings an arm around my shoulders, and I can feel her biceps press against the skin of my neck. She's been doing pushups, or CrossFit, or something like that. We only have five years between us but sometimes I feel at least twenty years older when she talks about compound movements and deadlifts and whatnot.

"Why does it have to be so hardcore, babe?" I asked her once. "Why can't our after-work life consist of gentle yoga and wine and dinner parties?" But Kate wouldn't have any of it.

"I want to be strong," was all she said, and how could I argue with that?

"Look," she says, while pulling me up, her arm still around my neck. "Look at the color of that ocean."

And it's true, it's very blue, and the waves crash photogenically against the rocks, but I'm too busy tallying up all the places where I'm in pain to fully absorb the beauty around us.

"Once we get to the top, we'll have an overview of the entire bay."

"Argh," I moan—dramatically. "I'm not sure I can do it, babe."

"Of course you can. The body is always capable of much more than you think." Another Fit-for-Forty Kate-ism. Statements like that drive me crazy. They don't lessen my pain in any way, only promise more.

I grumble under my breath. It's her birthday and I'm trying to keep up my good spirits, but I lost my sunny disposition a few blisters ago.

"It's fucking gorgeous," she says in a way that bears no contesting. "Nature at its very finest." She slips her arm from my shoulder and just stands there gazing into the blue in front of her. The sky is a few shades lighter than the ocean, surrounded by the vivid green of the bushes and the darker green of the mountain looming ahead, and it is, objectively speaking, staggering. But fuck me. I'm still panting after having stood still for several minutes, and the prospect of finding the willpower to tackle the rest of the mountain is killing me.

"You're right, babe," I mumble, still trying to be the bigger person.

"Shall we continue?" She looks at me with those dark eyes of hers, but Kate comes across more like a drill sergeant—a really hot one—than my wife right now.

"I need a few more minutes. You've been resting for ages."

"Fair enough." She sends me one of those loopy, crooked smiles I fell so hard for years ago. Hairstyles change, and the way jeans are worn switches from pulled high over the waist to slung low on the hips, but the shape of a smile always remains. And it's that very smile that got me here in the first place, the one I can never resist.

"Let's take the day off on the fifth," she'd said, "and finally go on that hike." I'd barely woken up and she was grinning down at me, her lips all asymmetrical and seductive. I'd pulled her back down under the covers with me and I guess that meant yes to her. My bad.

Kate hands me the water and I gulp it down. I'd rather splash it all over my face and neck, but I refused to carry my own backpack and I don't want to run out later. There are only so many sacrifices my out-of-shape body can make.

A few minutes later, we start climbing again. I'm too out of breath to complain but my inner monologue is going bonkers. This feels more like bloody rock climbing than a hike. The path we're on is thin and ridged with tree roots, and some stretches are covered with bits of rock and stones. I'm hardly a princess who fancies high heels, but this is fucking dangerous. Not life-threatening, but I bet bones have been broken on this surface. I focus my attention on maintaining my balance, which is a blessing because it keeps my mind off the steepness of the slope.

The torment continues for an eternity, only interspersed with brief breaks to admire the view, which, according to Kate, grows more impressive with every step. But my eyes are exhausted, and twisting my head to look would burn too much energy.

Then, when we've almost reached the top, the bushes around us growing denser, and it looks like we're entering previously unchartered territory, I feel something akin to pleasure. The maddest, craziest, most masochistic pleasure you could imagine, but pleasure nonetheless. Because, fuck, I'm about to reach the top of this damned mountain. No one else operated my feet. No machinery was involved to hoist me up. I did it all myself.

And then there's the absolute quiet around us, except for the forest sounds and the distant slap of the waves against the majestic shoreline beneath. And the fresh air in my tortured lungs, and the subsiding ache in my glutes, and the sweat on my brow dripping down my cheeks into my mouth. And I must admit, I'm feeling it. I get why she wanted to come here. It feels as though, because it's just us on this mountaintop, we're alone on the planet. A foolish notion, and perhaps I'm suffering from lack of oxygen to the brain, but I'm enraptured nonetheless. God knows which permanent injuries this hike will cause, but right now, when I'm at the top with my girl on her birthday, I don't care about anything but this moment.

Below, the ocean is ink-blue in bits, while other patches are indigo and the caps of the waves are the purest of white. The sky stretches endlessly in front of us and for a minute, I feel like I might cry.

"Happy birthday," I say, and press a kiss to Kate's sweaty cheek.

She turns towards me, folding her arms around my waist. "Thank you for coming with me, babe. I know it was hard."

"No sweat," I lie, fooling no one.

"I feel so, so good. Like I can do anything." She tilts her head a bit. "It's hard to describe, but let's just say I feel exactly how I wanted to feel on this day."

"And it's only midday." I pull her a little closer towards me.

"Well." There's that smile again. "As outstanding as this view is, it could be enhanced."

"Oh, really?" I play dumb, but I know what she's getting at. You can't spend two decades with someone and not be aware of their love for alfresco hanky-panky. We've done it in more parks and alleyways and deserted parking lots than I can count.

"I see a tree with your name on it, babe." Kate doesn't look at the tree though, she looks straight into my eyes, sporting that look she gets when her mind goes there. This hike was foreplay for her. I guess when you're fit at forty it can be more than torture. Not for me, though. I'm happy I made it to the top, exhilarated, in fact, to share this moment with her, but I'm nowhere near horny. This, however, doesn't worry me in the slightest. I know Kate. I know what she can do to me.

"Do you now?" I play along. "And, say you get to push me up against said tree, what would you do?"

"Oh, I will push you against it, babe. There are really no two ways about it."

This is how it starts. This is how she gets my blood to heat up in my veins, and the hairs to stand up on the back of my neck.

"Once I do, I will make you come so hard, make you scream so loud, the birds won't know what hit them. They'll all fly off in submission, convinced there's a new top bird on the mountain. Which will be true. At least for a little while."

Kate doesn't touch me while she says this, doesn't try to sneak a hand underneath my top and brush a finger against my sweat-drenched flesh. And I realize that I knew this would happen—how could I not?—and it's most likely what kept me going in the end.

"Now, tell me," she continues, narrowing her eyes. "Do you want a sea view with your climax or do you prefer a mountain view?" She cocks her head to the right a bit.

I try to hold back a snicker, but fail. I burst out laughing, which might not be conducive to the atmosphere she's creating. My brain is flooded with endorphins from the climb, my limbs loose, and my psyche not quite where she wants it yet.

"It's your birthday babe. You choose." I trace the back of my fingers over her glistening upper arm. Her skin is soft, but underneath her biceps is flexed and hard.

"I say sea." Her hand approaches my belly, catches the waistband of my shorts. She pulls me close. She doesn't smile. I know what that means. "Why don't you have a look in my backpack? I brought us something." She ducks down quickly to pick it up and offers it to me.

Shaking my head at her audacity—because I can easily guess what I'll find—I zip the backpack open. Sure enough, wrapped in a towel, but poking ostentatiously upwards nonetheless, is my favorite purple dildo. The one she got me for my fortieth.

"You are unbelievable." The sight of my preferred toy makes my pussy twitch. I look up and stare into her dark, dark eyes. I'd better not burst out laughing again. I don't think her backpack is big enough to hold a paddle as well, but I know what her hands can do.

"It was a rough climb, babe. I intend for us to stay here a while." A soft smile breaks through the serious expression on her face, then she goes all stern on me again. "For my birthday, I want you to come four times on this mountain. I just turned forty, after all."

"But, what if someone comes along?" I object, although I don't feel much like complaining.

"That's why we came on a weekday." That grin again. "And if someone were to pass by, well, good for them then."

"But—" She moves in closer, taking the backpack from my hands.

"No buts. Time for Number One." She curls her fingers around my wrists and coaxes me towards the tree. Adding another year to her life hasn't made her less bossy.

The trunk of the tree is rough and I can easily feel it scratch my skin through the fabric of my Lycra top. But fuck, the view she has me facing is breathtaking, and then she kisses me. A soft peck at first, followed by another, after which her tongue demands access and I happily surrender my mouth. Our lip-lock seems to last forever, and I feel it tingle in every extremity of my body. I haven't tasted another pair of lips in decades, and I know I haven't missed much. Ever since meeting Kate I've wondered if there's such a thing as meeting your perfect kissing companion, sort of like a soul mate, but for lips. From the very first time her mouth touched mine, I knew. I knew I would never need to be kissed by anyone else again because our lips met in such a definite and determined way that all other lips suddenly seemed obsolete. I'd found my matching pair.

Kate's mouth is soft on mine, and sometimes hard, like now, when she sinks her teeth into my bottom lip. Soon, she has me gasping for air—and I prefer the reason for this particular bout of breathlessness infinitely over the previous one.

When we finally break, and she looks into my eyes, I know that Number One won't be far off. My only worry is how the hell I'll ever get down this mountain after four orgasms. She'll have to carry me on her back. Maybe this is what all the CrossFit was about. "It's functional," Kate said, and up until now, I had no idea what that was supposed to mean.

"I'm going to take your top off," she says. It's not a question, and I know there's no use in contesting it.

"As long as you take yours off as well." I can't help myself. The mountain air must be making me mouthier than usual. Plus, I really want to see her take her top off. The mere thought of drops of sweat shimmering on her taut skin is enough for another round of clenches between my legs. I do hope she packed spare underwear in that bag of hers, because the pair I'm wearing now is as good as ruined.

"You know I like to bare it all when I'm outside." It's true. If it were up to her, we'd go on holiday to a nudist enclave every year. She doesn't waste any time and starts hoisting up her top. It's tight and clings to her flesh, but her strong arms have no problem with that. The sports bra, with extra support she wears for activities like this, comes off quickly and I have to catch my breath again. I'm floored by the sight of her naked breasts. I have no eyes for the wild beauty of the ocean behind her. It's all Kate for me.

She cocks her head again, as though saying, "Like what you see?" But she doesn't ask because she knows the answer all too well.

"Come on." She reaches for my top next and peels it off my skin slowly, gently exposing my flesh to the air. When my bra comes off, the faint breeze catches my nipples and the sensation is overwhelmingly pleasant. In no time, they grow hard, and I already know what will come next. Although, I wouldn't be entirely surprised if she produced a pair of nipple clamps from the backpack, but I'm guessing she didn't want to carry our entire drawer of sex toys on her back.

Kate presses her body against mine, our stiff nipples meeting, her breath husky in my ears. "I want you naked," she whispers, and her voice is low and gravelly, as though she's losing control a little.

It's a bit of a kerfuffle to hitch my shorts over my sturdy

hiking shoes, but she gets the job done. And there I stand. Naked from the ankles up. I have to draw the line somewhere. I'm not taking off my footwear in this place.

"Look at you, babe," she says as she overlooks the situation. "Gorgeous."

"How about you?" I ask, and motion with my hand towards her shorts, but she swats it away.

"No need." Her lips curl into a grin. "You know that."

I've been with Kate for such a long time, I can't even remember if I was such a pillow princess before we met. I am now. Well, at the moment more of a tree princess, but still. It's where she wants me, so that's how it is.

"Now." She inches closer, her nipples denting my skin, her lips hovering over mine. Her hand is sliding down my belly. "Spread your legs, babe," she asks, but does it for me anyway. She slants her body away from me and cups my breast with her other hand.

Her fingers are on my pussy lips, ever so gently sliding through the wetness there. Suddenly, the wind in the trees intensifies to a roar, and the sound of the sea is loud in my ears —despite our altitude and the distance separating us from the ocean. I have to hand it to her, there is something to be said for sex surrounded by nothing but the elements. She catches my nipple between two fingers and squeezes hard and quick. Her hand between my legs remains gentle, soft even, just gliding back and forth, staying too far away from my clit. She gazes into my eyes while she continues to pinch my nipple. Every tweak sends a fresh jolt of lust straight to my pussy, as if what her two hands are doing separately connects there. If she weren't such a tease and lavished some attention on my clit, Number One would soon be a fact.

"I'm going to fuck you against this tree," she says. And then she does. A finger slides all the way in, and everything I have clamps around it. She brings her other hand to my face now, fingers rubbing my lips, negotiating entrance. She has one finger in my cunt and one in my mouth. That's new. And incredibly arousing. I suck on her finger for dear life. My knees give a little when she pushes deeper inside of me. Soon, a second one follows, spreading me wide—everywhere. I twirl my tongue around her fingers in my mouth and shove my pelvis towards her other hand. I can't say it out loud, but we've been together long enough for her to know. I want more.

"Come for me like this," she says, slipping a third finger in both orifices. Earlier, while suffering on that steep incline, I never imagined this was the view she was talking about. Her view of me, like this, totally at her mercy. Her fingers in my mouth are a huge turn-on and, yes, I think I might be able to do what she asks. I close my eyes and focus only on what my body is experiencing, on the tight grasp of her fingers deep inside of me, inhabiting me—that's what she calls it and the word seems to fit—and taking me there.

My breasts bounce slightly, and the breeze and sun on my skin awaken other senses, stir up an unusual sensation, seizing my entire body through the expanse of my skin. It all comes together in a point somewhere deep in my body. That's where it starts, somewhere below my stomach, or perhaps in my brain, who knows? All I know is that Number One is coming. My birthday present to my wife, because to her, it is a gift when I come for her the way she demands it. She knows what it takes. It's not mere rubbing of fingers and manipulation of body parts. It's trust, and the years between us, and all this love that has blossomed, and now she's forty and more gorgeous than ever.

Oh, fuck. I can't say it out loud because my mouth is full of her fingers, full of her, and so is my cunt. It starts the way the waves crash onto the rocks below us, with a steady, sturdy slap, but then it transforms into an explosion of heat in my flesh and lightning in my blood. Her fingers in my cunt touch that spot over and over, and my knees give a little more, and that's how she knows.

She removes her fingers from my mouth and presses a kiss on my lips instead. Kate's usual M.O. after she's fucked me like this is to have me lick my own juices from her fingers. Today, she surprises me again and brings them to her own lips and stares deep into my eyes as she licks my wetness from her hand. Already, I can't wait for Number Two.

"Isn't it amazing?" she asks when she's done sucking her fingers.

"Oh yes," I say, not referring to our surroundings at all.

"Are you cold?" It's true that my skin has broken out in goosebumps, but that's hardly because of a drop in body temperature. I notice the gooseflesh on Kate's skin as well, and although there's some sweat on her brow, I realize it's due to the exhilaration of fucking on this mountaintop. I can't keep my eyes off her breasts. Off her small, rock-hard, earth-colored nipples, and how upwards they point, like an invitation to take them in my mouth. And fuck, I want to, but long ago, it was decided that Kate is calling the shots. It wasn't a decision as such, more of an organic unfolding of events over and over again that established patterns along the way. We both have very few reasons to complain.

If she hadn't said anything about four orgasms, I'd be content right now, sated, ready for one of those protein bars she packed in that seemingly bottomless backpack of hers, but now that I know there will be encores, a stirring remains in my blood—a sense of unfinished business.

I pull her towards me and kiss her, smelling and tasting myself on her lips. Her body is warm against mine, comforting, and restoring.

"Let me know when you're ready," she breathes into my ear after we break from the kiss. "I'm nowhere near done with you yet." She nuzzles my neck, before finding my eyes and painting that wicked grin on her face again. "On second thought, you'd best be ready now." She throws in a quick wink before grabbing me by the shoulders and spinning me around. Her knee is between my thighs, spreading them again. Her hand curves around my hip and pushes against my belly, indicating that I should stick my bottom out. My tummy tingles at the prospect of what that could mean—as if I don't know.

She bends her body over mine. I feel her nipples poke into the flesh of my back as she finds my ear.

"Permission to touch yourself," she says, "while I do this." With that, her hand glides down my spine, until it reaches my crack, and it still doesn't stop. She just spreads my cheeks. She wouldn't venture further without some preparation. My clit tightens with the confirmation of her plans for Number Two. And, yay me, I get to touch myself. What does she have in mind for the dildo, though? Then my thoughts freeze because Kate starts kissing her way down my back. She kisses with lots of teeth and tongue, and soon enough her teeth bite down on the curve of my ass. She must be on her knees behind me, but the view beyond the tree I'm facing is too overwhelming to look back, and I know she didn't put me in this position so I could check up on her.

The first drizzle of saliva slides down my cleft, and it's as though the entire expanse of my skin is hyper-sensitized and I feel everything tenfold. The birds in the trees chipper away in high-pitched tones, and the smell in my nose is decidedly green. Fresh. Alive.

There comes her tongue, and I immediately know she doesn't want to draw this one out. She's insistent, firm, entering my pussy with the tip from the first go. So I rebalance and steady myself against the tree trunk with one hand while my other goes to my clit. It's still a little delicate, but also throbbing wildly. I circle my finger without hesitation. The same way Kate is feasting on my ass.

I rest my forehead against the tree for extra support, because I know what comes next. Kate's finger, the same one that fucked me earlier, will soon seek entrance, and once it does, the fireworks will come. And I'll be lost.

She doesn't push it deep, barely skirting the rim, but it's enough—it always is. That glorious, tight, all-in sensation engulfs me from the first little probe, like a promise of much bigger things to come. But there they come already. I can never help myself when she touches me there, especially not now, out in the open on this mountain with the sun warming our skin. The exposure adds an extra, illicit, earthy awareness, and I rub my clit frantically while Kate fucks me very carefully, very controlled from behind. I open my eyes when I come, but everything blurs into a big smudge when my brain gives up its power to pure sensation, to the utmost pleasure of my wife possessing my ass.

"Oh god." My forehead presses against my arm as I try to regroup and I hear Kate shuffle behind me. I can just imagine the smug grin on her face. I can't wait to kiss it off her.

She spins me around with those strong, dark arms of hers, and I swoon a little. This particular type of climax is still rather new to me, and was only discovered because Kate kept gently coaxing me onto my belly, venturing a little bit farther every time over the course of months. It has only made me fall in love with her all over again.

"Let's sit for a minute." Her dark-brown eyes sparkle as she points towards a flat, wide rock skirting the spot where we've stopped. She grabs her tank top from where she let it drop on her backpack earlier and fashions a tiny blanket out of it. The rock is cold and hard, but I'm glad to be sitting for a bit, even though I'm completely naked for all the mountain creatures to see.

Kate reaches for her backpack and, instantly, the thought of what's inside ignites something in my belly again. But, damn, I need a break. I'm not an orgasm machine. Also, this spot doesn't seem ideal for a bout of dildo-fucking. I eye her as she rummages inside her bag and wonder how she's going to swing this one.

She produces a towel and bunches it up before handing it to me. "For your head," she simply says.

"What?" My brain is still a bit fuzzy from Number One and Two and I don't know what she means.

"The rock is big enough for you to lie down on. You can use the towel as a pillow."

"Lie down? What, erm, I don't know." I can't really seem to find my words either. They stall even more when the dildo materializes from the gaping mouth of her bag.

"For my birthday," she says as she crouches beside me, "I would like you to fuck yourself with this." She brings the dildo towards her mouth and slips it between her lips, coating it in saliva. "You should be wet enough, but just in case." She gives me the dildo and takes the towel from my hands, bunches it up some more and puts it behind me. "Take all the time you need, babe." She pushes herself up, ducks down one more time, and shows me her phone. "I'm going to take some snaps."

She doesn't mean of the view.

I open my mouth to speak, but no words come out.

"As a souvenir."

I scrunch my eyebrows together and realize she must have planned this entire day to a tee. She must have come here and scouted this spot, this rock, and the trees.

"Ready when you are." She just stands there grinning, mightily pleased with herself.

Heat rises from my belly to fill the tiniest cells in my body. Of course, she knew exhibitionism times two would turn me on exponentially.

I stretch out on the rock as instructed, putting my head on the makeshift towel-pillow, spreading my legs wide for her, and her camera. The rock cools my overheated body, and a subtle breeze skims along my pulsing pussy lips. I take the dildo into my own mouth to warm it up some more, because Kate was right, I should be plenty wet to provide it easy access to my cunt. I slip and slide it between my lips and Kate takes pictures, or a video. I have no idea, but I'm sure she'll show me later. After we watch it, we'll fuck again.

"Fuck yourself, babe," she spurs me on, and she must be so aroused from all the things she has done to me. Doesn't she need some relief?

I bring the toy between my legs, easily finding my opening with the tip, and it slides in swiftly. It's big, and a little bit curved towards the top, and I'm spread so wide—even wider than when she fucked me with three fingers—that it feels like surrender all over again. I imagine what Kate is seeing, what the pictures will show, and it speeds up my heartbeat, which seems to be in direct connection to my pulsing clit.

I fuck myself for her with slow, luxurious strokes of our purple dildo that she carried with her up this mountain. I have to admit it's freeing, exhilarating in its boldness. More than the thrusts I deliver myself, it's the entire picture that excites me most. Kate with her camera and intense gaze—and walking around with her top off. The green and blue above me, the crisp air, the heat of the sun, that inexplicable delight of engaging in these acts outside, and me buck naked on a rock in the mountains. It's a feast for all my senses, so I have no trouble going there again. As though my previous orgasm still lingers and I can easily tune back in and pick up where we left off. As though it's not a string of climaxes but an interwoven pattern of highs with some breathing room thrown in.

Then again, I know this toy well. I know exactly how to position it for maximum effect, the slightly upward curve touching me precisely where I need to be touched. When extreme arousal and excellent knowledge of mechanics meet, in a steady rhythm, there's only one outcome: me, panting on a rock, crying out loudly as I come at my own hands, for her.

She takes the dildo from me after it slips out of my pussy. All the smugness has left her face. Is that a tear glittering in the corner of her eye? She's touched by my complete abandon for her, I can tell. In return, it moves me deeply, too. Usually, I'm the one doing all the crying in the bedroom. But we're not in the bedroom. We're in the wilderness, giving in completely to our animalistic, base urges, and it's sensational.

"Make me come," she says, completely out of character. "I need to. Now."

I'm more than happy to oblige. I push myself up from the rock and kneel next to her, not caring about what I'm shoving my knees into. "Take my spot."

As soon as she's on her back, I tug off Kate's shorts and underwear, exposing her to me, and the elements. Number Four will be for her, then.

She lets her legs fall open, and the sight of her like that sends my heart aflutter. I find a semi-comfortable position between her legs so I can lick her until she howls. I hunker down, bringing my face towards her glistening cunt. I want to lap at it as though it's the first drop of water I see after climbing another mountain like this, but first I take a moment to admire my view. So much better than any I've seen today.

"Please, Birgit." Kate is not the pleading kind—more the commanding one—so I know her need is urgent. I let my tongue wander over her slick lips for a few seconds. She grabs me by the hair. She can't wait. I don't have the heart to try her patience. Not after Number One, Two, and Three. I suck my lips around her clit and let my tongue go wild. Her nails dig into my skull; her pelvis pushes towards me. She's trapping me with her body, welding my mouth to her pussy, and it feels just as freeing as being naked on the rock.

I revel in the little sounds she makes; tiny, throaty guttural groans fill the air around us, and it makes a nice difference from the bird chatter. I taste her, drink her in, lick her clit until she's writhing underneath me. Until she loses control.

"Oh fuck," she screams, and presses her palms against either side of my head, before slowly pulling me away from her.

"Happy birthday," I say when she opens her eyes, her mouth slightly agape.

"Come here." She motions for me to join her on the rock, which seems rather unrealistic to me, but I try anyway. I sit on the ledge, my hips glued to her side, and stroke her face with my fingers.

"Definitely the best hike I've ever been on." I shoot her a schmaltzy grin.

"Shall we make it a weekly thing then?"

"Maybe, but either way, let's keep these particular antics for special occasions." Although I'm not sure I can ever go hiking without this sort of incentive again.

"Our wedding anniversary is coming up." She smiles up at me from her spot on the rock, her head still pressed into the heap of towel.

"And the anniversary of when we first met and a few weeks after that, the one to celebrate our first kiss." I'm starting to come back to my full senses though, and it hits me that we're both sitting on this rock stark naked. "It's going to be a fun walk down." I bend over and kiss her on the lips.

As it turns out, on the way back, we walk hand in hand, the pair of us smelling like sex, that strong, heady scent that even nature can't erase. We're giddy, and loved-up, and I brush my hand against Kate's biceps now and then, just to cop a feel of exactly how fit she is for forty. My legs are light, my spirit soaring high, like the birds above us, and a new benchmark has been set for celebrating birthdays.

RATHER

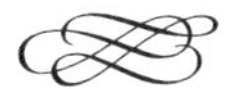

I close my eyes and listen to her voice. No one speaks like Catherine. My brother Andy sometimes imitates the way she pronounces the word 'rather', like someone from a different century. I always snicker, but nobody knows what it does to me inside.

"I'd rather not venture into town today," Catherine says.

I widen my eyelids a fraction at the mention of the word. Catherine has intertwined her fingers behind her neck and rests the back of her head on her palms. The pose seems almost too bold for her, too un-ladylike. I can't keep my eyes off her.

"Of course, love." My dad's Yorkshire accent sounds crass next to Catherine's noble use of vowels. "You stay here and enjoy the pool."

"Tilly will keep you company." Mum pinches me in the bicep. "If she ever properly wakes up."

I shoot Catherine a slow, sly smile and, in silence, we count the seconds until my parents leave. The seconds are long and hang between us like the heavy summer air, rich with the promise of beautiful days and humid with the sweat from our skin.

This is all the foreplay we need.

Catherine fixes her gaze on a spot just below my neck and my blood picks up speed in my veins. This is my family's summer house and I didn't bother to put on a bra for breakfast. I'm suddenly very aware of how my breasts, only covered by a flimsy, pale yellow tank top, rise and fall with my breath. Already my mind drifts to that delicious moment when Catherine will scoop them in her hands, just for a brief second, before pinching my nipples hard between her fingers.

I let my gaze drift to her hands, which now rest in her lap. Her fingers are long and her nails are always impeccably painted. A tight-fitted linen summer dress hugs her frame. No matter how high temperatures rise here, Catherine doesn't do loose-hanging clothes.

Slowly, she lifts a finger to her mouth—the one she'll fuck me with later. She drags the tip over her bottom lip. When my mum's heels clatter on the tiles behind her, she lets it trail to her chin and assumes a pensive pose. Her eyes don't leave mine.

"We'll be gone a few hours." Mum begins to clear the breakfast dishes.

"Leave it, Mum." My voice comes out much hoarser than I had expected. "I'll take care of that."

She shoots me a look as if she knows something, but she doesn't. Her mind wouldn't even go there. Catherine is her most respectable friend, with the best pedigree, the right designer clothes and—inherited from her deceased husband—a fortune to her name.

"Very well, then." Mum straightens her back. "Are you ready, George?" She calls for my dad who stumbles out of the kitchen.

"Have a wonderful time." Catherine gets up to kiss them goodbye. "I'll make supper tonight." The way she says it already makes it sound like a feast.

I wave my mum and dad off from my seat in the morning sun. We don't move while we listen to the sound of tires screeching through gravel. We wait until the hum of the motor has completely died down. My cunt doesn't wait though. I can feel moisture gather in the pyjama shorts I'm still wearing.

"Now then." Catherine picks up a jar of strawberry jam. "We'd best clean this up." She unscrews the lid and dips a finger in the red goo. Four nights we've spent together, but I already know better than to move without permission. "You'd best take off your clothes, Tilly. This could get messy."

It doesn't take me long to slip out of my tank top and shorts. Naked, I stand in front of her. My skin shivers with anticipation. The sun warms my exposed nipples. I resist the urge to squeeze my legs together because I know she'll want them wide. Heat pools in my blood.

She inches closer, her finger still in the jam jar.

"Toast is so inadequate." Her voice is near and posh. My nipples harden. She lifts her finger from the jar and smears a dollop of jam right above my left nipple. It feels as if she's grabbed me between the legs. My breath hitches in my throat and my nipples stiffen further. A droplet of hot moisture trickles down my upper thigh.

"This—" She eyes my jam-topped breast. "—looks so much better." With the tip of her finger she rubs the jam all over my nipple, before dipping her head down to lick it off.

When her tongue connects, my muscles tense, then slacken. My spine ripples.

She wipes her fingers on the skin of my belly as they travel down. What's left of the jam mingles with my wetness. The sun is hot on my scalp and when she enters, her lips still stuck on my nipple, I think I will explode with heat.

Instead, my legs give way and I crash onto the lawn next to the terrace.

"Talk to me," I say as I lay down on my back and spread

wide. The grass tickles my back. The breeze cools my lips. I want to hear her voice when she slips her finger inside again.

"You look extraordinary..." She drapes herself across my flank, her skin moist against mine. "...in strawberry." Her lips graze my neck before finding my ear. "I hear it's all the rage this summer." Her voice is a soft whisper. Her fingers have reached my clit and the mere presence of them so close to my cunt makes me gasp. I want to open up wider for her, buck my hips higher.

"But let's not talk about fashion." She slides two fingers over my clit to my entrance. "I'd rather fuck you instead."

LOVELY RITA

Sweat trickled down my temples as I danced for the first time in months. I didn't care if Rita showed up. I boogied myself into a state of indifference I'd been craving for weeks. Pushing my arms above my head, I relished the predatory looks my exposed belly button received. Being declared too monogamous for Rita's standards didn't spoil me for this crowd. Just because I wasn't one for sharing loved ones, didn't mean I couldn't enjoy the thrill of a one-night stand.

A girl dressed in black leather pants and not much else swayed closer to me. I'd been working on my abs tirelessly since Rita had left me, and now they were working for me. She pressed her hips into my behind and left them there, finding the rhythm with me. I guess you could call it dancing.

"Want a beer?" she yelled into my ear over the thundering bass.

I spun around to get a good look at her face. Hair tied back in a loose ponytail, some curls springing free. Intense black eyes and no makeup on her face. Zero resemblance to Rita.

"Yes, please." I shot her a smile. I was out of practice and fairly certain the sexy grin I was aiming for looked more like an insecure smirk, but she nodded and headed for the bar. I exhaled and brushed a strand of hair away from my forehead.

That's when I saw her.

A bundle of platinum-blonde hair. Lips red and full. A smile to die for. That glare that sent my heart racing and clit throbbing.

I gasped for air and scanned for emergency exits. Rita was not alone and I didn't feel like being introduced to her new girlfriend, who, no doubt, would still be so charmed by her she wouldn't mind all the talk of open relationships and the enrichment polyamory can be to one's life. I'm not one to judge —I just wanted Rita all to myself.

"I'm Liz." Leather pants girl handed me a cold bottle of beer. I wanted to rub it against my cheeks to make my burning blush disappear.

"Ali." I clinked the neck of my bottle against hers. "Thanks."

Liz followed my gaze, because, try as I might, I couldn't stop looking at Rita. She was the most beautiful woman I'd ever seen, with her big brown eyes and racially ambiguous skin.

"Do you know Rita?" Liz asked. I noticed the sudden twinkle in her eye, and I knew the score. This was a small-town club and Rita had probably taken half of the girls home at some point.

"She's my ex." It still stung when I said it. "It didn't work out."

I did try, but my heart had never hurt as much as when Rita had picked out a voluptuous redhead for us to have a three-some with. As if I wasn't enough.

"How long were you together?" Liz couldn't let the subject go. I totally understood.

"Seven months. Broke up three months ago." My night of forgetting Rita was not going as planned. Not only was she here, but I was trapped in a conversation with a stranger about her. That was Rita. Ever present and always on the tip of everyone's tongue.

Liz whistled through her teeth. Any attraction I had felt toward her seeped out of me.

Through the crowd, Rita made her way to where I was standing, resulting in a crazy pitter-patter of my heart.

"I've been looking for you," she said, her voice breathy and low. "Where have you been hiding?" As if she didn't know.

The woman trailing behind her was so pretty it hurt. She had a relaxed hipster way about her. Maybe it allowed her to stand things I couldn't possibly accept, no matter how much I wanted to keep Rita.

"I take it you've met Liz," I mumbled, avoiding Rita's question.

"Oh yeah. Good times." She poked her girlfriend in the ribs and flashed her a knowing smile. "Remember, honey?"

The gorgeous hipster was the honey now.

It wasn't so much anger rushing through me. After all, I could only blame myself for not being more compatible with Rita's ways. It was a big surge of raw lust gripping me at the sight of Rita's neck and her skin the color of brown butter. I had always wanted Rita. From the first second I laid eyes on her until this moment in the club, downgraded to the word ex, huddled between her current girlfriend and a lover for one night.

It was madness, still my blood pulsed with desire. Hot pangs of want were speeding through my veins. Heat gathering between my legs already. One look was always all it took.

"Please, meet Anya." When Rita smiled at Anya it was as if someone had reached into my chest and squeezed a cold fist around my heart. I'd never get that smile again. I'd relinquished all rights to it the day I disagreed with Rita's rules.

"Hey." Anya waved a long-fingered hand at me. She was a

skinny jeans and tank top kind of woman, with long ash-blonde hair falling to her shoulders and subtly painted lips.

"Let's dance." Rita grabbed Anya's hand and pulled her onto the dance floor. Then she had the audacity to wink at me. My breath hitched in my throat and all I wanted was to drag her away from Anya and take her home. Have her do that thing she did to me. That thing no one else ever did.

Liz and I followed. She seemed as entranced as I was, the twinkle in her eye still present. We slithered our bodies between sweaty arms and backs and I started moving with the rest of them. Whenever I glanced in Rita's direction, which was about 95 percent of the time, her eyes were fixed on me. I knew that look. She knew I did.

No one danced like Rita. The music flowed through her bones and her muscles flexed and relaxed to the beat of its drum. It inhabited her and she was all the more mesmerizing for it. Plus, she kept eyeing me.

I finished the beer Liz bought me in a few long drags and made for the bar to replenish, needing a break from Rita's stare. It was obvious what she was playing at.

Drops of sweat flickered on her bare shoulders when she joined me at the bar. I ordered four beers and thrust one in her hand.

"Thanks," she said, while letting her finger glide over the back of my hand. "I'm so thirsty." She tilted her head back, exposing the delicate skin of her neck, and swallowed for what seemed like an eternity. "Anya likes you."

In a perfect world, I would have been over Rita by then. I tried to look away and ignore her, but the muscles in my neck didn't allow me to—as if they were still as infatuated with her as the rest of me. Instead, I stared into the brown of her eyes, took in the enormity of her smile and surrendered. I'd never be done with her.

"Do you want to play?" She inched closer. So close I could

feel her breath on my cheeks. "Liz is welcome to join as well, of course. She's fun."

It was her unwavering confidence that always got me. Not a lot of people said no to her, because she acted as if the word wasn't even a possibility.

She brought her lips to my ear. "I know what you like."

I could barely move. She'd whispered me straight into a frenzy of desire. I inhaled and exhaled slowly to regain composure.

"I'd better get these to the others." I pointed at the bottles of beer on the counter.

She slanted toward me again. "I'll take that as a yes."

She wasn't too far off.

I weighed my options as if I had any. As if Rita's proposal hadn't erased all other outcomes to my night.

I could go home alone. I could take Liz home. All four of us could go somewhere together. Or I could ditch Liz—one less contender for Rita's attention. None of the possibilities had me alone in a room with Rita, but beggars can't be choosers.

My hands trembled when I brought the bottle to my mouth. My body wasn't giving me a lot of options. Throughout the seven months of our affair it had been reduced to nothing more than a bundle of want. Attraction-wise, no one came close. If she was offering it on a silver platter, I wouldn't say no —even if it meant including Anya. Even if it meant I was the extra for the night.

I found Rita's eyes, bit my lip and nodded. The smile she shot me alone was enough to send me reeling. She arched her eyebrows and tilted her head in Liz's direction, silently questioning her inclusion. I shook my head. If I was sharing Rita, one other person would do.

Fifteen minutes later, Rita, Anya and I sat huddled together in the back seat of a cab. I felt my blood beat through my veins as Rita's thigh flanked mine. It was only fitting she resided in the middle, like a queen amidst her minions. I wondered if Anya was as much a sucker for Rita's touch as I was. The answer was obvious.

Rita's flat hadn't changed. It was all red mood lighting and shag carpet. A faux fireplace guarded by life-size leopard statues in black marble. In anyone else's home they would have looked tacky.

"Hey." Rita pounced on me like a wildcat while Anya watched. Was she more of an onlooker? I hoped she was.

Rita's blood-red lips came for me. Her heady perfume hit my nostrils hard, and I inhaled as if my life depended on it. Her nipples poked into my skin through the fabric of our tops, and the prominent display of her arousal flattered me.

"You're in for a treat." There was that unflinching confidence again. There was no doubt in my mind that she was right. Every second with Rita was a treat.

Her fingers dug into my scalp as she kissed me, and my legs turned to jelly. Her smile shifted from generously broad to mischievously narrow as she pulled her mouth away from mine and glanced at me. She all but licked her lips.

"Come on." She grabbed my hand and guided me to the bedroom. I had fond memories of Rita's king-size bed, which, from my point of view, was a total waste of space because I always slept glued to her caramel-skinned body. She probably bought it with more advanced sexual activities in mind. It could easily fit three.

Anya followed us and hoisted her top over her head as soon as we entered the bedroom. All my attention had been so focused on Rita, I hadn't even noticed she'd gone through the night braless. As if it was a practiced routine, Anya inched closer and Rita stepped back.

"Kiss for me." Rita sat down on the bed, sucking her bottom lip between her teeth.

Anya's nails scraped over the flesh of my arms. A crooked,

full-lipped smile played around her lips. She looked so pale compared to Rita.

She pressed her naked chest into me, rigid nipples stabbing into my breasts, and traced the tip of her tongue along my neck, over my chin, to my mouth. The room was silent except for the agitated coming and going of our breath and the touching of our lips. Rita sat stock-still on the edge of the bed, her eyes on fire and her head tilted sideways.

Despite it not being Rita on the receiving end of my kisses, the fact that she sat watching us was enough of a turn-on. Anya tugged at my T-shirt and I lifted my arms to allow her to take it off. After she one-handedly unclipped my bra, she leaned into me and breathed heavily into my ear.

"We're going to make you come so hard," she said, and it made me shiver. That was Rita's line. That's how I knew she spoke the truth.

My nipples stiffened into hard peaks as they grazed Anya's porcelain skin. She slid a finger under the waistband of my jeans and flipped the button open. Before coaxing me toward the bed, she lowered the zipper with her other hand, and pushed me down.

I found her eyes and saw the madness, the same madness I'd seen flicker in Rita's gaze so many times. The yearning for this kind of activity. The desire to live with an abandon foreign to me.

From the bottom of the bed, Rita yanked at my jeans until they slid off. Anya removed her own pants faster than I could blink. She didn't appear to be wearing any panties either. It figured.

Anya lay down next to me and, while circling one finger around my belly button, allowed me to enjoy the show of Rita undressing. The spectacle wasn't in the way she did it, slowly and totally aware of the effect she had on me, but more in how she held my gaze throughout it. The intensity brimming in her eyes left me panting underneath Anya's tickles. Her glance skimming over my bare skin was plenty of incentive for my clit to swell beneath the flimsy fabric of my panties.

As soon as Rita was undressed she hopped on the bed and pressed her body against my side.

"Let me prove to you once and for all"—Rita looked me square in the face—"that three pairs of hands are so much better than two."

Anya's circling motions traveled up to my chest, while Rita started stroking my inner thighs. She might have had a point.

Their lips found each other over my head and, instead of jealousy, bursts of sweltering lust rushed through me.

Anya, on my left, pinched my nipple hard as Rita, on my right, trailed the top of her finger over the crotch of my panties. They broke their lip-lock to bestow all of their attention on me, and yes, it felt as if I were being fondled by a million hands at the same time. Fingers were everywhere. A frenzy of pecks, lingering tongues, and thrilling pinches descended on me.

Rita dragged my panties off me and my swollen pussy lips pulsed for her. Anya let a fingertip skate over my hard nipples while driving her tongue deep into my mouth. Instinctively, I spread my legs for Rita. I was so hot for her, so ready. The club, the cab ride, the little show—rehearsed lines and all—they had put on for me, it was all foreplay and I didn't need any more gentle coaxing. Juices oozed out of me as my clit throbbed to the quickening beat of my heart.

Anya moved the action of her mouth to my breasts and sucked a nipple between her lips. Rita trailed a finger through my wetness and I shivered in my skin. My muscles trembled and I pushed myself up to meet her, eager for her to enter me. Her lips parted slightly as she slipped a finger inside.

"Oh god," I moaned, because Rita's finger inside of me was all I ever wanted. She soon added a second one, while Anya nibbled on my nipples, her hands kneading and her teeth grazing.

With her free hand, Rita pulled the skin away from my clit, exposing it to the musky bedroom air. She didn't touch it; she just watched it as my juices gathered in the palm of her hand.

"Ready?" she asked, a surprisingly solemn expression on her face.

"Oh," I hissed in reply, no longer able to form words. I knew what she meant though, and my skin flared with anticipation. I was lost beneath their hands and tongues. A willing victim of their double act.

Rita curled her fingers inside of me and found the spot. The one, somehow, only she could reach. In response, I arched my back, my muscles stiffening. Anya's hand and lips kept arousing me, propelling me to new heights. Rita's fingers pushed inside, circling, curling, bringing me to the brink.

I found Rita's eyes and drank in her desire, because in that moment, she was mine. Or I was hers—again. All signs of irony had left her face. She pinned her gaze on me while her fingers touched me inside, the intent of them displayed in the twitch of her lips. Witnessing how Rita wanted me was all I ever needed. It wasn't a magical spot inside of me yearning to be stroked; it was the passion in her eyes and how it connected with every fiber of my being.

It started in my belly, a wildfire spreading through my flesh, seizing me. My pussy tingled and my nipples reached up. Flames tickled my skin. Desire burned through my bones.

I cried out as I came, fingers on my nipples and in my cunt. The climax echoed through me, bouncing through my body, again and again. I clenched the walls of my pussy around Rita's fingers, as though I never wanted to let her go again, before collapsing into the mattress, spent and voiceless.

Rita gently slid out her fingers, dragging them along my

belly, coating my skin in my own wetness, and kissed me on the mouth.

"I told you," she said.

Anya kissed my left cheek and Rita pressed her lips against my right cheekbone.

I curved my arms around the pair of them before turning my face to Rita. "Lesson learned."

WETTER

Spin class seemed to last forever. Rachel pushed down hard on the pedals, but didn't have sufficient strength left to follow the cadence of the music. She should have gone for that long hot bath instead of rushing to the gym again. Her cat, Jamie, should have been balancing on the edge of the tub next to her, shooting her disdainful glares every time he nearly slipped in. She was getting too old for this kind of fitness regime. Rachel looked up and, through the drops of sweat raining from her forehead, caught a glimpse of Toni's strong arms. The instructor's skin was soaked and her top clung to her body so tightly that Rachel could make out her abs gleaming underneath. To hell with that bath, she thought, this is by far the best place to spend a Thursday evening.

"Come on, Rachel," Toni shouted, her voice brimming with authority, "try to keep up." Rachel silently thanked whoever had invented the spin studio for the darkness she found herself sitting in, obscuring the no doubt bright shade of red currently flushing her cheeks.

She sat in the front row, right across from Toni—not her

bike of choice but her photography teacher Jimmy had taken her apart after class again.

"To discuss the shadow lines in that picture of your cat in private", he had said, but they both knew better. Jimmy had fancied her from the start. Rachel hardly wore her sexual preference on her sleeve, but she believed that, even to the not so keen observer, it must be fairly obvious she was a lesbian. Or perhaps Jimmy liked a challenge. Thanks to him she'd arrived late at the gym and the only available spot happened to be directly opposite Toni. Rachel usually hid in the back, cultivating her crush from a safe distance, but she had to admit the view up front was so much better.

"Rise," Toni yelled dramatically and Rachel pulled herself up, clinging to one last flicker of willpower, for a hill climb. Maybe she was just as bad as Jimmy, but at least her mild obsession with Toni was increasing her fitness levels. She did, however, realise you couldn't judge a woman's sexuality successfully if you'd only seen her in workout clothes—the margin for error was simply too big. Nevertheless, she had a good feeling about Toni, even though she didn't know much more about her than her name. She knew she had rock hard abs though, and triceps to die for.

A current of sweat trickled down Toni's forehead while the toned muscles of her arms bulged spectacularly as she tamed the imaginary mountain.

"Come on, team," she shouted at the top of her voice, "one more minute and you're free to do whatever you like."

If only she knew, Rachel pondered, what I'd like to do to her.

Rachel, weary of people this late in the day, checked if the steam room was empty. She inwardly chuckled when she saw there was no one inside because, as in life, she had learnt that it was small signs of good fortune like this that mattered most. Late night spin classes, for some reason, were quite a male affair. She'd only counted three other women in the studio—and Toni of course.

This near to closing time the female locker room was almost deserted and Rachel let her back fall lazily against the damp chair, safe in the knowledge the steam cabin was hers alone tonight. She closed her eyes and immediately visions of Toni's sweaty arms and shoulders occupied her mind. The strength and stamina they promised filled her with both instant desire and disappointment. Sure, Rachel had been lusting after Toni long enough to acquire a more than acceptable body for a woman her age, but apart from the occasional polite chit-chat before and after class, they'd hardly exchanged words.

Still, maybe it was wishful thinking, but Rachel did feel like she had some small signs to cling to. Not a class went by in which Toni didn't call her out—not an honour bestowed on anyone. Then again, maybe it was simply a perk of being a regular. They had exchanged appreciative glances in passing in the locker room, but then again it was Toni's job to train the gym's members and guide them towards firmer bodies. So, basically, she was only acknowledging her own work.

Steam hissed around Rachel and condensation drops seeped down from the ceiling. She'd give it another minute or two and then head for the shower. At least Jamie would be waiting for her at home and he was excellent at cuddling. A soft thud caught Rachel's attention and she opened her eyes. Seriously, she thought, someone's really going to ruin my blissful solitude now?

"Hi," a voice cut through the steam. Rachel couldn't make out a face through the vapours but she would have recognised that clipped low voice anywhere. Instinctively, she wrapped her towel around her chest, then changed her mind and let it slip to the side again.

"I thought you'd have perspired enough today." Rachel fixed her eyes on Toni's shape, which was becoming clearer by the second. Please drop the towel, she prayed.

"There's always room for more." Toni took the seat opposite her and unfurled the towel from her upper body.

Rachel swallowed hard and thanked all the heavens and the stars and all the gods she didn't believe in. She tried to regain the composure she'd lost the instant Toni had set foot in the cabin, but the heat enveloping her and the sight of Toni's bare breasts wasn't helping. She'd have to leave the steam room soon if she didn't want to faint. Or maybe Toni would resort to some inspired mouth-to-mouth if she did.

"You've been working hard," Toni said, her eyes focused on an area beneath Rachel's face.

"All praise goes to this gym's excellent instructors."

Toni flashed her a sly smile and Rachel couldn't keep her eyes off her instructor's magnificent shoulders. So close, she thought as a mild dizziness crept up on her, but yet so far away.

"I'm sorry, but I've been in here too long." Rachel rose and had to steady herself against the soaked wall. "I need to get out."

"Careful." In a split second Toni was by her side, her towel left behind on the chair. She supported Rachel's arm and the firm grip of Toni's fingers around her bicep made her head swim even more. "Walk slowly. I'll escort you out."

Not that Rachel had a plan, but still, this was not the plan. What was the point of boasting toned muscles and a lean body if you nearly lost consciousness in front of the hot instructor? She let Toni guide her out and sat down on the wooden bench flanking the cabin. She took a few sharp breaths and felt her strength return. Rachel had lost her towel along the way as well and Toni towered over her, a worried look on her face and her body covered in nothing but sweat.

"I'll get us some fresh towels," Toni said. "I'll just be a minute. Will you be all right?"

Rachel nodded and watched Toni scoot off around the corner, but not before getting a decent look at her well-shaped behind. The wall clock reminded her it was half an hour to closing time and Rachel was relieved to not hear any signs of other members in the changing room. All the showers were quiet and no locker doors were being slapped shut. She only heard the sopping sound of Toni's footsteps as she arrived with two clean towels.

"Thanks," Rachel muttered, slightly mortified. At least she got to see Toni naked, although not in the exact circumstances she would have wished for. "Time for a shower."

"Take the cubicle across from me," Toni commanded in her strict teacher's voice. "I want to keep an eye on you." Rachel was more than willing to oblige.

The shower cubicles closed with glass doors on both sides and Toni left hers ajar, inspiring Rachel to do the same. She set the temperature control to cold and the water was a shock to her system. Her nipples jumped to attention and blood pulsed through her veins. It was nothing compared to the effect catching glimpses of a showering Toni was having on her. A sizzling fire burned in Rachel's belly. It was now or never. This kind of opportunity wouldn't come knocking again anytime soon. Maybe the fuss Toni had made over her was a pure act of kindness or plain professional concern, but Rachel believed it left a lot of room for alternative interpretations. Either way, she had the dizzy card to play again.

She gaped at Toni through the crack in the shower doors, at the white foam sliding down her skin and caressing her taut muscles. Rachel had been vaguely aware of it before, but there was no more denying it now, something was throbbing between her legs and she had twenty minutes to do something about it. She wasn't planning on doing it herself.

"Oh," she yelped and let her back slam against the slippery wall, making enough noise to get Toni's attention. It only took Toni two seconds and three long strides to reach her side, her hands planted under Rachel's armpits and her eyes scanning Rachel's face for signs of an imminent blackout. Rachel realised she may not have to fake that dizzy spell after all. Blood rushed to her cheeks as she took stock of the situation. Two naked women crammed together in a shower cubicle with no one else around. No, not just two women—Rachel cornered by Toni's strong arms against the wall, which was getting colder against her hot skin. Rachel couldn't help but notice Toni's hard nipples, dark circles standing out against the light mocha complexion of her skin, like candy waiting to be licked.

"Shit," Rachel whispered as she heard the door of the changing room swing open and then shut. Toni put her hand in front of Rachel's mouth, curling her long fingers across her jaw.

"Shhht," she hissed. "If we're lucky, she'll be in and out."

Distant footsteps pattered about and Rachel prayed for them not to come any closer to the showers. Toni fixed her hazelnut eyes on Rachel, her hand still curved over Rachel's lips. Water drummed down around them and bounced up over their feet. Things could hardly get any wetter, Rachel thought, but immediately had to correct herself. It wasn't just water from the shower seeping down her legs. Her entire body pulsed and throbbed, aching to be touched more intimately by Toni.

Toni still had one hand underneath Rachel's armpit, but now withdrew it. She used it to shove the shower doors together and then gently ran a finger across Rachel's collarbone. Her finger travelled between Rachel's breasts, down to her belly. Whoever had come in was still fumbling with locker keys and Rachel heard precious seconds ticking away in her head. The presence of the other woman didn't seem to faze Toni, who took the opportunity to drive Rachel wild by skimming just one finger over her upper body. A nail trailed over Rachel's abs now and she was grateful for the extra crunches their body pump instructor subjected them to at the end of every class.

Beneath Toni's other hand, the one still clamped over her chin, Rachel widened her mouth and ran her lips over Toni's drenched palm. Soon she was licking her fingers and sucking them into her mouth—at least it kept her quiet.

Bam. The unwanted visitor left the locker room and a heavy thud of the door was the signal for both of them to crank up the heat. Time was not on their side and the cleaners would be in soon. Toni seemed to get the message as well, pushing her body against Rachel's, finally lavishing her with the touch she craved. Before pressing her lips hard against Rachel's mouth, she peered into her eyes one last time and the longing shining through them was inescapable. Rachel felt her knees go wobbly again, only this time it wasn't because her body couldn't cope. Toni's hands explored her breasts and they had no time for soft strokes. Rachel's nipples hardened under Toni's tugs and, instinctively, she spread her legs.

"Fuck me," Rachel moaned. Toni's lips moistened her already soaked neck and her ears were right next to Rachel's mouth. Rachel grabbed Toni's head and yanked it up to face her. "Fuck me now," she repeated and thrust herself against Toni's hard wet body. She snagged Toni's hand and pushed it down, unable to wait any longer.

"I need your fingers inside me." Rachel was ready to resort to begging to quench the lust dripping from her, flooding her inner thighs. Toni's fingers didn't delay and slipped inside Rachel as if they were made for nothing else.

"More." Rachel couldn't stop herself. Toni fucked her with

two fingers, burying them deeper with every thrust. Sweat mixed with soap and lusty juices and all Rachel heard was water coming down around them and the sound of Toni working on her pussy. Toni didn't need coaxing to add a third finger and when Rachel opened her eyes for a split second she could see how the strong muscles in Toni's arm bulged with every stroke.

Rachel dug her hands into Toni's wet hair and pushed her down. Not that she needed it to climax—she could already feel the orgasm building, tingling in her fingertips and toes—but she desperately wanted to feel Toni's tongue on her clit. Toni dropped to her knees on the rubber shower floor and didn't hold back. She started with one careful, almost hesitant flick of the tongue but soon transitioned into confident licks and nudges while her fingers continued to fuck Rachel to a screaming orgasm.

Rachel marvelled at the feeling of Toni's tongue dancing around her sensitive clit and increasing the tension in her body. She adored the tiny explosions her sexy spin instructor's fingers caused to ripple through her blood. She wanted to lean against that cold damp wall forever and have Toni go at her until her trained muscles gave up—not a thing Rachel would expect to happen any time soon. Toni's fingers drove upwards inside of her, touching her in all her most sensitive spots and filling her until Rachel believed she couldn't take anymore. The friction on her clit increased as Toni sucked it in and out of her mouth between puckered lips.

It felt as if all her insides were collapsing, swallowing each other only to be spat out again with big joyous bursts. Every thrust of Toni's fingers ignited a fresh round of swirling fireworks inside Rachel's bones and a satisfying warmth swarmed through her. She clasped her fingers in Toni's hair as her body tensed and relaxed, first in big slow waves and then short intense ones. Rachel pushed Toni's mouth away from her clit and revelled in the strong, unrelenting strokes of her fingers deep inside of her for just one moment longer before pulling Toni up and kissing her with all she had.

"Best wash up," Toni said, looking almost unflustered. She glanced at her waterproof watch. "We have five minutes."

Rachel still stood panting against the wall and it felt as if she'd spent the last five hours in the cubicle, while, in reality, it couldn't have been longer than ten minutes.

"I owe you one." Rachel curled her fingers around Toni's wrist, not wanting to let her go just yet.

"Same time next week." Toni pecked her low on the cheek, next to her lips, then slipped out of her grasp.

Rachel couldn't wait.

DRESS CODE

I hate these forced occasions of merriment, but I'm the boss and I need to set a good example. It's the last afternoon in the office before everyone goes on Christmas break and, as per tradition, my team and I spend it around a bowl of weak punch pretending we're friends instead of co-workers. I like most of them enough to get along with on a daily basis in a work environment, but out of the eight other people crammed in the small meeting room with me, there's only one I would voluntarily socialise with outside of business hours.

Emma is always dressed inappropriately for work, not because her skirts are too short, but because her trousers are made of leather and the shirts—obviously purchased in the men's department—hug her frame a bit too tightly, accentuating her breasts. I tried talking to her about her outfits once, in a friendly, understanding boss kind of way.

"This is who I am, Beth," she said, leaning her tall torso against my door frame. "Would you prefer that I wore a pinstriped suit and performed below par?"

There were so many things I could have said. The words swirled in my brain, fighting to get out, to find their way to my mouth, but I suddenly found myself unable to speak. That day, she wore a red tie over a starched white shirt on top of the tightest pair of faded jeans I'd ever laid eyes on.

Instead of reprimanding her, I forced myself to reassess the dress code at work. She had that effect on me. Still has.

Today she's dressed as a lesbian hipster tomboy Christmas elf. Emma didn't need to come out when she first joined our team. She walked in and we knew. She was swag personified in her knee-high leather boots with matching jacket. She didn't even take the jacket off when she found her spot behind the desk assigned to her and started typing data into a spreadsheet.

Emma does things with numbers I, as her immediate superior, should instantly understand, but I don't. Her brain works differently from most people's. It allows her to get away with murder—or at least circumvent what is socially and sartorially expected of her in the workplace.

"What are your holiday plans, Beth?" David, the person who always ends up standing closest to me at events like these, asks.

With difficulty, I drag my gaze away from Emma, who appears to be engaged in a passionate discussion with my assistant Drew. I'll have to interrogate him discreetly later as to the subject of their conversation.

"Turkey with the family," I quickly say. I know how my team sees me. A single woman in her mid-forties who appears to be only interested in work. If only they knew where my interests really lay.

"Just like last year, then." David obviously prides himself on remembering every bit of small talk he and I ever shared.

"How about you?" I try to inject some casual politeness into my voice, which is difficult, because Emma has torn herself away from her conversation with Drew and is headed in my direction.

"My missus is from Italy and she always cooks—" I can't for the life of me focus on what David has to say. Emma halts next to him, letting him finish his sentence, while peering at me over the rim of her glasses.

"Hey, Boss," Emma fixes her gaze on me. Maybe I didn't make the punch weak enough this year because it seems to have left me feeling a bit dizzy. "Drew is convinced your shoes are LV but they're Miu Miu, right?"

She might as well have asked me about the colour of my undergarments, that's how instantaneously heat flushes my cheeks.

In the opposite corner of the room, I see Drew stooped into a solitary giggle. He tries to stifle it unsuccessfully when he notices my eyes land on him. As the boss, I'm supposed to effortlessly rise above silly office bets—especially at the Christmas party. I try, but it's difficult with Emma standing so close to me, her body heat rising between us.

"They're Gucci, if you really must know."

"Oh." Emma doesn't lose her cool—she hardly ever does. "Could have fooled me."

"My wife prefers McQueen or something like—" David tries to insert himself into the conversation. Emma keeps looking at me with a gaze so intense I feel it between my legs. God knows what else she and Drew have been talking about concerning me. Or maybe that's just wishful thinking on my part.

"With all due respect, Emma," I hear coming out of my mouth. "But you actually do strike me as someone who could easily be fooled on that front."

Her lips curve into a smirk and she lifts her palms skyward. "You've got me there, Boss." Then she has the audacity to wink at me. "Drew dared me to ask you about your shoes. I do apologise because, frankly, I couldn't care less."

"Apology accepted." I paint a faint smile on my face. For some reason, maybe because I'll be going home to an empty house after this party, I find it hard to take it in jest. Not because of the utter silliness of the joke between Drew and

Emma, but because, and this thought is not new to me, the image of Emma's fingers unbuttoning my designer blouse flashes through my brain again. I know from experience it's only the beginning of the fantasy.

I want to flirt, but I can't. I'm her boss, and David keeps hovering around me, as if it will impact his year-end bonus.

The three of us stand around in awkward silence for a minute. "Drew and I are taking this party back to my place later," Emma suddenly says. "You're both very welcome to join."

I see hesitation flash across David's face. "Thank you for the offer, Emma." He's never really warmed to her unconventional ways. "But I need to get home to the missus."

I, on the other hand, have no doubts. "I hope your drinks are stronger than these." I lift the cup of punch I'm holding to chin level.

"Everything at my place is." Emma's smirk has transformed into a warm smile that melts my core. She winks at me again before turning around and walking back to Drew.

For obvious reasons, I'm suddenly anxious to end this tedious office party. I reach for my phone in the pocket of my pinstriped blazer. Faking a surprised expression, I pretend an important e-mail has just come in.

"I'm sorry, David. I need to nip back to my office for a bit. If I don't see you before you leave, merry Christmas to you and your family." I address the rest of them in my loud, authoritative voice. "Ladies and gentlemen, I'm sorry to say Wallace is having a bit of a crisis over the latest numbers. No need to ruin your Christmas, I'll deal with it. Happy holidays, everyone." My eyes scan the room. Most of the people present are in holiday mode already, their expression blurred by too much punch—no matter how low its alcohol percentage. My gaze falls on Emma who, somehow, always appears to be leaning against something. Her eyes narrow and she sucks her bottom lip between her teeth. She gives me a slight nod as if to say, a very merry Christmas to you too, Boss.

I retreat to my office hoping they'll all leave sooner rather than later, the number of them substantially thinning before joining Emma's after-party. I shut my office door and sit behind my desk. There's always work to be done, but, truth be told, I had switched off already as well and I'm no mood to attend to the never-ending avalanche of e-mails that rolls in—no matter what time of year.

I lean back in my chair and close my eyes. Immediately, images of Emma in various too tight outfits—and in a state of undress—assault the back of my eyelids. I've tried to stop it, but the longer she works for me, the harder it gets.

A soft knock on the door breaks me out of my spell. I expect it to be Drew who, while being an incorrigible prankster, takes his job very seriously.

"Yes?" I sit up straight and pretend to be focused on my computer screen, which isn't even lit up.

The door creaks open and to my surprise, Emma stands in the doorway. As if unable to remain upright, her shoulder finds the frame instantly and she leans against it, crossing her legs at the ankles. "I usually crunch Wallace's numbers so I was wondering if you needed help." She wears pointed brown leather boots and as I let my gaze roam across her body, from shoes to face, I know she's not here to help me with my imaginary task. The grin on her face is too crooked and the glint in her eyes too sparkly.

"Well, uh..." I stall because I don't want her to go but I also very much don't want to be on the receiving end of a sexual harassment lawsuit.

"Can I come in?" Her voice has dropped into a low register I haven't heard before.

"Sure," I nod.

She closes the door behind her and flicks off the lights in

the process. The room is only illuminated by the desk lamp I'd forgotten to switch off earlier and the city lights blinking outside.

"I don't mean to be presumptuous," she says as she slowly walks towards my desk. "But I know for a fact that Mr. Wallace is very happy with his accounts. Seeing as I'm his primary point of contact and all that." She plants her palms on the wooden surface of my desk. "Obviously, I won't ask you to explain yourself." There's that smile again. "Not because you're my boss but because..." She pauses extremely strategically. "...I know, Beth."

"I'm not sure I know what you mean," I stutter.

"Get up." Her tone is commanding, but I can't just obey. I get paid too much to just acquiesce.

"W-what?" I try.

"You heard me." She bends her elbows a little. "Get up." Briefly, her tongue flicks along her lips. "Your Christmas wishes are about to come true."

I swallow hard and slowly, trying to process the moment. I can hardly deny it's what I have wanted since the day Emma started working for me, but it doesn't make it less problematic.

"I'm not sure this is the time or place for—"

Emma scrunches her lips together. Her dark eyes don't leave mine as I rise from my chair. My knees are a bit wobbly, but the sensation is nothing compared to the heat tumbling through my veins. It engulfs me in long, luxurious waves. Emma hasn't even touched me yet and already I find myself having to catch my breath.

Her mouth stretches into a wide, cocky smile—the one she walks into the office with every morning, as if she owns the place—as she, by wiggling just one slender finger, beckons me towards her.

Like a puppet on a string, I march to where she's standing on the other side of my desk.

"Let's lock this door, shall we?" Emma breathes into my ear when we stand face to face.

She grabs me by the wrist and leads me to the door in a few quick strides. We've barely reached it when she twirls me around and pushes my back against it, her body inches away from mine.

"That should do it." She cocks her head to the left a little. "Now, before we begin… I need you to tell me something."

Begin? My heart thunders so hard beneath my ribs I'm not sure how much more I can take.

"I've seen you watch me, Beth. I've felt your eyes on me and I've noticed how they glaze over with lust at times." She traces a finger along my jaw bone. "But I need you to tell me. Do you understand?"

Am I supposed to reply? Is this foreplay? I'm not that much of a talker in bed; then again, I couldn't be further away from my bed.

"Tell me, Beth." Her finger has dipped down to my neck. "What would you like me to do to you?"

It's as if her finger is made of fire, leaving my skin scorched wherever it passes. And I know what I want her to do, the problem is I'm not sure I can say it out loud.

"Tell me," she urges as her finger travels even lower, into the opening of my Armani blouse. When she halts at the top button, my body takes control over my mind.

"Fuck me," I pant. "I need you to fuck me, Emma."

She slants her head so her mouth almost touches my ear. "All you had to do was ask." Her voice is a ragged whisper and I realise this is turning her on as much as it is me. We're in this together. When her lips briefly touch my earlobe, the first wave of tension releases and I feel my briefs grow wet between my legs.

"Exactly how expensive is this blouse?" she whispers in my ear, while her fingers tug at a button.

"Ridiculously overpriced," I hum back, hardly recognising my own voice. "Rip it off."

I feel her lips widen into a smile against the skin of my neck. "You're just full of surprises, Boss." As she pronounces the last word, she yanks my blouse open, sending its buttons tumbling to the floor.

I inhale sharply at the sudden exposure of my torso to air. I feel my nipples stiffen to hard pebbles against the fabric of my bra.

With a few swift movements, Emma slides both my blazer and blouse to the floor. She regards me from a small distance for an instant before bringing her face right in front of mine.

"I'd be lying if I said I haven't indulged in some fantasies myself."

Although she's barely touched me, my clit throbs wildly beneath the panel of my drenched briefs.

"Get on with it then." My voice sounds much more desperate than I want it to.

"Is that an order?" She curls her lips into a crooked grin again, one that melts every bit of me that hadn't surrendered yet.

"Oh yes." I barely manage to squeeze the words out of my throat.

Suddenly, her hands are on my breasts, and before I know it, a finger finds its way behind the fabric of each cup. She grazes her fingertips over my aching, swollen nipples and I all but sigh with relief. This is not relief at all, though. This is torture. I want at least one of her fingers focusing its attention elsewhere.

Just as quick as her fingers descended into the cups of my bra, she removes them to yank the fabric down, exposing my nipples to the air around us.

Through hooded eyelids I see her body heave with want and it only spurs me on. My hands have been hanging limply by my side, but they need action now. They need to feel skin. They reach for her neck and I pull her close, overcome with the desire to feel her lips against mine. Emma may believe she's running this show—and she has certainly started it—but this is my office and I need to get off fast.

Kissing her gives me pause, momentarily overwhelmed by the impossible softness of her lips and the tender way her tongue slips between mine. When we come up for air, I lock my eyes on hers. "I thought I told you to fuck me."

Without saying a word or altering the expression on her face, she bends her knees a little so her hands can reach the hem of my pencil skirt. It's a tight one and it takes some effort to hitch up, but when the fabric gathers at my waist I'm relieved to finally be able to spread my legs for her.

Already, her fingers graze the panel of my briefs. Her lips quirk up at the feel of them. Because my knickers are soaked, they offer no protection to my pulsing pussy lips. Just a hint of Emma's fingers skating along makes me want to buck my pelvis against her, makes me want to feel those fingers inside.

"Someone's a little bit excited," Emma says while, with the tips of her fingers, she slides the material to the side.

"Oh god," I moan, because I'm way past uttering any words of eloquence.

She stands in front of me fully dressed, and fully in command now. I'm at her mercy. My legs open for her, my cunt wet with want. Against the door of my office. I ignore the sheer audacity of it all, because my brain has transformed into the very definition of a one-track mind. Fingers inside. Now.

Of course, she teases. She slithers her fingers through my wetness, her eyes sparkling at the copiousness of it.

"All this for me," she says, her voice annoyingly controlled. "I can't possibly think of a better Christmas present."

A finger stops dangerously close to my clit. Lazily, she lets it circle around, again and again. She brings her face closer as she keeps making circles with her finger, close enough to drive me crazy but not enough to tip me over. I always suspected that, if it ever came to this, Emma would know exactly what she was doing.

"Merry Christmas, Boss," she says before pressing her lips to mine while her fingers, at last, enter me. They drive deep with the first thrust, leaving me trembling against the door.

"Oh." A guttural groan escapes me as Emma finds her rhythm. She curls her fingers inside me while her tongue meets mine.

I bury my hands in her hair, pulling her as close as I can. My pelvis reaches for her of its own accord, meeting her thrusts, always wanting more.

"Good god," I moan again when we break from our lip lock. I can just spot the mischievous glint in her eyes before her face disappears from my field of vision. The thrusts inside me stutter for an instant as she falls to her knees and I feel her tongue flick against my clit.

She's back at it with full force now, fucking me hard and deep, while her tongue dances around my clit. Because I need to hold on to something, I grab hold of her hair, my hands balling into fists as I twirl strands of it around my fingers.

Her tongue is relentless and when she sucks my clit between her lips, all the while thrusting high inside of me, my resolve gives. Heat crashes through me in shock waves of pleasure. Every cell in my body tingles as I come at Emma's fingertips. I tug wildly at her hair, but it doesn't deter her. She lets me ride out my climax, her tongue flicking and her fingers stroking. After the last contraction, which leaves my flesh sizzling with delight, my muscles go limp and I crash to my knees.

Our gazes meet while both of our bodies become a crumpled mess on my office floor. Immediately, I curl my hands around her neck and pull her in for a kiss. Her lips are hungry for me and I smell myself on them. When I start to push her down to the floor, my mind ready to forget about where we are again, she stops me.

"How about a private after-party at my place?"

I arch up my eyebrows. "Depends." I'm finally able to speak again, albeit only in short sentences. "Do you have mistletoe?"

She smirks up at me. "In every room."

STORMY WEATHER

Nic looked around for the waiter. He couldn't be far. She was the only patron at the bar—making her wonder where everyone else was hiding from the non-stop rain. She caught his eye and pointed at her empty daiquiri glass.

He nodded and sped off, visibly relieved to be at least of some service during low season. Relaxing at the prospect of more alcohol coming her way, Nic sagged into her chair. She'd made a mistake, that was obvious. She'd booked her trip to Vietnam in too much of a hurry, eager to get away from what had happened in Manchester—the confusing mess her life had become.

"I'm going on a soul-searching journey," she'd proclaimed to her best friend Daisy. Neither one of them had believed a word she'd said. She was running, but soul-searching sounded more acceptable.

With a revering tilt of the head, the waiter placed her drink on the table and scooped up her empty glass. The bright yellow liquid he'd served her could, to the unknown eye, be perceived as healthy. She could be drinking a mango smoothie, for all anyone knew. But damn, they made their daiquiris strong in this resort—probably to make up for the downpours.

As Nic watched him scuttle off, she noticed the door opening. The waiter made a big spectacle of securing the new customer a table by the window—for a spectacular grey cloud view, no doubt. Must be a new arrival, Nic thought, as she hadn't seen the woman around. Then again, since checking in two nights ago, Nic had divided her time between the spa—her skin had never been this silky-smooth and her muscles never this relaxed—the restaurant and the bar.

She had taken one walk along the beach, lasting about five minutes, before another storm had rolled in over the ocean.

"This year is very rainy," the receptionist at the spa had told her. "Normally not like this."

A fat lot of good that did Nic. She'd booked this resort to get away from the hustle and bustle of Hanoi for a few days. To relax. To escape the stifling, crowded heat and humidity of the city. To have a dip in the ocean, a swim in the pool. A few days of pampering. But this rain was having the opposite effect, leaving her more stressed out than before she'd left. The massages helped. And the daiquiris. Either way, if she'd wanted a rainy holiday, she might as well have stayed home—and faced the music.

"Been here long?" The voice startled Nic. Because she hadn't had a real conversation in days, it seemed to come out of nowhere, with its Queen's English accent and cultured tone.

"Two nights, three days," Nic replied, taking the woman in. She looked a bit tired, possibly from travelling, but kept her back straight. Her eyes shone like polished black pearls. "Two more nights to go."

The woman painted a small smile on her lips and nodded. "I assume the rain hasn't let up?"

"Nope." Nic sipped from her drink. The alcohol made her a

bit more forward than she'd usually be. "The name's Nicole, by the way."

The woman shoved her chair backwards. "Do you mind if I join you?"

"Please." Nic was dying for conversation, even if it was chit-chat with someone she didn't know. "Be my guest." She gestured to the empty chair at the other end of her table.

The waiter arrived with the woman's drink: a large pint of draught beer.

"Charlotte." She sat down, seeming completely at ease with herself. "But call me Charlie."

"Only if you call me Nic." Nic raised her drink, not her first of the day by a long stretch, and clinked the rim against Charlie's giant pint. Alcohol, easing pain and discomfort around the globe, she thought. At least for a few, blissfully forgetful hours. "Welcome to rainy paradise."

"I can see how it could be really beautiful under the sun." Charlie swallowed a large gulp of beer. "Which, truth be told, makes the presence of these billowing clouds all the more frustrating."

Outside, the rain had thinned to a drizzle, tapping lightly against the window—always lingering. Nic glared at Charlie. The skin on her arms had broken out in goosebumps.

"Are you cold?" Nic had learned to bring a cardigan to withstand the air-conditioned atmosphere of the bar and restaurant.

"To my great surprise, it appears so." Charlie chuckled. "You'd think I'd know better, but I'm still getting used to the difference in outside and inside temperatures in Asia."

"Have you been out here long?" Nic couldn't help but notice the flex in Charlie's biceps as she lifted the beer glass to her mouth.

"I moved to Macau for work six months ago. I'm here for a conference, but, unwisely, decided to head out a few days earlier." She sipped and stared at Nic over the rim of her glass. "How about you?"

Nic thought it too ridiculous to drag up the soul-searching phrase. "Holiday." She accompanied her statement with a sigh. "But hey, I guess in some ways, it still beats dreary Manchester."

"You're from Manchester?" A spark seemed to light up in Charlie's eyes. "I've only lived there half of my life."

"Are you kidding?" Nic raised her eyebrows. Like a blanket was slowly being lifted from her brain, a glimmer of recognition nestled in Nic's mind. Was Charlie one of the women in the bar she should never have gone to? Or was her subconscious playing tricks on her?

"University of Manchester. Class of 1995. Never left, until six months ago."

"Wow." Nic shook her head. "I'm a transplant myself. I moved there from Leeds for"—the word already had a false ring to it, even though she hadn't pronounced it yet—"love." And yet here she was, at the other end of the world, alone.

They sat in silence for a few seconds while the rain outside became bolder again. If Charlie had moved away from Manchester six months ago, she couldn't have been one of the women at Cherry Lane. Some of them skulking in the shadows against the wall, a few seated at the bar, chatting to the bartender as if they were in any other bar, the younger ones—too young for Nic, anyway—wearing skinny jeans, bopping on the dance floor. Nic had only spent thirty minutes there, knocking back two glasses of wine, feeling out of place and, at the same time, as though she'd finally found the spot where she belonged. She shook off the memory and regarded Charlie. She was sure she'd seen her somewhere.

"Where in Manchester did you live? You look awfully familiar." Nic drained the rest of her daiquiri.

Charlie shot her a crooked grin. "Alderley Edge for the past five years."

Then, as if some mechanism had clicked into place in the back of her brain, Nic saw it. "Wait a second..." Narrowing her eyes, she peered at Charlie, head slightly tilted. "Are you Charlotte Lau? The Charlotte Lau?" Nic had read an interview with her in one of Joe's business magazines. Charlotte Lau had been crowned 'Businesswoman of the Year' twice. And, as a mere footnote, as if it was the most normal thing in the world, in the last paragraph of the article, it had been stated that she was openly gay. Openly gay. Two words that just wouldn't combine in Nic's troubled mind.

"The one and only." She opened her arms wide. "I started a company in Macau to work with the casinos. I should be there another six months. I'm meeting some business associates here. The Chinese love to travel to places like this. It's all part of the game." A snicker followed her last statement. "Some might even say I sold out, but Britain's only so big, and damn, those casinos are interesting places."

Nic tried to listen attentively, but Charlie's proclamations about work didn't really compute. On that bright white T-shirt she was wearing, she might as well have it stencilled in blood red letters: openly gay. She barely resembled the image of the woman Nic had read about in the magazine. In the accompanying photo, she'd worn a tightly fitted black pencil skirt and matching blazer, a stark white blouse underneath, open at the throat, and Nic had thought, Really? This woman is gay? Ignorant at best. She could have said the same thing to the reflection staring back at her when she looked in the mirror.

Charlie rubbed her palms over her bare arms—making her biceps pop again. "I should really go get a sweater." She rested her eyes on Nic. "I'm in one of those beach villas over there. Private pool and everything. Can I interest you in a beverage at mine? At least the view will be better."

Perplexed, Nic nodded. She watched Charlie drain the last of her beer. Nic signalled to the waiter so she could sign the receipt for the three mango daiquiris she'd just consumed.

~

A bottle of wine later, they sat in Charlie's sea view villa with the air-conditioning turned off.

"What about you, Nic?" Charlie inquired. "I keep going on about myself, but I'm not that much of an egomaniac that I only want to hear the sound of my own voice." She sat in the sofa, legs folded underneath her body, one arm resting on the backrest, only occasionally peering into the dramatic stacks of clouds above the ocean.

Nic had gathered that Charlie didn't suffer from a lack of self-confidence, but, instead of displaying her success in life in a show-offish way, she radiated a self-assuredness that only people completely at ease with themselves possessed. "My life's not nearly as interesting as yours," Nic said. In the past hour, Charlie had regaled her with tales of her first two start-ups, how one of them had gone under spectacularly, and how she'd learned from her mistakes, eventually building one of the most successful software development companies in the world.

"It may be very different from mine, but everybody has a story to tell." She slanted her body towards the coffee table to deposit her empty wine glass, a bit like a sideways crunch that stretched the fabric of her T-shirt—once she'd switched off the AC, Charlie had, to Nic's delight, taken off the sweater she'd put on.

"I have a husband at home," Nic started, feeling the effects of the alcohol. A loosening in her limbs—like after a massage—and a gradual dimming of the voice in her head that usually stopped her from making confessions like the one she was about to make. "Who has no idea why I wanted to travel through Vietnam on my own for three weeks." She thought back to the time, now months ago, when Joe had last grabbed her shoulder in bed, spooning her, his desire for her clear, and how she'd rejected him—again—because, after fifteen years of marriage and despite loving him, it simply wasn't an option anymore.

"Now that's interesting." Charlie repositioned herself in the sofa, turning her body fully towards Nic. "Shall I pour us some more wine first?"

"Sure." Nic tried to sound casual. She followed Charlie with her eyes as she rose and walked to what seemed like a fully stocked fridge in the neighbouring, open kitchen. She wore tiny, black shorts, and the definition in her legs spoke of hours in the gym.

To Nic's surprise, after refilling their glasses, Charlie didn't return to her spot in the sofa across from where she was sitting, but sat down next to Nic, in the settee facing the window.

"Tell me," she said, placing a gentle hand on Nic's shoulder. "I can see that you want to."

Successful, hot, openly gay and clairvoyant, Nic thought.

"I love my husband," Nic heard herself say. It sounded like such a cop-out. Like she was a fraud. "But, um,"—she paused to drink—"well, the past, I guess, five years, I've been questioning, erm, some things."

Charlie, her hand still resting on Nic's shoulder—burning through the fabric of her top, it seemed—nodded and blinked once, slowly, as if that small movement of her eyelashes held all the encouragement Nic needed. Strangely, it sort of did.

"I don't know." A glow of exasperation clung to Nic's voice. She barely recognised the sound of it. "I wasn't raised—I mean, I've been married for so long, it just never seemed like an option." She drank more and rolled her head back on her shoulders. "I think I like women," she blurted out, and as she said it, she released the hold on her wineglass—all her muscles seemingly going limp—and it tumbled to the floor in a high-pitched clatter of broken glass. "Oh shit." In a flash, her body went rigid again—swinging to the opposite side of the pendulum.

"It's all right. I've got it. Don't move." Charlie's hand slipped off her shoulder as she rose from the settee and tip-toed to the kitchen.

Nic stared at the floor, at the mess she'd made. A perfect metaphor for her life. She slid down, crouched next to the broken glass and started collecting shards.

"Don't hurt yourself," Charlie said as she kneeled next to Nic. "I'll call housekeeping. They'll take care of it." There was her hand on Nic's shoulder again. That hand. Ever since Nic had realised who Charlie was, images of what that hand could do had been flashing through her mind—like the strikes of lightning outside, flickering with sudden white light but dissolved in the blink of an eye. "Come on." Charlie raised herself up and held out a hand to Nic, who reached for it and let herself be hoisted up. "We'll sit over there for a while." She gently tugged Nic towards the dining table, pulled out a chair for her and sat her down. "I'll just be a minute."

Nic heard Charlie make a call. She was glad that, after the turmoil, she had a few moments to let the magnitude of what she'd just said sink in. Had she really said it? Out loud?

Still on the tips of her toes, Charlie pattered back from the phone mounted to the wall near the entrance. She pulled up a chair and positioned it so she sat across from Nic. "I take it you know I'm gay?" She arched up her eyebrows, widening her black eyes.

"Y-yes," Nic stammered. "I read an interview."

"I'm glad." The feet of Charlie's chair scraped over the wooden floor as she dragged it even closer. "That you got to say it. It can only be a good thing."

A good thing? Nic puffed out some air. “God no,” she shook her head in desperation. “How can it ever be a good thing?”

“Because,” Charlie placed both of her hands on Nic’s knees. “It’s the first step to accepting who you really are.”

“But…” Nic felt goosebumps spread across her skin, starting from where Charlie’s hands rested on her body. “I’ve never even… erm.” She couldn’t say it. She’d said enough out loud. And, though it was a relief, having acknowledged her sexuality to another person for the first time ever, it now presented Nic with a whole slew of new problems. When it was still just a dawning idea in her head, a constant nagging in her mind, it hadn’t been concrete. Now, as she sat opposite this gorgeous, openly gay woman—the only one she’d ever encountered in her life as far as she knew—she had concrete desire rushing through her veins, all sorts of thoughts tumbling through her mind, making her stomach drop.

The breaking glass had sobered her up somewhat, but there was still enough alcohol diluting her blood that she could allow herself to put her hands over Charlie’s on her knees without too much guilt wrecking the moment. Her eyes found Charlie’s, and to just be with someone who was like her, to experience that kinship, although silent and with a virtual stranger, made her heart beat in her throat.

A discreet knock on the door interrupted the moment and, once again, Nic was brusquely pulled from the natural flow of things.

“Hold that thought,” Charlie said, as she gave her knee a quick squeeze, and sauntered to the door. A hotel employee dressed in a sharp suit assessed the damage and made quick work of making it disappear. He was in and out in minutes.

“Where were we?” Charlie asked after she’d sat back down, a benign smile on her face.

Nic burst out in a sudden bout of laughter, the hysterical, uncontrollable kind, starting in her stomach and engaging all her muscles. "I'm such an idiot," she said as she came to. "What the hell am I doing? Thinking?"

"You came here for a reason." Charlie didn't touch her this time. "Better make it count."

Nic shook her head. "This is ridiculous. Really." The giggles subsided and her abdominal muscles relaxed. An image of her wedding day popped up in Nic's mind. Had she really not known? Had it been that much of an impossibility—even in this day and age? She stared at Charlie, who, for some reason, had started to resemble her picture in the magazine more. Her clothes were still summery and casual, but her glance had become intense, her eyes black and shiny like coals about to be lit on fire.

Nic didn't know this woman. She knew which companies she'd founded and that she could rock a business suit—and be openly gay and successful—but she didn't know her personal story. Obviously, she didn't need to be much more acquainted with her to feel that gravitational pull towards her, a drowning sensation in her mind—perhaps still the alcohol—and that ceaseless throbbing somewhere deep between her legs. She wanted Charlie, and it only made her feel more ludicrous.

"I should go." Nic started getting up. Outside, a loud crash of thunder broke in the sky. Startled, she steadied herself against the edge of the table.

"Easy." Charlie was by her side within a split second. "Why don't you lie down in the sofa for a few minutes. I'll get you some water." Charlie guided her to the lounge area, her hands burning on the skin of Nic's arms.

Dazed by everything that was going on—the storm outside as well as the one rumbling inside of her—Nic felt out of breath by the time they'd crossed the three feet to the sofa. Grateful for it, she stretched out, closed her eyes and let her mind wander. By the time Charlie returned with a glass of water, she'd drifted off into a restless, fitful sleep.

When Nic opened her eyes, for an instant, she had no idea where she was. The curtains were drawn and the room was dark. A splitting headache started at the base of her skull, making its way forward. She sat up and her eyes landed on an empty glass, a bottle of water and a box of Panadol. Without thinking, she pressed two pills free from the strip and swallowed them with large gulps of water.

Had she really said the words out loud? And where was Charlie? What time was it, anyway? Disoriented, she rose from the sofa and walked towards the window. Pulling back the curtain a bit, she stared into the blackness of the beach and the ocean. The storm had calmed. It wasn't even raining anymore.

"Hey." Charlie's voice was soft and quiet. "How are you feeling?" Where had she come from?

Nic turned around and watched her descend the stairs. She wore a different pair of shorts and just a tank top—oh sweet Jesus, what a shoulder line—and as she headed towards Nic, who was still a little sleep-drunk and a whole lot hungover, it felt like a dream. "W-what time is it?" Nic stammered.

"Two in the morning. You were out for a while." Charlie remained at a small distance. Still, Nic could see her top was wrinkled, as was the skin of her left cheek.

"Sorry for waking you." There was that pulsing hot sensation between her legs again—and a sudden shortness of breath.

"I couldn't sleep anyway." Charlie inched closer until she stood next to Nic, whose fingers were still curled around the hem of the curtain. Charlie positioned her hand just above Nic's and pulled it away a bit further. "Has the storm quieted?" Her voice sounded different in the dark and Nic could feel her body heat radiate onto her back.

"Looks like it." Nic barely managed to squeeze the words out of her throat. Then, that hand on her shoulder again. Nic tried to keep her breath steady. She focused her gaze on the waves outside; they were the quietest they'd been since she'd arrived.

"I want to show you." Charlie's voice was a mere hot breath in her ear. "How it can be."

Nic's knees gave a little and she had to use her free hand to steady herself against the window. In the reflection, her eyes locked on Charlie's. Two blurry mirrored faces in the dark—and again, the persistent idea that this was a dream. Nic turned away from her reflected self, spinning on her heels, to face Charlie.

One shallow breath, one blink of the eye, one split second was all it took for her to decide—because the decision had been made for her long ago already. Nic's hands lunged for Charlie's neck and she pulled her close for the first kiss she would ever share with another woman. Soft lips met hers as Charlie curved her arms around Nic's waist and tugged her closer. Overwhelmed, Nic sank into the embrace, leaning against Charlie's strong frame, glad for the support.

When they broke for air, Nic's head spun and her skin was covered in goosebumps. "I've never..." she tried to say.

"I know." Charlie nodded. "Come on." She let one hand slip to Nic's side and curled her fingers around Nic's wrist. "Let's go to the bedroom."

Nic regarded the stairs and had no idea how her trembling legs would make it up there. But her body was fired up as well, with the thrill of what was to come, with the nervous giddiness of the first time. She let Charlie guide her while the first tremor coursed along her spine, erasing her headache and releasing the tension in her muscles.

Upstairs, the bedroom was as big as the whole downstairs area, with wall-sized windows facing the ocean. A bed that could easily fit five adults was positioned in the middle of the room, as if put there for one purpose only.

But Nic didn't have the time—or the inclination—to enjoy the view. Charlie still stood close to her, her breath on Nic's neck and her hands roaming upwards across her arms.

"Are you sure?" she asked, while cupping the back of Nic's head. "I know this is a big deal for you."

"God yes." She planted her hands on Charlie's sides, already tugging at the fabric of her tank top, although in the wrong direction.

"Good." The smile Charlie shot her melted every cell in her body that hadn't surrendered yet. "Because oh, how I want you."

Really? Nic wanted to ask, but her lips were soon otherwise engaged, and any remnant of doubt or guilt or lingering questions got squashed with the rippling sensation in her blood, as if warm liquid was making its way through, rocking and rolling like the waves on the beach outside.

This kiss lasted longer, growing from tender to demanding quickly. Their lips stayed locked while Charlie pushed Nic down onto the bed until she sat on the edge.

"Let's take these off," she said, and crossed her arms in a downward X along her chest, pulling her tank top off in one swift movement. She came for Nic's top next, but Nic was so mesmerised by the sight of Charlie's stark naked upper body she hardly noticed her clothes being yanked off her—bra included. "Lie down." Charlie gently gave her shoulders a push and Nic fell back—as if in a trance—and crawled backwards until her entire body was supported by the mattress.

Nic had often imagined this moment, all the while thinking that it may never really come. But now, as if in slow motion, Charlie lowered her body on top of hers, their breasts touching in a crash of soft flesh, and it was enough for the fireworks in Nic's tummy to start their first course of explosions. In a frenzy she grabbed for Charlie, kissing her, while her nipples grew hard.

And, perhaps, Nic had never truly experienced desire like this before, but nonetheless, her actions came easily, flowed naturally, as if everything had always only led to this moment. Her hands lunged for Charlie's shorts, tugging at them—in the right direction this time—because she wanted her naked.

Charlie pushed herself up and glanced at Nic for a moment, a wild smile slipping along her lips. Nic seized the opportunity to negotiate her own shorts off, baring the pulsing, moist mess between her legs to the air. She watched Charlie watch her and it only made everything throb harder. With a flick of her leg Nic threw her clothes off until she lay completely naked in front of Charlie.

Charlie bit her lip and narrowed her eyes while she swiftly disposed of her shorts, before draping her body next to Nic's, her breath heavy in Nic's ear. She slipped an arm under Nic's neck while she trailed imaginary lines over Nic's body with her fingertips. Trailing figure of eights around her belly-button. Ever-receding circles around her breasts, until the circles were so small, her fingers hovered over Nic's nipples, seemingly making them grow harder with every light caress. Instead of touching them with her fingers, Charlie manoeuvred herself half on top of Nic and closed her lips around Nic's left nipple.

A lifetime of desire pooled between Nic's legs at the connection of lips on her skin, and she buried her hands in Charlie's raven black hair. Charlie treated her other breast to the same sensation, sucking softly before baring her teeth and clamping down, forcing a tremor of lust to travel downwards from Nic's chest to her clit.

White hot desire crackled in Nic's brain, taking her out of her body—a level of abandon completely foreign to her. Charlie's lips travelled down, retracing the figure of eight she'd drawn with her fingers earlier, stopping just above Nic's triangle of pubic hair. Her entire body was pulsing, as if charged by an electric current—as if someone had finally, after all these years, located the power switch.

Nic looked down at Charlie's tangle of hair on her belly and her fingers, at last, pinching her nipples. Instinctively, she spread wide. She was ready. She'd only waited forty years for this.

Charlie looked up, their eyes meeting. The storm that had brought them together that afternoon seemed to rage in her pupils now, dark and loud and deliciously brooding.

Nic braced herself, but not in her wildest dreams had she envisioned it ever being like this. That first furtive but promising touch of Charlie's tongue to her clit. The promise of everything she'd ever wanted, everything she had denied herself her entire life. This particular storm brought rain in the shape of tears, trickling one-by-one out of Nic's eyes as Charlie started licking her more purposefully, but soon streaking her cheeks wet as Charlie's tongue ventured between her pussy lips, sliding up and down and in and out of her.

The undercurrent of pleasure that had been hiding beneath her skin since meeting Charlie gathered in her clit, intensifying, speeding to ever-dizzying heights every time Charlie touched down with her tongue, which was going a mile a minute.

"Ooh," Nic heard herself moan. Her voice much lower and more guttural than it had ever sounded. As if, in finding herself, she was losing herself as well.

She felt Charlie shift, her tongue losing contact for a fraction of a second, only to launch a new onslaught on her clit that quickly sent Nic on the way to a core-shaking climax. But it wasn't just Charlie's tongue down there anymore, probing at her slithering lips. There were fingers, two of them, perhaps even three. Slowly, Charlie pushed them inside of her, cutting off Nic's breath in the process. She held her tongue still for a moment, while going deep and spreading Nic wide, stroking her from the inside. The subtlety of it, the effortlessness with which Charlie seemed to reach that spot inside of her, floored Nic, and when Charlie lowered her tongue to her clit again, all the while moving gently inside of her, she lost herself completely.

The storm took over. Her body was nothing but fluid motion and wetness, lightning striking in her blood, thunder in her brain. It raged on, heavy waves crashing into her, as if her body was the beach that afternoon—defencelessly tackling the storm, because what other choice was there?

A loud long shriek pierced the bedroom air as Nic came to herself again. Charlie let her fingers slip out and Nic relaxed her body against the soft covers of the bed. Her muscles needed some more time to recover, her limbs still trembling with the force of the orgasm, but it wasn't just the climax that had made her rise and plummet to and from such great heights. It was Charlie, who was now crawling back to her, a satisfied but sweet grin on her face.

Nic curled her arms around Charlie, wanting to hold her close. She'd shown her all right, but it was nowhere near enough. She needed to do the same to her, coax the same sort of pleasure from Charlotte Lau as she had from Nic.

"Your heart's thumping like crazy." Charlie broke the silence, her head resting on Nic's chest.

"No wonder." Nic chuckled. "I can barely believe this is happening."

Charlie pressed herself up and looked her in the eyes. "You'd better."

Nic had so many questions burning in her brain, but they could wait until later. After all, the weather forecast for the next two days wasn't predicting a lot of improvement. First, she needed a taste.

"I'd better what?" Nic asked, tossing Charlie off her as she pushed herself up. "Lick your pussy, too?" Not words Nic had ever spoken, but a new kind of freedom had settled inside of her. She could say things like that now. She painted a wicked smile on her lips and sat in front of Charlie on her hands and knees. "Because I was just planning to."

"You don't have to." Worry crossed Charlie's face. "No need to rush into things."

Rush? What a joke. "For me, this is the final sprint after ten back-to-back marathons." She inched closer to Charlie. "Under extremely strenuous weather conditions. I need to finish. Now."

Charlie nodded her understanding, reciprocating Nic's smile. In response, she stretched out on the bed, her legs wide from the start.

A new kind of heat started pulsing in Nic's blood. She did her best to focus her attention on Charlie's perfectly shaped breasts, dark pert nipples, and glorious abs, but she couldn't resist the pull for very long. As if it was gravity itself tugging her down to earth, she was irresistibly drawn to what lay between Charlie's legs. First, she probed with her hands, the ocean of wetness galvanising her. But she needed to taste. Needed to press one of her own intimate organs to one of Charlie's.

Positioning herself between Charlie's legs she glared at the shiny wetness beneath the black patch of her pubes. Her clit stood out, blood-shot and distended. Her pink pussy lips glistened with juices Nic couldn't wait to quench her lifelong thirst with. She bent over for that first taste, her hands curved around the bend of Charlie's hips. Charlie's musky, earthy, intoxicating aroma nestled inside of her, like a memory of a perfume she would never forget, as she let her tongue swirl over her clit.

There's no way back now, Nic thought, as she did what she had been born to do. Lapping at Charlie's pussy as if she'd never done anything else in her life. Taking in her essence, her most secret of scents, and guiding another woman to ecstasy seemed to provide Nic with even more pleasure than when that final shot of lightning had crackled through her.

Still, it wasn't enough. She needed to feel. Needed her fingers to be enveloped by the warmth of another woman. She glanced up at Charlie, whose head was tossed back in the pillows, her abs contracting and releasing in quick, steady intervals, and brought her fingers to Charlie's entrance. Only one at first, slowly venturing in, flooring Nic once again with a powerful, previously unknown, sensation. Soon, two of her fingers stroked inside of Charlie, whose pelvis shot up with every one of Nic's thrusts, while she kept circling her tongue around Charlie's clit.

"Oh baby," Charlie groaned. "Oh yes." And of all the new sensations Nic had experienced that day, this one threw her the most.

Another woman coming on her fingers, the walls of her pussy clamping down hard as she rode the waves of her climax. The tears that dripped from Nic's eyes then were as much for the fact that she had finally arrived, as for all the years she hadn't allowed herself to be who she was.

"Aah." After one last, throaty moan, Charlie gripped Nic's head between her hands, indicating her to stop.

But Nic knew it was only the beginning.

NEW GIRL

"Does it still hurt?" Nina asked.

Liz fingered the purple-blue bruise above her cheekbone. She glanced back at Nina in the mirror and tried not to scoff at her new teammate's concern. This massive shiner was all her fault and she didn't even realise. Too wrapped up in the impossible glossiness of Nina's legs, Liz hadn't seen the ball coming. It was a powerful smash delivered by the opposing team's star player and, as stupid as it may sound, Liz had forgotten to duck. She'd been so enthralled by the flexing muscles in Nina's calves that she'd ignored the most important reflex of any volleyball player: protect yourself.

"Kind of." Liz removed the useless make-up from her face. She remembered the days when half the team was made up of lesbians and they drove home after an away game, no matter how far. Nowadays, it seemed imperative that they book a cheap B&B so the youngsters could flirt all night with the male teams lingering about the cafeteria. Nearing twenty-nine, Liz knew she was on her way out and maybe it made her a tad bitter. Her lifetime volleyball companion, Kate, had bowed out of the game due to a knee injury—no doubt caused by too much wear and tear, they were the same age after all—leaving Liz to share a room with the new girl. Not that she minded that much. Her gaze followed Nina as she brushed her long unruly curls before tying them into a ponytail for bed. It was just a bit embarrassing at the moment.

"She was really gunning for you." Nina shook her head and her ponytail bopped from left to right. "What a bitch."

"It was my own fault. I was distracted." Still looking at Nina's reflection in the mirror, Liz pinned her eyes on her teammate's hazel ones and stared for a moment too long. Nina had slipped out of her summer dress and wore nothing but a flower-patterned pair of shorts and a skimpy tank top. Didn't she realise they were about to share the bed? As soon as Liz had heard she'd be bunking with Nina she'd invested in a pair of silk navy pyjamas which covered most of her skin—mainly as a measure of self-protection. The thought of inadvertently touching Nina during the night had made her a bit too moist for comfort.

"Oh yeah. By what?" Nina had moved to the edge of the bed and was applying moisturiser to her legs. Liz tried not to stare at them but, just like during the game, she couldn't pull her gaze away.

"I don't know." Liz had to swallow before she could continue to speak. "Someone in the crowd, I guess."

"Someone special?" Nina shot her a sly smile.

"Hardly." Liz hadn't met someone to refer to as special in a while. "Excuse me." She grabbed her pyjamas, stepped into the tiny bathroom and closed the door behind her. Before splashing cold water in her face she examined herself in yet another mirror. Her cheek was swollen, narrowing her left eye. The bruise seemed to mock her and, admittedly, despite the dramatic purple-red edge of the contusion, it was her ego that was wounded most. She had no business lusting after someone who'd just graduated from university. Nina was barely twenty-one and even though they were only eight years apart in age, somehow, it felt more like eighteen—or eighty, now that she was feeling especially melodramatic about it.

Liz ran her fingers through her blond bob and sighed. She undressed and let the soft silk of the pyjamas envelop her limbs. Her nipples perked up against the smooth fabric. Liz certainly hadn't counted on a pair of PJs making her feel frisky. Who was she kidding, anyway? She had plenty of silk garments and none of them had this effect on her. She relied on another deep breath to calm her down and headed back into the bedroom.

Nina lay on her side, her nose buried in an Ian Rankin thriller. She looked up as Liz entered the room. "Nice PJs." Nina gave her a quick once-over and curled her lips into an innocent smile.

"This old thing?" While scolding herself for behaving so pathetically, Liz switched off the overhead light, leaving Nina's face solely illuminated by a small reading lamp. At least her legs were covered, Liz noticed, torn between relief and disappointment. Either way, some miracle would have to happen for this not to be a feverish sleepless night for her.

"Do you mind if I read?" Nina lifted her book up and presented it as a piece of evidence. "Never had time at uni to read a decent thriller. It was all Jane Austen here and Emily Brontë there."

"Could be worse." Liz found herself tongue-tied and unable to engage in intelligent conversation with this girl.

"I understand if you're tired, what with barely escaping a concussion." Nina pulled the covers away on Liz's side of the bed and Liz didn't know what to make of the gesture. It was so easy—so tempting—to see more in it than it was.

"That's all right. I don't mind the light." Liz slipped under the sheets and the pressure of the blanket reminded her of the stiffness of her nipples. Sheer fabric like silk was quite revealing and Liz was suddenly mortified. She pulled the sheets up to her chin and lay there with no idea of how to relax, let alone fall asleep. She listened to Nina's breathing and the rustling of the pages. The rate at which she turned them made Liz suspect the book was worth staying up late for and she made a mental note to buy it. At least they would have something to talk about next time they had to share a room. If there ever was a next time. Kate was not one to miss out on many games and it had only been the distance—and the fact that she had to put her knee up—that had kept her from joining this trip.

After twenty minutes Nina switched off her reading light and turned to her side. "Are you asleep?" she whispered as soon as it had gone dark.

"Mmm," Liz mumbled. She was wide awake and had spent the better part of the last ten minutes wondering if she should lie on her hands, hoping to prevent inadvertently touching herself. Nina's body heat seemed to multiply under the sheets and the thought of those legs mere inches away from hers made Liz's skin sizzle. It was a good thing she had on an extra layer to hide the goosebumps that were now breaking out all over her body.

"How long have you been on the team?" Nina obviously took Liz's grumble as willingness to talk. As long as the subject was the team, Nina could handle it.

"Twelve years and barely missed a game." Inside, Liz swelled with pride. She'd given a lot for the team, but had gotten much more in return. Two girlfriends for instance, and a lot of pent-up lust, it seemed now.

"And still the best player. Amazing." Nina hesitated for a split second. "I really look up to you."

Liz lay there blushing in the dark, gobsmacked but with pure joy rushing through her veins. "They just keep me on because I'm so tall." She shuffled nervously under the covers. "My reflexes are not what they used to be. You saw what happened today." Liz heard the sound of skin rustling against sheets.

"Are you kidding?" Nina had propped herself up on one elbow, half her body towering over Liz.

Don't come too close, Liz prayed, not sure if she had the necessary willpower to refrain from curling her hands around Nina's neck and pulling her in for a kiss. "You're not so bad yourself."

"I'm nowhere near as good as you and never will be."

Liz's eyes were used to the dark now and she could make out the contours of Nina's face. A few strands of hair had come loose from her ponytail and crinkled along her cheeks. Nina sank down into the mattress and her bent elbow hit Liz in the bicep.

"I'm so sorry." In a flash Nina sat back up, a hand stroking Liz's upper arm. "And you're already so bruised."

"It's okay." Liz flexed her bicep a little to give Nina a good feel. "I can take it."

Nina's thumb gingerly trailed along the sleeve of Liz's pyjama top. "I was just babbling, trying to make conversation." Her face was close enough for Liz to feel her breath when she spoke. "Sharing a room with you is a bit nerve-wracking."

"Don't worry," Liz sighed, "I won't touch you inappropriately."

"Oh." Nina's grip on her arm intensified and left Liz feeling quite confused. "I was sort of hoping that you would." Nina's fingers snuck up to Liz's bare neck and their touch electrified her skin.

Liz brusquely put her hand on Nina's and pushed it down. She wanted to brush it away, but something stopped her. "Don't play me." Her voice didn't sound as harsh as she had set out to either.

"You're the most beautiful woman I've ever seen." Nina's nails dug into Liz's skin, making a point Liz couldn't ignore even if she wanted to.

"But—" Liz stammered, clearly having lost use of her mental faculties again. "You're not even gay."

"Says who?" Nina lowered herself until her lips almost touched Liz's unblemished right cheekbone.

"Have you ever even kissed a woman?" Liz felt as if she were digging her own grave, but she still had some decency left.

Nina pressed her lips against Liz's skin and then trailed them to her ear. "I have now," she whispered.

Liz had to gasp for air. Her nipples poked against her pyjama top and a moist heat spread between her legs. "I'm serious." Her mouth was dry and she had to swallow multiple times to lubricate it before she could continue. "We can't—"

"I'm serious too," Nina interrupted her, her mouth still tantalisingly close to Liz's ear. "I've had a crush on you since I first saw you."

"Don't be silly."

Nina pushed her body against Liz, her nipples pressing hard into Liz's arm. "Methinks the lady doth protest too much."

"We'll see about that." Liz slung her leg over Nina and pressed her down until she was on top of her. She peered into her brown eyes. "Are you sure?" she barely managed to ask.

"One hundred percent." If she was uncertain at all, there was no sign of it in her eyes. They brimmed with lust and desire and Liz was slightly taken aback by the sudden reversal of the situation.

Liz leaned down for the first kiss. The way she brushed her closed lips against Nina's was almost chaste, until Nina dug her fingers into Liz's hair and drew her near. Nina opened her mouth, allowing Liz's tongue to enter. Liz's nipples writhed against the silk of her top and her fingers trailed along Nina's neck as they lost themselves in moist kiss after kiss. Liz's knee rested between Nina's legs and her right hand kept moving down until it reached the curve of Nina's breast.

The time for hesitation had passed and, over Nina's skimpy tank top, she curled her fingers over her breast, its nipple perking up against her palm. Soon she was squeezing and tweaking and the tank top got in the way of her plans. Without interrupting the kiss, Liz slid one hand under Nina's top and the touch of soft skin on her fingertips sent an electric current straight to her pussy. Liz expected her PJ bottoms to be drenched by now and her juices to be leaking through onto Nina's flexed thigh muscles.

Liz's fingers found Nina's bare nipple and she gently pinched it until soft moans escaped from the mouth underneath hers. Shifting her body to the left, Liz gave Nina's other breast the same treatment. The supple flesh under her hands ignited throb after throb to pulse through her pussy. Their passionate lip-lock had to be broken then, because Liz couldn't wait any longer. She had to see the breasts she'd been stroking so feverishly.

Nina stared up at her as Liz nibbled her younger teammate's bottom lip one more time. Her glance alone, with those huge brown eyes glinting with desire, was enough to entice Liz to rip off all her clothes and ravage Nina, but, despite the lust leaking from between her legs, Liz knew she had to go slow. Unhurried, she pulled up Nina's tank top until her breasts were exposed. Liz had seen them before, in passing in the locker room and, more in detail, while soaping up in the communal showers, but this couldn't be more different. Nina's pert mounds lay at her fingertips now and their taut nipples looked more than ready to be savoured.

"You're so beautiful," Liz mumbled before leaning in again, lower this time, and tasting Nina's left nipple. It was hard against her tongue and Liz sucked it between her lips and gently trailed her teeth along the tip. With one hand she squeezed the soft flesh of Nina's breast together so she could take as much as possible into her mouth.

Nina tugged at Liz's top, yanking it upwards. "Take it off." Liz interrupted her glorious feast of dark nipple and velvety breast and allowed Nina to pull her silk top over her head. The sudden rush of air pricked up her own nipples until the skin around them couldn't stretch any further. Liz repositioned herself and hovered over Nina until their breasts almost touched and their nipples grazed against each other. Keeping the pressure in her arms, Liz didn't let her body's full weight come down. Instead, she let her nipples dance across Nina's upper body, occasionally bending her elbows and pushing the rigid brown buds into Nina's belly and breasts.

Liz followed the erratic path her nipples had taken earlier with a trail of kisses leading down to the waistband of Nina's shorts. She appeared impatient and started pushing her shorts down before Liz had a chance to luxuriate in the thought of slowly exposing her pussy. She locked eyes with Nina and covered her hands to liberate them from their task. She lowered the shorts lazily, as much a test for her as it was for Nina, and bared her black pubic hair first. Again, this was not a first for Liz—team sports have their perks—but it didn't stop her from being floored by the musky sweet scent tinging the air and, as the shorts came off, the sight of Nina's swollen pussy lips glistening with wetness.

"Yours as well." Nina sat up and tugged frantically at Liz's pyjama pants. Their eyes met and Liz saw no reason in them to deny such a heartfelt request. Both naked, Liz coaxed Nina down on the bed and kissed her. Skin to skin and nipple to nipple, their hands roaming freely over each other's body, Liz felt her juices spill onto Nina's glorious legs. They may have been the start of all of this, but Liz's focus lay elsewhere now.

She pushed herself up and cast a longing glance at Nina's pussy.

"Fuck me," Nina said and the unexpected words sent a shiver up Liz's spine.

She crouched between Nina's legs and flexed her elbows just low enough for her left breast to brush the lips of Nina's pussy. Liz shifted her weight onto her left knee and arm and with her free hand guided her breast, its nipple protruding stiffly, to Nina's throbbing clit. Nina moaned at the touch of flesh on flesh and Liz repeated the action. She skated her nipple up and down Nina's pussy and nudged her clit with it. The sensation of Nina's hot wetness on her nipple made Liz's knees tremble with delight and her clit now stood firmly to attention.

"Oh god," Nina grunted and dug her fingers into Liz's hair. Liz couldn't wait any longer. As magnificent as the nipple fuck felt, she needed a taste now. She brought her mouth down to Nina's gleaming lips and ran her tongue along the length of them. Nina tasted salty and moist and intoxicating. Just as she'd done with Nina's chest a few moments before, Liz let her tongue follow the path her nipple had traced earlier. Every time her tongue stroked Nina's clit, her entire body tensed under Liz's mouth. Low whimpers of ecstasy drifted from Nina's lips into the room. Liz dug her tongue as deep as she could into Nina's pussy and let its aroma coat her mouth and chin.

She focused her attention on Nina's clit, circling around it in a steady motion until Nina's grunts intensified and her grip on Liz's hair strengthened. Liz needed more though; she needed to feel the inside of Nina's pussy on her fingers, needed to feel her muscles contract around her knuckles. Interrupting the motion of her tongue on Nina's clit, she lifted her head to get a good look at what she was about to enter. Through the darkness, to which Liz's eyes were now fully accustomed,

Nina's pussy glistened with juices, her lips a deep swollen red. Before the irresistible urge to feast her mouth on them gripped her again, Liz brought one finger to the rim of Nina's pussy. She circled it around and up and down and then let it slip inside. Nina immediately let out a hoarse yelp as Liz's finger was covered in slithery juices. She explored Nina's inner walls and, before finding a more steady rhythm, inserted another finger.

Nina buried her nails into the sheets and moaned louder with every thrust. Liz revelled in the sensation of fucking her teammate who was indirectly responsible for the painful bruise on her cheek—it didn't hurt that much anymore now. Liz watched her fingers slip in and out of Nina, a small puddle of juice gathering in her palm. She brought her head back down and went straight for Nina's clit. She flicked it back and forth with her tongue to the same rhythm as her fingers delving inside.

"Oh my god," Nina exclaimed and repeated. "I'm—" Before she had a chance to say it she released a stream of juice onto Liz's palm and her pussy clenched and unclenched multiple times around Liz's fingers. Liz kept fucking and licking Nina until her voice grew hoarse and her body stopped shaking.

When Liz looked up and sought Nina's gaze she saw a wide smile plastered across her face. Liz hoisted herself up on her elbows until their eyes met.

"Is this even allowed?" Nina asked slightly out of breath. "Making a teammate scream like that?"

"Remember how I yelled when that ball hit my face?" Liz planted a kiss on the edge of Nina's mouth. "I needed to get you back for that."

"And the game's not over yet." Nina licked her lips and cast her glance down, in the direction of Liz's pussy.

"You don't have to." Liz was suddenly reminded that this was Nina's first time with a woman. "We can take it slow."

Nina eased herself out from under Liz's embrace and topped her. "Like you did with me, you mean?" A naughty grin curled around her lips. "We'll see about that." She shot Liz a wicked wink before pushing her body down, her breasts tickling Liz's skin and her breath caressing her clit already. Liz knew slow was no longer an option.

BAR SERVICE

Veronica didn't really do anything at the bar. She just sat there. Every night. Scanning the room from under dark lashes. Selecting prey. I'd go in at least twice a week, begging gods I didn't believe in that she'd pick me one night. I'd seen her leave with girls half my age and women old enough to be my mother. Veronica's random selection process filled me with hope as much as it did with dread.

"Stop gawking, Marie. Really." Charlotte poked me in the ribs. "If you're so desperate for some V, get us another drink." Veronica even had her own verb. When she chose you, you got V'ed.

"With great pleasure." Before getting up from my chair I winked at Charlotte. If it weren't for her, I'd have been here on my own again. I strutted towards the bar, smoothing a wrinkle out of my tank top.

"Same again?"

I nodded at Mimi, who had seen me coming. Did Veronica ever pay her in kind? Or was being in her proximity enough of a perk? As Mimi fixed two gin-and-tonics, I let my gaze drift to the corner of the counter. Veronica held court on a high bar stool to my right. She played with an unlit cigarette, bouncing it between her long fingers. A pair of leather pants clung to her legs. In all the times I'd come here, I'd never seen her wear anything else. What drew my eyes to her most, though, were her blood red lips.

The wet thud of glasses on the counter yanked me out of my daydream before it could get out of hand.

"Ten bucks, darling." Mimi smiled her knowing bartender smile. She realized the excellent mixing of drinks was not the reason why I came here so often.

"They're on the house."

A chill ran up my spine as Veronica's low voice pierced through the air. I turned my head and looked straight into her bright green eyes. I knew better than to protest. If the stories I had heard were anything to go by, this was how it started. This was how you got V'ed.

"Thanks." I wanted to stand there and bask in the glory of the moment until everyone left, but I was pretty sure that was against all protocols. Veronica placed being cool above anything else.

"Loyal patrons deserve a treat once in a while." She drew out her words, which accentuated the iciness in her voice. She fixed her eyes on mine and I immediately felt it between my legs. "I hope you stay until closing time."

I had to swallow before I could speak. My nipples poked against the flimsy fabric of my bra, no doubt denting my tank top. "I always do." I shot her a wide smile. This was going to be my lucky night.

By the time I got back to our table my hands were shaking so hard, I'd spilled a good portion of our drinks.

"What's up with you?" Charlotte scrunched her eyebrows together.

"You don't happen to have any Valium on you?" She was a nurse so it was worth a try. I checked my watch. Two more hours before closing time. I needed something stronger than a G&T to not crumble entirely before then.

"Oh, I see." Charlotte chuckled. "You've been stung by the V."

"Not just yet." My whole body tingled with excitement. "But, if the next two hours don't kill me, the waiting will."

Charlotte, ever the pragmatist, grabbed my hand. "Don't forget you have to work in the morning."

"Hey, Miss Buzz Kill, I'm having a significant moment here."

"Well, as much as I'd love to stay and watch you sweat. I have the early shift tomorrow."

"No worries. I'll just stop watering down my gin with tonic."

"As a health professional, I would strongly advise against it." Charlotte clenched her fingers around mine. "That is, of course, if come the light of dawn, you want to remember this night at all."

It was my intention to cling to every second of this night for the rest of my life. I'd been dreaming of Veronica for months. Of peeling those tight pants off of her. Of her long fingers claiming me.

"I'm just kidding." I held onto Charlotte's hand for an instant longer. "I'll switch to Pepsi, I swear."

"Water would be better." Charlotte let her fingers slip out of mine. She looked me over and let a small sigh escape. "Be careful. Veronica looks like she might have a well-equipped dungeon in her house." She planted a kiss on my cheek and got up. "Call me tomorrow."

I watched Charlotte exit the bar and scanned the room. Only six other barflies left. Maybe they were all hoping for the same outcome, but tonight was my night—and I didn't feel sorry for them. I strolled to the bar and ordered some ice water before settling on a stool two seats from Veronica.

When her boss went out for a smoke, Mimi craned her head towards me. "Say yes to everything she asks," she whispered, "and you'll have the time of your life."

My mouth went a little dry and there was that itch between my legs again. I wasn't naturally submissive, but for a woman like Veronica, I'd gladly make an exception.

The clinking of heels on the wooden floor announced Veronica's return. She chose the stool right next to me and pivoted towards me.

"We could sit here and make conversation, but I'm not much of a talker."

I was enthralled by the glossy redness of her lips. I wondered what they would taste like and speculated if she would let me chew them—probably not.

"Let's go then." I stared into her eyes with a boldness completely foreign to me, instantly fearing I had overstepped and she'd change her mind.

"Can you close up tonight, Mimi?" It was more a command than a question. "I have something to attend to upstairs."

"Sure thing, boss." Mimi raised her eyebrows expectantly when we locked eyes—the things she must have seen.

"This way." Veronica slid off the bar stool and spun around. She escorted me up the stairs as if we were stepping into her back office for a business transaction. My body didn't feel business-like at all. My temples throbbed and my breath caught in my throat as I followed her up a dimly-lit staircase.

She flicked her long blond hair over her shoulder while she opened the door of her apartment for me. It looked exactly like the bar downstairs. A lot of exposed brick, black leather, and tinted lamps. She fit right in. I half-expected her to plant her behind on a bar stool and instruct me to strip.

"My house, my rules," she said and positioned herself in front of me, a sparse smile tugging at the corners of her mouth.

"Take it or leave it." She was right, she really wasn't much of a conversationalist.

I nodded while secretly hoping she'd produce a large bottle of gin to calm my nerves with.

"Rule number one." She spread her long legs and crossed her arms in front of her chest. "Don't touch me."

Despite the effortless authority with which she delivered it, this rule confused me. I silently agreed anyway.

"Number two." She uncrossed her arms and brought a crimson-nailed finger to the edge of my chin. "I'm in charge." She lifted my chin skyward with a flick of her finger. "Understood?"

"Sure," I began. "But isn't—"

She moved her finger to my lips and I smelled a faint whiff of tobacco on it. "I'm not really one for pillow talk either." She pinned her eyes on me and I blinked once in agreement. I thought it a good idea to follow Mimi's advice. Veronica let her finger slip off my chin and I already missed her touch.

"Come on." She grabbed hold of my dangling hand and pulled me towards a closed door. Dungeon or bedroom?

Veronica didn't give me time to process. As soon as we entered the room she slammed me against the nearest wall and one-handedly pinned my wrists above my head.

"I won't hurt you." She leaned in a little closer, until I could feel her lips brush against my ear. "If you do exactly what I say." She bit down hard on my earlobe and it hurt like hell. After she released my ear, her lips traced a moist path over my neck, down to my clavicle, and back up to my mouth.

After the brutal assault on my ear, the first kiss of her scarlet lips was surprisingly tender. She let her tongue slip into my mouth with a gentleness that made my legs wobble.

With her free hand she hoisted up my tank top and used it to tie my wrists.

"Keep them above your head."

"Sir, yes sir," I wanted to say, but thought better of it—my earlobe still stung a little.

I stood there, feeling a bit ridiculous with a white piece of fabric wrapped around the top of my outstretched arms—binding me as if ready to surrender.

Veronica lodged her knee between my thighs, spreading my legs with gentle force. She took a step back and let her green eyes wander from my head to my toes while she started to undo her blouse. It was a tight black number made of silk. She flicked open the buttons with slow expertise.

She was all black and red, just like her bedroom. The sheets were as dark as the night. The light she'd flipped on upon entering cast a hazy red glow over the shadows it created. Except for her eyes. They were green and mysterious and, most of all, brimming with the promise of ecstasy.

Veronica left me no time to ponder on her interior design and fashion style choices. The red of her nails contrasted with the black of her blouse as she let it slip off her upper body, creating a dark puddle of silk on the floor. My heart hammered in my chest at the sight of her red lace bra, and the hint at what lay beneath. She'd have to tie me up with a lot more than a tank top if she wanted to stop me from touching those breasts.

She took a step towards me and lifted her arms to grab my hands, pushing her chest into my face.

"Let's see what you're made of." Yanking my arms down, she dragged me towards the bed and pushed me on my back. She bent down and roughly pulled my shoes off before instructing me to move closer to the headboard.

I used my shoulders to shuffle upwards until my hands touched something cold. Straddling me, the curves of her breasts right in front of my eyes, she untied my wrists and immediately clinked them into what felt like fur-lined handcuffs. She really was serious about not wanting to be touched.

Still, I had lips, and a tongue dying to lick any bit of her that came close enough.

Then, for the first time, she smiled. Not measured like before, but wide and generous, as if saying, "I've got you where I want you now."

Veronica's hand shot to the button of my pants. Witnessing how her fingers undid my jeans sent pangs of anticipation up my spine. I couldn't wait for her fingers to slip inside. She tore down my pants with an ease betraying her level of experience —as if she never did anything else but sit on a bar stool and take women's trousers off.

My skin sizzled under her scrutinizing glance. Her distant kind of foreplay surely worked on me. She'd hardly touched me but had me more than raring to go.

She tangled up her leather-clad legs with mine and draped her upper body over my chest. The lace of our bras touched and it ignited as many sparks in me as if our breasts had been bare. She hovered her lips over my mouth while boring her eyes into mine. Every time I anticipated she was leaning in for another one of those heavenly soft kisses, she withdrew, the retreating glow of her glossy lipstick taunting me more every time.

I couldn't grab hold of her head and pull her close. I could barely lift my own head without pain shooting up my shoulders. When she finally planted her lips on mine, my body shook with relief. This time, she exchanged her gentle manner for a more savage approach and, after the softest of pecks, sank her teeth into my bottom lip. I stifled a wimpy cry while my clit responded vigorously to Veronica's antics, throbbing beneath the soaked fabric of my panties.

The leather of her pants collided with my frisky skin as she coaxed my legs apart with her knee. She slithered her body down, making sure the lace of her bra touched my belly and her protruding nipple brushed my clit on the way down.

She traced her tongue along the waistband of my panties and her saliva scorched my skin. When she slid one finger under the seam my breath hitched in my throat. She used both hands to escort my panties down, pulling them over my ankles in one swift movement. The fresh rush of air blowing over my pussy made my clit stand to attention even more.

I half-expected her to tie my ankles up next, but instead, she reached up and pulled the cups of my bra down, finally exposing my aching nipples. With two scarlet-nailed fingers, she pinched me right back into submission and, this time, I couldn't hold back a gasp.

Veronica didn't speak but I could see her eyes asking if this was all I could take, a manic sparkle betraying her joy at this discovery. I hoped she wasn't getting out the nipple clamps next.

She lowered her lips onto my nipple and I braced myself for teeth impact. Surprising me again, she spread balmy saliva over it with her tongue, licking me straight into paradise.

"Ooh," I moaned, which was obviously a sign for her to stop.

She shot me a smile again, a wicked one this time, conveying only lust and the intention to push me to my limits. Her lips meandered to my belly button, stopping to dip her tongue in and take the sensitive skin that stretched above my lower abs between her teeth.

When the first rush of her breath reached my pussy lips I was ready to explode. Fluids leaked out of me, onto her silk black bed sheets. I wanted nothing more than her fingers in me, exploring me, taking all I had. She could gag me for all I cared; she could spank me until daytime, as long as she buried her red fingernails inside of me.

"Fuck me," I said, despite knowing better.

Our eyes locked and I caught her desire. Her pussy might have been safely tucked away beneath black leather—and her breasts guarded by the lace of her bra—but I clearly saw. She wanted to fuck me as much as I wanted her fingers inside of me forever.

"Please, fuck me," I urged.

Her eyes softened and, for the second time that night, I knew I had her. She crawled up until her face was parallel with mine, the hard lines etched around her mouth relaxing into a friendlier, more accessible pout. I almost asked her to unlock the cuffs but I didn't want to push her too far out of her comfort zone.

She skated her tongue over my lips before letting it dart inside my mouth. A whole new tenderness took hold of her, standing in stark contrast to the aloofness she had displayed before. She poured her body over mine, grinding the leather of her pants into my pussy.

Goosebumps broke out all over my body as she ran her fingernails over my outstretched arms and pressed her breasts against mine. I found her eyes again and there was nothing left of the stern top who'd dictated rules to me earlier. Her body molded over mine like hot liquid, seemingly covering all of me at the same time.

After an avalanche of kisses, Veronica pushed herself up and, with one hand, unclasped her bra.

Bewildered, I gazed at her breasts as if they were the eighth wonder of the world. I'd already accepted they would stay hidden behind her bra forever. I noticed a hint of doubt creeping along her face before she reached over my head and freed my hands from the cuffs.

While I rolled my wrists to breathe some life into them she sat back and unbuttoned her pants, which came off with surprising ease—I'd thought them glued to her skin. She kicked off her boots, which she hadn't bothered taking off before—no doubt to enforce her image of being the one in charge.

I pressed my torso off the mattress and unhooked my bra

and then, against all expectations, we were both completely naked.

She launched herself at me and the touch of her naked skin all over mine unleashed a fresh stream of juice to seep from my pussy. But, despite the shift in power balance, some things had remained the same. I still wanted her to fuck me.

Her hand was already between my legs, exploring, roaming over my pussy lips.

"You're so fucking wet," she whispered in my ear as her long hair fell over my face.

"Fuck me," I said for the third time. "I can't wait any longer."

She sought my eyes while slipping two fingers inside of me. She pulled them out after one stroke and brought them to her red lips. Without breaking eye-contact, she licked my juices off her fingers, sucking them into her mouth again and again before bringing them back down, back between my legs, before entering me again.

I buried my liberated hands into her hair as she fucked me and, at last, spread her wet fingers into a V inside of me.

PERSONAL TRAINING

"This is not good enough." I always shout at Ali ten times louder than any of my other clients. Not that she needs the extra encouragement. The swell of her biceps when she performs a push-up rivals mine, and I do this for a living.

Ali lifts her leg higher and kicks the punchbag harder. The black leather quivers when she flicks her leg back. I shudder at the sight of her contracting hamstring, but by now, I've learned to mask my weakness behind an even louder scream.

"Give me more, Ali. This is ludicrous." I inch closer. My heart hammers so frantically in my chest, I feel I need to cross my arms and cover myself. "Ten extra. Same leg."

She doesn't even look up. She just continues to pound the leather with her foot, her elbows protecting her face. Exactly like I taught her months ago. Her breath comes out with a short, hushed puff every time she attacks.

"Nine... and ten." I steady the punchbag. "Good job."

Her eyes meet mine and I give her a quick, approving nod. Does she see it in my glance? Does the curve of my lips give me away at all?

She shoots me a small smile and heads to the corner of the

gym. Bench presses. Both my favourite and most feared part of our work-out. What if one day I get so entranced by the rise and fall of her breasts, my strength gives way and I drop the bar? It would be the end of me.

She squats as she loads the bar with two twenty pound plates on each side. A few blond curls have come loose from her tight ponytail and cling to her forehead, soaking up the sweat.

"Add two extra fives on each side." I slip back into drill sergeant mode. It's the only way I know to ignore the throbbing between my legs.

She cocks up her left eyebrow. She can arch them independently from one another and it never fails to crack me up. I hide the glee bubbling inside of me and stare her down.

"For real?" A drop of sweat trickles down her temple. I have to restrain myself to not crouch beside her and wipe it away.

I simply nod, lifting my palms to state that what I say should not be questioned. I don't shout, because I'm not sure I have it in me at this point.

She screws on the additional weight, straightens herself and backs down onto the bench. Her legs are spread wide and her tummy lifts with shallow breaths. I can see the outline of her abs through the drenched fabric of her tight tank top and I wonder who should be paying who for this work-out.

I pick up the bar and its weight catches me off guard. I have to work hard to keep my features straight. Towering over Ali, I hand her the bar, my pinkies briefly grazing her thumbs. The touch startles me, but I know this is nothing compared to what's to come.

Ali's entire body tenses under the weight of the bar—exactly the way I would want it to tense under my touch.

"Let's start with ten slow ones." My voice sounds gravelly and strangled, but Ali doesn't seem to notice.

When she brings the bar low her biceps strain to not let it gloss against her nipples.

"Elbows out," I say, more to distract myself, because she's doing it perfectly as usual. Nevertheless, I push her elbows out with the palms of my hands and this time the touch of her skin causes a cold ripple to run up my spine. My skin transforms into gooseflesh and I need to inhale and exhale deeply to steady my nerves. It doesn't help that her face is so close to my thighs, I can feel the heat of her breath as she exhales.

After she has finished the first set I take the bar from her and place it in its holder. Ali sits up and stretches her body left and right to loosen up her back. Her shoulders are shiny with sweat and her tank top rides up as she twists. I catch a glimpse of myself in the wall-length mirror opposite the bench, of the lust shimmering in the black of my eyes. I know I'm about to lose control. Three sessions a week for five months have taken their toll. I'm all out of restraint. I can't yell at her anymore to make it go away.

Heat flashes through me as I approach the bench from the side. I sit down next to her.

"What are you doing after this?"

She widens her eyes in mock-amazement. "Small talk?" She brings the back of her hand to my forehead. "You must have a fever, Jan. If not, you're freaking me out."

"I'm sorry," I stutter. "I didn't mean to—"

"Don't be sorry." She swivels her body to face me better. "Do you have any idea how exhausting it is to please you?" Her lips curl up into a smile. "Always one more, always harder, always better. Nothing is ever good enough and you never utter more than two words that are not an instruction."

I have no idea what she says next. I'm enthralled by the flush in her cheeks and the excited tone of her voice. I hardly notice that I bring a finger to her lips, silencing her. My body seems cut off from the common sense that's supposed to keep me from touching her. Reputation is everything in this town. If word gets out…

"Jan?" I feel lips moving against the tip of my finger. I focus my gaze and meet Ali's big blue eyes. I know I should retract my finger and apologise as profusely as possible, but I can't. After hours of admiring her strong body, her tenacity, and unbreakable willpower, something inside me gives.

She goes wide-eyed, but doesn't push my hand away. I move in closer, cupping her chin with my palm. Maybe I should say something, but I have no idea what. So I kiss her. I lean in and plant my lips on hers. Instantly, I'm dizzy with lust. Until she pushes me away by the shoulders.

"Excuse me?" Ali's expression is more amused than annoyed. I can see in her eyes this is not a dismissal. I can see it in the way she tilts her head and bats her lashes.

This is my gym, I think. I'm in charge. I stand to face her. "I've wanted you since the first day you walked in here." I bring my hands to my sides, as if I'm casually explaining a new exercise. "I thought it was time you knew." In the frenzied state my mind is in, there's no room for rejection.

Ali gets up from the bench. She's one inch taller than me, which hardly allows her to tower over me, but that's how it feels. She draws her mouth into a crooked smile. One I haven't seen before. I never give her a lot of reason to smile. "Time I knew?" She repeats. "Do you really think I can't see through all your macho bravado?" She takes a step towards me, and despite the burning desire inside of me to be as close to her as possible, I back away. "That I don't see you ogling my backside in between your yelling matches?"

Maybe it's the tension, but I can't suppress a giggle bubbling up from my throat. "Any interest I have in your backside is purely professional," I lie.

Her mouth widens in feigned surprise. She shakes her head and corners me next to the TRX cables. "Is there anything else I should know? Now that you're being so honest."

My back hits the wall and Ali is so close I can smell her. The scent of her sweat stirs something in my blood. When I dreamed of this moment, and I've spent hours picturing it, I was the one backing Ali into a corner. I was the one in command. I imagined it would come naturally to me. Now that the moment is here, I feel I'm losing more control with every passing second. I respond by grabbing her arms and pulling her close.

Her breath warms my already flushed face. Her blue eyes bore into mine. As far as truth goes, I can only repeat my previous actions. I move my hands upwards, trailing my nails along the flesh of her arms, and pull her in.

This time, she responds to my kiss by parting her lips and allowing my tongue to slip into her mouth. She withdraws and traces a moist path to my ear with her lips. "You have no idea," she whispers. And it's true, I have no idea what she means. But I don't care as I inhale her closeness and revel in it. My nipples harden under my top. They poke into the fabric of my sports bra and I can't wait for them to be freed.

I make a play for Ali's tank top, wanting to lift it and expose the abs we've been working on so hard, but she's quick to intercept me. She grabs me by the wrists and, in one swift movement—as if it's all she does in life—she pins my hands above my head.

Her eyes don't leave mine. Her face is unreadable. Maybe this is what she does in life.

"No shouting," she says. "None of that loud PT shtick you love to hide behind." She holds my wrists together with one hand, while she traces two fingers of the other along my cheekbone. "And you'd best keep your hands above your head."

She scans the room briefly. "Actually, I have a better idea." Something in her eyes has changed. A thrilling darkness has taken over. A desire to discipline that I wouldn't dare contradict. She lowers my hands and guides me to the wooden wall bars. While pressing me against them, she positions my hands above my head again. "Don't move," she says as she scoots for the nearest TRX cable. Her eyes shine as she fastens it around my wrists.

When I went to work in the morning, I had no idea I'd end up tied to my own gym equipment. I'd only envisioned another frustrating hour of lusting after Ali while I worked her body so hard, I couldn't feel the signals my own was sending me anymore.

"For all the pain you've caused me in this gym…" Ali's voice comes out ragged. I can see she's turned on by the sight of me at her mercy. "…and for all the unnecessary insults you've thrown my way, this is only a mild punishment, don't you think?"

I don't know what to say. After all, I was only doing what she paid me for.

"Don't you think?" She growls more than asking, while yanking my top over my breasts.

I quickly nod.

"Glad we agree." Her fingers teasingly meander along the hollow of my neck. Raw lust glints in her eyes and I have no idea what she's going to do next. Judging by the wild throbbing between my legs, I'm quite enjoying this role reversal though.

With a quick tug, she lowers the cups of my bra, exposing both my breasts. My nipples crinkle into hard peaks, as if begging to be touched. Ali peers at my chest from under hooded eyelids. Her fair complexion can't hide the heat that has rushed to her cheeks. She really does get off on this. I can't help but wonder if she has dreamed of a moment like this as well. She leaves me no time to explore her desires though, as she submits my yoga pants to the same treatment as my top. In one go, she drags them down, underwear and all. This is not the kind of foreplay I'm used to, nevertheless, I feel wetness pooling between my legs. My clit reacts to the sudden air exposure by swelling between my folds.

I stand there, tied to the wall bars, hands in the air, all my intimate parts on display for this woman I've lusted after for months. This is what it has come to. I don't feel vulnerable or punished in the least. Lust flares through my flesh as I stare into Ali's face.

She presses her fully-clothed body against me and finds my ear with her lips. "What would you like me to do next, Jan?" I feel her mouth stretch into a smile against the delicate skin of my neck. She trails her tongue along my jaw and ends its journey by sinking her teeth into my lower lip.

"Well?" The back of her hand grazes my nipple. "What's it going to be?"

I believed it to be a rhetorical question. I have to swallow before I can speak. "Fuck me." My voice comes out choked already. "Please."

"You'd like that wouldn't you." My right nipple is caught between two of her fingers and she squeezes hard as she speaks. "But the time for me to follow your orders has passed." She shoots me a tight smile. "Which is only fair, I think."

She gives my nipple one last squeeze before dropping to her knees. Moisture trickles out of me at the sight of her blond curls stopping so close to my throbbing pussy lips. She now drags my pants all the way down and manoeuvres them off one leg so she can spread my legs wide.

For an agonising moment, she just sits there, as if pondering whether to proceed or not. First, I feel her breath on my lips—hot and promising. Then her tongue is on my clit, just like that, without warning, she goes for the money shot. My legs buckle at the sudden contact and my wrists tug at their restraints.

"Aah," I moan as her tongue draws circles around my clit. I

can feel the beginning of an orgasm dance through me already. I groan louder as heat crashes through my muscles. I push myself into her, wanting more of her. She brings her hands to my butt cheeks and digs her fingernails in deep. She sucks my clit between her lips, gives it another flick of her tongue, and withdraws. I'm left panting against the wall, so close to climax, yet unsatisfied.

I feel her lips against my inner thighs, kissing a path down my left one and back up along my right thigh. Her fingers travel lower along my butt cheeks, meeting the moisture that has spread from my wet centre.

I'm not sure if I'm allowed to speak, if saying something would increase or decrease my chances at release, so I stay quiet and swallow my frustration. Her mouth has kissed a wet path to my belly. My legs tremble with aching lust. I want to push her mouth into my pussy, make her finish what she started, but I can't because she has me tied up.

She waits for what seems like another lifetime, until the pulsing of my clit has returned to a bearable level, to launch herself at me again. This time she focuses on my lips, sucking them into her mouth and letting her tongue dart in and out of me. She avoids my clit, because she knows that the instant she touches it, I'm there. All the muscles in my body are tense, screaming for release. She works my pussy for a while longer, and as thrilling as it is to see her head work between my legs and to feel her tongue luxuriate on my pussy, I need her to refocus her attention on my clit.

"Please, make me come." The words float out of my mouth against my better judgement. "Please." I realise I'm begging, but I don't care. Maybe, if I'm really lucky, it's exactly what she wants to hear.

She retracts her head from between my legs and my heart sinks. She looks up at me, her chin glistening with my juices, and I see it in her eyes. She's lost control as well. She licks her lips and tucks back in. I relax against the hard bars poking against my back, and let all the tension rush out of me as her tongue, at last, finds my clit again.

White noise crackles in my brain as the thunder of my climax travels through me. Heat shoots through my blood and my clit pulses in her mouth. Five months of pent-up lust are expelled from my tortured flesh as she skims the opening of my pussy with her finger. As I come violently, she thrusts deep, and I clench all I have, all my lust contracting in the walls of my pussy, around her.

I'm still speechless when she hoists herself up. For a minute, I fear she'll leave me there, tied to the wall bars, waiting for my next client to find me. But she grins at me foolishly, a little sheepishly even, and unties me.

When I find my voice again, I say, "You do realise you've only given me more incentive to shout at you."

"Maybe I like it." She wipes my wetness from her mouth with the back of her hand. "As long as I get to punish you for it afterwards." She turns on her heels and heads for the showers. I can't follow her fast enough.

THE POWER OF WORDS

Alice fought the urge to cover her legs with a beach towel. Who did this girl think she was, anyway? Prancing around here half-naked like that. Had Miranda not taught her about the untowardness of it all? Ah, who was she kidding? Young women didn't get instilled with the same values anymore the way Alice had been. Everyone was liberal now, even conservative people. You had to be. Shower your children with compliments so as not to bruise their fragile little egos. Hug them at the most inopportune moments—at the meat counter at Harrods, for instance, where toddlers always seemed to burst out in a tantrum and Alice always rolled her eyes at how their mothers fussed over them. Her own mother had certainly never given her that sort of unbridled attention.

"Come into the water, Alice," Joy shouted.

Who even calls their daughter Joy? She'd been wondering that for three full days now, ever since Joy had arrived. She hadn't brought a lot of joy for Alice, but what was she supposed to have said? "I know it's your house, Miranda, but I need my privacy, and no, your daughter absolutely cannot stay here at the same time as me?" Alice had been able to deduct from

Miranda's tone of voice that she was embarrassed, just as—most likely—Miranda had known in advance that Alice wouldn't be able to refuse. Solely because it would be impolite not to allow the owner's offspring access to her own home. And impoliteness was not in Alice's blood.

But it just goes to show, Alice thought for the umpteenth time, that children hold all the power these days. Not that Joy was still a child. She must be twenty-five now, Alice guessed. She could ask, but she was still getting over the shock of seeing so much brazen, loose-mannered youth on display at all hours of the day.

"Maybe later," Alice replied. There was no way she was sharing the swimming pool with a topless woman. She had asked. The first time Joy had emerged from the house in just a pair of slinky yellow shorts. At first, Alice had been too flabbergasted to speak but, when she'd found her voice again, she'd said, "Would you please put something on?"

"Why?" Joy had asked in return. "This is my home."

Alice could present no arguments against this statement. But Joy could have, perhaps, inquired if it bothered Alice that she darted around the house half-naked, and now, pulled herself half-way out of the pool, her young breasts on full display. It was quite obvious the girl didn't care about anything or anyone but her precious self. All Miranda's fault, Alice concluded. This is exactly what happens when you pamper children too much. And when you take them on holiday to the Algarve twice a year, to your family's summer house, as though it's the most normal thing in the world. Look at the sense of entitlement it breeds. Alice couldn't stop herself from giving in to these thoughts and, basically, ruining her holiday. Even though she needed the time off. Unlike Joy, she guessed, she had an actual job to escape from.

"Oh, come on." Joy had the audacity to splash her with a few drops of water. The nerve of this girl. "Don't be such a sour-puss, Alice."

Deep breaths, Alice repeated in her head. Deep, deep breaths. But really, how could she possibly tolerate being spoken to like this? She was a peacekeeper by nature, avoiding conflict as best she could, but this was too much. First, the totally unanticipated arrival of Joy, disturbing her much-needed quiet time, and now the manner in which she addressed Alice.

"I would appreciate it if you didn't speak to me like that," Alice said in her most stern voice. It came surprisingly natural to her.

"It was a joke, Alice." Joy rolled her eyes. Did she not have any social awareness at all? Any other person would at least be mindful of their adverse effect on someone else, but Joy clearly wasn't perturbed by that. "Just relax."

Relax? That's exactly what Alice had come here to do.

"I was perfectly relaxed before you arrived," she heard herself say. For Alice, the words came out of the blue. The thought had, of course, occurred to her many times, but to actually articulate the words... She had to apologise this instant. "I'm sorry. I shouldn't have said that."

"It's probably the first time you've spoken the truth, so I can take it," Joy said. She pushed herself out of the pool completely and sat on the edge next to Alice's deck chair. "Why don't I give you the rest of the day to yourself? I was planning to go to the beach, anyway."

"That's not necessary at all," Alice said, kicking herself inwardly. Why was it so hard to just speak her mind? The way Joy did. "After all, this is your home."

"Actually it's my mother's house and I crashed your solitude party without any notice." Joy rose. A thousand drops of water slid down her slick, tan skin, collecting in a puddle by her feet. "I'll go."

Alice watched her trot off into the house. She didn't even dry her feet before entering. It was exactly this sort of carelessness and lack of respect for others that was driving Alice mad. Her eyes briefly lingered on Joy's firm bottom, the cheeks perfectly visible through the wet fabric of her shorts. Alice's body had been like that once. A body men found desirable. Alan had found her desirable enough for about ten years. Then he'd found someone else more desirable and Alice couldn't be bothered to find a replacement. Fifteen years of being single had worked out perfectly well for her. No one to get on her nerves when she arrived home from her busy law practice. No children to beg her for money or any other kind of help. Alice was perfectly content.

"See you later," Joy said. "Enjoy." She didn't even look back at Alice as she walked off the premises. At least she'd put on a top. Alice was in half a mind to sneak after her and check if Joy was as liberal with showing off her body on the beach—and how other people would react.

Truth be told, it wasn't that she minded the view. But she had been brought up to find such actions highly impertinent, and it wasn't easy to shake off an ingrained sentiment like that. Now, when she let her gaze glide over the pool, its water a pristine blue, it was as though she could still see Joy sitting on the edge of it. Top off and all.

"You should have bought your own house here years ago," Miranda had said the last time they had come here together. There had been no sign of Joy then. But Alice wasn't one to invest her money in a summer house. Even the notion of such an extravagant folly. "And wearing a bikini instead of that eternal one-piece wouldn't kill you, either," Miranda had continued. Alice had been too offended to argue. She did enough arguing in her professional life.

Alice had brought a bikini on this trip. She'd even worn it on the one day she'd had the house to herself. As soon as Joy had arrived, Alice had gone straight back to wearing her black one-piece swimsuit. And she'd hardly ventured into the pool at all. Perhaps now, when she had the place to herself, would be a good time to unearth her bikini.

Ten minutes later Alice lay in a deck chair wearing just a pair of bikini bottoms in a loud floral print. The way the sun warmed her nipples was, indeed, an exquisite sensation. Additionally, Alice was still basking in the glory of actually having taken her top off. She'd just done it. First the straps, then the clasp, finally letting it fall by her side—after which she'd picked it up and draped it over the back of her chair. Joy was entirely to blame for this. Alice didn't take any responsibility for putting her upper body on display like that. And she would certainly never even consider doing so in front of someone else. But it was just her now. The blue sky above. The cool water of the pool next to her. Some birds chirping in the bushes surrounding the garden. This was what her holiday was made of. Joy would be leaving again in a few days. In fact, Alice might enjoy her holiday even more, what with the contrast of being all alone again—and the new-found pleasure of baring her chest to the sun.

"Wow, Mama," Alice heard someone say, followed by a wolf whistle. "Glad to see I inspired you."

Alice blinked her eyes open. The sun was all the way on the other side of the garden. What time was it? "I must have dozed off," she muttered. Joy stood next to her chair, her eyes fixed on Alice's bosom. Only then did Alice remember she'd taken off her top before falling asleep.

"Oh shoot." She quickly covered her breasts with her arms, looking around for her top.

"Looking for this?" Joy held Alice's bikini top between two fingers. "Nice fabric, by the way… Very unexpected, but hey, life can be full of surprises like that."

"Give it to me," Alice snapped.

"It doesn't matter anymore now, Alice. I've seen them already." Joy shot her a wink. "Not bad at all." She painted a crooked smirk on her lips. Alice felt she would die right there and then. This surely was one of the most embarrassing moments of her entire life. Only her GP, her gynaecologist, and Alan had seen her like this, and now, this… crass girl, with her loud mouth and loose manners. For all Alice knew, Joy could have taken a picture of her while she was snoozing, with that smartphone that never seemed to leave her hands.

"Here." Joy handed her the garment and, in order to take possession of her much-needed top, Alice had no choice but to extend a hand, thus offering another glimpse of her breasts to Joy.

Alice snatched it out of Joy's hands and hurried into her room, of which the French doors opened into the garden. When she caught a glimpse of herself in the mirror, her cheeks were flushed bright red. She threw the bikini top on the bed and glared at herself for a few seconds longer. Had Joy meant what she had said? Not bad at all. For a woman of fifty-three, Alice looked damn good. She worked hard enough for it. Alice never understood how other people could be so careless with their bodies, drinking countless units of alcohol, eating fried food, and failing to exercise at least four times a week.

"I don't have time to occupy myself with all of that, Alice," Miranda had said once when Alice had questioned her about the topic. "I have a bloody life to live."

A knock on the door startled Alice. She hadn't locked it, just let it fall to when she had rushed in.

"Hey," Joy said. "I'm sorry about earlier. I didn't mean to embarrass you."

You're doing it again, Alice thought, covering herself up. She didn't say it out loud.

"How about I make it up to you? I'll cook for you tonight. I make a mean sangria as well." Joy winked again. "No need to dress up."

What was that supposed to mean? And was she really expecting Alice to accept her invitation when she kept alluding to what had happened earlier?

"Fine," Alice said, despite herself. "Please put on a T-shirt when you cook."

Joy just grinned and turned on her heels.

Alice let her arms fall to her side. Something must have chipped away a tiny bit at her sense of decorum. Otherwise, she would never have said yes. Nor checked herself out in the mirror again.

"That's a very inappropriate question," Alice said.

"I'll go first then." Joy refilled Alice's glass. "I can tell you need some more liquid courage."

"I think I've reached my limit for today." Alice obstructed the opening of her glass with a flat hand.

"You're on holiday, for Christ's sake. Live a little." Joy just swatted Alice's hand away and filled her glass to the brim with sangria. The drink was strong and had gone to Alice's head after the first few sips. That was more than an hour ago. She was well aware that she was beginning to slur her words, but the piri piri chicken Joy had prepared had been surprisingly delicious and at least for the first part of the evening, the girl had, for once, displayed excellent manners.

Joy put the jug down and took a sip. "I last had sex with Alex Anderson, one week before I came here."

"Good for you," Alice said, not feeling half as uncomfortable as she ought to. "Will you be seeing this gentleman again?"

"Gentleman?" Joy scoffed. "Alex has nothing gentlemanly about her."

Alice nearly choked on the sangria swirling down her throat.

"What? Oh, please don't tell me Mum never brought it up. She likes to moan to me about it every chance she gets. I swing both ways, you see, and Mum has a really hard time getting that through that thick skull of hers."

"W-what, erm, I'm not sure what you mean," Alice stammered.

"I'm bisexual." Joy just shrugged. "It's no big deal." She fixed her gaze on Alice. "Anyway, back to you. When did you last have a really good shag, Alice? You're keeping me in suspense here."

"I, uh, don't really talk about subjects like that."

"Enough of the avoidance tactics. We're sharing this house in gorgeous Quinta do Lago. You've seen my tits, I've seen yours. I may only be twenty-seven, but I've seen a few pairs in my life so far, and yours stack up really nice. So… out with it. Whatever gets said here tonight, stays here. I'm not going to tell Mum if that's what you're worried about."

Did she just say that Alice has a nice pair of tits? And that was supposed to encourage her to divulge details about her intimate life? Today's youth was just so careless with their personal information, what with publishing everything on social media and such. Alice shook her head, indicating that this subject was closed.

"Has it really been that long that you don't remember?" The girl just didn't know when to stop.

She was right, though. Had hit the nail squarely on the head.

"It was with Alan, probably a few years before he left me… which he probably did because he wasn't getting any at home anymore," Alice blurted out, heavily influenced by the alcohol in her bloodstream. "Not that it was ever very satisfying."

"Aah." Joy leaned back in her chair. "Now we're getting somewhere."

"I doubt it," Alice said. "I haven't gotten any in a very, very long time." Lack of an intimate life was not something Alice had ever paid much attention to.

"Men will probably disappoint you," her mother had said to her when she was in her teens. That was as close to a personal conversation they'd ever had.

"You have, erm, you know... experienced an orgasm though, haven't you?"

"What?" Alice masked her discomfort with a smile. "Of course, I have." A girl like Joy could probably see it on her face, though. It was just that orgasms were not very high on Alice's priority list in life either. She wasn't sure a sexual climax made it onto any of her lists—and Alice lived and died by lists. In the end, her mother had been right. Alan had turned out to be a massive disappointment. She was in her fifties now. What use was it trying to change any of that now?

Joy didn't say anything. She just sat there, staring back at Alice, as though looking straight through her, but catching a glimpse of her soul in the process. Then, as if she'd just reached an important conclusion about something Alice wasn't privy to, she nodded. She folded her features into a determined expression, but kept her eyes on Alice. "We have to do something about that, Alice." The nodding turned into a shaking of her head. "That's really no way to live your life." She cocked her head now. "It explains a lot, though." Joy curled her lips into a warm smile. Was that a smile of pity? The last thing Alice needed was anyone's pity.

"I think I'll go to bed now." Alice pushed her chair back. "I've said enough for one night."

"Before I leave this house"—Joy paused to think—"in four days, you will have an orgasm. That's my promise to you."

Alice scuttled off wordlessly. How had a semi-pleasant

evening turned into this embarrassment? Maybe she should see if any hotels were available in the area. She doubted they would be at this time of year, but it was worth a try. Anything would be better than staying in this house with Joy.

~

The next day, Alice went out of her way to avoid Joy, which meant she spent the better part of the day—a beautiful, impossibly blue one—in her room overlooking the pool. She couldn't help but catch glimpses of Joy's naked upper body. Alice didn't see her with a top on for a single second. She waited for Joy to nap in a deck chair before getting her breakfast and lunch from the kitchen. Alice had just laid down on her bed for a siesta when a knock on the door surprised her. Although it could really only be one person.

"Yes," she said reluctantly. Alice knew deep down she was behaving like one of the petulant children she so often criticised.

Joy appeared in the doorframe wearing only her yellow shorts. "I must have really upset you," she said. She was only upsetting Alice more by standing in her room like that.

"Would you please cover yourself," Alice snapped and averted her gaze.

"This is how I am, Alice. I believe there's nothing wrong with being naked."

"Oh, so you're a bisexual nudist. I see. Your mother must be so proud."

"What does it even matter to you what I am? Just chill."

"It matters because we are sharing this house and you've been nothing but disrespectful to me."

"Disrespectful? Says the woman who's been sulking in her room like a wronged teenager all morning. Why, Alice? Did you finally try to masturbate?"

"Please, leave." Alice walked further away from Joy. "And close the door behind you."

"No, I'm not going to be living with a ghost who only ventures into the common areas when I'm sleeping. We had a nice time last night. Drank a bit too much. Some things were said. That's life. That's just how things go. Get over it."

Alice turned around—and was startled again by the flawlessness of Joy's skin, and the springy bounce of her breasts as she gestured with her hands. "You and I are very different people, Joy. You're young. Carefree. And that's all fine, but I would appreciate it if you could make a little bit more effort to respect my boundaries."

"Fine. At this point, I'll do anything to lure you out of your room." Joy leaned her shoulder against the doorframe. "Except..."

"Except what?"

"Except if, after what we talked about before your dramatic exit last night, you've actually been trying to lure me here..."

"What?" A flush crept up Alice's neck. "I've done no such thing. Even the—"

"Relax, Alice. I'm just winding you up. It's so easy, you know?" Joy stood there chuckling. "After a few glasses of sangria you were perfectly enjoyable company, though. I've made a fresh jug. Why don't we have some by the pool?" She cocked her head again in that way of hers. "No tops required." With that, she quickly winked at Alice and left her standing there flabbergasted.

As a sign of goodwill, Alice wore her bikini—top on, of course—when she joined Joy poolside.

"That's better," Joy said.

"I'd like to say something," Alice announced. Joy was already pouring her a large glass of sangria.

"Be my guest."

"You're very direct. I'm not used to that. It unsettles me.

Especially when you address topics that, huh, I never talk about. I think there's a middle ground here, however. I'll try to be less uptight if you limit your conversation to... normal topics."

"Normal, huh? Like what? The weather?" Joy had applied a fresh layer of sunscreen and her skin gleamed in the sunlight. Alice's own milky white skin stood in stark contrast.

"This is exactly what I mean. It's as though everything you say is said to provoke a reaction out of me. It prevents me from relaxing. I feel like I need to have my guard up all the time."

"Okay. I'm sorry. It's just how I am, I guess." Joy let her head fall back. "I've been thinking about extending my stay."

"Another joke, I presume." Alice was slowly starting to get the hang of this verbal sparring.

"Maybe." Joy closed her eyes and they sat in silence for a while, enjoying the sun and—in Alice's case and to her utter amazement—the sensation of being in this spectacular location with another person.

After two more glasses of sangria, a boldness had built in Alice's gut. She dipped in the pool to cool off and when she came out, she took off her top. She sat down across from Joy defiantly.

"What were you going to do about it, anyway?" Alice could tell Joy had trouble averting her gaze from her chest. It served her right.

"About what?"

"About not leaving this house until etcetera etcetera..."

"Etcetera? Can you not even say it? We should really start with that then. Your generation harbours so much sexual shame, Alice. It's such a waste. You're a woman in her prime. You're at your sexual peak at this very time of your life. Have probably been for years. You should take full advantage of that instead of fussing over whether you should wear a bikini top."

"I didn't realise Miranda had sent you to feminist school.

No need to burn your bra, though, since you hardly ever wear one." Alice was getting good at this.

"Just say it, Alice. Just one time. Just say that you would really, really like to have a mind-blowing orgasm, just once in your life."

"What happens then?" Alice asked. "I say it, but nothing changes. They would just be words."

"Words are the single most powerful tool we have." Joy pinned her dark-brown gaze on Alice. "Trust me. Just saying something out loud can be so transformative."

Alice knew this wasn't a time to cling to values that had, quite honestly, left her rather frustrated all her life. With most of her inhibitions washed away by the sangria, she said, "I, Alice McAllister, would like to experience an earth-shattering, life-changing climax at some point in my existence."

To Alice's surprise, Joy didn't even attempt to mock her. Instead, she gave her a tender smile, her eyes narrowing into a kind expression. "All you needed to do was ask," she said and rose. "Come on."

"What?" Heat travelled through Alice's flesh at high speed. "What do you mean? Where are we going?"

"We're going to your room and I'm going to show you what it's all about." Joy extended her hand and waited patiently. "Think about it. I'm here and I'm more than qualified to initiate you into the joys—no pun intended—of self-love. I mean, somehow, it's almost as though I was meant to be here."

"I'm not sure this is appropriate."

"Who gives a damn about appropriate? What's even appropriate in your mind, Alice?" She shuffled a little closer and put a hand on Alice's shoulder. Alice felt Joy's nipple skate along the skin of her arm. "We both know it's time."

Alice's feet acquiesced first. They planted themselves firmly on the ground so she could push herself out of her chair. Her hand came next when she put it in Joy's palm.

The walk to her bedroom, which was easily reachable through the French doors, was quiet, almost reverent. Alice had tried touching herself a few times, but that was years ago, and always unsuccessful.

She didn't have many clothes to dispose of, but Joy set the example by taking off her bikini bottoms first. She didn't use words to urge Alice to do the same, which made it easier for Alice to do so. They stood naked in front of each other for an instant.

"You're beautiful. You know that?" Joy said.

I'm beautiful? Alice wanted to ask in return. Have you looked in the mirror recently? Have you seen the reflection of your unblemished skin and strong muscles flexing underneath? All your youth still so brazenly on display. But she remained silent. She needed quiet in that moment and she accepted the compliment with a simple nod of the head.

"Why don't we lie down?" Again, Joy set the example by hopping on the bed and stretching herself out and beckoning Alice over with a movement of her arm. "Lie on your back. Spread your legs a little, if you like." It was the addition of 'if you like' that made all the difference.

"May I?" Joy asked, her fingers slicing the air above Alice's belly.

"Yes," Alice managed to squeeze out of her throat. She hadn't been touched in years. Not like this. And now she was in a bed in Portugal with a girl young enough to be her daughter. But Alice didn't have children. She'd never wanted any. And Joy was definitely not a child. She'd just presented her womanhood in all its glory to Alice... The endless tailspin of thoughts in Alice's mind stopped abruptly when Joy's fingers touched down just above her belly button. So that was what was required to make the world stop in its tracks.

Joy let her fingers meander up the slope of Alice's breast

and soon they were circling around her nipple, as though wanting it to grow even harder than it already was.

"Does that feel good?" Joy asked.

"Yes," Alice moaned. "Very."

"I don't want to do anything you don't want me to do, okay?" Joy said. "If at any point you want me to stop, please tell me." She pushed herself up on one elbow and looked into Alice's eyes. "Okay?" she insisted.

"Okay," Alice repeated, but she'd already reached a point where she couldn't imagine saying no to anything Joy might do to her. Alan had certainly never touched her in such a gentle, exploring way. Not that he'd ever been rough, just manly, and mainly focused on himself.

Joy traced her fingers to Alice's other breast, but they were bolder this time. Instead of circling around her nipple, she pinched it hard between her thumb and forefinger. So hard Alice had to gasp for air.

"Too hard?" Joy asked, but she didn't look as if she might regret it if it had actually been too hard. Alice responded with a satisfied smirk. "Can I kiss you?" Joy asked next, and that did take Alice aback, even though it was, for once, a very polite request—natural, even, under the circumstances.

"Please."

When Joy's lips touched hers she repeated the pinching motion of her fingers and something in Alice just came undone. Years of neglecting to admire and caress her own body—in the absence of anyone else to do it for her. A lifetime of missed climaxes. A sense of loss being replaced by pure pleasure. Alice threw her arms around Joy's neck and pulled her closer. She was done lying here paralysed like a first-timer, although she sort of was.

Joy responded in kind and deepened her kiss, her teeth grazing Alice's lips, her tongue growing bolder. All the while, she kept pinching Alice's nipple and every time she did, Alice felt it all the way down to her clit. Oh, to have those fingers touch her there. And then, while they were still frantically kissing, those fingers did venture down, going back on the path they came from, but not stopping at Alice's belly button. They dove straight down to her pubic hair and when Joy touched her there, she pulled back from the kiss, as though in shock.

"You're so wet," she said and, instead of embarrassing Alice, it only made her wetter. Joy kissed her on the cheek and then let her lips follow the lines her fingers had traced earlier. Every time she planted her moist lips on a patch of Alice's skin, a jolt of electricity skittered through her flesh. How could this feel so good? Why had she denied herself this exquisite pleasure for so long? And what if Joy hadn't turned up at the house? Perhaps it had happened for a reason—a very specific one. Then, Alice's mind went blank again. Joy's lips had reached the point where her fingers had stopped before: her long-neglected clitoris. Alice couldn't possibly remember a time when it had pulsed like it was doing now, as though screaming for attention—and, if possible, immediate release.

Joy found Alice's eyes and said, "I'm going to lick you until you come." It was almost enough to make Alice come there and then. The power of words, Joy had said earlier. She'd been right —again.

Joy scooted over a bit and positioned herself between Alice's legs. Alice could hardly lie there and claim she had dreamt of a moment like this, but if she ever had, the dream would certainly not have included a person of the same sex half her age. She could easily imagine what Joy would have to say about that. That's life, Alice. Live a little.

Joy's breath was already rushing over her lips. Her tongue hadn't even touched Alice yet, but it was as though Alice could feel it already. Her muscles tensed with anticipation. Had Alan ever gone down on her? If he had, she couldn't remember—so he'd probably never bothered. Neither had she.

Joy pressed her mouth to Alice's clit, and another wave of the same sensation as earlier was released from its shackles. A sense of freedom. Of new beginnings. Because if this was feasible—and it was—then what was not in the realm of possibilities? This gorgeous woman with the supplest skin Alice had ever seen was licking her clit. What had the world come to? This was Alice's last thought before she surrendered to the fire in her belly. To the pleasure building in her muscles. To the years of neglected physicality catching up with her, clawing their way to the surface of her soul.

Alice couldn't pinpoint exactly what Joy's tongue was doing. One moment it seemed to circle around her clit, while the next it seemed to seek entrance to her... What should she call that body part she spent most of her time not thinking about. Her vagina? How clinical. Pussy? How pornographic. Her cunt? That was a crude curse word, wasn't it? It didn't matter. Joy's tongue danced its way expertly around her nether regions. And then she started sucking Alice's clitoris between her lips. A brand new wave of arousal washed over Alice. She'd never experienced the likes of this before. She was not a woman of extreme emotions, nor of crazy actions—and definitely not of tears. So what was happening to her now? Some sort of deliverance at the tongue of another woman?

Alice clasped her hands around the back of Joy's head. She pushed Joy's face deeper between her legs—lest she thought Alice was giving a sign that she should stop. Alice never wanted this to stop. She was on a journey. The one Joy had promised to take her on. Well, actually she had said that she would show Alice, but this was no time to argue over semantics.

Would she return the favour? If a woman pleasured you in this way, was it common courtesy to do the same to her? Alice imagined positioning herself between Joy's legs, bending herself towards her, and inhaling her scent. It drove her right over the edge.

"Oh, Christ," she muttered. "Oh my good Lord." She delved her nails into Joy's skull. Joy licked and sucked, until Alice's muscles stopped spasming, until her toes uncurled, and she released her grasp on Joy's head.

Joy immediately smirked up at her, her chin glistening with Alice's juices. Her juices. What a strangely arousing thought.

"And?" she asked, eyes glittering. It was a needless question, answered extensively by Alice's earlier groans.

"Come here," Alice said and opened her arms wide. Joy rushed to her side and fell into her embrace. Alice had never dared to dream she'd lick her own juices off another woman's chin so enthusiastically.

If you enjoyed this short story, you might want to check out Harper's novel Seasons of Love, which was inspired by it.

FAIR AND SQUARE

I focused on the sound of my shoes hitting the track. If I concentrated on Sofia, who ran in front of me as usual, I'd never win this race. It was hard to keep my gaze off of her flexing calf muscles though, and the way her white shorts contrasted with the glistening ochre of her skin. But this was not the time to indulge in enticing images. This race was important. This was our own personal fight for who should be top.

I knew she believed she had me already. A force of habit I could hardly blame her for. With her strong, stocky body she always outmanoeuvred me in the bedroom before I had a chance to even realise what was going on. It came naturally to her, whereas I had to fight for it. Or at least win this race.

Sofia liked to wear old, oversized T-shirts when she ran, but today she'd opted for a tight-fitting tank top—all part of her strategy. She'd rather wear a dress for a month than let me win.

I gained a little ground on her, enough to witness a drop of sweat making its way out of her hair onto the nape of her neck. Her tank top was black and so soaked it showed the outline of her shoulder blades. They flitted up and down along the inside of the fabric as she cleaved her balled fists through the air. My heart pounded inside my ears and I wasn't sure if it was from the exertion of trying to keep up with her or from the sheer pleasure of watching her run.

Sofia was never more beautiful than when she ran—as if she was made for it. Her shoes landed on the track with an elegance so incongruous I simply had to look up that first time I spotted her a few months ago. My gaze had shifted from her toned thighs to the sweat shimmering on the skin of her arms and I had ended up looking straight into the cockiest smile I'd ever seen. Everything about her oozed dominance. From the way she tilted her head when she addressed me, eyes blazing with confidence, to how she untied her shoelaces after a run. As if the miles she'd just put in were nothing but a leisurely stroll in the park.

I rounded the bend and increased my speed, prompted by an urgency to see her face. I ignored the stitches in my side and ran alongside her. She shot me a crooked grin, accompanied by a quick wink. She allowed me to run by her side for a few strides before taking off. I cursed myself for allowing my desire to catch a glimpse of her dark stare, to be with her in the moment, to knock me off my game. But I wasn't ready to throw in the towel just yet. I fixed my eyes on her behind, and pushed images of my flat hand landing on it—leaving the molten gold of her skin flushed a delicate red—out of my mind.

My breathing grew shallower and sweat trickled down my temples. It was neither a case of being unhappy submitting to Sofia, nor a matter of pride. I just knew this was the only way she'd ever let me. Sofia would only willingly surrender if I beat her at the one thing she considered herself unbeatable at.

I might not have been as strong as her, but I was taller. For every step I took, she almost had to take two. If I pushed through the pain in my lungs and the cramp in my thighs, I could still win. I took a deep breath and accelerated again.

Immediately, my pulse quickened and I felt heat rise to my head. This was our final lap and I could see the finish line looming around the next bend. Sofia had about two metres on me. The rise and fall of her shoulders were as steady as ever. The rhythm of her feet was so natural in its cadence, it almost felt like a crime to disturb something as effortlessly beautiful as Sofia running on the track.

I remembered what was at stake and connected with a longing buried deep inside of me, a longing I never even knew I possessed. I lengthened my strides and sped past her. Spurred on by the glorious sensation of running ahead of her, of smelling victory, I held on to the last scrap of strength in my muscles. Strangely, my feet seemed to bounce higher now that I had surpassed her. More air seemed to fill my lungs and I couldn't feel any more pain. All I saw was the finish line, a simple white line marking my impending glory. Because I knew I would win. Not because Sofia would let me, but because I wanted it more than anything. I wanted it more than Sofia tying me to the bed, leaving me there for long minutes as she retrieved ice cubes from the freezer. I wanted it more than the delicious bite of her riding crop just below the curve of my behind.

I passed the finish line a mere second before she did. I would have loved to have seen her cross that white line—my white line—but I was too busy trying to avoid collapsing from sheer exhaustion. Doubled over, my hands resting on my thighs and my breath wheezing in my lungs, I glanced at her. A flash of abs peeked out from under her tank top and her nipples grew hard underneath. She was as excited about all of this as I was.

"I didn't know you had that in you," Sofia said in between panting and wiping the sweat from her brow. "My bad for underestimating you." A darkness gathered in her eyes. Above anything, Sofia was a proud woman and despite trying hard to keep her features neutral, I knew her pride was hurt. But I'd try to make her forget about that soon enough.

"You ain't seen nothing yet, baby." I'd caught my breath and inched closer. "I may need to borrow some of your toys though."

The smile she shot me was not as sly as usual, as if she was already trying on her new, less cocky role. I hunched over her and buried my nose in her black, musky hair. My knees went a little weak at her scent and I grabbed her hand to lead her off the track.

We walked to Sofia's apartment in silence, contemplating the role reversal our race had brought about. My body slowly recovered from the physical exploit it had just endured, the feel of Sofia's moist fingers against mine speeding up the process. The beat of my heart returned to its normal rhythm only to pick up again as I realised I would be in charge tonight. I glanced over at Sofia and gripped her hand tighter. I was hardly a pillow princess and I gave as good as I got, but when it came down to control, I was always happy to relinquish.

I tried to reconnect with the desire that had driven me to victory moments earlier, that struggle for power I had found roaring inside of me. It seemed to have faded to a faint tremor in my gut—faint, but still present. Maybe I was just afraid. Maybe it had been a part of me all along. Why else would I have run my heart out for it?

When we arrived at Sofia's front door I cupped my hands under her keys and waited for her to drop them. It didn't feel right to be let into an apartment in which I was expected to call the shots. She locked her eyes on mine and I observed signs of sceptical amusement in the twinkling blackness of them. She let the keys dangle between her thumb and index finger and drew them away when I tried to snag them from her—as if to say that if I wanted control, I would have to work for it.

I took a step towards her, towering over her, and shot her a cool smile.

"I'm not sure your neighbours would agree if we engaged in what I have in mind in the hallway, honey." I accompanied my statement with another step towards her. I could feel the heat radiate off her skin. Suddenly, I couldn't wait to dig my nails in her well-shaped biceps and see her muscles tremble under my touch.

Sofia let the keys tumble into the palm of my hand and, without further protest, I let us into her apartment. Insecurity washed over me as I scanned her living room. I'd been there plenty of times, but this wasn't home turf for me and I missed the easy confidence that comes with being in your own place. It didn't help that she positioned herself in front of me, legs spread and arms crossed over her chest. She didn't say anything but her entire attitude screamed for me to show her what I had.

Over her head, I caught a glimpse of myself in a wall mirror. My hair clung to my forehead in moist strands and my skin was oily from the exercise, but my eyes sparkled with something I had never seen before. I'd beat her in the race. I had won and, perhaps for tonight only, she was all mine in exactly the way I wanted her to be. I looked my mirrored self in the eye and slipped into another version of me.

"Come here." My voice sounded lower than usual.

Without any apparent sign of reluctance, Sofia inched closer. She let her arms drop to her sides. Her tank top had ridden up high over her stomach, baring taut skin stretched over prominent abdominal muscles. I momentarily lost composure and swallowed hard. Sofia took advantage of my weakness and lifted her arms to curve her hands behind her head. This made her breasts rise on her chest, stiff nipples protruding. I had to gasp for air again.

That's when I realised it wasn't necessarily a matter of Sofia being the more powerful top. It was, for me, a matter of not being able to harness the lust coursing through me at the sight of her. One glance at her light-olive skin and I was lost. One wink of her eyes, as dark as the night, and I was gone. If I were to have any chance of embracing this possible part of my personality, it would have to start with self-control. Not easy when I already felt a moist heat glowing between my legs and a flush creep up the skin of my cheeks.

"Take your top off." This time I barely recognised my own voice. The words leapt from my mouth strangled and choked, yet with an urgency foreign to me.

Sofia obliged and slowly peeled the tank top off her skin. She stood in front of me in just her sports bra and I felt my composure slip again, but I regrouped much faster this time. It was hard, though, to resist the urge to tug the black straps of her bra off her square shoulders and to not trail a finger over her pronounced collarbones. Sofia's body was a work of art requiring hours of hard work. Her breasts sloped perfectly under the fabric of her bra and her belly was a flat plain of muscle.

"Bra as well." I squeezed my legs together, hoping it would calm the throbbing there, but the flimsy Lycra of my running pants was no match for the heat pooling between my legs. I stood there soaked, while Sofia, with the icy glare of a seasoned stripper, unhooked her bra. She clutched it to her chest for a moment before letting it drop to the floor.

She locked her eyes on mine, a question in her stare, but all I could see were the rigid peaks of her nipples, piercing the air. I had to call upon every ounce of willpower inside of me to not kneel in front of her and close my lips around those stiff, dark buds. If I was strong now, I still stood a chance. But she knew. Oh, she did. I could see it clearly then. The corners of her mouth curved upwards ever so slightly and her eyes, questioning before, had turned into a pool of simmering lust that sucked me in, regardless of what I had told myself or wanted to make myself do.

Sofia didn't make the mistake of giving in. She could have cracked a quick joke about the situation—about my glaring lack of self-control—and undermined me, but instead, without being asked, she tugged her shorts off, heeled her shoes and socks off her feet and presented herself to me in just a pair of tight white boy shorts. She backed away from me until she hit a wall—the same wall against which she had turned me around one day, spread my legs wide, and whipped my bottom until I had come so hard my knees had buckled and I had sunk to the floor in a puddle of my own wetness.

She slid her undies off and spun around. She planted her hands high against the wall so her perfectly-rounded behind lifted towards me. I could have wondered who was topping who at that point, but I was too mesmerised by the glow of her skin in the evening light and the way her bottom arched, beckoning me. My blood beat faster in my veins and my clit hammered against the constraint of my running shorts. I hoisted my top over my head as I strode towards Sofia's sculpted body on display for me against the wall.

I didn't have time to take off the rest of my clothes. The need to touch, to devour, was so overwhelming I launched myself at her, covering her body with mine. I dug my nails into the strong muscles of her arms while my lips landed hard on her shoulder. I felt my body go limp against her hardness, all resolve draining out of me. My skin prickled into gooseflesh at the touch of her toned back against my nipples. My lips found her ear and I said the words.

"Fuck me." My fingers kneaded through her flesh and my voice had transformed into a raw growl. "Please, fuck me."

As quick as a flash she turned around. With able, well-trained fingers she disposed of my bra and, before I had a chance to process how the tables had turned once again, one of my nipples was caught between her thumb and index finger. Her other hand ducked into my running shorts, into the unbearable wetness there, and found my clit.

"You," she said, as she spun me around and shoved me hard with my back against the wall, one finger grazing my opening, "are such a big fat bottom."

I wanted to tell her it was all her fault, that I'd lost command of all my faculties when I was with her. That the mere sight of her fit body rendered me completely useless, but the words got swallowed by a long overdue moan escaping from my throat.

She looked into my eyes as she slid two fingers deep inside of me. "I'll fuck you," she said. "I'll give you three more thrusts and then you'd better come for me." She pulled out slowly, flicking my clit with her thumb on the way out.

"One." She pinched my nipple hard as her fingers dug into me. I kept my gaze on her, fighting the urge to lean my head back and enjoy the climax my body had been aching for since long before we left the running track.

"Two." Her biceps flexed as she took me again, her fingers twisting inside of me. A flaring heat travelled through my flesh and invaded my blood. She didn't have to count to three anymore. I was there. For her. Obeying, as ever.

"Three." Sofia slipped out of view as I closed my eyes and a million stars burst on the back of my eyelids. She was there when I opened my eyes again and I pulled her close, panting into the dampness of her hair.

"Next time, I won't let you win," she said, before sinking her teeth into my earlobe. But I knew I had won fair and square.

THE CLIENT

I sat across from Claire like I did every week. Every Thursday evening from seven to eight. She was my last client of the day, but that wasn't the only reason I looked forward to her visit. I loved the way she crossed and uncrossed her long, smooth legs whenever we reached an uncomfortable point in the conversation. I couldn't get enough of her thick-rimmed, fashionable glasses slipping down the bridge of her nose when she tipped her head forward. I was mesmerized—sometimes not even fully listening to what she was paying me to hear—by the dip of her neck where the collar of her blouse spread wide.

Usually, it was the other way around. Clients projecting, sometimes even reluctantly admitting to indulging in a sexual fantasy about me. I always patiently explained, my face drawn into the most solemn expression, that it was normal and logical, but that, of course, nothing could or ever would happen. In my ten years of practice, I'd never once been tempted. Until Claire came along.

I wanted her from day one.

Today's session was drawing to a close and I let my eyes

linger briefly over the New York skyline sparkling behind her. I stifled a sigh at another hour of reveling in her presence coming to an end. Lust drummed in my veins and pooled between my legs. Every week, after Claire left, I was a sodden mess of desire. I sat in my plush office with the shag carpet and spectacular views and tried to rationalize my way out of this inappropriate lust. I'd even considered going into therapy myself.

"Are you listening to me, Angie?" Claire's voice had shot up. "You charge a bit too much to not give me your full attention."

"I'm sorry." My response came quickly, my heart thundering in my chest. I rested my eyes on her, hoping she wouldn't see the turmoil rushing through my flesh. "I was distracted. Long day."

She arched up her eyebrows in disbelief. She had every right to.

"This week's session is on the house," I corrected myself. "And I'll throw in a free drink as well." I rose from my chair and headed for the liquor cabinet, hoping she didn't have anywhere to be.

"Really?" Her voice was behind me. "Is that ethical?"

Ethical. The last word I wanted to hear. Before turning to face her, I grabbed two glasses and a bottle of Scotch.

"I highly doubt it." I shot her a wide smile—the one I use for seducing. With every second that passed, I felt boundaries crumbling. Up until now, I'd always managed to keep myself in check, to ignore the throbbing of my clit when her voice grew low with desperation. I crossed back to where she was sitting and set the glasses down on the small table between our chairs, pouring a generous amount of liquor in both.

Silence filled the room. My office was too high up for traffic noise to filter in. My assistant had gone home at seven. It was just Claire and me, and a bottle of booze. And the lust crawling up my spine, clinging to my skin. Finding a way out.

"But I'm only human," I continued. "I suffer from the same imperfections as anyone else." I took a large swig of the whiskey and relished how it burned my throat, like punishment.

"Rough day?" She leaned forward and snatched the other glass from the table. I hadn't dared offer it to her, afraid of the trembling of my hands and how it would appear. I still had some sense of decorum left. "Too many sob stories?"

We'd been working on Claire's easy refuge into sarcasm, which I secretly loved. I chuckled nervously, then shook my head. I locked my eyes on hers, on the impossible blue of them. I'd been trying to come up with a suitable adjective to describe their dazzling color but they were all inadequate.

"It's not something I can talk about, I'm afraid." I shrugged my shoulders. "Confidentiality and all that."

She nodded her understanding, but a sly smile played around her lips. "What were you thinking about earlier? When you were distracted?" She'd deposited her glass back on the table and curled her fingers into air quotes.

A flush spread from my neck up to my cheeks. I sipped from my drink and twirled the glass between my fingers before glancing at her again. She'd taken off her glasses and her eyes seemed too close, too knowing. "Do you really want to know?"

"I do." The tone of her voice, even in those two short words, indicated that she already did.

I cleared my throat and swallowed the sudden dryness out of my mouth. "I think you're the most beautiful woman to ever set foot in this office." I resisted the urge to look away. I witnessed how a small sigh escaped from her lips.

"Apart from yourself, you mean?" She picked up her glass from the table again and drank from it without losing eye contact. Our glances stayed connected over the rim. The skin of my arms pricked, the hairs reaching up. I sat stock-still for an instant, listening to the furious beat of my heart. Her face broke out into a smile.

"It would be foolish to compare." My voice came out strangled. "Such a waste of time."

She slanted her body backwards. "What are we going to do about this?"

Wet heat gathered between my legs. Would it be better if I waited for her to make the first move? Or just plain silly because the time for considerations like that had surely passed?

I drained the last of my drink and stood up. My knees felt weak as I bridged the small distance to where she sat. I extended my hand to hers, fingers shaking slightly. She gripped me by the wrist and the sensation of her fingers curling against my skin made me dizzy with delight.

"I've always admired your view." She twirled me around to face the window. "Let's take a closer look."

The blue light of dusk clung to the sky. I loved how the city lit up in the darkness, as if never wanting to go to sleep. The splendor outside paled in comparison to the wicked sparkle in Claire's eyes as she spun me back around.

"Wonderful," she hummed. "Truly beautiful." She grabbed me by the waist and pushed me up against the narrow windowsill.

Desire zapped through my flesh at the touch of her fingers on my body. Was I dreaming? Was this actually happening? The window was cool against my back. A stark contrast to the heat spreading through my muscles as she raked her fingertips from my waist to my thighs.

"Is this what you were thinking of?" Claire asked before her lips found mine. She tasted of whiskey and lipstick. Her tongue was soft in my mouth, intertwining with mine, exploring. My legs turned to jelly when her fingers snuck beneath the hem of my skirt.

I traced a wet path of kisses to her ear. "Every day since we met," I whispered. I licked her earlobe and retraced the steps my lips had taken earlier, inhaling her scent and committing it to memory.

Her thumbs pressed into the flesh of my thighs and I was glad I had the windowsill as support. My panties grew wet between my legs. My pussy throbbed violently. I pressed my palms against her chest, wanting to feel more of her. My fingers tore at the buttons of her blouse, eager to discover what lay beneath.

She broke our lip lock to hike up my skirt and I took the opportunity to slide her blouse off her shoulders. The black straps of her bra strained deliciously over her pronounced collar bones. I leaned forward and trailed my tongue along her soft skin there, biting into the right strap and guiding it off her with my teeth.

Claire moved in closer, pushing my chin up. She locked her eyes on mine as she brought her hand between my legs. With my skirt hitched up, I was able to part my knees wider. When her fingertips reached the wet panel of my panties, my pussy lips felt so puffed up I could feel them press against the constraints of my undies.

She traced a line along the fabric, up and down, and again. Our gaze stayed connected and the lust glimmering in the blue of her eyes was almost enough to set me off. I might have imagined a moment like this a dozen times per day for months, but I'd never dreamt she'd take me like this, propped up against my office window, the city glistening below us and Claire's gaze on me as effective as what she was doing with her fingers.

Her eyes narrowed a fraction when she slid a fingertip under the hem of my panties, lifting it before sliding it to the side. My clit reacted by standing to attention instantly, eager for her touch. My pussy pulsed with want and I lifted my pelvis towards her in response. A small smile played on her lips before her face disappeared from my field of vision.

A split second later her tongue skated along my clit, briefly teasing it. I clenched my fingers around the edge of the windowsill, imagining my knuckles going white. My toes barely touched the floor and I had to engage my core muscles to retain balance. I glanced down and saw her blonde hair bobbing up and down between my thighs. It was the most beautiful thing I'd ever seen.

Her tongue darted in and out of me, licking along my sensitive opening—as if she instinctively knew that was what I liked. My office was quiet except for the strangled sound of my breathing and the lapping noises rising up from between my thighs. Moisture trickled out of me as Claire sucked my pussy lips into her mouth.

When her tongue hit my clit again, my knees buckled. Heat travelled through my veins, spreading like wildfire through my body. I wanted to trap her head there, keep her there forever. All the things I knew about her, all the secrets she had told me fell away when she let a finger slip inside of me. She curled it up and hit my sweet spot with the tip. I had seen it in her when we talked—I had seen that she would know exactly what to do with a woman.

The waves came fast then, my blood smoldering in my veins and my muscles ready to explode. Her tongue trilled against my clit at high speed while her finger rubbed inside. I was beginning to wonder if I had told her about this. If I had told her what makes me tick more than anything else. My eyes went wide and my shoulders tensed—my fingers still clamped around the windowsill—as a bolt of electricity took root deep inside of me.

"Oh my god," I screamed, as my pussy released a stream of juices, the walls of my cunt trapping her finger inside. I knew it was only the beginning. My muscles went limp as my pussy released its hold on her and shot a line of liquid down my lips, moistening everything. I had no choice but to sink to the floor, landing on my knees next to Claire.

Her eyebrows were fully arched up when I found her gaze and she held a hand in front of her mouth. Her chin glistened with my juices, my wetness dripping from her. "Wow," she said. I could only nod. My flesh was spent. My voice was gone.

I breathed in deeply to regain some kind of composure, to at least regain the power of speech. Grabbing her by the neck, I drew her near and kissed her, my teeth tugging at her lips and my tongue licking my scent off her. My fingers snuck behind her back to unclasp her bra and I pressed her down onto the floor.

"Thanks for the generous tip," I said, finally laying eyes on her breasts. Her nipples peaked hard, denting the air. I couldn't wait to taste them, but I needed to get her skirt off her first. I traced my fingers over her collarbone, in between her breasts, along her belly and down to the side zipper of her skirt.

Her chest rose and fell rapidly with the increasing rhythm of her breaths. I zipped her out and she lifted her bottom to help me guide it off her legs. I wanted to feast on the smoothness of them for hours, but my office was hardly the place for that. I tugged her panties off next. They were black and soft and skimpy and I had to keep myself from pressing my nose into them and inhaling her most secret scent.

For ease of movement, I slipped out of my own skirt before settling down next to her on the floor. She lay next to me completely naked, and, as gorgeous as her body was—just as soft and sexy as I had imagined it—it was her face that got to me the most. The look in her eyes as the back of my hand made its way to the swell of her breasts. The way the corners of her mouth tugged upwards as I caught a nipple between two fingers. The rosy blush on her cheeks and the bliss spreading across her face as I shot her a smile. It dawned on me that I hadn't been the only one fantasizing about this. Claire came across a little too eager for this to have come completely out of the blue.

I wanted nothing more than to make her come as hard as she had made me. While nuzzling my lips against her neck, I pinched her nipple between my fingers again.

"Aah," she moaned, and the sound of her voice sent a fresh shiver of delight up my spine.

I licked my way to her lips and kissed her, trapping her moans in my mouth. As much as I wanted my lips to stay locked on hers for a long time, I needed a taste of her nipples. I hoisted myself up on one elbow and pecked my way down to her collarbone. I stopped to worship the hollow of her neck, the only body part I'd been able to gawk at freely for hours until now. Catching her breast in my hand, I lifted the tip to my mouth and sucked her nipple between my lips. This time her groan couldn't be heard over my own. I squeezed the flesh of her breast between my fingers while suckling on her nipple. Her skin was soft, inviting and intoxicating.

"Please," she said, as she gently pushed my head down.

I understood. I nipped at the hard pink bud of her nipple one last time and headed south. Her bush was neatly trimmed, allowing her clit to peak through the apex of her pussy lips. Crawling over one of her legs, I kneeled between her thighs. I marveled at the sight in front of me. Puffed up pussy lips glistening with wetness. At last, I thought, as I leaned in and kissed her there.

Her scent was heady and I felt my clit throb as I traced my tongue along her slit. I dug my hands under her behind and clenched my nails into her flesh, pushing her closer to me. When I probed the tip of my tongue into her opening the first time, she let out another sigh, her pelvis bucking up to meet me. The time for teasing had passed.

My lips latched onto her clit, sucking it into my mouth.

"Oh god," she said as her fingers found my hair, her nails digging into my skull. "Oh yes."

I flicked my tongue over her clit a few times before releasing it from my mouth. She responded by shoving my head deeper between her lips.

"Don't stop," she hissed, and I had no intention of stopping. I sucked as much of her lips into my mouth as I could before trailing my tongue from the bottom of her pussy all the way up and launching a frenzy of licks on her clit.

Instantly, I felt her muscles tense beneath me. I lapped at her clit, flicking it from left to right, until she came, shuddering, her pussy releasing a jet of juices that I happily swallowed.

"Jesus," she sighed. Her body relaxed and, as happy as making her come had made me, I wanted so much more. I crawled up to her, pouring half of my body over her, my own pussy lips pulsing with need again.

"I don't charge for house calls," I whispered in her ear. "Any chance we can continue this in your bed?"

"Oh yes." She held me tight in her arms, her fingers stroking my neck. "But you need to recommend a new therapist first."

MATCH POINT

Before I even hit the ball, I know it will land in the net again. I've lost my mojo and, glancing at the other side of the court, it's not hard to see why. I used to be the star player of our club, almost effortlessly winning every championship—until Ruby came along. On paper, we're a match. But when we face off on the court, she always wins.

Thank goodness this is not the final, I think as I prepare for my next serve. In my mind's eye, I can already see the ball whizz limply over the net—no spin, no glory. Ruby will cross it with that mean forehand of hers and I won't even feel disappointment. Only awe. And the incessant thumping between my legs.

Ruby joined our club six months ago, amidst a scurry of whispered gossip in the dressing room before games and—alcohol-fuelled and more daring—at the bar afterwards.

"She's renovating the old Slater house all by herself," my friend Sarah, who's always the first to know, told me after we watched Ruby park her black BMW Z4 at the club's parking lot one day. "She moved here from the city after a bad break-up… with another woman."

I'll never forget how my heart seemed to jump all the way to the back of my throat. When Ruby first arrived I was still very much in denial. Now, six months later, it has never been clearer. It crystallised in my mind, in my heart, and in my blood after our first match against each other. I lost that one too, and no one could explain why I missed all those easy balls except me—and maybe Ruby. She held my gaze a bit too long before each serve—the way the pros do it to intimidate their opponent, her light blue eyes sparkling with something so confusing, yet enthralling. My gaze was still fixed on hers when the first ball zipped past my head. I didn't even lift my racket.

I gather my thoughts and tear my eyes away from Ruby's tan skin. I need to win at least a few points to avoid too many questions. Ruby usually gives me a few. She's kind like that. And good with her hands. And she's a lesbian.

Slam. Ruby serves another ace. After this game, we're switching sides and there's a slight possibility our skin may brush together when we cross each other. I've only had sex with women in my head. I want Ruby to be my first.

"What's going on with you?" Ruby is suddenly by the net. "I'm afraid I may hit you in the head if you stay distracted like this." She has the voice of someone who strips whole houses by herself—commanding and gravelly like sandpaper. The way she slings her racket over her shoulder and shifts her weight to one leg, makes my blood go hot. She's so close now, only that wretched net between us. Did she ask me a question?

"Jasmine? Are you all right?" I spot the genuine worry in her eyes and my legs almost go limp.

"I'm sorry. Severe off day, I'm afraid."

She arches up her eyebrows as if to say, "Again?" She looks like a smart woman, a woman who's been around and knows a thing or two about life. She must see it when she looks at me. She must see how my skin glows brighter when she approaches and how my nipples harden when she speaks.

"How about a short break?" She nods as if my reply will automatically be yes. "I'll arrange it with the umpire."

"Sure. Thanks," I stutter.

"Take a seat and drink some water." Her tone is not one that would accept defiance.

Scuttling over to the bench on the side of the court, I watch her explain something to John, our umpire for this match. He shoots me a wink I don't understand and gets out of his chair.

"We have five minutes," Ruby says when she sits down next to me, her bare thigh not even an inch away from mine. "Do you want to talk about it?"

What could I possibly say? My blood picks up speed in my veins. I know she's single. What have I got to lose? But I don't know the protocols of girl-on-girl dating. What if she doesn't want to make a move on someone who's supposedly straight? Why is this all so difficult?

"It's obvious that you throw me off my game." To my surprise, my voice doesn't tremble when I say it. My body knows what it wants and is going for gold. "I've never played this appallingly in my life."

"And here I was thinking I was just that good." Ruby's knee brushes against mine and I relax into the sudden touch, relishing it. Something in the back of my mind tells me this has gone on long enough.

"You're much more than that." I have to swallow, because despite knowing what I want more clearly than ever, all of this doesn't come easily to me.

"Am I?" Ruby's voice sounds raspy now—more sexy as well.

I respond by letting my hand slip from my knee to hers. The throbbing in my clit, which hasn't stopped since we first set foot on the court, intensifies and I find myself digging my nails into her flesh. My cheeks flush and I'm afraid to look at her.

"Ready to resume play, ladies?" John's low voice interrupts

the moment. I lift my hand from Ruby's knee and we both shoot up from the bench.

While finding my eyes, Ruby grazes a finger along my wrist. "After," she whispers and I melt inside.

The short moment of revelation on the bench has freed me. I lose the first few points by a small margin, but by the next game, my confidence is back. It's as if I've drawn a new sort of strength from Ruby's finger on my skin. As if she has infused me with the ever-renewable energy of a born winner.

Shuffling along the court, I only take my eyes off her when they need to be on the ball. It's as if I see her again for the first time, her image all new to me now that something inside of me has changed for good. Because I know there is no way back. It may be too late for me to win this match, but I can get something much greater out of it.

I make her sprint to the net to reach deftly placed drop shots, make her stretch her long arms to reach balls landing on the line with a precision I haven't reached in months.

When we switch sides at the height of the final set—the score unexpectedly tied and my muscles fuelled by a sexual energy quite foreign to me—she blocks my way briefly.

"If you beat me I won't play hard to get," Ruby mutters under her breath, which comes out more strained now that I'm competing like a worthy opponent.

Instantly, her words settle under my skin and play tricks with my mind. Will she make me seduce her if I lose? Do I want her to take the lead or is this my show?

I'm so caught up in questions I lose my service game. If I don't break her serve, I'm done. If I lose, she'll make me fight for her. Maybe that's the only way it can be.

Her first serve is an ace. Instead of pumping her fist, she winks at me from across the court. She tucks a few blond curls behind her ear before preparing for the next one. What does playing hard to get really mean, anyway?

Her next serve lands in the net and I brace myself for an easier return on her second serve. Knowing approximately where it will land, I shuffle to the right a little—my move as much intimidation as strategy.

Surprisingly, she launches her next ball to my left and my backhand falls short. My return doesn't make it over the net.

"Thirty-love," John says. If I lose the next point I'm up against a match point. I'm not sure what else I'll be up against if I lose but it does suddenly become clear that Ruby is a much better strategist than I am, what with whispering that challenge in my ear.

She makes a show of getting ready for her next serve. When she wipes her brow with the back of her hand, her eyes are locked on mine. She's too far away for me to read the details of her expression, but I feel the intensity of her stare. What does Ruby want? Does she want me to win and try to conquer her?

She serves and I see her approach the net for a follow-up volley. I anticipate and hit the ball in the far wide left corner, way out of her reach. I'm still in the game.

"Nice one," she compliments me and I know now that I want to win. I don't want Ruby to play hard to get. I need someone who knows what they're doing to guide me through my first time. I have everything to play for now. I easily return the next few balls, breaking Ruby's serve with a two-point lead.

It's five all in the last and deciding set and I have my groove back.

There's never been a better time, I think to myself, and serve two aces in a row. This time, it's Ruby's turn to look stunned on the court. It's kind of cute when her jaw drops and she bunches her fists in frustration. Something I can work with.

I don't give away any more points, ending the last set seven-five. Not only did I kick Ruby out of her first club championship, but I also won my first match against her.

"Well played," she simply says when we shake hands over the net, but her fingers linger and her nails already dig into my flesh. I can't help but wonder how it would have been had she been victorious.

"Back on form then," John says as he gets out of the umpire's chair. He walks away unassumingly.

Ruby and I stroll to the locker room in silence. I don't know what her quietness is about, but mine is filled with anticipation, nerves, and the relentless throbbing of my pussy lips.

"Let's shower at my place." Her voice is low when she breaks the silence.

When I turn to face her, a whole new sensation takes hold of my body. As if something that's been fast asleep for ages is suddenly awoken. Tension tingles in my stomach and blood rushes to my cheeks. Is this it? Will nothing ever be the same after I say yes?

"Okay." I want to make a joke about the unfinished state of her house, but my throat is swollen with nerves and quipping doesn't seem like the right thing to do.

Ruby's demeanour becomes serious when she packs up her bag and leads me to her Z4. I ignore the fact that I drove my own car to the club and get into the passenger seat.

"Ideally, we should talk first," her voice hums over the roar of the motor. "But that last set came a bit too close to foreplay for me."

Shocked by her sudden directness, my eyebrows hike up when I look at her. I watch her drive for a second. Her hands look confident on the wheel of a sports car. Her tan skin contrasts with the white of her tennis shirt and the natural honey-blond of her short but wavy hair. Ruby looks so healthy and in control—maybe wholesome is a better word. As if, no matter the task in front of her, she'll always know what to do. I revel in the air of capability she exudes. It makes me feel safe and comfortable. And turned-on.

"I've never been with a—"

"I presumed so," Ruby cuts me off, as if she doesn't want to focus on the fact that it's my first time. She takes her eyes off the road for an instant and bores the light blue of them into mine. "It's all I've been thinking about for the last hour or so."

What does that mean? I should ask her. I should start an adult conversation about this. Isn't that what lesbians do? But the words stall in my throat again. Maybe because I don't have the right ones for this. Maybe it's too new and too overwhelming. Maybe it's even too much.

Even though it feels as if we only just left the club, Ruby is already pulling up to the short driveway to her house.

"Are you sure?" she asks before exiting the car.

I may not know how to say it, but I've never been surer of anything in my life. I reply by opening the door, getting out of the car with all the swag my trembling legs can muster, and waiting for her on the driver side.

"I'm sure," I tell her when she stands in front of me.

With a soft thud she closes the car door. "Good." She shoots me a smile that seems to lodge itself somewhere in my chest. "Welcome to Ruby's den of love."

The ball of nerves in my stomach shatters into a million pieces as I genuinely snicker at her words. I follow her inside, not a trace of doubt in my mind.

"Can I get you a celebratory drink?"

At first, I think she's referring—somewhat prematurely—to me losing my lesbian virginity, but I realise just in time she's talking about my win on the court, which I've all but forgotten about. "I don't want a drink." I shake my head and extend my hand. Because, despite not really knowing what I'm doing and being a novice at this, I know what I want and I can't wait any longer. Years of denial and months of longing for Ruby bubble to the surface, glow beneath my skin and burn in my bones. "I want you." My words seem to flow naturally now, as if this is how it was always meant to be.

Ruby bites her lip before pulling me closer. "How about that shower?" Her lips are inches away from my neck.

"Only you," I whisper in her ear as I inhale her scent. She smells musky from playing tennis but also lightly of perfume, something deep and heady that fills my nostrils.

"Come on." She takes my hand—her fingers burning against my skin—and leads me up the stairs to her bedroom. "I don't mean to be impolite." Her smile is crooked because we both know the time for politeness has well and truly passed. "But how old are you, anyway?"

"Thirty-one," I sigh. "You must have heard about the woman of the two failed engagements. This is a small town."

"Hey." She draws me in again. "It's never too late."

"I always thought it just wasn't for me, you know. That I'd end up an old—" She shuts me up by kissing me. Her lips are impossibly soft on mine and nothing like I had imagined. Everything is softness and tenderness. Her fingers crawling up my flesh, her skin glued to mine. The world rocks on its axis when the back of her hand brushes lightly against the side of my breast, but it also—for the very first time—presents itself as so incredibly right.

In a heartbeat, I stand in front of her in just my underwear. I have no idea how my tennis clothes and shoes came off. The only evidence of them is a puddle of white on the floor. At the sight of her hard nipples straining against the fabric of her sports bra, my pussy clenches and I feel a moist heat leaving me from between my legs.

Ruby's breath is ragged when she pulls me toward the bed. She drags me on top of her and my knee slips between her thighs. Her skin is hot. Her lips are everywhere. Her tongue dances in my mouth and then trails along my neck and it would be so easy to get lost in this frenzy of new sensations—

so easy to get lost in her—but I want to remember this night forever. I want to etch it in my memory so that, no matter what happens, I'll always have it.

Her hands are behind my back, looking for the catch of my bra, but I'm wearing the kind that closes in front. I push myself up, fix my eyes on hers, and remove my bra while she watches. It's the single most freeing moment of my life.

Ruby's fingers ride up my stomach, as if drawn magnetically to my naked breasts. She looks beautiful below me, her blue eyes blazing and her hair framing her face, like a lustful angel sent to save me from what I always thought my life would be—devoid of passion and desire like this.

She pinches both my nipples between her fingers and a storm rises up in my flesh. I was engaged twice and had plenty of premarital sex, but, somehow, it feels as if I've never been touched like this. I bend my elbows and let my mouth crash down on Ruby's, her hands still firmly planted on my breasts. I feel her shift beneath me and, before I know it, she has me on my back. Her eyes stare down at me. Her knee presses into my clit, which hasn't stopped pulsing violently since I first met her six months ago. That's a lot of pent-up lust for one person to bear and I realise I'm grinding my pelvis against her leg. I need some sort of release, and fast. I can feel it overtake me, a lust that's been with me forever but is only now finding a way out.

"Please," I beg, because I don't know what else to say.

But Ruby understands me. She sees the desire in my eyes and she can read the want expressed in the lines of my face. She pushes herself up, away from me, and starts peeling off my briefs. Before she touches me again, she removes her own underwear. I revel in the brand new sensation of being completely naked in front of another woman in the intimate setting of a bedroom.

I can't keep my eyes off her breasts. They sit up high and

firm and are tinged with drops of sweat I want to lick off, but I resist the urge and let her take charge.

She drapes herself against my side, her eyes on mine, and traces two fingers over my skin. It almost tickles, but more than that, it takes my breath away. She's barely touching me, but already I'm a panting mess and—in a flash—I realise this is how it was supposed to be all along. I recognise I've wasted years of my life believing I was straight, and the fire that burns inside of me now must be visible in my eyes because I can see Ruby react. A new urgency takes hold of her fingers and they travel down, over my belly, down to my pubic hair and, at last, between my legs. Her eyes don't leave mine and are as much a caress as what her fingers are doing. It's an intimacy I'm not really used to, but I couldn't look away if I tried.

Her fingers glide through the wetness between my legs and circle my entrance. Instinctively, I spread wider and grunt. "Yes," I hear myself mumble.

Ruby narrows her eyes and slips a finger inside. Everything falls away in that second. It's just her eyes on me and her finger inside of me. It's just us and the fire in my belly and the heat of her finger. Slowly, she starts moving and I gasp for air. Ruby's flesh is hot against my flank, our skin slithering together as she pushes deeper inside. Her other hand rests behind my neck and I can feel her nails digging into my shoulders.

She adds another finger, but instead of driving in hard and deep, she retracts and circles her fingers around my aching clit. Her fingers are wet and slippery and they slide over my swollen, aching bud.

"Jesus," I hiss, because I'm already beside myself. She repeats the movements. One second she's deep inside, filling me with delicious thrusts, and the next her fingers skate over my clit. It's a rhythm I won't withstand for long, but Ruby reads me again and lowers the intensity with which she's fucking me.

Her fingers slip and slide, dancing around a sweet spot

inside of me I didn't even know existed. Without her even going near my clit, something builds in the depths beneath my skin.

"What..." I utter and then it's too late. Then it's all red flashes and Ruby's blue eyes and her finger pressing down on my entire body and wave after wave of intense release rolling through me.

Ruby's eyes are wide and her fingers tremble a little bit inside of me. Slowly, she lets them slip out and looks at them in wonder. As if she can't believe what they've just done.

I can't really believe it either, but I'm there and so is she. I pull her on top of me, wanting her entire body weight on me—as if needing to be grounded.

"I'm so happy you're not a sore loser." I bury my lips in her hair, that boyish mane of blond curls, and nip at her ear.

"Oh, I was just being nice." Her breath is heavy in my ears. "You'd best brace yourself for what's to come."

I smell her hair and giggle—I haven't giggled so much in a long time. No matter what comes next, I want it more than anything.

FREEDOM

At first glance, I'm not certain it's Brooke, and, once I am, I'm not sure if it's appropriate to approach her.

She makes the decision for me. "Ella, is that you?"

"In the flesh," I say, a stupid joke going nowhere. I put the book I was thinking of buying back on the shelf.

"How have you been?" Brooke is holding a stack of thrillers. She goes through at least three every week.

"Yeah. Good," I mumble. "You know, adjusting to the single life." Instinctively, I want to inquire about Jamie's health, but it still seems to hurt too much to say her name—even to her own mother.

We stand around in the awkward silence that follows for a few seconds.

"Do you want to grab a coffee next door?" Brooke asks. "Catch up?"

I don't really know what to say. Am I still obligated to be polite to this woman? It's not her fault Jamie swapped me for her new colleague after seven years together. "Maybe it's just the seven-year itch," I had tried to tell her. "Maybe you'll regret this in a few weeks." Six months have passed and I've noticed no signs of regret.

"Sure," I say to Brooke. "Coffee would be good."

"Let me pay for these and I'll meet you at the exit in a few." Brooke says it as if we're simply old acquaintances who've run into each other. As if her daughter never broke my heart.

"Okay." I watch her saunter off in her mink coat and heels that are not suitable for Saturday afternoon shopping. I never really belonged in the Stevens family, anyway. They were always too posh for me.

While I wait for her I make up a dozen excuses in my head why I suddenly have to go, but when she meets me at the door, a tote bag full of books in one hand, gently touching me on the shoulder with the other, I meekly follow her. At least, I know Brooke is smart enough to spare me tales of her daughter's newfound happiness.

At the café next door, she insists on buying the coffees. I glare at her from my seat while she places our order at the counter. All long limbs and no trace of a protruding waistline. Everyone in that family is so skinny. Another reason why I didn't belong.

She places the cups on the small round table between us, sits, and slings one leg over the other.

"Thanks," I mumble, wishing I had some whiskey to pour into my coffee.

"After, uh, it happened, I tried to call you several times, but I understand why you didn't want to speak to me."

It? I remember Brooke's number appearing on the screen of my phone. And how I had to keep myself from picking up and yelling at her for producing such a cruel child, fresh rage still boiling in my blood. "I'm sorry." Inwardly, I scoff at my apology. Does Debby now sit in the chair I occupied at the Stevens' table for Sunday lunch? Do she and Brooke go for coffee together?

"I was so worried about you, Ella. I would have come to see you, but I didn't know where you had moved to and I didn't want to ask Jamie."

"It's fine, really." She has Jamie's eyes—or Jamie has hers, I suppose. Wide and grey-greenish in color with long, long lashes. Long lashes and limbs. And cruel hearts. That about sums up the Stevens.

"It's not. I understand things can happen in a relationship, but Jamie didn't handle it very gracefully." Brooke takes a sip from her latte. Some milk froth clings to her lip. She licks it off gracefully. "And this Debby…" She shakes her head.

My ears perk up. This situation may be awkward, but any negative comments about my replacement will surely make it better.

"She's not like you. You knew how to handle Jamie, were a good influence on her. Two party girls together, I'm sure it can't end well."

Does she mean I'm boring? That Jamie left me for someone far more exciting? Me wanting to stay home more was a constant bone of contention between us. I'm thirty-three years old and I think there's nothing wrong with staying in on a Saturday night to watch five consecutive episodes of Game of Thrones.

"I tried," I say, as the feelings of hurt catch up on me again. "I truly believed our relationship was strong enough to withstand the excitement of meeting someone new, but bam, Debby worked there for barely three weeks before Jamie left me." I briefly look into Brooke's eyes, but even that hurts. As I look away, a tear makes its way out of the corner of my eye. I quickly wipe it away, hoping she didn't see.

"Hey." Brooke leans over the table and cups my hand with her palm. "Did you know I sold the house? I live in a flat ten minutes away from here. Why don't we continue our conversation there? I'll pour you something stronger."

I'm not sure I want to go farther down this road. I just wanted to buy some books this afternoon and order a couple of cases of wine to be delivered to my flat downtown. I had not prepared for reminiscing. But maybe it will help. Maybe Brooke can shine a new light on matters. And perhaps she can say more unflattering things about Debby. I also don't want to cry in the middle of this coffee shop. "Okay." I nod and quickly empty my cup. I hope the contents of Brooke's well-stocked bar have survived her move from the suburbs.

The city sidewalks are crowded, so I walk behind Brooke until the ocean of people clears up and we arrive at one of the posh streets alongside the park.

"The house simply got too big. You've no idea of the amount of maintenance a place like that requires, and just for little old me. I was fed up with it." She gestures at a building a few feet away. "I live there now and I can walk everywhere. It's fabulous."

"I bet," I say, as I follow her inside, past an obsequiously nodding doorman.

Brooke occupies one of the lower floor apartments, but the view of the park is still breathtaking.

"Lovely." I scan the living room and recognize some pieces of furniture from the old house. I'm surprised Jamie didn't talk her mother into getting rid of that sofa, considering what we once did in it. Twice, actually…

"Now, for that drink." Brooke shrugs off her coat and heads to a cabinet in the corner of the living room. "Do you still like a good brandy?"

"Oh yes." I perk up at the mention of it.

She grabs the bottle and two brandy snifters, and deposits them on the coffee table, gesturing for me to take a seat next to her.

After pouring us both a generous amount, she hands me a

glass and clinks the fat belly of her glass to mine. "You look good, Ella, don't let anyone tell you otherwise."

"Thanks." Immediately, a flush burns on the skin of my cheeks. I wasn't expecting a compliment. The brandy helps. Now both my throat and my cheeks burn.

"How are you coping with being alone?" She draws her lips into a lopsided grin. "As you well know, I'm an expert at that particular activity."

I asked Jamie a dozen times, shaking my head in disbelief, why a beautiful, classy woman like her mother would prefer to remain single for so long after her father's death. "She likes her independence," Jamie would say. "And why don't you ask her yourself if you're so keen to find out?" I wouldn't have dreamed of asking that question back then, but now Brooke practically brings it up herself.

"It sucks." My eloquence has let me down a lot since the break-up. "I mean, I'm not very good at it. How do you, um, go about it?"

"Jamie may have been foolish enough to let you go, but you won't be alone for long, Ella. I'm sure of that." She brings her lips to the glass and sips. "As for me, I just can't seem to find anyone to my taste. Let's just say some of my preferences have changed since Gareth and I got married." She locks her eyes on mine and drags the tip of her tongue across her teeth.

I drink to recover from the sudden intensity surrounding us, from the change of air. What am I doing here, anyway? I look away and my eyes land on a picture of Jamie, all blond and healthy and beautiful. Brooke's hair is blond as well, but more golden and quite probably dyed.

"I should go," I say, suddenly overwhelmed by an alien emotion. I can't identify it as grief or anger—the two main ones I've been suffering from of late. It's more a mixture of apprehension and the rush of being flattered by a member of the Stevens family. I don't get up, though. I remain firmly planted in my seat.

"Stay." Brooke reaches for the bottle and refills my glass, which isn't even empty yet. "I've just remembered something... funny, I guess."

I arch up my eyebrows.

"Remember when we went to the coast a few years ago? The summer of 2010, I think it was."

I nod. "Yeah." We'd stayed in a small house by the beach and all had to share the same bathroom. It was the only time I ever saw Brooke in pajamas and without makeup.

"I overheard a conversation you and Jamie were having on the front porch. I wasn't eavesdropping, I just happened to walk past you girls."

She has my full attention. Somewhere, in the back of my mind, I have an inkling of where this is going, but it hasn't fully registered yet. But maybe I'm wrong.

"You said something like 'I'd do your mother in a heartbeat. She's smoking hot for her age.'"

For an instant, my jaw slackens and my brain stops working. I narrow my eyes and lock my gaze on Brooke's. "I didn't mean to be disrespectful. I was just trying to wind Jamie up."

"I took it as a compliment." A small smile plays on her lips again. "I've always liked you, but ever since then, I've liked you a little more." The skin around her eyes crinkles as her mouth breaks into a wide smile.

If I had to hold up my hand and swear on a bible, I wouldn't be able to claim the thought never crossed my mind without perjuring myself.

"I'm sorry, but I don't quite know what to say to that." I may have said those words—years ago—but she invited me into her home, poured me brandy, and brought them up.

"What's your stance on the subject these days?"

Can't say I saw that one coming. "Seriously?" The brandy is

starting to go to my head, and I've been played by members of the Stevens' clan long enough to know how to play along.

She sips and nods.

"I stand by my words." I say it with much more bravado than I feel.

"Mmm." She scrunches her lips into a semi-pout, her eyes drawn into slits. "I can only admire that. I'm not getting any younger."

Is she fishing for more compliments? Or is she after something else? Either way, Brooke has barely changed since I first met her about seven years ago. I can't remember her exact age, but I'm guessing late fifties, or perhaps sixty already. She looks at least ten years younger. Because of the direction this unexpectedly strange conversation has taken, the thought crosses my mind again. I immediately reject it. Fantasies are just that for a reason. "You don't look a day over forty," I say, exaggerating, possibly to make a point.

She chuckles. "I'm sorry for making you feel uncomfortable, Ella." She deposits her empty glass on the coffee table and places a hand on my knee. "All I wanted was to cheer you up. Gosh, you looked so sad an hour ago. At least now I can spot a hint of a smile." She squeezes my knee and shoots me a big grin.

My glance drops from her smile to her hand on my knee. She leaves it there, zapping shots of lightning through my flesh, as if her fingers are electrically charged. I haven't been touched by another woman in a long time. Not that it's an excuse for anything, especially not for the thoughts in my mind getting racier by the second. But am I dreaming this or is she coming on to me?

Despite certain body parts starting to throb violently, I say, "I should probably really go now."

"Why?" She scoots closer to me on the sofa, the leather creaking under her legs, her fingers digging deeper into my flesh. "No longer standing by your words?" The light of the late afternoon sun slanting through the window catches in her eyes. She tilts her head and finds my ear with her mouth. "Here's your chance to… do me." After her lips have touched my earlobe briefly, she continues, "I want you to."

"But, what about—" I protest.

"No." Her voice is suddenly stern, still low and gravelly, but harsher in tone. "Don't go there. This is about you and me."

How can she even say that? How can it ever be just about her and me? The only reason I'm even here is because of her daughter. But I know what she means. She's asking. It's my choice. The phrase "consenting adults" springs to mind. Plus the fact that, because of the dismissive way Jamie treated me in the end, I'm in no way obligated to keep her feelings from getting hurt—I'm not her mother. She certainly didn't seem to care a whole lot about my feelings, when it was her time to choose.

I nod, my breath already catching in my throat. I bring my hands to the back of Brooke's neck and pull her close. I stare into her eyes—Jamie's eyes. Is it a twisted sort of revenge? Unexpected comfort? A few words from years ago catching up with me? It stops mattering as soon as our lips connect. I don't need to know her motivation. The kiss crashes through me and destroys at least a little bit of my pain in the process.

The hand she put on my knee earlier travels upward and every tiny movement of it shudders through my flesh. Her other hand is on my throat, her breath in my mouth, her lips on mine.

"Come on," she whispers when we come up for air. She stands and reaches out her hand. I take it and follow her to the bedroom. A brief interlude during which we could both come to our senses. I don't, and by the time she slams the door of the bedroom shut behind us, I'm glad she, clearly, hasn't either.

From the start, it's evident this can only be a one-night-stand, but far from a frivolous, playful one. Strings are already attached. Strings that can never be undone.

She shifts her weight to one leg and starts to unbutton her blouse. In response, I pull my top over my head. In a flash, she comes for me, and I see the need in her eyes. She cups my jaw in her palms before kissing me again. Softly at first, tiny nips at my bottom lip, but soon her tongue darts into my mouth and I start to lose myself again.

I curve my arms behind her back to find the clasp of her bra. Her hands go in search of mine, but my bra closes in the front, so I push myself away gently and show her by undoing one hook. She cocks her head, as if to say, "I think I can manage," and swats my hands away. Slowly, she frees my breasts, my nipples already hard as pebbles, ready for her.

I reach for the button of her pants next, lowering her zip in a frenzy. After stepping out of them, she unbuttons my jeans and pushes them down over my hips.

When she pulls me back in for a kiss, our breasts touch, and we both catch our breath simultaneously. She drags me with her as she walks backward to the bed and crashes down on it, pulling me on top of her. I let my lips wander to the hollow of her neck, her collarbones. I have to taste her nipples. She has her hands in my hair and I could swear she's pushing me down, coaxing me to explore her body.

My lips find her nipple, hard and the darkest of pink. I cup her breast in my hand and suck her nipple between my lips.

She moans and I suck harder while my other hand finds her other breast. How long has it been since Brooke has been touched? I roll her nipple between my thumb and index finger, and the guttural cry that she utters above my head indicates it may have been a while, but I have no way of knowing and I certainly don't intend to ask.

I feel her hands on my ears and she hoists me up, pressing her lips to my mouth, her tongue dancing with mine. When we break free and I look into her eyes, the desire pooling in them lights a fire under my skin. This time, when my mouth travels down the same path it did before, my hand goes lower, first tracing the waistband of her panties, but soon finding the soaked panel between her legs. Maybe she's been thinking about this since the day she overheard me say she was hot.

My lips clamp down on her nipple again, I let one finger slip under the panel of her panties, more probing than touching.

"Jesus, Ella," a voice above my head says. I barely recognize it.

I push myself up and lock my eyes on hers while yanking down her panties. Brooke Stevens lies completely naked in front of me, her legs already spread, ready for me to take her.

I was only going to buy a book this afternoon. Instead, I ended up here.

I lie down next to her and place a hand on her stomach. Her skin shivers under my touch as I draw a circle around her belly button. I kiss her neck and let my finger go down, slowly, stopping briefly just above her clit.

Brooke has one hand curved under my neck, her fingers on my shoulders, her nails digging deep.

I dip lower, circling her clit, before spreading her pussy lips wide with two fingers. Her hips are already bucking up against me, her head thrown back in the pillows. As slowly as I can muster, I let one finger slip inside of her. Then another. I fuck her gently, controlled, increasing my speed with small increments. When she starts meeting my strokes with thrusts of her pelvis, I push my torso away from her and bend over. The first flick of my tongue against her clit is just a warning shot. Then I get serious. I launch an assault of licks while my fingers drive down deep inside of her.

With her long limbs, she can easily grab a fistful of my hair in her hands. She pulls it roughly, as if losing the last scrap of self-control.

A loud sigh, followed by a moan, precedes an instant in which her body goes rigid. She yanks at my hair so forcefully it hurts, but I take it easily, because I can feel the walls of her pussy clamp around my fingers as she bucks up higher.

She puffs out a large breath of air as her body relaxes onto the covers. After I let my fingers slide from her I quickly push myself up, eager to read her face. But Brooke's face is entirely covered by her hands and I don't know what to think. I can hardly start feeling guilty now, though.

"Jesus," she says, the sound muffled by her hands.

"Are you all right?" I ask when she peeks at me through her fingers.

"I have no idea." She lets her hands drop down, one of them landing on her chest, the other on my shoulder. "But that was..." Her lips crack into a wide smile, lighting up her face. She narrows her eyes and shuffles around until she's on her side, watching me, elbow bent, her head resting in the palm of her hand.

"Insane?" I offer. "Disturbing perhaps? Or maybe just a little twisted?"

She brings a finger to my lips and presses down. "Shh." Her finger trails down along my chin, in a straight line, until it's just above my breasts. "We're not done yet." Her finger wanders in between my breasts, tracing a line underneath each of them. "And I was going to say wonderful, by the way." She tilts her body until half of it covers mine, her nose buried in my hair.

My skin breaks out in goosebumps as she hitches her body on top of me, her knees spreading my legs in the process. She plants her hands on either side of my head and looks down at me, not saying anything, sinking her teeth into her bottom lip. Then, she bends at the waist, briefly kisses my nipples, before going for the prize.

Brooke Stevens, I think, when her mouth connects with my clit, is about to go down on me. And then she does. The tip of her tongue trails across my pulsing pussy lips, before she sucks my clit into her mouth. I'm so wet I can feel it trickle along my inner thighs, all the way onto her duvet cover.

And, if I ever dreamed of taking things this far, it was only furtively, in unguarded moments just before sleeping or waking, and never with the intention of turning it into reality. But here I am. Legs spread. Brooke's blond head moving between my thighs, her tongue lapping at my most intimate parts. If I close my eyes it may just as easily be Jamie down there, so I keep them open. I take in my surroundings. This is a new place. A new life. A different person. Both her and me.

I don't say any of the things I used to say to Jamie in the bedroom. I don't need to, anyway. I've already got Brooke where I want her: her lips locked on my clit, her tongue twirling around. What happens next is as much physical as it's emotional. The juices that flow from between my legs, coating Brooke's chin and lips, free me from more than the sexual tension that has built up over the course of this afternoon. When my muscles tremble beneath the touch of Brooke's tongue, and the first climax in years not administered by Jamie or myself rushes through me, I burst into tears. The tears are not for Jamie. They're for me. For the joy of this moment. For Brooke's lips on my clit and the way she looks at me when she comes up for air, her face flanked by my thighs, her green eyes sparkling.

And I know all too well this is not the beginning of romance. Only freedom.

ONE-ON-ONE

"Kris, with a 'k'," she told me when I introduced myself three weeks ago before class. "Everyone always assumes it starts with a 'c'. It doesn't." I had wanted to look away, laugh it off, but a sudden seriousness had taken hold of me and I couldn't stop staring into the green of her eyes.

She'd left me distracted throughout the hour of Body Balance I teach, making my muscles tremble inexplicably while demonstrating exercises I do every day. Since then she's attended my classes at least three times a week, not that I've been counting. The tremor in my hamstrings has subsided—it never takes me long to regain control over body parts that can be trained—but a dull ache tucked deep behind my stomach has remained.

"Everyone," I address today's group, "move a little closer to the front. I get lonely up here." I search for Kris's eyes, but she's still focused on the screen of her mobile. "And let's switch off those phones, shall we? Time to disconnect."

I keep my gaze on her and revel in the apologetic look she sends me. I shoot her a small smile and nod. I run through the warm-up without even glancing at her—a new personal record.

"I'm going to show you something new today." My heart vibrates in my chest. I've waited for this moment. "Can I have a volunteer, please?" I ignore Celia's outstretched arm on my right. "Kris? How about you?"

Kris arches up her eyebrows. It's hard to say whether that's a twinkle of amusement dancing in her eyes, or just plain annoyance. I decide to go with the former.

"Come on. Don't be shy." I somehow manage to keep some authority in my voice. "I need a regular with a strong back."

She inches forward and my pulse quickens. Will she feel the heat radiating from my skin?

"What makes you think I have a strong back?" Kris says quietly as she approaches.

I can hardly say I've been studying her shape with keen interest. "It's my job to notice." She's so close my throat tightens and the words come out thin and high-pitched. I cough to cover my growing desire. I should have prepared for this better, but I had no way of knowing that inhaling her faint floral scent would throw me so off guard. "Lie down on your back, please." I scan the studio to remind myself there are other people around. Maybe this wasn't such a good idea, after all.

Kris does as asked and stretches out on the yoga mat in front of me. I kneel next to her, hoping she won't hear the foolish thudding beneath my ribcage.

"Bend your knees." As she complies, she shifts her body on the mat and her tank top rides up over her belly, exposing a sliver of skin. To distract myself, I grab her ankles and push them in a bit more. A mistake. The touch of her flesh sends a shiver up my spine.

"Hands by your sides." My voice lets me down again, sounding pinched and desperate. I refrain from touching her again. "Now push your pelvis up." Kris's tank top slides down as her lower body angles up. Her abs are not pronounced but her belly looks the right kind of soft and flat. Maybe I'm in the wrong business, but I prefer a smooth layer of flesh over hard muscles any day of the week.

"Make sure you don't over-arch your back." I bring a hand underneath Kris's body and gently glue it to her skin for support. My other hand hovers over her stomach, hesitant to make contact. "This." I glide my hand through the air, a mere inch away from Kris's skin, travelling from her thrust-up pelvis to just underneath her breasts. "Has to be a straight line."

"I can't hold this much longer." Kris lowers her back onto my hand. My fingers want to dig into her flesh.

"I've got you." I find her eyes and push her down gently. Her belly is caught between my hands, descending towards the mat, and I'm about to forget I'm in the middle of a class when my fingers hit the ridged surface of the mat.

I refocus on the group. "All right, everyone. Lie down. Let's try this." My hand is still trapped underneath Kris's back and I want nothing more than to keep it there. I rely on my best poker face to not display any of the turmoil crashing through me.

Kris scrambles up and with the breaking of contact between our skin, I snap out of the moment and help her get up. "Thanks," I mumble and, while she patters back to her mat, I wonder why I did this to myself.

Every time I try to look at Kris throughout the rest of the class, I feel my face flush. I scold myself for my childish, unprofessional behavior. I touched her and now what? More feverish dreams laced with increasing guilt? At least she doesn't know, or if she does, she has enough courtesy not to show it.

During the five-minute relaxation at the end of the class, I dim the lights and survey the studio. I know that for most people attending, this is the best moment of the entire class, but for me, it's the worst. All is quiet around us except for the low hum of deep breathing. They all have their eyes closed, emptying their minds for a few precious instants. As for me, I sit up, and I can't keep my gaze off Kris. My body is far removed from a relaxed state. My brain works overtime, alternately coming up with new strategies to get closer to her and ways to absolve myself for feeling this way. It fails on both counts.

"Give yourself a round of applause." I clap my hands together. "Good job, guys." I watch how Kris exits the studio while chatting to one of her classmates. As usual, Celia hangs around the studio until I've gathered my belongings and am ready to leave. I shoot her an obligatory smile.

"See you tomorrow, Lucy. For another round." Her face is drawn into a hopeful smirk.

"Well done, as always." I give her a quick pat on the back and scuttle past her, out of the door. My senses are frayed, my nerves brittle. I need to get out of this gym, or maybe attend one of my colleagues' Body Combat classes to punch this madness out of me.

"Lucy." Goosebumps prickle up along the skin of my arms at the sound of her voice. Kris sits on one of the low benches in the lounge area, a half-empty bottle of water on the table in front of her.

"Hey." I shuffle my weight from one foot to the other, not quite sure what to say or do.

"Can I ask you something?" She scoots over on the bench.

Is she making room for me? Do I need to be seated to answer this question?

"Sure." I sit down next to her. Instantly, I feel my blood pump in my veins. It's been like this since that time she told me her name.

She twirls the bottle of water around between her fingers, as if deciding on the best way to start this conversation. "Are you available for personal training?" She fixes her eyes on me. "One-on-one, I mean."

My heart flutters, skipping a beat. My throat goes dry. This wasn't what I was expecting. "Not through this gym." I hear myself say. "Though I am available for private sessions."

"Sounds good." Her gaze is still on me. "After you called me to the front today, I concluded I might benefit from some one-on-one training."

"What would you like to focus on?" My legs are trembling beneath the table, my muscles letting me down again.

"It would be really great if I could have arms like yours." She giggles and stabs me in the biceps with her elbow.

I have no idea how not to blush. I don't know what to say. Usually, I have this sort of small talk down to a tee. It's how I make a living. I should follow up with an obvious compliment, but no sound comes out of my mouth. I rise from my seat and look at her.

"Follow me." I try to convince myself I'm not reading this situation wrong. My mind is cluttered with images of Kris pressing up from cobra into downward facing dog. Of my hand floating over her belly, almost touching, but not quite. Of the green of her eyes and how it seemed to shine a little brighter when she said "one-on-one".

I walk her back into the gym, past the area hosting all the cardio equipment, into a small cubicle reserved for personal training sessions. Technically, I don't have access to these rooms because I only teach group classes at this gym. I shut the door behind us. It has no lock.

"How about a taste right now?" I scan Kris's face. My actions could be interpreted either way, though the clipped, tortured tone of my voice, and the way my nipples poke hard against the Lycra of my top, must be a dead giveaway.

Her lips quirk up into a smile. She brings her hands to her sides, as if contemplating the implications of what she's about to say. I've seen enough, though. Or maybe I just think I've seen enough and I'm blinded by the lust blasting through my veins and the desire for her that settled in my bones the day we met.

"Show me," she says. Small laughter lines bracket her eyes and, at last, there is no more room for misinterpretation.

"Lie down on your back." I point at the mat taking up almost the entire surface of the floor. "Just like you did in class." I wait for her to stretch out before crouching beside her.

"I'll show you the difference between a group class and a personal training session." This time, my hand lands on her belly without qualms. "Bend your knees." I repeat the same words as in class earlier, when a dozen glares were pointed at us and my actions were still tinted by uncertainty and doubt.

I pry a hand under her back and lift her off the mat. "Push up." Her back muscles tremble against my fingers. I lock my eyes on hers. Her face is fixed in a focused expression, lips slightly parted and eyes narrowed to thin slits. I keep my left hand under her back for support, but my right one travels from her belly to the waistband of her yoga pants.

"And down." She drops her back onto my hand.

I sink my nails into her muscles while my other hand skims a little lower. "Up again." As she thrusts her pelvis up, my fingers glide between her legs. The heat radiating through her pants almost makes me lose my grip on her back.

A short moan escapes from her throat. With her pelvis still suspended in the air, I let my fingers trail over the hot fabric of her pants.

"Down." I need to use all the strength I have in my left arm to not let her backside crash to the floor. Her breathing becomes more ragged. My fingers slip under the waistband and into her pants.

"Up." She digs her heels into the mat and drives herself up—making it only half as high as before. My hand wanders further until my fingers meet her bush. I suppress the urge to tug down her pants and bury myself between her legs. My own clit is a throbbing mess, blood racing thickly through my veins, leaving my skin flushed. My fingers drift deeper still, until they encounter the wet heat of her cunt.

"I can't hold..." Her back collapses onto my hand. I flex my biceps and catch her falling down. I remove my hand from under her and use it to hoist up her top. I am now free to ogle the smooth plain of her belly without apprehension.

The fingers of my other hand circle around her clit, but the angle of my arm disappearing into her pants is wrong, limiting my access. I search for her eyes, still wanting to ask for some sort of permission. It's no longer necessary. Kris's hands tug at her pants, shoving them down, off of her. I retract my hand and help her, exposing her to me.

The usual clatter of gym noise filters through the thin walls of the cubicle. I should have checked the schedule. Someone could burst in at any time, but I'm too far gone to worry about that now.

On my knees, I shuffle from Kris's side to between her legs. I remove her pants and underwear completely and look down at her. Three weeks of pent-up lust crackle through me. I lean in and sweep my tongue over her puffed-up pussy lips. As soon as I make contact, her hands are in my hair, her nails digging into my skull.

I lick her up and down, fully aware of the pulsing between my own legs, but this is no time to be selfish. My tongue encircles her clit. I can't distinguish my own groans from hers. I pull back briefly to gorge on the sight of her slick cunt as it takes two of my fingers. First, they explore, but then they dig deep, juices gathering in my palm. Her breathing grows heavier. Her grip on my hair intensifies. I start to lick her again while my fingers continue to thrust inside of her.

"Oh, Lucy." Her voice is so full of everything I want to hear. Desire. Satisfaction. Pure need.

I fuck her harder, going deep, while my tongue flicks over her clit. Until her moans stifle and her body flexes tight, all her muscles contracting at the same time, all her strength gathering in her cunt.

She releases with a lengthened sigh, loosening her hold on my hair. “Damn,” she giggles, tiny bursts of laughter slipping from her mouth. “You showed me all right.”

I wipe my mouth with the back of my hand and hoist myself up. I allow myself to lie down beside her on the yoga mat for a brief moment, ignoring the want strumming beneath my skin. “I take payment in kind.”

“Good.” She draws her lips into a wide smile. “I probably couldn't afford you otherwise.”

I press my lips to her cheekbone. “Let's get out of here before I lose my job.”

A MATTER OF INCLINATION

I look out for her on the twenty-fourth of December every year. It has become our unspoken, informally agreed upon annual appointment. When we first met fifteen years ago, Amelia O'Brien's hair came to her shoulders, and she walked along the shoreline with two toddlers at her feet. So much has changed since then.

This year, she's late. For the first time in my life, I spend Christmas day alone. I had to stop Charles from flying down, what with it being only my second holiday season since Bill passed away so suddenly just after we returned from Seal Rocks at the beginning of last year. I had expected Amelia to be here—and I didn't want Charles to miss out on the busiest day of the year at the beach club he works at in Melbourne during his summer break.

Amelia and I exchange the occasional e-mail over the year, and that's how I know she has finally divorced Ralph. From what I've witnessed, it's been a long time coming. I never told her about that time he made a pass at me when we were alone on the beach one night, and about how I would surely have reciprocated if it had been her propositioning me. I've never told anyone any of that.

I guess we are seasonal friends more than anything, but over the course of fifteen summers by the beach, I have told Amelia much more about myself than I've told my 'everyday' friends back home. There's one thing she doesn't know, though. The thing I had hoped to perhaps address this summer.

Her eldest daughter Phoebe is spending the summer—winter there—in Barcelona, I know that much. I have no idea if Katy will be joining Amelia this year. In fact, it's beginning to look as though no one will show up at all. But I have it in writing. At the bottom of Amelia's last e-mail, sent a few weeks ago: 'See you on the beach this summer.' The stretch of beach connecting our houses has been mightily empty so far. I've had too much time to envision worst-case scenarios and I've concluded that the most disappointing outcome for me personally would be if Amelia showed up with a rebound lover.

"Is it too soon to set you up with someone new, Mum?" Charles asked me a few months ago. "You're obviously way too young to spend the rest of your life alone. I think Dad would have wanted you to be happy more than anything."

It was a very unsettling question. One I waved off immediately. As far as I'm concerned, Bill is and was the only man for me. We had a happy marriage. One that didn't leave a lot of room for questioning certain things, like that giddiness that descended on me every summer when we undertook the long drive over here. For fifteen years, I was able to just categorize it as a mere enjoyable sensation. It's not as though Amelia and I ever engaged in any flirtatious behaviour, or that even the slightest of hints has ever passed between us. I've just always found her fiercely attractive, but more in an admiring way than in a sexual one.

Until after Bill's heart attack.

On Boxing Day, I venture out of the house early for a walk

along the beach—and past Amelia's empty house. But the windows have been thrown open and the breeze rolling off the ocean is playing with the curtains. My heart is in my throat instantly. First, I fear she may have rented out the place to strangers, but—as though she's been waiting for me to walk past—the next instant she appears outside the house, her hand shielding her eyes from the sun that is rising in deep, hopeful oranges behind me.

"Merry Christmas," she shouts as I head over to her.

When our bodies meet in a quick but sturdy hug, my heart picks up even more speed. I try to mask my excitement by drawing a few discreet, shallow breaths.

"Katy decided rather last-minute to go horseback riding with Max instead of joining her old Mum at the beach, but I insisted we spend Christmas together, what with Phoebe gallivanting off in Europe. It's all so complicated when they grow up." Amelia is her usual waterfall of words. "I thought it was only supposed to become simpler." She sends me a smile that hits me straight in the gut. Perhaps it's the semi-unexpectedness of seeing her this early in the morning, or all the thoughts about her I've indulged in since I last saw her.

Last summer, everything was still different. It was my first time at the beach house without Bill, and Ralph was still in the picture. This summer—this day to be exact—is the first time I feel free to even have these feelings. To luxuriate in the wave of happiness that washes over me now that I've finally come face-to-face with my friend again.

"How's Charles?" she asks, and I inform her of his academic progress and his job at the St Kilda Beach Club.

"Have you had breakfast?" I ask, guessing that her pantry is probably empty. "I made fresh bread overnight."

She shoots me a seductive smile, of which I know it's not supposed to be seductive, but my brain interprets it that way nevertheless. "You're a lifesaver. I arrived late last night and just fell into bed."

I don't regret not seeing or hearing her arrive. We have weeks here together. At least, I think we do. "How long are you staying?"

"As long as nobody needs me in Sydney. You?"

"Three weeks, until school starts again."

"I would say we should drink to that, but it might be a bit early. Even for a fresh divorcee like myself."

If the divorce from Ralph was painful at all, it hasn't left her with any visible marks of distress. If anything, Amelia has a freed look about her. As though she's turned over a new leaf—one that had been stuck for a very long time.

"I know he cheats," she said to me a few summers ago. "And I don't sleep with a man who fucks other women." The shortest of probing questions has always been enough to instigate a monologue in Amelia. She's the sort who likes to talk—and uses ten words when one will do. "If it weren't for the girls, he'd have been out years ago, but I just… can't do it to them. Not yet. I feel as though I need to protect them just a little while longer."

"That's why mimosas were invented," I say now, and, arm in arm, we walk back to my house.

"I like the way you think, Rachel," she says. "Always have."

"If you haven't had a proper Christmas, we'll have one this afternoon," Amelia says. "I'll drive down to the shops later and prepare us a turkey." She's on her third mimosa—perhaps the divorce has left some scars—so I don't really see that happening.

"Let's just relax. Catch up. I haven't seen you in a year." I don't care about turkey. It's too hot for roasted meat. And sitting on the front porch of my house with Amelia, my gaze flitting from the ocean to her, is all the Christmas celebration I need.

"And what a year it has been." Amelia stretches her arms above her head. "But—silver lining—with the way Ralph carried on, I truly managed to squeeze every last cent out of the divorce settlement. I thought it was time he paid up for the shit he put me through." She shakes her head. "Men." She spits out the word as though it's a foul piece of meat. "How about you, Rachel? Or is it too soon to inquire?"

Again with the 'too soon'. I don't know when 'too soon' or 'appropriate' would be for me to start being interested in another man. "I don't find myself particularly enthralled by men my age."

Amelia lets the back of her head rest on her intertwined fingers. I don't think she's wearing a bra underneath that T-shirt. I have plenty of pictures of her in a bikini and I've seen her with her top off many a time. She can never keep it on when we swim to the small wooden jetty a few hundred feet into the water. "The sun on your nipples, Rachel," she would say. "What is better than that?" After I worked up the courage to lose my bikini top—and making doubly sure no one was around—I quickly learned to agree.

Amelia quirks up her eyebrows. "Oh really? Looking for a toy boy, are we?" Her hair is short in the back these days, with a fringe that falls over her eyes at times.

I blush. I can't help it. I can see how my comment might have been misinterpreted. "That's not what—" I start, but she cuts me off.

"I've considered it myself." She sits up and lets her hands drop onto the armrests. "A good fuck by a young, ultra-virile man who still has enough testosterone flowing in his veins... if you know what I mean? Not that Ralph ever had a problem with that, I assume. I just didn't want him near me for that."

She peers into the ocean. "But really, who needs that sort of hassle at our age?"

I know better than to reply this time. This is an Amelia monologue moment.

"All I'm saying is that it's been a very long time since I've been touched by anyone but myself." She locks her gaze on me. "Have you?" She makes a sideways gesture with her head. "Since Bill?"

I refill our glasses. Little did I know that our first conversation this summer would take a turn like this.

"No," I say, after having taken a good sip.

"Do you want to?" Something glitters in her eyes.

My earlier blush hasn't properly receded yet before I'm hit with another heatwave on my cheeks. "W—what, erm, do you..."

"There are websites for that, you know? We could get some studs out here. It's probably not cheap, but Ralph's money has to be good for something."

My stomach drops. There's no viable reason why Amelia would have the same thoughts as I.

"I'm just kidding, Rachel. I know you're not the type." She slaps the table with her fingertips. "And I would never stoop to Ralph's level and pay someone to have sex with me."

"He did, erm, that?" I still haven't recovered. The images in my head are too vivid. It doesn't help that Amelia is sitting across from me with no bra, her breasts bouncing a little when she laughs.

"I don't really know. But it wouldn't surprise me." She shrugs. "Anyway, new rule!" She takes her refilled glass off the table. "Let's not speak the bastard's name anymore." She holds her glass out for a toast and we clink rims. "At first, I wasn't sure I wanted the beach house. For starters, God knows who he brought here? But I have so many good memories here. Witnessing the change in the girls every summer. And if I let go of the house I wouldn't see you anymore, Rachel."

I think my neck is blushing now too, as well as my forehead and my ears. Amelia pins her grey-blue gaze on me.

"Are you okay? You look a bit flushed. Is it the alcohol?"

"Must be," I mumble. I know at that moment I will never be able to tell her. Some secrets are better kept buried. Doesn't mean I can't enjoy her company. The meals we will share. The wine we'll drink as the sun sets on the horizon. The tales we will tell about our children and what happened in our lives over the past eleven months. How is it even possible to have a crush on someone I only see for three weeks every year? A woman, no less. It's madness. I could never get those words over my lips.

"Here." Amelia hands me a glass of water. Our fingertips brush against each other briefly and I feel as though my ears may catch fire, burn to ashes and fall off my head. "I'll make us some coffee, shall I?"

She ventures inside my house. She probably knows it as well as I do. It's strange to be so well-acquainted with someone I don't see very often. I'm glad for the moment's respite of her presence. I steady my gaze on the ocean and draw air between my lips in rapid gusts. I hope it's not going to be like this for the next three weeks: me unable to control myself.

The next day we meet on the beach after breakfast. It's silly to each keep a house, I think, as I wander over to our meeting spot. But perhaps our children would disagree.

"I can't contain myself any longer." Amelia is wearing an earth-coloured bikini. "I need to swim to the jetty."

In the fantasy I visited before falling asleep last night, it was the first thing we did as well. I nod.

We drop our towels on the beach, slip out of our flip-flops and tip-toe to the edge of the ocean. At least in the water my cheeks won't turn as red, and if they do, I can blame the strain of swimming the few hundred feet into the sea.

Amelia is a few years older than me, but her limbs are longer, and she has more purchase on the waves. Still, when you've swum in the ocean all your life, you don't forget how to move in it, and I reach the jetty only a few minutes after her. Her hands are already crossed behind her back. I can't keep my eyes off her when she drops her bikini top and stretches it out to dry next to her. She leans back and lies down, her breasts exposed to the sun—and me.

"Aaah. I've only waited all year for this moment." Amelia has closed her eyes, leaving me with ample opportunity to stare, but I avert my gaze. The view is too much. Like being offered something on a silver platter only to have it taken away again just as you're reaching for it—over and over again.

I sit down next to her. Spin my head from left to right a few times to see if no one is around, but if this place is known for one thing, it's privacy. I live thirty miles from Melbourne. If Bill and I had just wanted the ocean, we could have bought a summer house on that coast. But Seal Rocks is different. It's drenched in the most beautiful solitude I've ever encountered. Blue skies, strong surf, white beaches, and no one around.

Assured that we're alone, I bring my hands behind my back and unclasp my top. The sensation of the hot sun on my wet nipples hits me much harder than previous summers. A throbbing ignites between my legs—I'll need some private time later. I stretch out next to Amelia and look up into the blue sky. I wish I had one of those drones so that I could take a picture of us lying side by side, chests bare. It's easy enough to imagine, however. I pretend I take flight and my gaze is trained on the jetty. Amelia's face is blissfully calm. Mine is also—that's how I know I'm just pretending.

I didn't get a lot of sleep last night, what with alternative versions of Amelia's arrival assaulting my mind, but then I do find a sense of calm. The sun dries my skin as my eyelids stop fluttering and I feel myself drift off into a light, sun-soaked, summer nap.

"Rachel." Amelia's voice reaches my ear, but I don't want to open my eyes because her fingertips brush against my arm and my skin seems to break out in goosebumps despite the increasing temperature. When her fingertips tap against my side a moment later my eyes fly open nonetheless. "If we stay here too long we'll be red as lobsters later."

I stare into Amelia's eyes. She's sitting up, watching me. I have to swallow a lump down my throat. Instinctively—perhaps still drowsy from my nap—my fingers curl around her wrist. Her gaze flits from my face to her arm, then back. The sun may have dried my bikini bottoms, but I'm sure they're wetter now than when I pulled myself out of the sea onto the deck of the jetty.

"I'm sorry." I chicken out and let go of her wrist. "I'm just glad we're here together."

It's as though I can feel Amelia's eyes on my breasts. My nipples stiffen under her gaze.

"I can tell," she says, then just smiles and pushes herself up. I take in her long shapely legs as she bends over to pick up her top. She throws me mine in the process. She has no idea—and I have no idea what to do with myself.

"Yours or mine?" Amelia asks after we've made it back to shore.

"I, uh, just need a little time. A bit of an upset tummy, I think," I stammer and start in the direction of my house.

"Do you need anything? I have tablets for that," she shouts after me, because I had to take a few long strides away from her.

"I'm fine." I briefly turn my head. "I'll see you later."

When I reach my house I stand under the ceiling fan for a long moment. It must be menopause, I decide there and then. These hot flushes. These inappropriate feelings for my friend. After all, I've never felt anything of the sort for any other woman. Or perhaps it's sunstroke. I can't believe I grabbed her wrist, can't believe I lost control like that. I'll need a better excuse than just being happy to see her. Or maybe Amelia will just forget about it. She's the type who would.

I resist the urge to go into my bedroom, peel off my bikini and pleasure myself. It seems too crass. As if I were reducing Amelia to someone I fantasize about during masturbation. Not that I'm not guilty of that already. But the moment isn't right. I need to find the strength to see her later, and every day after that.

Besides, this irrational crush—but aren't most silly infatuations devoid of logic?—isn't just a physical thing. It's something that's been building inside of me for years, and suddenly I think that in my life I've only had eyes for one man and one woman. I'm that type of person, I guess.

"I was worried about you, Rach," Amelia says when I finally dare to venture to her house a few hours later. She's preparing lunch. "Want some?" She points at the avocados she's slicing. "Or will your stomach not agree?"

I'm actually starving, but I'm not sure I should admit to that. "Maybe I'll try a little."

"I'll fix us both a plate. Why don't you take a seat in the shade?"

As if she was expecting me, the table is set with two sets of cutlery and two wine glasses. A bottle of rosé chills in an ice bucket on a stand next to the table. I pour us both a generous portion.

"You've found the wine," Amelia says with a smile as she comes out of the kitchen. "Good."

We eat in silence, which is strange. Not for me, but for Amelia, who is never at a loss for words.

"We've known each other for a long time, Rachel." Amelia deposits her knife and fork on her plate, indicating she's done with her meal. "But in all that time, I've never known you to be so... I guess skittish is the right word." She leans back in her chair.

I haven't finished my salad yet, but my stomach is instantly closed for business.

"It's as if you can no longer fully relax around me." Her bikini top shines through the flimsy T-shirt she's wearing. It only reminds me of what lies beneath. Of what I've seen. "Tell me honestly... is it because Ralph hit on you and you don't know how to tell me, but you feel like you should now that we're divorced?"

"You know about that?" For a minute, I consider this a viable excuse for my erratic behaviour around her. Although it won't pardon future occurrences of it.

"Does everyone just assume I was blind when it came to my husband? I have eyes in my head and two ears"—she taps her fingers against her earlobes—"right here."

"I'm sorry." I drink from the chilled wine to counter the flush I already feel creeping up my neck.

"Don't apologize for him, Rachel."

"I didn't give him even the slightest of leeway. Perhaps I should have told—"

"Stop!" She holds up her hands, palms out. "I know I brought it up, but I meant what I said. Let's not waste another word on that bastard. He'll always be the father of my children, but that's where it ends for me for the rest of my life. No more talk of bloody Ralph O'Brien."

"Okay." I hold the belly of my glass against my cheeks. "Gosh, it's hot today."

"It's not that, though, is it, Rachel? That had you speeding to your house earlier?" Amelia doesn't let up.

"What do you mean?" My cheeks must be the same colour as the discarded tomato on my plate.

"You keep on blushing for no reason. Stammering your words. It's... strange. That's not the Rachel I know and love." She grabs her glass. "And before you even contemplate it, you can't run away this time. Just tell me, Rach. It's me."

How can she have me cornered like this? Not that I believed I was doing a stellar job of hiding my feelings. I don't have a lot of experience when it comes to that.

"It's nothing, really. Just having a bit of difficulty adjusting to the new, erm, situation."

"What new situation?" Amelia narrows her eyes to slits. "You mean just the two of us here together?"

"I guess." I really can't say any more. I'm not doing the best job of defending myself, but why do I need to?

"We've spent hours together just the two of us. Walking on the beach. Sunbathing on the jetty. Drinking wine after we put the children to bed. What's so different now?"

"Only everything." I take another sip. My fingers are curled dangerously tight around the stem of my glass. "Bill died. Ralph is out of the picture. Our children are all grown up."

"Well, yes. But I don't see what that has to do with you acting all silly around me. Like we've only just met and you—" She pauses. Her eyes narrow further. I take a few quick sips. My heart is in my throat.

"Do you, huh..." It seems as though I've rendered Amelia O'Brien speechless by not saying much at all.

I put my glass down. I can't stay quiet now. I have to say something. Or at least make it clear that this is not a situation that requires anything from her.

"I'm sorry—" I start.

"Stop apologizing, Rachel. For crying out loud." Amelia sighs. She pushes herself up a bit in her chair, erasing the relaxed position she was in earlier.

"I seem to have developed… feelings for you. I don't know where they've come from or why or how it happened, but they're there, and they're driving me slightly insane."

There, I said it.

Amelia doesn't speak for a long time. All my hopes are stretched out in those seconds of silence. I don't dare look at her anymore. Instead, I cast my gaze to the bench on the edge of the patio. It was Bill's favourite spot in the shade. Is this happening because of him? Because I miss him too much and I need someone else to dump my affections on and Amelia is the only viable candidate?

"Shit, Rach. I wish I knew what to say to that."

I steal a glance at her. "You don't have to say anything."

"My brain is working very hard to process this information." Her words are starting to come quickly again. "How long have you felt this way?"

"Oh God, I don't know." I'm not the most expressive person, but this is too much for me to hold in. "It doesn't matter. I mean, it's fine. I have no expectations. It's just a silly feeling." Fear tightens my stomach. I really shouldn't have eaten any lunch. I wouldn't have if I had known this conversation was going to be our dessert.

"How can you say that when it's obviously much more than that?" Is she scolding me now? For sitting here with my heart on my sleeve?

"I didn't say anything because I don't want anything to change between us." Words as hollow as how I feel inside.

"How could things between us not change when every time I merely glance at you, you freeze like a deer in the headlights?"

"Let's just… ignore it," I blurt out. "Now that I've gotten it off my chest, we can just go back to normal."

"No, we can't. Well, I surely can't. You can pretend all you like, but I can't un-hear what you've just said."

"I'm sorry, Amelia." I push myself out of my chair. "I'm not running, but I need a break from this conversation right now."

"Hey…" She holds out her hand. "If anything, I'm flattered that a woman like you would fall for someone like me."

Am I supposed to grab her hand? And is that supposed to make me feel better? She's flattered? Although, I guess, it's better than offended.

"Come here." She beckons me with her fingers. I touch my thumb against the heel of her hand. The wine seems to have gone to my head, that's how dizzy I suddenly am. "There are not a lot of things a fifteen-year-old friendship can't withstand, Rach. We'll figure it out."

"Yeah." I want to cry. A wall of unshed tears is ready to crumble behind my eyes, as though they've been waiting until I admitted it out loud.

"Go have a lie-down, or whatever it is you want to do, and we'll talk tonight. Okay?"

I want to run away from her but want to stay near her at the same time.

"I need some time to think about this." She gives my fingers a quick squeeze before dropping them from her hand.

"Yeah," I say, again, and make my way back to my house along the shoreline without looking back.

"Knock, knock." Amelia mimics a knocking motion with her fist in the air. "Care for a G&T?" She holds a bottle of gin in her other hand.

It's after nine. I haven't had dinner. A G&T now could give

me the confidence to continue the conversation we aborted earlier. "Sure."

"At your service." Before I can get up, she heads into the kitchen adjoining the deck where I've been sitting since I came back from hers after lunch.

Ten minutes later, she's back with two glasses and a packet of crisps. She hands me a glass, tears open the crisps bag and starts munching on a few straight away. "I missed my supper, but this will do."

I drink from the G&T and flinch. She made it a double, then. Perhaps it's the only way for us to talk about this further. I don't even know where to begin, nor how to explain the turmoil in my heart. I try, anyway. Silence is no longer an option. "I guess I first noticed something that time we walked all the way up to the lighthouse seven years ago. The wind was blasting in our faces all the way up there, and I didn't feel a thing, was light on my legs even, because it was just the two of us that evening, and your company lifted me up somehow."

"Seven years ago?" She knits her brows together.

"It wasn't so much a conscious feeling. Just flashes. And the desire to want to spend as much time with you as possible during the time we were here together." To give my hands something to do, I grab a crisp but don't eat it. "After Bill died, I started seeing those feelings in a different light. As if him no longer being around gave me free rein to properly think about it for the first time."

Amelia pops another crisp into her mouth. She even looks good doing that. The sky is a stunning shade of purple-pink above the ocean behind her. The picture is almost perfect.

"I didn't come here so you could explain, Rach. I don't need you to explain yourself to me. You probably can't even explain it properly..." This is more babbling than I'm used to from Amelia. These are strenuous circumstances for both of us, of course.

"And I just want to make it perfectly clear that I don't expect anything from you."

Amelia scrunches her lips together before speaking, as if she's organising the words in her head first. "I did some research this afternoon. It's not as uncommon as I first believed."

"What isn't?" I need more gin in me pronto.

"Latebians." She says it with an almost shrug. "You know, women who prefer the company of other women later in life. Like you said yesterday. Men our age are so unappealing."

I chuckle, and it feels so good to just have a little laugh. To release some of the tension from my strained muscles.

Amelia goes into monologue mode. As if she's teaching one of my sociology classes in school. "More like a preference that develops after a certain age. And I have to say, the articles I read made some damn good arguments." She makes a tempering motion with her hands. "But, before I get too carried away, let me just say that I'm not sitting here and proclaiming it would be for me. I don't know that. Unless I try, I guess."

My eyes widen. My mouth follows.

"Maybe we should go on a date." She sips from her G&T without taking her eyes off me.

"A d-date?" I stutter.

"Well, it would basically just be a meal together, the way we would usually enjoy each other's company, just with an added… bonus. And perhaps a different outcome."

"Are you serious?" I don't know what to do with myself. This pragmatic approach is not what I had expected at all, but here sits Amelia O'Brien telling me that she's not dismissing my feelings for her.

"Yes. Why not?" She straightens her spine. "It doesn't only have to be a matter of inclination."

Inclination? I never really questioned that. Mostly because I never truly allowed myself to question my feelings for Amelia. I was happily married to my husband for twenty-five years. The matter of inclination never really presented itself.

"Okay." I have to keep myself from nodding vigorously.

"Can breakfast be a date?" she asks, a smile so sexy on her face, I wish the sun would set and rise already.

"Our lives, our rules," I say. "So yes."

"Breakfast it is then. I'll make pancakes. Say nine?"

As though she has a pressing other engagement, Amelia finishes the last of her G&T and makes to leave. "Keep the bottle," she says, before spinning on her heels and heading for her house.

When I reach Amelia's porch the next morning, I'm fairly certain my stomach is not up for pancakes—it's too much aflutter for any solid food. I also realize why breakfast isn't deemed the perfect time of day for dates: the absence of booze.

"Good morning," she says. She's freshly showered, her hair still wet, her fringe tucked behind her ear. "Sleep well?"

"No." I follow my reply with a nervous giggle.

"Neither did I, really. I did some more research... of the more physical variety." She cocks her head to the side. "Men really can be obsolete, I guess."

It feels to me as if Amelia's skipped the date part and moved straight into foreplay. My skin tingles underneath my sundress. She pours me some coffee while I deposit the bowl of fruit salad I was cutting at four AM this morning on the table.

"Sit. Eat." Amelia prances around some more, bringing condiments to the table. "You know I make a mean pancake. Charles can eat at least five of them, if I recall correctly."

Then, we find ourselves sitting across from each other, a

stack of pancakes between us. Silence descends. Even Amelia can't keep up that sort of nervous chatter for too long.

"I've been thinking, though, Rach. I mean, technically we've gone on so many dates already." She cuts up a pancake into a dozen small pieces but doesn't eat it. "I think it's the 'want-to-come-in-for-a-coffee?' part that really needs exploring in our case. I already know that I like you. All I need to find out now is how it feels when I kiss you."

A sudden bolt of audacity hits me. Uncharacteristically, perhaps, but not really, because I've wanted to kiss Amelia for years. I've wanted to test what that feels like in real life for a very long time. "Then kiss me," I say.

"I will." She eyes me for a second, and I feel lust pool between my legs. She pushes her chair back. I do the same with mine. We stand up at the same time and meet halfway.

"I always knew there were hidden depths behind those eyes of yours, Rach." She sends me a half-smile before putting her hands on my neck and pulling me close. When our lips touch, in that fraction of a second, I know. I'm definitely a latebian.

I wrap my arms around her neck. My tongue slips inside her mouth and she leans into me a little. This is not the kiss of someone who doesn't want another, I conclude, as our lips and tongues meet again and again. When we finally break, her fringe has come loose from behind her ear and covers half of her face. I tuck it back and ask, "And?"

"So much better than pancakes," she says and tugs me close again.

THE OPPOSITE OF DARKNESS

"Ready?" Doctor Matheson asked.

Erica had grown close to the man over the past year. And now he was about to give her the one thing she'd never believed she'd have again. Her sight.

Everyone was here. Lauren squeezed her right hand. Her mother did the same with her left. Erica heard her father expel some agitated breaths from a corner of the room and, although she couldn't see her—yet—she sensed Jenny's presence at the end of the bed.

"I've been ready for seven years, Doc," Erica replied. Seven years of darkness is a long time. Seven years during which so much had changed and she hadn't seen any of it. Erica remembered what her parents looked like, of course. Her dad's gruff forehead with the deep worry lines. Her mother's button nose and ever-shifting gaze. But she'd never seen Jenny's or Lauren's faces. She had an image in her head of what Lauren, her partner of the past four years, looked like, and she'd let her fingers flit over her face almost every day of their life together, but she'd never actually seen her. Not with her eyes.

"Do we really want our parents in the room when we first meet?" Erica had asked Lauren before the surgery.

"Don't be silly, babe," Lauren had whispered in her ear. "We met years ago."

Erica knew Lauren hadn't said that to brush off any concerns. She'd said it because it was true.

"As we discussed before, everything will be blurry at first, and it will take some time before objects truly come into focus," Doctor Matheson said. "It can take months before vision is fully restored."

"Yes." Erica nodded. She'd waited long enough. "I'm ready."

In the few seconds it took the doctor to bring his hands to her eyes and start peeling off the bandages, the past seven years flashed through Erica's mind. The accident. Cory leaving when Erica needed her most. Hiring Jenny to help her adjust to life as a vision-impaired person. Jenny introducing her daughter, Lauren, to Erica. And now this.

It had taken numerous surgeons seven years to amass the knowledge—and work up the nerve—to accomplish this. But now, after seven years of only sound and smell and taste and touch, Erica would be able to employ her fifth sense again.

She'd often discussed with Jenny if it was worse to be born blind and never to have seen and hence not know what you'd been missing, or to become blind, and have all the images stored in your memory, but not be able to add new ones, or see the old ones again. It was a never-ending discussion, with arguments in favor of both cases depending on Erica's mood, but most of the time she was glad that she'd been able to see before. Even though it didn't make the darkness easier to deal with.

Erica felt the bandage over her left eye loosen as Doctor Matheson slowly removed it. Lauren's fingers wound themselves a little tighter around Erica's.

Erica kept her eyes closed—she wanted to open both eyes at

once. Doctor Matheson started on the other bandage, repeating the process. That was when the nerves really hit her. Everything would change again. What if the surgery hadn't been entirely successful? What if she only got her vision back for a day, or a few weeks? What if some other mistake had occurred? Because, as Erica knew only too well, accidents happened.

"Okay, Erica," the doctor said. "Slowly open your eyes. Take your time. There's no rush."

Erica was determined not to let her newly acquired vision be blurred by tears. She'd done enough crying. If anything, this was a time for smiling. She hadn't seen the reflection of her own smile in years. Then again, she hadn't had that much reason for smiling. Not the first few years, anyway. Not until Jenny and Lauren saved her not only from the physical darkness she'd been dumped in, but also from the encroaching mental darkness that was starting to take more than her ability to see. The one that was chipping away at her ability to live.

There's no such thing as slowly opening your eyes. Either they're open or they're closed. So Erica opened her eyes, and blinked a few times. She saw light. A few dark, smudged shapes. But it didn't matter what she saw, as long as she was seeing something.

Everyone around her had gone quiet. Were they waiting for her to say something? Something meaningful, perhaps? Or for her to confirm that the surgery had been a success? But Erica wanted to remain in that moment a few seconds longer. The moment the world presented itself to her again, in light, and color, and shadows—and reverent silence.

"I can see," she said, still blinking, her brain trying to adjust to her retinas absorbing and translating light into images—just shadowy shapes, really, but images nonetheless.

"What do you see, honey?" her mother asked.

"Just..." But Erica couldn't describe it. She'd no longer have any need of other people describing themselves to her, either. Like Lauren had, on Erica's request, when they'd first met.

"Which celebrity do you look like? It needs to be someone who was famous before my accident." She'd sat there grinning like a fool, because Lauren's voice was low and sexy and her energy when she entered Erica's flat had done something to her. It had been a blatant set-up by Jenny, who had said, after giving Erica the tough love she needed those first few difficult months, "I know you and I know my daughter. Believe me, this will be a match made in heaven."

"But I'm blind," Erica had said. It had been enough reason for Cory to leave, although that wasn't entirely accurate. Erica's attitude had greatly contributed to Cory's decision for them to "go on a break."

"So?" was all Jenny had replied. It was her go-to response when Erica was feeling sorry for herself.

"I don't look like anyone famous," Lauren had said. "I'm just me."

"Oh, come on. Meet me halfway here," Erica had insisted. "I know I have some Sandra Bullock in me."

They'd both broken out in giggles and it was never established whom Lauren resembled.

Soon Erica would be able to see for herself. Soon, when this blurriness made way for more defined pictures. For now, she could make out the blueish hue of the sky behind the flimsy hospital curtains. And the hulking outline of her father on the far side of the room.

"You don't need to say anything, babe," Lauren reassured her. "You have all the time in the world to process and talk about this. All the time in the world." She leaned over—and Erica actually saw Lauren's torso approaching, instead of just sensing a shift in the air—and kissed Erica on the top of her head.

Erica brought her hand to Lauren's face; let a finger slide

along her cheek. She'd established long ago that she had high cheekbones, and a strong chin, but she couldn't feel the color of her eyes—coffee brown, she'd been told—or the shade of pink of her lips.

Erica would have to remain in the hospital for observation a few days longer, but once she got home, she knew what she'd be doing first. Taking in the colors of Lauren. Laying eyes on the freckle on her inner thigh that Lauren liked to guide her finger toward. Determine whether her hair was ash-blond or dirty blond or just plain blond. See her appendectomy scar instead of just letting a fingertip skate across it.

"What have you done to my apartment?" Erica said when she and Lauren arrived home. It had taken another week before Doctor Matheson had allowed her to be discharged from under his watch. In that week, everything she saw had become more distilled. When she'd watched the news on TV the presenter had, incrementally as the days progressed, transformed from a gray and pink blob into an actual person. Erica had cried then. When she'd first been able to make out the contours of another human being's body in all its details, she hadn't been able to keep the image from becoming blurry again. But that was only temporary, and at least that way she'd already shed her tears by the time a real person came to visit her. That person was Lauren.

"Just made it a bit prettier." Lauren had quite quickly moved into the apartment Erica used to share with Cory. Now, though, they'd finally be able to move somewhere else. Somewhere Erica didn't have to feel her way around. Somewhere where she didn't need to know everything by touch.

"I guess I never realized you have questionable taste," Erica joked, casting her eyes around the living room where she had spent the last decade of her life. A vase filled with tulips now stood where Cory's rather ridiculous toy soldier collection used to be. Everything that had belonged to Cory had been replaced by Lauren's belongings. Erica knew this, of course, but witnessing this change with her own eyes for the first time made her go a bit soft on the inside regardless.

"And I guess your lack of vision made you miss the past years' evolution in interior design," Lauren replied. It was exactly this sort of take-no-prisoners humor that had made Erica fall for Lauren. After she'd stopped wallowing in her misery, someone like Lauren by her side had been what she needed. Jenny had been right.

"Can't wait to see what you've done to our bedroom, babe." Erica dropped her bag and shrugged off her coat. As overwhelming as it was to come home and to be able to see her apartment again, it wasn't nearly as urgent as the heat building in her blood. Since the first second she'd truly been able to make out Lauren's contours—those alpine cheekbones, that curve of her hip—she'd only been able to think about coming home and feasting her eyes on all of her lover. She wanted her naked before it went dark. For Erica, it was essential to have daylight streaming in through the windows when she looked at Lauren's intimate parts for the very first time. Artificial light would simply not do.

"Come on." Lauren grabbed her by the hand and dragged her in the right direction. Moving through the apartment unencumbered was also a freeing experience, and it only made Erica's desire grow bolder.

Strangely, Lauren always slept with a sleep mask covering her eyes. She had one hanging from the bedpost at all times and as they came to a stop by the bed, Lauren presented it to Erica and said, "I thought I'd blindfold you."

Erica snatched the mask from Lauren's hands and tossed it to the floor, but not without wondering if she would ever be able to sleep in a non-pitch black environment. At the hospital, sleep had been elusive at best since the bandages had been removed. Erica had drifted in and out of it, exhausted by all the emotions and the new sensations, day and night, not caring that a hospital room rarely went dark. She didn't want darkness, anyway. All she'd wanted was the opposite of it.

"You'd best lay off the dark humor and strip, babe. I've never been more ready in my life." Erica's hands reached for a button of Lauren's blouse and she couldn't help herself—she had to start tugging, had to start undoing clothes, had to see naked skin. She'd felt every inch of that skin, had explored it for hours with her fingertips, her cheeks, her tongue, but now she was ready to examine it with her eyes as well.

"What? No gentle lovemaking? And here I was thinking this would be a tantric experience. The pair of us at opposite ends of the room just staring at each other until we couldn't take it anymore." Lauren grinned. She had a bit of Michelle Pfeiffer in her when she cracked a crooked smile like that.

"As far as I'm concerned, this is our first time. One I've waited a very long time for."

"Oh, I see. The chastity belt has finally come off." Lauren pulled her close by the neck and kissed her.

This must be exciting for her as well, Erica thought. To surrender to my gaze for the very first time. This did not quench Erica's lust. Their kiss grew frantic, their lips mashing together, their tongues meeting in a darting frenzy.

"Fuck, you're so hot," Erica said, slightly out of breath, when they came up for air. "Like... what's her name... from that TV show." But Erica didn't have a brain that remembered faces, nor TV shows for that matter. Seven years without vision also had left her quite oblivious to today's ridiculous body standards and fashion hypes. Lauren might as well have walked around in nothing but sweatpants for the entire time Erica couldn't see. Nonetheless, she'd dressed up today—for the day she was taking a seeing Erica home. She wore a baby blue blouse tucked into a tight pair of jeans, and Erica thought that, perhaps, that was one of the things she had missed the most. To see a woman fully clothed one instant, and stark naked the next. The contrast. The urgency. The desire displayed in the seconds the clothes came off.

"Téa Leoni?" Lauren asked.

"I don't even know who that is." Erica pulled Lauren close again, but instead of kissing her, she flipped open a few more buttons of her blouse. A navy blue bra with lace skirting the cups peeked through. Erica didn't recall ever coming across much lace when touching Lauren's undergarments. She must have gone shopping for the occasion. Meanwhile, Erica had been forced to wear the comfortable clothing she'd gone into hospital with. And the same old beige bra, of which she'd never known the color before. After this—perhaps a few days of this—a shopping trip was in order.

Erica dragged her finger along the skin above Lauren's bra—just like before, but entirely different at the same time. Before, she would have used her finger to gain arousal and information. Now, it was purely for arousal. Erica already knew what the slope of Lauren's breast felt like, but the sight of it curving out of that bra cup left her gasping for air.

"Hey." Lauren put her hand over Erica's. "How about we take it slow? All this visual stimulation will have you climaxing in minutes, otherwise."

Erica already felt her clit pulsing against her panties, and her nipples poking hard against the fabric of her bra. "Yes." She nodded and took a deep breath. Her hand was still on Lauren's breast, and her eyes—her eyes were everywhere. Her gaze flitted from the unruly curl on the side of Lauren's head, to the three freckles on her nose, to the hollow of her neck, and the promise of her half-open blouse.

Lauren loosened her grasp on Erica's hand and trailed her fingers over it. "Why don't you sit back and... watch," she said.

Erica's lips curved into a grin. She didn't need a mirror—or the power of eyesight—to know it was a leery, horny grin. "Oh yes." She took a few steps toward the bed and sat. Out of habit, her hands touched the mattress before she allowed her bottom to crash down. "A striptease." Before she'd lost her vision, Erica would have scoffed at the idea, but now, it made her flesh sizzle —and feel very constrained underneath her clothes despite their comfortable nature.

Lauren sank her teeth into her bottom lip and proceeded to open the buttons Erica hadn't got to yet. She let the sides of her blouse hang open while trailing a finger from between her collarbones, down the cleft of her cleavage, over her belly button to the button of her jeans, which she undid painfully slowly, her gaze locked on Erica's.

Most of all, Erica thought, it's her eyes. Oh, what she had missed not being able to look into her partner's eyes.

"You want more?" Lauren asked.

Erica failed to reply. She couldn't. Her throat was so dry, she feared she might choke if she tried to speak. Heat traveled through her veins. Her panties were damp against her ever-swelling pussy lips. So instead, she simply nodded.

Lauren pushed her jeans off her legs. Her panties matched her bra. A thin strip of lace edged the waistband and the blue looked so delicious against the porcelain of her skin, it made Erica's mouth water. Lauren had been wrong. This was already too much. She needed that frantic, early release Lauren had alluded to earlier. Not only because regaining her vision and seeing her lover on full display rendered her beyond hot, but also because of all the pent-up emotions that were clawing their way free of her soul. Most of all, she needed to see. Now.

"Take off your bra, please," she pleaded, her voice hoarse and low.

Lauren obliged and let her blouse slip from her arms. Erica watched as it landed in a puddle of light blue on the bedroom's hardwood floor. Lauren brought her hands behind her back and held her bra up for a brief moment before sending Erica a warm smile, and letting it tumble down the same path her blouse had taken. She stood with her hands at her sides, her gaze on Erica, but Erica, for the first time, averted her eyes from Lauren's. She knew the shape of Lauren's breasts, of course. The size of her nipples. But she'd only ever heard about the light-brown birthmark the shape of Asia to the side of her right breast. And the color pink she'd imagined Lauren's nipples to be was much darker than reality. They pointed upward in the most arousing display of lust. Erica realized that conjuring an image of breasts in her mind, no matter how perfect they might be, never lived up to casting her gaze upon the real things. The mounds heaving with ragged breath. The person they belonged to being the woman who'd entered her life and brightened it beyond the ability to see.

Lauren's hands slid toward her panties and, slowly, she started pushing them down. Her breasts swayed in the process, and then Lauren stood completely naked in front of Erica.

"Oh, Christ," Erica muttered. "You are so unbelievably beautiful." It was doubly true, because for the longest time Erica had believed she'd never see her partner like this.

"Oh, but so are you, babe," Lauren said, and came for her. "Fuck, I want you naked too." She tugged at Erica's sweater and it came off easily. No striptease required.

Erica got up and stepped out of her panties, unclasped her bra and tossed it as far away from her as possible—she'd never wear that particular one again. By the time all her clothes had gone, Lauren had lain down on the bed in front of her, her knees clasped together chastely.

Erica wasn't having any of that. She moved onto the bed and kneeled in front of Lauren's closed legs. She put her hands on Lauren's knees and gently pushed them apart. Erica had seen plenty of lady parts before things became serious with Cory, but she'd never seen Lauren's. And now, at last, her gaze was fixed on Lauren's pussy. Gleaming lips. Wetness already spreading to her upper thighs. A neatly trimmed bush. Before she'd lost her sight, she'd been too young to have lovers with gray hairs down there, but Lauren had a few lighter threads running through the curls on her mound. Her clit protruding the tiniest amount through her slit.

Erica had been told so many times—until she'd had no choice but to believe it—that having use of all your senses wasn't a requirement for happiness. Perhaps it wasn't. She had found happiness in her life after the accident. But it was nothing compared to this sensory feast. The sound of Lauren's and her own breath blending in her ears. The smell of Lauren's arousal teasing her nostrils. Erica's hands firmly planted on her lover's knees, holding them apart although that wasn't necessary anymore. She'd taste her soon enough—as she had done many times before—but first, she had to look a while longer.

Lauren found Erica's hand with hers. Not to urge her to take action, Erica was sure of that, but to enjoy this moment together. There would only ever be a first of this. If Erica were to go blind again tomorrow, she wanted this view etched into her memory—along with an image of Lauren's smile, and her body naked in front of her.

Neither one of them seemed to have the nerve to crack a joke at this point. Nor did Erica have the time or the inclination to consider the visible changes to her own naked body. Lauren had seen it before. It didn't matter.

As though in a trance, Erica bent and pressed a kiss to Lauren's nether lips. She inhaled deeply, but she didn't want to be between her lover's legs for this. It impaired her vision too much. She pushed Lauren's legs down and found a position next to her.

"I want to see you," Erica said. "When you come."

Lauren nodded and pulled her in for a kiss and her hand trailed down Erica's stomach. They'd often done it like this because of the aural stimulation it provided. Lauren's gasps in her ear had always been a huge turn-on for Erica. This time, it wouldn't only be Lauren's moans and groans spurring Erica on.

Erica traced a finger back to Lauren's soaked pussy lips and let it skate along the pooled wetness there. Oh, the things she wanted to do. Watch her fingers disappear in her lover's cunt as she fucked her. Take in the curve of her behind for long seconds when she spun her around. But as Lauren had said at the hospital: they had all the time in the world. And right now, lust was consuming her flesh, making her clit pound and drenching her pussy in its own juices.

Erica pushed a finger deep inside of Lauren, while gazing deep into her eyes. They narrowed a fraction as her lips parted. Erica found a rhythm, and added a second finger, before Lauren touched her thumb to Erica's clit and started strumming it.

"Oh fuck." The full sensory overload was already having spectacular effects on Erica. This wouldn't be just another climax. This would be her first climax seeing Lauren. That and the fact she was simultaneously fucking Lauren, and witnessing what that was doing to her face, drove more and more blood rushing to her clit. Her heart full of love, her eyes full of light, and her lover's cunt full of fingers. There really wasn't anything more to it for Erica then. She gave herself up to the moment, to the heat rushing to her extremities from that one point between her legs, rolling back and forth.

"I'm close," Lauren said. "Oh god, I'm close."

"Me too," Erica grunted. And while she came, she tried as hard as she could to keep her eyes wide open.

STEPPING STONE

Her eyes rest on me for a fraction of a second. I don't blink. I never do. When she looks away, I feel it though. I always do. I feel something contract in my stomach, flutter in my blood. The day is hot for the season. The sun slants through the window next to which I'm seated, but I don't look out. How could I when what I see in front of me is so much more enthralling than anything that could go on outside? Not until she's there—hopefully with me behind her.

"Annie," Professor Worthington says, addressing the girl next to me. She's dressed entirely in black today. As though she had to attend a funeral before class. Tight black pants. Equally black boat-neck top in a fabric that doesn't leave a whole lot to the imagination. Her black blazer is draped over her chair. "Can you tell me..." But the professor doesn't have time to finish her question because the chime of the bell interrupts her. I can hear Annie visibly relax next to me; her limbs go soft and a breath of relief leaves her body. But I'm not looking at Annie. No one in this classroom is of any interest to me. Not since Professor Cilla Worthington walked in the door. That was last September. It's May now.

Professor Worthington pulls her blazer off the chair with a casual gesture and lets it fall across her forearm. The blackness of her clothes contrasts heavily with the paleness of the rest of her. Her eyes are the lightest of blue—although I've seen them turn darker at times. Her light blond hair is pinned away from her neck, a few curly strands framing her forehead. She has the thinnest lips I've ever been attracted to, and when she smiles, it doesn't really look like a smile. It's more like an invitation, like her letting us in a little.

I wait until my classmates shuffle out of the room. Some of them—always Tyler and Sammie—nod at the professor with an inappropriate sneer as they walk past her. The things they say behind her back are too foul to repeat. She nods back solemnly, with just the slightest tilt of her head. I don't even pretend to still be packing books into my bag. The need for pretense disappeared long ago.

When the last student has filed out, Professor Worthington leans her hip against the front desk, her blazer now hanging from her index finger and slung across her back. In her other hand, she holds her briefcase. This time when her eyes rest on me, I do blink.

She would be foolish to say anything in this room at this moment, so she doesn't. Instead, she pulls up her eyebrows, wrinkling her forehead in the process. In response, I nod once. It's enough. She heads out the door and I count to ten. Then I follow.

I don't need to look to know where she's going. Our spot is a mile away from campus. We meet there twice a week, unless the rain gets too heavy. Nowhere else. Only there. On campus, we don't communicate. We don't text, don't email, don't call each other. We might as well not know each other. Once I see her disappear around the bend, I sit down on a bench and count to ten again. I've taken to doing it in different languages.

I can count to ten in Chinese and Italian, as well as in French and Spanish.

"You'll never know what it might be good for," she replied when I told her. "I take your education very seriously." She'd smiled her non-smile then, and my knees had gone weak. When I get up this time, my knees go weak again, because I know what's coming. The anticipation has been building for hours, since before class. Since I woke up this morning. No, since I went to bed last night, my skin hot and feverish under the covers at the prospect of Professor Worthington's hands all over it—even though she's not that hands-on a person.

The place where we meet is a tiny patch of dense woodlands. Like a peninsula of trees just off the big forest next to campus. It's unappealing in its smallness compared to the forest, but it suits us just fine. I like to believe it's 'our spot' but the truth is that I don't know if she brings other people here. We don't have a relationship that lends itself to exclusiveness, nor any talk of it. Some might call what we have something barely covered by the word relationship—although nobody knows, so nobody else's opinion matters—but the sort of intimacy we share, however brief between the rustle of the trees and the sounds of the nearby forest, in my mind, is definitely worthy of the term.

I skirt the larger forest following the dirt path that meanders around it, my footsteps quickening, like the beat of my heart. I live for these moments, the minutes just before I see her standing there, waiting for me—me!—in the sort of casual stance she seems to specialize in. My heart is in my throat, my skin becomes so sensitive I can feel the shift of the air as I almost trip over myself to round the corner. On a couple of occasions she has hidden behind a tree. "I heard someone coming and I knew it wasn't you," she said the first time it happened. The first time I arrived at our spot after our silent agreement and I didn't see her, and my stomach seemed to drop from a thousand feet high, every muscle in my body clenching with disappointment.

"How did you know?" I asked, after my mind had calmed down.

"Their steps weren't so eager," she'd just replied and given me one of her lopsided semi-smiles. Some people just don't have warm smiles in them. Perhaps that's what draws me to her so much. The absence of easy overindulgence. Flash a smile and get your way. Flash a smile and make others feel welcome. Flash a smile and drain the tension from any given situation. Not with Professor Worthington, whose name, as I approach, slowly changes into Cilla.

And, then, there she is. Shoulder leaning against a birch. Her blazer draped over her briefcase.

"If I cared at all about keeping things clean I certainly wouldn't be here with you," she said once when I made a remark about the proximity of the dirty soil to her clothes.

No smile today, either, but I see it glittering in her eyes. She wants me too. There's no question, no doubts. When I slip my hand inside her panties later, she'll be so wet, so ready, so consumed by anticipation for the moment, and lust for one of her students, it will astound me all over again.

"Girls like you are my eternal weakness," she says, now, as I adopt my own faux-casual posture in front of her. It pleases me more than the laconic "I was disappointed with your participation in class today" she greeted me with last time. Cilla always has a one-liner prepared for my arrival. I believe she may get off on how she's able to deliver the words so coolly before falling apart in my arms afterwards.

"What kind of girls would that be?" I ask and take a step toward her.

"Look in the mirror and you'll know."

This is just posturing. Our version of small talk. We can hardly exchange 'I-love-yous'. Love is not on the agenda here.

And if it were, it would never be expressed with words. Not while we have so many other means of expressing ourselves. So, I swallow the question that follows naturally in my mind: "Do you have one every year?" It has no place in this moment—and the answer doesn't matter. Finals are approaching quickly. Two more classes with Professor Worthington and one final exam a few weeks later, and I'll be out of here. It'll all be over. This outdoorsy string of sexual encounters that has injected my last year in college with a slew of memories I will never be able to erase.

"Come here," she says, pushing herself away from the tree she's leaning against.

Unlike her, I have a vast arsenal of smiles, and I shoot her the one that says, 'oh no, I don't think so'.

She sinks her teeth into her thin bottom lip because she knows what it means, just as I know what she means when she says 'girls like you'.

"Turn around." My voice has descended into a lower register. The one that drives her mad. I know because I've witnessed it over and over again.

She spins on her heels and faces the tree she was leaning into earlier. The things that tree has seen. It's always the same one. A long, stately birch with a rough trunk and a comfortable girth to plant your hands against.

It's all shadows here, in this spot where we come to fuck out of sight. Where we come to pretend we are people we are not. When we walk into our tiny circle of nature, green above and green below, I cease to be her student and she's no longer my professor. I do the teaching here.

I move behind her, inhale a whiff of her scent. It's powerful, like Cilla in front of a classroom, but when I feel my knees buckle, I straighten my spine and ignore the sensation. I bring my hands to the hem of her ink-black top, lift it just a fraction, gaze at the brightness of her skin peeking through the gap I've created, and let my fingers snake up the length of her back. The first touch, the first skin-on-skin contact, is a sensation so intense I can't ignore it. Not even girls like me can. But it's okay, because Cilla can't see me. I give her three seconds of gentle fingertip-caressing until my nails dig in. Her body goes stiff, her hands falling against the tree, arms outstretched, as though she's recovering and looking for support after a long, exhausting run.

"I've brought something," I whisper. "Had it in my bag all through class and only thought about that, about what I'd do with it later."

She doesn't ask what it is that I've brought. Not because she's not interested, but because she knows I'll only tell her if she doesn't inquire. My hands have reached her shoulders and her top has ridden all the way up. Out of nowhere, the sight of her spine rippling beneath her skin makes me bend my torso over her and kiss all her vertebrae. Two more weeks and this will all be over. The thought nestles itself in the forefront of my mind, unwilling to retreat. So I kiss her more than I otherwise would. As long as it's only her backside, she will never know. When I push my lips away from her flesh, I see her skin has broken out in goosebumps, despite the muggy air surrounding us. Just another instance of us not saying I love you.

Without waiting for my command, she turns around to face me. Her thin-lipped expression is blank, but then changes as she lets her gaze wander over the length of me. I expect a fight for top at first—it's not the first time she's challenged me—but there's something new in her glance. A tenderness I haven't yet encountered. Maybe she's feeling it too. The end of the school year blues. It's messing with our discipline.

"Next week," she starts to say, but then pauses, as if unsure.

I cock my head, curiosity brimming within me.

"Next week, come to my house." She finishes her sentence

and lets her back drop against the tree, pulling me with her with a sudden grasp of her hand on my arm.

This is no time to change the rules, I think, despite the crazy leap of my heart into my throat.

"I'm sick of seeing you walk away. Just once, I want to wake up next to you. Just once before you leave for good."

Her sentimentality floors me and I have nothing else to hold onto than to her.

"Jamie," she breathes, "I want to spend the night with you. Just one night."

Perhaps she does this every year. An unexpected parting gift to girls-like-me. Part of me is keen—and wants nothing more than to look at Cilla when she opens her eyes for the first time in the morning, revealing the strange breakable blue of them. But, then, where do we go from there?

"We'll see," is my provisional reply. Because don't we need the outside air around us? The sense of danger that comes with doing what we do hidden behind some trees? Isn't that particular urgency an essential part of us? Can we just transport this to the bedroom? All we've ever given each other has been given here, with large trees as sentinels, and flickers of sky reflecting in our eyes—making hers grow darker—the immovable scent of green in our noses when our muscles spasm into orgasm.

She corrects herself. The shift is subtle. A squaring of her shoulders, a quick blink of her eyes, after which the urgency of her question has faded. "Show me what you brought."

And now I have to, because now I don't have it in me anymore to not give her what she asks for. I can only say no so many times to Cilla Worthington. I duck down to grab the toy from my bag. It's brand new—bought especially for her, like some crazy sentimental adieu gift—but I've taken it out of its box and wrapped it in a towel for easy access in the woods.

From the sudden glimmer in her eyes, I can tell she knows what it is before she sees it. She unfolds the towel and unveils the dildo in its full glory. The smile her lips curve into is as close to a conventional one I've ever seen on her. "I know just what to do with that," she says, while re-wrapping it in the towel. "Thank you." It's her turn to crouch down now and stash it in her briefcase.

Not what I had in mind. I glare at her silently until she speaks because I'm definitely owed an explanation.

"Perfect for when you come to stay at my house next week."

I shake my head. A big part of what we do in these woods is this never-ending struggle to determine who calls the shots. We'll never really know. But, at least, the woods are a level playing ground. Not hers, not mine. Just ours. "Not next week," I counter. "Take me to your house tonight."

She regards me for an instant, one corner of her mouth drawn up into the sort of semi-condescending quizzical expression that makes my blood boil with rage and lust at the same time.

"Deal." For an instant, I think she's extending her hand so we can shake on it. "I take it you know where I live?"

Touché. Of course, I do, even though she's certainly never told me. I have to acquiesce and nod.

"Come by after nine. Be discreet."

Is this where our meeting in the woods ends? I wonder. Perhaps the last one we'll ever have? But Cilla doesn't move, just stands there, waiting. It's my move, I guess.

When I reach for her, wanting to stroke the back of my hands across the soft porcelain of her cheek, she grabs me by the wrist and stares into my eyes. "Oh Jamie," she says, and with that twirls me around and pushes my back against the tree.

And I know it's one of those days when nothing goes according to the plans I've made in advance, the plans that have been swirling in my brain since the last time we met. The image of me fucking Cilla with the dildo, of her mouth opening while she gasps for much-needed oxygen which the trees around us provide aplenty. Of her surrendering to my touch—and my plans. But how can I mind when I know what she'll do next? When the mere thought of it makes me crave more oxygen, almost more than the birches have to give.

She stares into my eyes—a stare that touches me in many places but mostly between my legs. And if I'm truly honest with myself, setting aside all my habits and beliefs, it's instances like these that excite me the most. When the professor takes control. When she leaves me no choice but to be hers. When I lose myself in the blue of her eyes, because she never—never—looks away. Not when she starts unbuttoning my blouse one-handedly. Not when she zips open my jeans, her finger exerting a gentle press against my panties, just because she can.

Her eyelashes are almost translucent. Her eyelids narrow a fraction as she starts pushing my jeans down. And god, I do want to spend the night with her. I want to be reckless with my heart because of the opportunities it brings. Having Cilla spread her legs for me on the forest floor comes with a certain romanticism, and that primal element of doing what we do in nature—the abandon of it, and the sense that it needs to happen no matter where we are. But after all these months of braving the weather to fulfill our needs, the conventionality of a proper bed is very appealing. The promise of being able to take all the time I want with her, to remove the rushed quality that always lurks in our outdoor encounters, and replace it with more attention for each other, for what we've learned about each other's bodies, and apply it in the safety of her bedroom, is suddenly much more alluring than a fresh breeze on my clit as I help her push my jeans all the way down.

But the bedroom is for later. Now, I stand in front of her, my blouse open, my legs wide for her. Her eyes are so close to mine, her fingers on my throat, her thumb stroking the line of my jaw. And then she kisses me. The touch of her lips on mine instantly makes my clit throb. She wraps her fingers gently around my throat—a gesture of possession that drives me wild. Sometimes, in class, she brings her fingers to her throat, rests them there casually, and shoots me a quick look, and a shudder of lust spikes in my blood.

Her tongue invades my mouth now, twirls itself inside of me, and I pull her close, curl my fingers through her hair and the pins that keep it up at the back of her head, and draw her as near to me as I possibly can.

The kiss doesn't stop, but the hand that was on my throat slithers down. A finger briefly strokes the skin above my left bra cup, then inches further south, to where none of my clothes are left. Because we don't have the luxury of time here, two of her fingers scoot straight down, wandering along my pussy lips, pulling them apart, as though wanting to expose my most secret spot to the elements around us.

We break from the kiss because she'll want to gaze into my eyes for what comes next. She always does. The treetops above us shake in the wind, and allow a sliver of sunshine to slant through, lighting up her eyes. You're so beautiful, I want to say, but as much as what we're doing is a display of wildness, of breaking rules, it's also an exercise in restraint, in knowing what is and what isn't possible. I play my part well and swallow the words.

When she enters me with two fingers, her mouth widens as if in amazement, as if what I'm letting her do to me is the greatest gift anyone has ever given her. Of course, this is only my interpretation of that crooked O her lips form, and perhaps a mere projection of my own amazement at what is happening, at Professor Cilla Worthington's fingers disappearing inside of me, claiming pleasure from me. As her fingers start sliding up and down inside of me, and my blood heats up under her stare, her lips curve into her version of a smile, accented by the fire in her eyes.

"Oh, I know the spot, Jamie," she says, "I know exactly what to do." And she does—oh, she does. First, she gives me a few high, deep strokes, her face only contorting a tiny bit as her arm muscles do all the work, just to let her presence be felt, to let her long fingers explore as much as she can inside of me. But then she retreats, just for an instant, leaving me breathless and wanting more against the tree, until her lips part again, and she pushes three fingers inside of me. She splays them from the start and with one—or two, or all, I really don't know at this point—hits the spot she knows so well. She knows because I let her know, because I invited her in. No bedrooms required.

"Later, you can fuck me, Jamie. I want you to," she says, while she's fucking me, and her words intensify what her fingers are doing and, all the while, her eyes are on me, examining the tiniest shift in my facial expression, the amount of lust and pleasure displayed in my own glance. "With that dildo you brought." And there's something so unseemly, so thrilling about hearing my professor speak the word dildo, just when her fingers are busy inside of me, that it sets me off, breaks through any resistance I had left.

"Oh fuck," I moan. "Oh fuck, Cilla." I close my eyes then, when the walls of my pussy start clenching around her fingers violently, trapping her within me, wanting them to linger after what they've just given me.

When I open my eyes, as the final shudders of orgasm make their way through my flesh, and look into hers, I'm glad that, most likely only for today, it doesn't end here. Because leaving the woods is always awkward, and always ignites a sense of loss as I walk away—always me first.

Her fingers slip from between my pussy lips and she plants her hands against the tree on either side of my head. "If only you could see your face when you come," Cilla says. She's never said anything like this before. I'm still panting, my brain still a bit frazzled from my climax, that I don't know how to respond. So I focus on her face instead. On the smattering of freckles just above her nose, so pale they're only visible in the right kind of light. On the slant of her high cheekbones, and her lips as they move towards me again, kissing me on the right corner of my mouth first, and then fully on the lips, her tongue claiming entrance immediately.

"I can't wait for tonight," I blurt out when our lip-lock ends. I don't fear her reaction though—fear has no place here either. Because by then I've realized that her invitation to her home tonight is more than a chance for her to fuck me in her bed. It's an open invitation to take this affair from the woods into a more real world. Not everyday life just yet, but a space in between the secrecy of hiding and the openness of the other life we lead. It's a stepping stone to more. Because in only a few weeks, I won't be her student anymore. Other rules will apply, and really, who knows what will happen then?

"Neither can I," she says, and starts kissing me again.

COMMANDING OFFICER

I was the first person to raise my hand when Captain Betts asked for volunteers to work on Christmas day. Even before she said, "I'll be here as well. If that's any incentive."

It's an unwritten rule that single officers without children volunteer to work holidays. The captain's divorce has been widely discussed among all ranks and pay grades, what with her marriage having ended so abruptly and without dignity. I knew the score way before any of my colleagues did, because I could see it in her eyes so clearly. Day after day, I witnessed how the light in them dimmed a little more—and all I want is for the sparkle to return to her gaze. But I guess the holidays are not the best time for that.

"Here we are," Captain Betts says when she arrives at nine on the dot. "Merry Christmas, Groves."

"Same to you, Cap." My shift started at 7 a.m. and, unlike the captain, I'm all decked out in uniform.

"Where's O'Mally?" she inquires while letting her gaze drift over the empty room where, on any other day, at least ten officers would be busy and hunched over their desks.

"Out on a call. Mrs. Brewers again. He figured he could handle it on his own."

Captain Betts tilts her head and scrunches her lips together. "Fair enough." She drops her purse on a chair. "So it's just us then." She accompanies her statement with a sigh. "I have a ton of paperwork to catch up on, but I also had the grimmest Christmas Eve ever, so you know what? Screw it."

I raise my eyebrows a fraction, then quickly lower them, lest the captain thinks I'm judging her in any way.

"It's Christmas, Groves. We can hope for some action, but Mrs. Brewers' imaginary burglars are probably the best we're going to get."

"At Thanksgiving it got pretty busy in the afternoon with that brawl at Phil's Bar," I say.

"Thanksgiving? You worked then as well?" She narrows her eyes. "You must really love being a police officer."

"I do, Ma'am."

"What's your story?" she asks as she crashes down into a chair. "I'm sure you know all about mine." She flashes a weak smile.

"I'm a rookie, Ma'am. Not that I mind working on holidays. But we all have to pay our dues."

Captain Betts shakes her head. "Nu-uh, Groves. There are so many things wrong with what you've just said." She raises a hand and stretches three fingers. "First, I don't feel like being 'Ma'am-ed' today. Second, if you worked on Thanksgiving, you should have gotten a break for Christmas. And third… While, yes, we all have certain dues to pay, that doesn't explain why you so greedily volunteered to take this shift in the first place. So, I will repeat my question to you, Groves. What's your story?"

"I simply don't mind, Ma—" I stop myself from 'Ma'am-ing' her just in time. "Captain Betts."

"My name's Olivia," Captain Betts says. "It's just the two of us here and we're getting paid to sit here while the rest of the town is preparing Christmas lunch or picking up relatives from the bus station or turning over in bed for a good old lie-in. So, Tasha..." She pauses and fixes her eyes on me. "Let's just have a relaxed conversation and cut all the formality. It's Christmas. We can live a little." She gives a heartfelt chuckle and her face actually breaks into a smile. Captain Betts—Olivia—has the kind of face that changes completely when she smiles. In fact, when she smiles, she is Olivia instead of Captain Betts. "How old are you, anyway? Aren't you too old to be a rookie?"

"Never too old, I guess." When I signed up for this shift, I had believed it would be a repeat of Thanksgiving, when Lieutenant Stix hid in his office from nine to five, and I was out here answering calls and finishing reports I hadn't gotten round to yet. The only difference this time, I had expected, was that Captain Betts would have taken up residence behind the door on my left, and I would occasionally allow my mind to drift to the thoughts it likes to drift to. Thoughts of knocking on Captain Betts' door and pulling that always tightly-tucked-in blouse from her pants and slipping my hands underneath. Or her calling me into her office and putting my baton stick to good—alternative—use.

"God, you really are an open book, aren't you?" She rises from her chair. "Well, keep up the mystery, Tasha. You've got me intrigued." She grabs her purse. "I'll be in my office, but drop by any time you'd like to continue this illuminating conversation." She tilts her head again to look at me for an instant, then walks off.

I feel disappointed I didn't stretch the conversation longer, but I've never been a woman of many words, and it's not as though the captain doesn't know my story—all she has to do is consult my personnel file.

~

About an hour later, I knock on the captain's door, which she has left open.

"An update from O'Mally, Ma'am," I say. "He responded to a call from the Bergs. Something about their dog being in trouble."

The captain chuckles and removes her reading glasses from her nose. "I guess it is too much to ask of a rookie." She leans back in her chair and stares at me. "To address me by my first name."

"Habit," I say, swallowing the 'Ma'am' that sits at the ready waiting to be released from the tip of my tongue.

"If I wasn't your superior officer, I'd have to conclude you enjoy calling other women Ma'am." Captain Betts dangles her spectacles between two fingers, but keeps her eyes firmly on me.

"I've been known to," I say, meeting her gaze. O'Mally will be out for a while longer—and I'm allowed some frivolity. "Have been called it a few times myself."

"Was that in your previous job?" Captain Betts asks.

I sink my teeth into my lower lip and just shake my head—leaving the captain to draw her own conclusions.

Captain Betts' eyes are still on me, and she has the beginning of a grin on her lips. This is quickly turning into a staring competition. Whatever will the winner get? Then she averts her eyes. I win.

"Thanks for letting me know about O'Mally," she says, straightening her posture.

I give her a quick nod and turn to leave. I haven't looked into a woman's eyes for this long in years.

~

"Care for some lunch?" Captain Betts asks. "I'm guessing O'Mally is being fed by the Bergs."

"Great gut instinct." I swivel my chair around so I can look the captain in the eyes—those gray-green eyes that have haunted me since we were first introduced ten months ago. "You should still be on the streets, Cap."

This makes her laugh which, in return, makes my belly tingle. "I haven't been on the streets in a long time, Tasha." She makes a show of emphasizing my name. "I keep moving up and up." Her voice sounds sarcastic now. "My life is basically a walk in the park."

I hesitate to inquire further. I don't know the captain that well. She's not my immediate superior—though I've often wished she was—and I'm not sure she'll want to divulge details about her private life to a rookie like me. But I'm here for a reason and now is the time to, ever so slowly, let my intentions be known. "How are you doing, Olivia?" My turn to let her first name roll off my tongue flirtatiously.

"How about I tell you all about it over lunch?" There's sadness in her eyes, but also something else. A glimmer of recognition, or longing, perhaps. I can only hope she finds some comfort in being trapped at the station with another woman of the same inclination.

"I'd be honored." I rise, holding her gaze.

She nods and heads for the break room.

While we eat our sandwiches she paints a broad-stroked picture of her divorce from Sally Pelham, Mayor Pelham's daughter. It's not so much an ugly picture as a profoundly lonely one.

"How about you, Tasha?" she asks, looking into my eyes again.

I shrug, quickly losing confidence I'll win this particular staring contest. The captain hasn't exactly shown her vulnerable side, but she has confided in me. "There's no one special in my life," I say, focusing on the laughter lines bracketing her eyes.

"How come?" She gives no signs of flinching any time soon. "Pretty young thing like you?"

I have to look away then. I get the unmistakable sense of being found out. Because, of course, I'm not just here today because of the sheer goodness in my heart. I'm here for her.

"I'm not that young," I reply, lifting my gaze from my half-eaten sandwich to her.

"That's right. You're the not-young rookie. We don't get many of those here." The captain puts down her sandwich and pushes it away from her. "That excellent gut instinct you were referring to earlier is trying to tell me something. Care to give me a clue?"

I put my own sandwich down and wipe my hands on a napkin, then nod. "There's a reason O'Mally has been out all day."

"I figured." She lets her bottom lip protrude, giving the impression she's thinking really hard about this.

"It's Christmas," I say. "We should live a little."

She replies with a quick, loud cackle of a laugh. "Good one." She brings a hand to where her blouse is open at the throat. "What did you have in mind?"

"You're the boss, Ma'am. I think I'll leave that up to you." A pulse quickens between my legs.

"You will do no such thing. I like a rookie who shows initiative." Her fingers caress the hollow of her neck.

I have to swallow, that's how much my mouth is already watering. Is she giving me carte blanche and, in the process, not giving a damn about the rules? Because what I've been dreaming of for months is not allowed—and could get her in much more trouble than me. "Why don't we go into your office, Ma'am?"

She just sits there, her eyes narrowing, as though pondering the ramifications of my request. Pros versus cons. Living a little versus abiding by the rules. "Okay," she says after a few seconds heavy with silence. "Why don't we?"

She doesn't make any motion to get up so I'm the first one to push my chair back and rise. She follows my lead. I walk out of the break room and head to her office, praying that no phones will go off in the next hour—and that O'Mally will stick to our deal. I promised to swap him two weekend shifts if he stayed out all day. But, more than that, I'm aware of the heat in my blood and the quickening of my breath. The captain's urgent footfalls behind me make my heart beat faster—in rhythm with her step.

I'm the one who opens the door to her office, lets her in as though it's mine, and locks it behind us. I wonder if I can get her to call me Ma'am—but I don't want to get ahead of myself.

"Now what?" The captain stands with her hands at her sides. She's wearing a white blouse with thin pink stripes and her stance accentuates the tightness of it around her waist.

"Now this." I take a step in her direction. "Now this," I repeat, before covering her hands with mine and pressing a kiss to her lips. The touch of her mouth instantly connects with my throbbing clit. I've wanted to kiss Captain Olivia Betts for such a long time, this doesn't just feel like living a little, it feels like a Christmas miracle.

She pushes both our hands away from her sides and, leaving my arms to dangle purposelessly for an instant, cups my cheeks and pulls me closer. Our mouths open and our tongues meet and the wetness I encounter must be evenly matched by the one between my legs. I curve my arms around her waist and her breasts press against mine.

"I don't need to make you sign a disclaimer that this is consensual?" she says in between gasps when we break from our kiss.

"I want you, Captain," I say with a forceful tone. "I've wanted you for months and months."

In reply, she pulls me closer again, until our lips are so close they almost touch. "Big surprise," she says, then kisses me again.

My mind translates it as a definite 'Ok Go' sign, and also the exact moment to let my dreams come true. I let my hands slip down and start tugging at her blouse. As arousing as I've always found the way she looks in her ultra-tight blouses, it is nothing compared to how thrilling it will be to let my hands roam freely across the skin underneath. When my fingers meet flesh, and the hardness of her toned body, I let go completely. At the end of this, she will be calling me Ma'am.

I break from our kiss and, while I stare into her eyes, start unbuttoning her blouse. My fingers are quick but in control as I open Olivia's blouse and push it down her shoulders. I let my gaze drift down then, to the mounds of her breasts sloping out of her bra. In my dream scenario, we would get totally naked, but this is a real-life police station and if I have to make a choice, I'd rather focus on getting her pants off than her bra.

"Take off your shoes," I say. It's not a question.

She raises her eyebrows. Of course, she does.

"We don't have much time," I urge. And how else can I bury my face between your legs?

She lifts her leg behind her and brings a hand behind her back to push off her shoe, then repeats the process with the other foot.

I'm up next. I flip open the button on her pants and start tugging them down, not touching her underwear. When her pants are off, Olivia holds up her hand, and says, "Hold on." She reaches down to pick up her discarded pants and hangs them over the nearest chair. "Can't look too crumpled when we're done." Her tongue flicks along her lips and it tells me how much she wants this.

I fold my arms around her neck and pull her close again. I kiss her lips, her cheek, her neck, drinking in her scent—and her arousal. "Sit on the desk," I say after dotting her collarbone with a string of kisses.

"Jesus, Groves," she says, her voice nothing but a breathy whisper.

"Do it." Beneath my own pants and underwear, I can feel my clit press against its constraints. But I can wait. This is all about the captain.

I'm surprised by how easily she complies with my request. It also makes me break out in a hot sweat. She shuffles to her desk, her legs bare, her belly exposed, her blouse hanging open. She pushes a few items to the middle of the desk and hops onto it, then locks her eyes on mine again.

Best Christmas gift ever, I think, as I approach and push her knees apart. The captain's blouses always looked like the most delicious wrapping paper to hungrily tear off of a present.

I step in between her legs and put my hands on her sides. She's not slender—she's strong. I feel hard muscles pressing against my thumbs and, this time, she tugs my head close and kisses me hard. Need coils in my stomach as I kiss her back greedily, feeling her abs ripple under my fingers. My uniform feels too hot on me and part of me wants her to take it off me, but the other part wants to make my dreams come true. Not that Captain Betts undressing me isn't in my repertoire of dreams. Still, I have urgent business. Our lips still glued together, I slip one hand from her belly to her panties. Gingerly, with one finger, I trace a line along the length of it. I can feel the contours of the captain's swollen lips and clit.

Her mouth falls open and her head tilts back slightly—just enough for me to catch a glimpse of her face. My fingers keep tracing that invisible line over her panties while I gaze into the captain's stunned face. I keep looking as I hook my fingertip underneath the gusset and pull it to the side.

She gasps, as though the flow of air on her nether lips shocks her. I guess it does.

"We need to get these off," I whisper, my voice no longer able to reach its normal volume. Beneath my black uniform shirt, my heart is racing and I can feel my skin going damp.

Without words, she scoots backwards onto the desk, plants her hands behind her, draws up her legs and pushes her ass off the desk. I take the opportunity to rip her panties down and, after she has lowered her ass again, take them in my hands. Ostentatiously, I put them in the pocket of my uniform pants. She's not getting those back any time soon. Unless, perhaps, she comes to pick them up at my house—on New Year's Eve for example.

And now I have the captain exactly how I want her. Her pussy exposed to me, on offer, for me to do with as I please.

"Come here," she says, and grabs a fistful of my shirt. "I want to see you." She hoists it out of my pants and starts lifting it up. I help by undoing the top buttons so I can just haul it over my head and toss it to the floor—I don't care how crumpled it ends up after the fact. "Take off your bra," she says, once I've disposed of my shirt.

For some reason—perhaps because she is my commanding officer—I don't hesitate. I liberate my breasts and, instantly, my nipples reach up.

She grabs for me and I don't stop her. She takes a nipple in her mouth and she might as well be sucking on my clit, that's how hard my legs start trembling. When she lets go, and I can regain focus, I take my chance to hunker down and get a good look at her pussy. My legs start shaking again—and not from the exertion of squatting between the captain's legs.

Because real life is always so much more intoxicating than the wildest dreams can be. I smell her. I hear her labored breathing. I have my hands on her thighs, my fingers pushing deep into her flesh. And now, I'm about to taste her.

I begin by pressing the gentlest of kisses on her inner thigh, and slowly making my way upward. Even though I know we don't have much time, this is the moment I need to treasure most. The moment my tongue greets her sex. And then it does. I let my tongue skate along the length of her swollen lips and my world spins on its axis. Even more so because the captain has brought her hands to my hair and is tugging at my short strands wildly. This Christmas miracle is really happening.

I unleash my tongue and don't hold back—the reverent moment has now passed. My tongue flicks along her clit while my hands dig deeper into the flesh of her behind. The captain's hands are in my hair, pressing my face into her, intertwining us in this instance of passion. We're breaking so many rules, and a phone could start ringing any second, and I'm eager to get the captain off quickly because, truth be told, I want to impress her as well. A sense of acute urgency floods my veins and while my tongue stays busy with her clit, tasting her most intimate spot, leaving me drunk on her juices, I bring a hand between her legs.

The captain keeps one hand in my hair, but brings her other hand to her ass to meet mine. She folds it over my hand, slipping her fingers between mine, and I'm so touched by her gesture, my tongue loses traction for a split second. Not for long though as my finger skids along her lips and gets soaked by her wetness. Oh, how wet the captain is for me—I will never forget. As I suck her clit between my lips, I push one finger inside of her. As a result, her thighs clamp themselves around my head, leaving me completely trapped between her legs. Did she have this vision of herself when she walked into the station this morning? She might not have, but I sure did.

The sounds she makes are muffled by her thighs covering my ears, but they still ignite a violent throbbing between my own legs. And they spur me on. I pull out my finger and add another. Then increase my pace. My tongue and fingers work in tandem as I try to stay in the moment and focus all my attention on the captain's pleasure. But I already know this isn't going to be enough. That's the thing with dreams and having them come true—greater, more daring ones are always waiting in the wings.

The captain is now meeting my thrusts with her pelvis and her thighs are banging against my ears, letting in her groans and moans and the intoxicating way with which she yells out my name.

"Oh, Groves," she screams. "Oh fuck." The captain is so much noisier than I had imagined and it doesn't fail to turn me on. My uniform pants will be soaked through. However will I resume duty after this?

The captain's sex contracts around my fingers, trapping me inside of her. And I know that, as soon as I let my fingers slide out of her, all I'll want is to get them back inside as soon as possible.

"Christ," she mutters as I retreat. Her legs fall down awkwardly, but I don't bother catching them because I need to kiss the captain on the lips like I've never needed anything before. I slide my hands around her waist and briefly look her in the eyes.

"Merry Christmas," I say and, before she has a chance to reply, slip my tongue inside her mouth again.

In response, the captain winds her arms around my neck. God, for that tongue to move on my clit the way it does now... I'm painfully aware of the pulse between my legs.

"You'd better take off those pants," the captain says when our lips part.

"I'm not sure we have time for that," I reply, though my words lack any conviction.

"You're going to be cautious now?" Her lips curve up into a smile. "Besides, I'm your commanding officer and you'd better follow my orders."

"Yes, Ma'am." I give her a smile back but don't move.

"If I invite you over to my house after your shift, will you still call me Ma'am?" she asks.

"We won't know until then." I do take a step back now, to take in the sight of the captain on her desk without pants one more time. Then, behind the closed door of her office, a phone starts ringing.

"Damn," we both say at the same time.

"You'd better get that, Tasha," the captain says with a smirk on her face.

"Here to serve." I start doing up my shirt while holding her gaze.

"Oh, I know." She slides off the desk. The phone keeps ringing. "Come collect your overtime payment soon." The wink she shoots me connects with my clit instantly.

But I have no choice but to get out of her office and pick up that phone. I head to the door and as I open it she says, "Oh and, Tasha, Merry Christmas to you too."

NOT YET

"Close your eyes," Ava says. "Trust me, you'll want to keep them open later. Give them a rest for now."

As if I can ever keep my eyes off her. But I do as I'm told, because this is Ava, and her command over me has incrementally increased in the time we've been together—and is now absolute. I can't say no to her pleading brown eyes and to that lopsided smile she puts on when she has things like this in mind.

I close my eyes and wait.

Nothing happens. But I've learned not to lose my patience. I don't peek through my eyelashes and try to figure out what she's up to. Like she asked me to earlier, I trust her.

She has me naked on the bed and a faint rush of air flows over my skin as she brushes past me. I've heard the sound of her rummaging through a drawer enough times with my eyes closed to successfully identify it. I also know what she keeps in that drawer.

"Give me your hands," she whispers in my ear.

I know better than to offer them to her in front of me. As part of our unspoken code, I bring them behind my back. She ties me up with something that feels like silk. It must be a ribbon of the red dress she made me tear up a few weeks ago. She'd come home looking ravishing in it, in full-on red carpet mode, still glowing from the attention she'd received. When I told her how good that dress looked on her, so good, in fact, that I wanted to tear it right off her, she instructed me to do so. And I did. The rip of the fabric in my ears, the touch of the silk in my hands while I exposed her glorious body to my gaze, was so intoxicating, she had me whimpering in minutes.

"That dress is a keeper then," she'd said jokingly afterwards, but she'd meant it.

I relish the memory of that night as she tightens the fabric around my wrists.

"Keep your eyes closed while you shuffle onto the bed. Make yourself comfortable." She follows up with a little chuckle because it's not exactly easy to make myself comfortable with my hands tied behind my back. Just standing up already makes me lose my balance a little, but, again, I've been in this position many times before. I take tiny steps backwards, turn around and, while bracing my core, bring one knee onto the bed. My other follows quickly and I only sway a little before finding my balance again.

"Better work on your core strength, Charlie," Ava said the first time she made me do this. I had toppled over face-first into the duvet, to Ava's great delight. Back then, she was still much more easily distracted and we'd both burst out into an uncontrollable fit of laughter. She untied me and allowed me to roam my hands all across her body while she fucked me. Not even if I fall over in the most comic fashion will she let me do that tonight.

The way she is with me now has been a gradual evolution of her pushing a tiny bit more every time we do this. The tone of her voice has changed from hesitant to incontestable. The touch of the paddle she sometimes spanks me with has grown from gentle grazing to determined smacking. Sometimes, in moments like these, when I clumsily shuffle onto the bed and try to find a comfortable position to sit in, overly aware of her eyes catching my smallest movement, I wonder where it will end. What she'll have me do a year from now.

I've tried fighting her for top, most times playfully but sometimes with such heartfelt passion it warranted a long discussion after, but in this combination of her and me together, this is how it is. And I've grown to enjoy balancing on that thin edge of curiosity, between wanting her to have her way with me in any which way she pleases, and the struggle that remains within me to resist. I'm by no means naturally submissive and we both know it—both get off on it.

"You can open your eyes now," Ava says.

I blink when I do and see nothing. I sigh, both with contentment and frustration.

"You'll figure out soon enough why I had to tie you up for this," she whispers in my ear from behind, then lets her teeth clamp down on my earlobe.

I've somehow managed to cross my legs underneath me and the touch of her teeth against my skin makes my clit pulse heavily.

Ava makes her way to the other side of the bed and I glue my gaze to her. She's still wearing the tank top and shorts she had on when she tied me up. I have no idea what her next move will be. She might delve back into the drawer, but she doesn't have me in the right position for a spanking. She might just leave me here to ponder her next action on my own for fifteen minutes, until my head is so full of possibilities—and my clit so engorged with lust—I'll be struggling to get my restraints off, yearning to put myself out of my horny misery.

Today, she does neither. Instead, she brings her hands to the bottom of her top and, slowly, pulls it over her head. I already knew she wasn't wearing a bra underneath, but the sight of her breasts being liberated, her nipples growing hard just by the feel of the air, unleashes another round of throbbing in my clit.

"It's really a courtesy to you that I've tied you up," Ava says. "You know what I'd have to do to you if you touched yourself of your own volition." There's that crooked grin again, accompanied by a wicked sparkle in her eyes. "I'm all about doing you favors, Charlie. That's how much I love you." With that, she hooks her thumbs underneath the waistband of her shorts and just stands there for a few seconds—mute and utterly delicious.

She's definitely doing me a favor by, ever so slowly, sliding her shorts over her hips and baring herself to me. As she bends over, her breasts fall forward and, by god, she was right to tie me up because if my hands had been free I would have grabbed for them in a split second. The combination of my impaired mobility, and the sight she has me behold, has me gasping for breath already. And I know her quick striptease is not where this will end, because that's not how she's wired. Not anymore. If I'm sure of one thing, it's that my hands will remain bound behind my back for a good while longer.

Amused and incredibly aroused, I watch her, waiting for what she'll do next. Even in the bedroom it's so clear that Ava was born to entertain—born for the bright glare of the limelight. She usually refuses to switch off the light when we make love, a decision I can always only wholeheartedly agree with because I'm at my happiest when I have my eyes on her, when the light—any light—catches in her glance and I can see how much pleasure she gets from sexually torturing me.

Ava now stands naked before me, her hands on her hips, a grin so triumphant on her lips it makes me fear the worst—or the best. I fully expect her to dig out that nasty flogger she bought a few months ago and have a go with it on my attention-starved nipples. Or maybe she'll go for the nipple clamps. She has that kind of look on her face that's not interested in mercy. Between my legs, I feel myself go wetter.

Instead of reaching for the drawer again and introducing another prop, she gingerly hops onto the bed and sits in front of me.

"How badly do you want to touch me right now?" Her face is a mask of mock-seriousness. As if she doesn't know the answer to that question already. As if it's not written all over my face that I want my wrists to be freed and my hands all over her magnificent body.

The only response that will preserve my dignity in this moment is complete silence. It's all part of the game. I purse my lips together, as though keeping them tightly shut will prevent any pleading words from spilling from them. I look into her eyes, trying to gauge her, the way I've done so many times before, but today, I truly have no idea what she has up her sleeve.

"Come on, Charlie," she spurs me on. "I'm not above letting you know that I really want to fuck you right now. Meet me in the middle here."

I remain silent, still fiercely braving her gaze. Though I'm getting distracted by the finger she brings an inch from my chin, by the promise of touch I know she won't deliver on. Not yet. She cleaves her finger through the air, the tip of it dangerously close to my nipple now, but our skins don't meet. Though for my nipple, she might as well just have pinched it hard the way it reaches upward, trying to catch her touch.

"Fine." She drops her hand and starts scooting backward. "But remember you asked for this. You know how I feel about these silences of yours." She pushes herself all the way to the other side of the bed, then clasps her arms around her knees chastely, her lips pressed together, as though giving great thought to something—like she didn't plan every single second of this before we entered the bedroom.

And there we sit. I on one side of the bed, hands tied; she on the other. My blood beats with anticipation. My clit feels like it might explode any second now.

Then, slowly, Ava lets her arms drop from around her knees and she spreads her legs, putting herself on full display for me. Instantly, my mouth goes dry. My heartbeat picks up speed. Because now I know how she's going to make me suffer. She's going to make me watch. We've done this over Skype a few times, but the big difference then was that my hands were not tied behind my back and I could take full advantage of the slew of stimulating images unfolding in front of me.

Her knees drop onto the bed and, her eyes pinned to mine, she inserts a finger into her mouth. She sucks it in deep, making a smacking sound when it leaves her lips. Then she drags it over her neck, in between her breasts, down her belly button, and holds it still in front of her sex. And it feels like she's doing this to me. In my tortured state, I can feel her wet finger drifting over my skin, halting a hair's breadth away from my clit.

Involuntarily, my wrists wriggle against their restraints. I want to break free. I want to do to myself what she's doing to herself. I want to mirror her actions and take the pleasure she's getting from them. But I'm not in charge of my own pleasure. Not tonight. Not yet.

She's not even moving her finger. It just lies there still. The only sound is the one I'm making trying to free myself and I know she must be getting off on the twitch of my muscles, just as I know that she has bound me tightly enough in order for me to not be able to set myself free. This pains me more than any smack she has ever delivered to my ass. The view in front of me is so sexy it hurts. My wrists ache from being bound, my shoulders from trying to wriggle free, but, most of all, my clit throbs so violently, I'm afraid I might climax just by sitting here. Just by exposure to air and the image of Ava spread open for me, about to touch herself. And that would be the worst sin of all. Not only because it would go against our unspoken rule that, in this particular situation, I am not allowed to come without her explicit permission, but, even more so, because for me, it would feel like a wasted orgasm. A quick shudder of relief that would not deliver on the anticipation that's being built up and up. I don't want a shudder from this, I want a dazzling thunderstorm.

I try to steady my breathing and, behind my back, clasp my fingers together solemnly instead of fidgeting with the fabric around my wrists. I focus on my breath and, when I look into Ava's eyes again, I see she's waiting for me to calm down. To enjoy this in a way that doesn't ruin my eventual pleasure. Oh, how I will explode when she frees me and finally touches me. One flick of her finger and I will fall apart underneath it. But we're not there yet. I take another deep breath and try to tap into the stamina that I've built up being Ava's lover.

Then, her finger starts moving. She slides it over her nether lips, into the wetness that has gathered there. Her other hand joins the party and, with it, she spreads her lips wide, opening up her most intimate spot, for me. Though we're a world away from touching each other, we're so close in this moment. So wrapped up in each other. So completely devoted to each other.

Ava's no longer wise-cracking. Her mouth has drooped open. Playing with me the way she's been doing must have aroused her greatly and now, in the smallest way, it's my turn to enjoy her torture. Because she's actually touching herself and how can she not surrender to that? She will come under my gaze. My eyes on her will make her climax much faster than she'd want to. Inside of Ava's mind, a war is waging now. I can tell by the intensified motion of her finger around her clit. And, oh god, she brings a finger of her other hand inside herself and the groan that subsequently fills the room doesn't come from her side of the bed.

"Jesus," I moan. This is too much. The desire to touch my clit is so overwhelming I fear I might pass out. But then I would miss out on the spectacle she's giving me. One finger circles, while the other dips in and out of her, until she wants more and she adds another finger and delves them deep inside, as deep as they will go. I wish those were my fingers feeling the warmth inside of her, giving her this pleasure. I wish it was my tongue circling her clit. I wish so many things, until all my wishes are drowned out by the sight of Ava's stiffening limbs.

She's coming in front of me. Even though I'm not the one delivering her climax, the fact that she's giving herself up to me this way, showing her most vulnerable side as the orgasm claims her, I feel it power through me. The river my pussy has become will surely leave an irremovable stain on the sheets—a memento to remind us of this night forever. Her two fingers go deep inside of her as her muscles spasm, as her pussy contracts around her, and she furiously strokes her clit.

When she comes to, opens her eyes and finds my gaze, there's no sign of triumphant Ava. Her smile is soft, barely there, her eyes narrow in what looks to me like compassion. Because I had to witness this while imprisoned by her control over me.

This moment is a culmination of everything, because it's the instant before she will release me, but it's also the aftermath of her climax she had me watch, it's what this entire night has boiled down to. She knows it. I know it. It's why I don't mind her waiting a few seconds before she pushes herself up and gazes deep into my eyes, affirming our love, and this chemistry between us, and what our sex life has become as opposed to what it was when we first met. It's recognition of the journey we've been on, inside and outside of the bedroom.

Then, finally, she comes for me.

She cups my jaw in her hands and kisses me as the smell that lingers on her fingers penetrates my nose.

"Untie me," I beg, when we break from the kiss, because I don't care about the game anymore. My skin sizzles with need. My clit aches with unmet desire. My entire body has become an extension of the want between my legs. I need her now.

Ava doesn't speak, just brings her hands behind my back and, as though she bound my hands together with the most uncomplicated knot, sets me free. My wrists are numb, but I don't take the time to shake some new life into them. Instead, I throw my arms around Ava's neck and pull her to me. Our breasts crash together, her skin on mine is hot.

I let myself fall backwards, pulling Ava on top of me. "Fuck me now," I say in between heavy breaths. "Please, fuck me now."

Not even Ava has the gall to not immediately honor my request. There's no more room for exerting control over me now. Time has run out. I'm sure, next time, she'll push me farther, but tonight, I've earned my climax.

She plants a flurry of kisses on my jaw, neck, nipples on her way down. I let my legs fall wide, allowing her to see the full extent of my arousal. I'm so wet I feel it trickle down my behind, coating my inner thighs. My clit is a pulsing heart of dire need, evidence of how her actions have aroused me. Wisely, she doesn't kiss it immediately. It would set me off straight away and she knows what I like when I come. One of her exquisitely long fingers inside of me at the very least. Or two or three. Wet as I am, three shouldn't be an issue at all.

I feel her breath move over me down there, feel her fingers skate up my thigh, along my lips, spreading my pussy wide. She plunges in two from the start, quickly adding a third, and I'm starting to lose it already. I'm in Ava heaven. Images of how she delved her fingers into her own pussy earlier pop up on the backs of my eyelids. Oh, those fingers and what they can do. They instantly connect with something deep inside of me, with the need she has created by tying me up and making me watch her, by the desire that's been running in my veins since the day we met. Already, I'm starting to crumble under her touch. But my neglected clit is still thumping wildly, still waiting impatiently for the touch of her tongue.

When I don't feel her tongue touch down as expected, I open my eyes and see her glancing at my face, her lips trembling with focus, her dark eyes glimmering with love. I don't have to say anything because how could she not know. I love her and I want her tongue on my clit right now. I need release. I've been tortured long enough.

Then, at last, she bows her head and, a split second later, her tongue is where I want it. Her fingers are still pumping, still bringing me to new heights, but the addition of her tongue, finally, lets me really break free. My hands are in her long, fanned-out hair. My pelvis is bucking up, trying to find some rhythm. My clit is melting under her tongue's caress. The sensation spreads through me. When my muscles start to shudder with orgasm, I relive the image of Ava sucking her own finger deep into her mouth. The same finger she's fucking me with now. It all blends together. What has come before and what's happening now. The touch of her tongue and her fingers. The smile on her lips when she undressed earlier. The memory of the ribbon of red dress cutting into my wrists. And I erupt under her touch. My body gives itself to her completely, resulting in a loud, syncopated moan from my lips.

I'm free and I'm hers as she claims me with her fingers and her tongue, as the orgasm dances through me, reaching every extremity, saturating my blood, singing under my skin. When I come down from the cloud I was just on, the one that transported me out of my body and kept me firmly locked in its pleasure at the same time, I know that it would never have felt like this—this liberating, this earth-shattering, this all-consuming—if she hadn't played me so expertly from the very beginning.

With a contented sigh, I sink into the mattress, as Ava's fingers retreat. That victorious smile is back on her lips, but there's a subtle difference compared to the one she painted on earlier. A tenderness has crept into it. A tenderness that emanates from her entire body as she drapes it over mine and whispers in my ear, "I love you."

If you enjoyed this short story, you might want to check out Harper's novel Release the Stars, in which Charlie and Ava meet and fall in love.

ABOUT THE AUTHOR

Harper Bliss is the author of the *Pink Bean* series, the *High Rise* series, the *French Kissing* serial and many other lesbian romance titles. She is the co-founder of Ladylit Publishing and My LesFic weekly newsletter.

Harper loves hearing from readers and you can reach her at the email address below.

www.harperbliss.com
harper@harperbliss.com

Printed in Great Britain
by Amazon

76259660R00203